MEADOWLARKS
Book One

Ashley Christine

Copyright © 2013 Ashley Christine

ISBN 978-1-62646-418-6

All rights reserved. No part of this publication may be reproduced, stored in a retrieval system, or transmitted in any form or by any means, electronic, mechanical, recording or otherwise, without the prior written permission of the author.

Published by BookLocker.com, Inc., Bradenton, Florida.

The characters and events in this book are fictitious. Any similarity to real persons, living or dead, is coincidental and not intended by the author.

Printed in the United States of America on acid-free paper.

Booklocker.com, Inc.
2012

First Edition

I know all the birds of the hills,
and all that moves in the field is mine.

Psalm 50:11

CHAPTER ONE

I'd planned on sleeping in on this beautiful May morning, but instead here I am, at six o'clock, in the barn helping Ivy deliver her first calf. She's been struggling for a while on her own. Now I'm finally able to get him out. I take a towel and dry him off. He is a cute little guy, with a creamy coat and a white face.

About an hour later, I call Jeremiah. Jer is my right-hand man on the ranch; we grew up together in Sheridan, and we've been best friends since kindergarten class back in 1987.

I tell him all about finding Ivy early this morning in a stall in the barn, struggling to birth her calf on her own. Jeremiah knows Ivy well; she gave him a few broken toes a few years ago during a thunderstorm. She, being the stubborn cow she is, would not come in from pasture. Jer and I had wrangled all of the animals except Ivy. She charged by, whipped back around, and stomped right on his foot. That night, she stayed outside, and Jeremiah—well, he was on crutches for a few weeks.

We agree to meet later today at the feed store in town to pick up some supplies. At one o'clock, I climb into my black Ford Super Duty, my new baby; my ear-to-ear smile is a side effect of owning something this beautiful. The diesel engine roars and I shift into gear. Driving down my lane, I pause at the boundary between what I own and the town road, and check for any other vehicles. *Nothing.* I creep onto the gravel and shift quickly into second, then third. Dust trails behind me as my big tires kick up stones, and I feel exhilaration when I push the pedal right down to the floor. When the dirt road turns to asphalt, and the stop signs become street lights, I know I have to slow down and stop driving like a teenager trying to impress his friends.

Zeke's is a small wooden building on the corner of Oakburn Street. Jeremiah's truck is already in the parking lot, and I find him inside.

Zeke is stocking some chicken feed on a shelf. "Hey, Blaine! What's up?" He smiles widely when I walk in, and he lets a feed bag drop on the floor.

"Oh, not much. Just in for the usual." I smile and walk over to a wooden pallet in the corner. It's filled with stacks of colored buckets. I set aside four blue and four red.

Jeremiah asks Zeke something about feed, and they go off to another aisle. I make my way to the dog food, stopping quickly at the gum ball machine to pop a quarter in. I turn the knob. The child in me smiles as the green ball travels down the steel chute and lands with a clink in the chamber. I lift the small metal door and pop the gum ball into my mouth, chew down, and crush the sugar coated candy between my teeth.

When I get to the aisle stocked with dog food, I stand for a moment and stare absentmindedly out the large window. I bask in the warmth of the sun and peer out the glass toward Lander's grocery store, where some children are outside selling baked goods. Their sign says the proceeds are for a class trip to Big Horn. I may just have to buy something from them later.

I choose the usual brand of dog food Rex eats; you know the one, with the happy running dog and the bright bold words on the bag explaining in detail how this brand is simply the best natural food for your best friend.

*Blah, blah, blah...*I've seen Rex eating cow patties. I'm sure this is a delicacy in comparison. Then I think about all the times he's licked my face. *Oh, yum.*

The ding of the tiny bell from above the door grabs my attention. I look up, expecting to see Jer with an arm full of feed bags, leaving to load the truck. Instead, I see quite the opposite. I see beauty. Breathtaking beauty, actually. Then, right behind the breathtaking beauty...a guy. *Shit.* He is fumbling in his pocket and pulls out a cellphone. He starts quickly thumbing keys on the touchscreen.

She is browsing the front counter, looking at homemade dog treats. With one hand at my side, the other holding the dog food bag slung over my shoulder, I stand there and watch her.

With my feet firmly planted on the old wooden floor, I feel as if I'm encased in an invisible box.

I hear Jer and Zeke's voices again and I peep over the shelving unit that divides the two aisles. They're at the front counter, with Breathtaking Beauty and her still-texting friend.

I hear Jeremiah make a suggestion about a dog treat and the girl smiles and giggles.

Damn, that was a beautiful sound.

She places a few treats on the counter and Zeke rings them into the register.

"That'll be $2.87, ma'am." He beams at her and she blushes.

Looking down, and still smiling, she riffles through her large purse and pulls out a wallet. The friend, still standing a few feet behind her, still texting, is clueless to the men with eyes glued to the gorgeous creature at the front counter.

I can't help but smile as I stand there, looking like a stalker.

Jeremiah catches my gaze, and gives me a *Dude, why are you just standing there? Check out this chick!* look, nodding his head in her direction.

I roll my eyes at him and slowly make my way to the counter.

The girl has long auburn hair, a deep red and brown mixture of beauty. She has half of it pinned back, and the rest cascades down her back in long flowing curls. She is wearing a light blue summer dress, with thin straps, revealing her beautiful skin and back. She is tall, too, probably five foot eight or so. All legs, and curves, and hips...*and damn!*

I feel like I'm walking in slow motion. I have to; I have to take in all of her beauty. Her long legs end with beautiful feet in white flip flops; clearly, she can't be from around here. I trail my stalker gaze back up her body and feel a familiar tightening in my jeans.

A pair of cold blue eyes meet mine, and I look away as fast as I can.

The friend caught me. *Shit.*

I feel like an adolescent caught peeping at his hot teacher as she bends over to pick up a pencil.

The guy snorts and grabs the bag of treats from Zeke's hand. "Let's go, Addy," he says and taps her elbow with his finger.

She smiles at Zeke and Jeremiah, and walks out the door, just as beautifully as she came in.

Putting the dog food on the counter, I look at Zeke who is still gaping at the sex on legs that just walked out of his store.

"Bro, why the hell did you stand back there? You totally missed that girl!" Jeremiah asks, shoving my right shoulder with his palm.

"I have no idea," I say, shaking my head. Honestly, I did not have a clue.

***

At home, Jeremiah backs his old Chevy up to the barn doors and we unload the bags of feed. I grab the red and blue buckets and place them in the tack room. We feed and tend to all the animals and by suppertime I'm starving.

"You want to get some beer and ribs?" I ask, while shutting the door behind me.

"Yeah, man," Jeremiah says, rubbing his stomach. "I'm starving!"

I laugh and pat his stomach, "You're wasting away, Jer."

"Hey! Not everyone has time to paint abs on in the morning, asshole!" he says, and gives me the middle finger to tell me to shut up.

There are really only two places to get good beer and ribs around here—well, at the same time anyway. Mulcaster's Mill serves to a more family orientated atmosphere, like a Chili's or Applebee's. Then there is The Wolfbarrow, a smaller place without salad forks and "mocktails". We hop in Jeremiah's old Chevy and decide on the usual, The Wolfbarrow.

Inside, a deep and sorrowful rock song is playing rhythmically from the old jukebox in the corner; the guitar whining and ripping through the chords. Jesse, the owner and the bartender, is standing behind the counter, pouring draft beer for a group of men sitting on the red bar stools in front of him.

I hear a familiar voice from behind and feel two arms around my neck. "Blaine! How are you?"

It's Gwen Wolf, Jesse's younger sister and a classmate of ours since elementary school. "You guys haven't been here in a while!" She lets me go and hugs Jeremiah.

He grins ear to ear and wraps his arms around the small of her back, trailing one down to her behind.

She pushes him back and slaps his chest. "Ass!"

He laughs and tells her she looks beautiful.

Gwen is tall and blonde, with pouty lips and deep green eyes. You know the type of girl that knows she's beautiful and loves the attention? That's Gwen. Sexy yes, yet unappealing to me. Most other men drool over her like cavemen to fresh meat. She seats us at a tall table facing two of the four flat screens in the small bar and hands us menus. Like we need them; we always get the same thing.

"I'll be right back, boys. Are you both having draft?"

We smile and nod, and she bounces off to greet three other people who just walked in.

"Damn, that girl does all kinds of things to me," Jer says slyly, looking in her direction.

"Yeah, you and three quarters of the guys in this town." I roll my eyes.

"Do you ever think she would date me? I mean, in high school, she always had a boyfriend, but now...you never know." He shrugs.

"True," I say while flipping over the cardboard coaster on the table. "You never know".

Gwen is back in less than two minutes with our glasses filled to the brim with cold beer. I take a long sip and wipe the remainder off my lips.

Gwen bites her bottom lip and looks down at the menu. "Have you boys decided?"

I raise an eyebrow and smirk.

We order our usual, two full racks, one honey garlic, and one spicy buffalo. Extra carrots and celery on the side, with ranch dressing.

There is a replay of a rodeo segment on the TV. From last summer, showing clips of the annual Sheridan WYO Rodeo. It is held in July each year, and only being a few weeks away I smile with anticipation.

"Dude, I can't wait for the WYO this year!" Jeremiah is looking at the TV and grinning too.

It isn't Gwen who brings us our food, but Josh, the kitchen kid who usually buses the tables. "Here ya go, fellas. Can I get you anything else?" he asks, placing our plates down ever so quickly.

"Nope, we're good Josh. Thanks buddy." I smile, grab a celery stalk and dip it in the ranch dressing.

He leaves and we eat the delicious, fall-off-the-bone ribs, have about four more drafts each and call it a night.

I'm not drunk, but I really shouldn't drive, so Jesse calls us a cab. Gwen hangs around the entrance while we climb into the cab. Jer tries to sneak a goodbye kiss, and she jokingly shoves him into the cab.

"Goodbye, my lady!" he calls to her, and she laughs and turns back into The Wolfbarrow.

***

Jer lives in his parents' house, about five minutes from my ranch. His mom and dad died six years ago in a car crash, leaving him, the only child, everything they had. The house was a typical farm house in the area at the time it was built, over fifty years ago. Big and white, boasting six bedrooms, yet they only ever needed two. A small chicken coop was off to the left side of the house, and a massive red barn lay behind it. After his parents had died, Jer sold off all of the animals, either to me or to the local auction house. He spends as little time as possible on his now empty farm. He's talked here and there about selling, but I know he just doesn't have the heart to do it.

"Buddy, thanks for the good eats," Jer says. He shakes my hand, thanking me for paying for the meal.

"Anytime, Jer." And we bump fists like we're kids again.

Laughing, he gets out of the cab and makes his way to the front door. He salutes when he steps inside, and I wave as the cab pulls away.

Once I'm at home I had the driver money for the fare and thank him for the ride. Walking up to the house I whistle for Rex, my German Shepherd. He comes from around the back of the house and picks up pace when he sees me, wagging his tail happily.

"Hey, boy." I rub his back, and we go inside.

I kick off my jeans and pull my t-shirt over my head. Putting on some blue striped cotton pajama bottoms, I pull back the covers on my bed and fall in—face first. When my body is immersed in my luscious mattress, my head hits the pillow, and I'm out like a light. I dream of Ivy, and her little creamy calf. I dream of him getting bigger and bigger and one day becoming a champion bull. He lets no man last eight seconds on his back, bucking and kicking his way around, owning the ring and sending the dirt flying.

Two days go by, and there's not much excitement around the farm. Long work days and long, lonely nights without sleep. Eventually, I close my eyes and drift off. Rex startles me awake by barking at the bedroom window. I sleepily rub my eyes and get out of bed. His wet nose leaves prints all over the window, and he stands rigid, with his hair is straight up on end. He sees something.

"What is it, buddy?" I squint as I try to look out into the darkness, but I see nothing. He's still worked up, so we both head outside—but not before I grab my gun from behind the door.

Rex is sniffing the ground all around the barn door, and I walk over quietly to him. He starts barking again, fiercely, and I open the barn door. He barrels in, and I'm quick on my feet behind him, one hand holding my rifle, and the other keeping my pajama pants from falling off my hips.

Flipping on the lights, I see the nothing but Ivy and her calf in their stall. All the other animals are outside in the pasture. Rex has something cornered and all of a sudden, I hear an ear-piercing yelp.

A fox.

Like a blazing orange streak, it flies past me with Rex on its heels, and they're out the door.

"Rex! Get back here!"

I hear him barking in the distant field, and I call him over and over again.

Finally he comes back, limping. He's holding his right paw up.

Oh, great.

"Ah shit, boy. What did you do?"

The fox could be carrying rabies, and I know I'll have to take Rex to the vet. Looking at my watch, I see it's 5:48 AM. Deciding to wait until eight o'clock when the office opens, I check Rex out for myself. He seems to be okay. I can't find any puncture wounds; maybe he just hurt himself while running after that sly little bastard. How did it get into the barn anyway? I'll have to look around when it's light.

CHAPTER TWO

Dr. Holly Jenkins is a short, older woman with jet black hair. She has lived in Sheridan her whole life too; she even went to school with my parents and was a good friend of my mother's.

"Blaine!" She smiles. "What has this big fella got himself into now?"

Dr. Jenkins has seen Rex a few times in the past, for quill removal when he got brave and chased a porcupine, and other minor things. She also saw him when he was neutered, and I won't begin to tell you the guilt I felt about that one.

I explain the late night encounter with the red-haired fox, and she rolls her eyes and frowns at Rex.

"I'll bring him in and check him out. You can stay out here and wait if you like. We will probably be twenty minutes or so."

I nod and sit down with a copy of National Geographic. There's not much of a selection on the old wooden coffee table. I smirk and shake my head at the thought of Rex chasing the fox, and as fast as it ran by me in the barn, a new thought crashes through my mind.

Red hair...*the beauty*. The breathtaking beauty. I haven't seen her again, not since my awkwardness at Zeke's.

Forget it, Blaine, she didn't even see you.

My mind tells another part of me to let the thought go.

Yeah, I know, I know...but her boyfriend did all right. He caught you, holding your dog food, peeping over the shelving unit and salivating like a 12 year old hiding in the girl's locker room.

I shake my head at myself and at where my thoughts are most likely headed.

It's been what? Seven months since Quinn? She was the last girl I dated. Well, if you can call only sex and nothing else "dating". Then okay—I dated the shit out of that girl.

Quinn Masterson was the girl in high school that didn't know she was beautiful, not like a Gwen Wolf. She wore clothes that were too far big for her, instead of something more her size that would let you appreciate her sexy curves. She moved to Arizona for college and then came back about two years ago with a teaching degree. She's now a chemistry teacher at Sheridan High.

If I had a teacher that looked like her in high school, I definitely would have flunked chemistry just to have her all over again. *Hot for teacher!*

Quinn and I reconnected at The Wolfbarrow over a year ago and hit it off. I didn't mention how I felt about her in high school; instead I played it cool, letting her think I didn't notice her until she came back to Sheridan. We spent more time in bed than anywhere else. We didn't do the dinner thing, movies or coffee. We had sex on almost every surface in my house, and even a few times outside when we didn't make it indoors.

We were great physically, but emotionally? We were complete opposites.

Quinn started to hint around the *L word* and I, like an asshole, shut that runaway train down before it collided head on with another. I don't know why I wasn't ready for that type of relationship. My parents had been happily married, and both of my older brothers are currently and have children, too. I guess I'm at a loss for a reason as to why I am so different.

"Blaine?"

I snap back to the present, and Dr. Jenkins has returned to the waiting room with Rex.

"Rex is fine. He didn't contract rabies, and his leg is okay too. Just a small sprain."

I smile and sigh with relief.

"I suggest he takes it easy for a few days, and then he will be back to good."

"Thanks, Doc."

I look down at Rex and purse my lips. He looks up at me, eyes lit up and happy as a clam. Heading over to the reception desk to pay for the visit, I catch something out of the corner of my eye.

A big malamute comes through the door and behind him...it's her.

This time I see all of her—large blue eyes and that flowing auburn hair.

Well, hello, again... Says the familiarity in my jeans that I felt at Zeke's the first time I saw her. I actually blush.

Finally her eyes meet mine, a moment that I wish happened a few days ago, but I didn't have the guts make it happen. She's perfect; I can't put it any other way. And this time, she seems to be without the texting friend.

I hope he's just her friend.

Her large dog starts sniffing Rex, but he doesn't seem to mind or even notice him.

"Luca! Mind your manners." She blushes and pulls on his leash.

"Ugh..." I stammer. "No worries, ma'am. Rex doesn't mind."

I collect myself and give her my big white smile. When I see her reaction, I start to feel like a man again. Her beautiful cheeks turn pink, and she looks down at the leash coiled in her hands.

There you go, Blackstock. Welcome back.

"Hi, I'm Addison. I called earlier about my dog, Luca." She peeks around me and speaks to the young girl behind the desk.

"Hi, Ms. Cole. Dr. Jenkins will see you and Luca in a few minutes. If you'd like to take a seat, she will be right out!" The all-too cheery girl motions for the seating area and chews noisily on her gum.

Addison smiles at me and walks Luca over to a row of empty seats and tells him to sit, which he does promptly.

I decide that I need to talk to her now, or I probably never will. I tap my leg and tell Rex to come. He hobbles behind me, and I slowly walk over to the chairs.

"Ms. Cole?" I stand a few feet away and put my hands on my belt buckle. She looks at my hands, then at my face, smiles, but doesn't say anything.

"May I?" I motion to the seat beside her.

She nods and slowly blinks her beautiful long lashes at me.

"I'm Blaine." I extend my hand to her and she shakes it. Tingles shoot up my fingers and down my forearm.

Oh, damn...

"Addison," she smiles, her blue eyes alight and sparkling. "Are you from around here?"

I reach out and pet the top of Luca's head.

"Born and raised. I live on a ranch on Porter Road. What about you?"

"Just moved into town. I'm from the east coast, actually."

Her smile leaves me breathless, and when the receptionist tells her it's her turn, I figure it's now or never. "Would you like to get coffee sometime?"

Maybe it is the adrenaline from our early morning fox chase, or maybe I just haven't seen such a beauty before and I can't let her get away. I need to chase my own fox, so to speak.

"I would love to, Blaine," she says completely taking me by surprise. "How about after Luca has his shots?"

She reaches to scratch her dog's head. He's panting.

I feel ya, buddy... I smirk at myself.

My cell phone rings, but I completely ignore it.

"That sounds great. I can meet you down the street at Bean There in about half an hour?"

Bean There, a comical name for a coffee shop, is locally owned by a friendly couple from New York who had enough of the city life and wanted to lay some country roots.

"Okay. I'll see you then."

She is gorgeous when she smiles. Her perfect teeth, the small dimples in her cheeks, and the way her hair falls around her face when she looks down to blush.

I almost trip over the coffee table when Rex and I make our way to the exit. I shrug my shoulders, and she giggles, a sound that makes me smile even bigger.

I have to take Rex back home. He needs to rest that leg, and I need to look in a mirror to give myself a pep talk to grow the nerve to actually see this girl for a third time.

Addison Cole...wow.

I open the rear door of my Ford and lift Rex in. He winces. "Sorry, boy." I pat his head and close the door.

Looking back into the window of the vet's office, I see her sitting in the same chair, Luca at her feet, and she's watching me.

Okay, Blackstock, show her the goods.

I open my door, give her a smile, and extend my arm to hoist myself up into my truck, ensuring the muscles in my biceps are at their best.

See you soon, gorgeous.

***

Rex is sleeping comfortably on his oversized dog pillow. I quickly check myself in the bathroom mirror, run a bit of water over my hands and rake my fingers through my hair. It's unruly, but when isn't it? I smell my armpits. Not bad. I spritz on a little body spray anyway.

I'm wearing my usual well-worn jeans with a few rips in the knees, boots, and white t-shirt. Unlike Quinn Masterson's wardrobe in high school, this does compliment my body very nicely.

I feel a buzz from my pocket, signalling me that I have a voice mail. Must be the call I ignored while engaged to the lovely Ms. Cole.

It's Jeremiah.

"Where are you? You will not believe what time I woke up this morning. We didn't even drink that much!"

He sounds groggy; he doesn't do hangovers well. I decide to call him back, and he picks up in two rings.

"Jer, buddy—you really can't handle a few beers anymore?" I laugh, and he groans. "Are you still coming over today?"

He tells me he is going to shower and be over within an hour.

"I have to go out for a bit, but I'll be back later." I don't want to tell him who I'm going to meet. Not just yet.

"Okay, bro. See ya."

We hang up and, shoving my phone back in my pocket, I head out the door.

Addison met me at the entrance of Bean There, and we walked in together. It's actually pretty cool on the inside. An odd Mediterranean theme for a coffee shop, but the warm peaches and cool blues tie in well with the brown tables and chairs. The young brunette behind the counter blushes when we approach her to order.

"Welcome to Bean There! What can I get for you today?"

I look at Addison, who smiles and orders a black coffee.

"I'll have the same, please." I hand the brunette, whose name tag says Kelly, a ten dollar bill. Addison and I look at one another and smile, her fingers twirling a small strand of hair.

"Thank you, Blaine." She picks up her coffee. "Where would you like to sit?"

I suggest a round table by the window, one with only two chairs close enough together that I'm hoping our knees will touch underneath the wooden tabletop. I hold out her chair for her to sit, and she smiles and thanks me. Sitting down across from her, I can't believe that I'm having coffee with the same girl I was staring at a few days ago at the feed store.

"So, tell me about yourself, Blaine," she says, and then takes a small sip of coffee.

"Well..." I reply, tapping my index finger on my chin, thinking of what people would usually say when asked this question.

"I'm twenty-nine. I have two older brothers, Nick and Owen. I'm a rancher. You know, horses, cows, chickens, you name it. I've lived there my whole life." That pretty much sums it up; I don't know what else to say. I've never met anyone in my adult life that I've had to tell myself about to. Everyone I've dated I went to school with at some point in time, and that makes me realize how small of a bubble I live in.

"I love horses. I actually used to ride them as a kid."

She takes another sip of coffee. I haven't touched mine; I can't take my eyes off her.

"I have a brother, too. Alex. He's twenty-two, dropped out of college last year and is staying with me until he decides what he wants to do with his life."

Ahhhhh, Texty is her brother! And, also not Texty, but Alex.

I smile and remember the look he gave me at Zeke's when he caught me gazing at her.

"Well, you will have to come out some time, and we can go for a ride."

I can picture her now, riding one of my horses. Bareback, beautifully cantering along, smiling at me. The thought immediately travels from my mind, sweeps past my heart and flows right into my lap with all the rest of the blood in my body. Tingling and heated, I shift in my seat.

"How many horses do you have?" she asks, awakening me from my quick daydream.

"Four quarter horses and two Arabians," I say with a smile. "Would you like to come see them today?" I surprise myself with the question but don't regret asking.

She inhales, and her cheeks are pink again, but she smiles. "I would love to."

I am elated, and I finally take a sip of my coffee, feeling like I've overcome some barrier and now can drink in celebration. We make small talk for a while about where she went to school (a university in Maine) and how she got a degree in nursing but decided not to pursue a career just yet. She moved to Wyoming after basically spinning a bottle on a map; she was at a crossroads in her life and needed a change. Her brother Alex tagged along out of sheer boredom.

I tell her about Nick and Owen, their wives and children, Nick having three boys, and Owen a boy and girl fraternal twins. She never once looks bored during our conversation. We are completely engaged in each other, and all the bustle around us fades into the background.

What seems like forever is only an hour and a half, according to the giant roasted bean-shaped clock on the wall. Addison looks outside and notices that it has started to rain.

She pouts her perfect and enticing lips. "Awe, rain! Maybe another day I can visit your ranch?"

"Well, if a little rain doesn't bother you, I'd still like to take you out there." I suggest and smile, praying she says yes. And she does.

Outside, I point to my truck, and we start running toward it, covering our heads with our hands like it'll make any difference. I open the passenger door, and she gracefully hops in, pulling her beautiful hair all to one side and over her shoulder. I don't realize I'm staring until she looks down at me and blushes.

Getting into the driver's side, I turn on the defrost setting to warm us up a little and take the fog off the windows. If I were a teenager again, I would be proud to have a hot woman like Addison in my truck with steamy windows. I smirk at my thought, turn the key, and shift into gear.

Addison is quiet for the first few minutes of our drive. I sneak a glance over at her, and she is sitting gracefully with her hands clasped together on her lap. Small drips of water are coming off her hair, trickling down her shoulder, down her back.

Damn lucky rain.

The brief shower of rain has let up as we make our way down Porter Road. She is quietly singing along with the song on the stereo.

Blackstock Ranch Est. 1927 is engraved on a large wooden banner across the top of the lane way. Held up by large posts, our family's roots have grown here for over 85 years.

"Wow, 1927." She lifts her head up to see out the window. "There must be a lot of memories here."

Pulling up to the house, I see Jeremiah's red truck. *Shit.* I forgot he was here.

I can see him in the field with Ivy and her calf. He's got a big stick and is keeping a good distance from the two of them. I laugh to myself at the thought of Ivy and Jer's history.

I shift into park and turn the quiet rumble off. I hop out and quickly go to Addison's side to open her door.

"Thank you," she says, smiling, and takes my hand to get down out of my truck's lifted interior.

"Ma'am," I reply, smiling back.

"Blaine!" Jeremiah is running over to us now. Ivy is still standing by her calf; she turns her head down to graze. "Oh...hi!" he says, as he ever so obviously recalls the last (and first) time he saw Addison.

"Hi. I'm Addison." She extends her hand to Jeremiah, who quickly takes it and kisses it.

I roll my eyes and snort.

"Jeremiah Sanford, but I'm sure Blaine has told you all about me!" He laughs.

"Yes, he did mention you, Jeremiah. It's a pleasure to meet you." She takes her hand back and clasps them together at her waist.

"Jer, how's the little guy today?" I ask him. Anything to get this awkward moment over with.

"Oh, he's good. She's a little moody, as usual, but he's strong, Blaine. He'll be a big boy for sure." He looks over at the cows, holding his hand over his eyebrows to shield the sun that's finally peeking out of the grey clouds.

"Good. I can't wait," I say, rubbing my hands together. "Addison and I had coffee today, and I was telling her about the ranch. She loves horses, and I thought I could show her mine." I felt the need to explain why this gorgeous woman was standing in my drive way.

"Oh, coffee. Isn't that nice," Jeremiah says, sarcastically. "And, you came to the right place for a ride..."

He says he's got to go into town for a while, which I doubt, but he's doing the best friend thing to give me alone time.

"Okay, Jer. See you in a bit."

He winks at me while she's got her back turned, gets in his truck, and leaves.

"So, Miss Cole. Do you want to change into something less...*wet*?" I ask, eyeing her body. The clothing is clinging to her in a way where it leaves little to the imagination. No wonder Jer was acting like that—I can see through her white blouse that she has beautiful breasts. I try not to let her see me looking at her, but I can't help myself.

She bites her lip. "You have women's clothes?" she asks, laughing.

"Well," I start to explain, my eyes wandering on her body. "No. But you can wear one of my t-shirts if you like."

Okay, Blackstock, enough of the eye-sex.

I pull open a drawer to find a dry pair of jeans, put them on, and open the closet. I decide not to wear my usual white, but instead a dark green vintage John Deere shirt and head into the kitchen. Addison is already there, standing by the window, looking out. She's wearing my shirt, and I have to clench my jaw at the sight—wishing it was all she was wearing.

"Hey," I say from the bottom of the staircase.

"Hi." She turns around and with one word makes me melt like butter in a pan.

"Want to head out and see the horses now?" I ask, even though I'd rather pull her into my arms and devour that gorgeous mouth.

Outside we find the horses all together in the pasture. "There's my boy." I point to one standing by the corner. Mischief is a stocky mixture of quarter horse and pinto, but doesn't have the patches like his father. He's a rich copper with a jet black mane and tail. I whistle, and he trots over to the gate.

"This is Mischief. He's a big suck; I don't think he realizes he's a horse." I laugh.

Addison runs her fingers through his mane.

"Hello, Mischief," she says. "He's beautiful, Blaine."

We're both quiet for a few minutes, and she finally breaks the silence.

"Is it weird that we're complete strangers, yet here I am, totally comfortable and enjoying this immensely?"

I run my hand through my now dry hair, letting out a sigh of relief. I was hoping that she was enjoying herself, as this was not a typical *"Hi how are you? Let's meet occasionally for coffee and text one another"* start to...well, whatever this is.

"I've gotta be honest—I feel it too. This is completely comfortable to me." I hold my breath and take her hand in mine.

An over-played pop song quickly plays in my head. *Hey, I just met you, and this is crazy...*

We walk through the field, talking about random things like movies, music, and favourite foods. She tells me her favourite meal is lasagna.

"I would like to make that for you, if you would stay for dinner," I ask while I rub her knuckles with my thumb.

"Mmm, how could I refuse?" she says sweetly.

A large boom startles us both; it seems a storm was looming. The rain from earlier must have just been the beginning. Instinctively we both turn and start running as the rain follows the thunder, and we reach the porch just in time. The rain comes down hard, and the thunder crashes loudly.

"I just can't keep you dry today..." I laugh and pull my boots off.

She bites her lip, and I'm no longer butter in the pan—I'm water. Steam, evaporation. She's blowing me away. The distance of a few feet between us is no longer as we find ourselves wrapped in a passionate kiss, my hands in her hair and her hands on my arms. I feel myself start to harden, and she presses herself against me. Her body flush with mine.

The kiss is never-ending. I am lost in time; I have no idea how long we have stood here and been completely engulfed in lips and tongues and heavenly taste. She is the first to unseal the bond and steps back breathing heavily.

I open my eyes and I am complete mush. I could just fall and I would be nothing more than a pile on the hardwood floor.

"Addison..." I start to say, but can't find any other words. The only thing I want on my tongue at that very moment is her.

"Blaine, I...ugh...how about that lasagna?" she says quietly, snapping me back to reality.

I smirk at her, tip her chin up with my hand, lean in for a kiss and instead I whisper, "How could I forget?" into her ear.

My phone buzzes and when I swipe the screen to open the message, I see it's from Jeremiah.

I won't make it back today. Oh, and U R filling me in pronto!!!

I smirk at his message and text back. ***OK, cya then. And...We'll see.***

There's no way he will let me just casually explain this one. He will want details. But do I want to share the specifics of this? Hell, no. Sorry, Jer. She's all mine.

"Can I help you with anything? Maybe chop some veggies?" she asks sweetly, while sitting on the stool at the island in the center of the kitchen.

"Sure, you can." I slide over a cutting board and knife. "There are some in the crisper." I point to the fridge behind me. There is no way I am going to get those vegetables myself. I want to see her beautiful body walk around me. And she does, leaping down off the stool. She is barefoot in my kitchen. Inside, I snort. I cannot help myself; I look over my shoulder and see her bending down, reaching for items in the crisper.

God, she is sexy.

She places a green pepper on the counter, along with some cherry tomatoes and a bunch of spinach. Rinsing them all in the sink, she places them on the cutting board and goes to work. Every so often she catches me looking at her, and smiles, never stopping the chopping motion.

"Music?" I ask, pointing to my iPod cradled in its dock on the counter.

She nods. Turning it on, I select Shuffle and it starts playing some upbeat country music. She is moving her shoulders to the beat of the music, smiling and mouthing to words to herself.

I am immersed, fully capsized and ready to sink to the depths of the ocean. Is this how Quinn felt about me? I have a feeling of guilt but quickly push it aside. There is no freaking way this is love—not yet, anyway. We've known each other for two seconds. It's just got to be lust. I want this girl in such a raw way, yet...I want to know her, too.

The smell of lasagna fills the kitchen and travels into the living room where we are sitting on the large leather couch. I am embarrassed that I haven't offered her a drink by now. When I do, I realize I'm a bachelor and only have water, milk, or beer.

She says she'll have a beer, and I'm pleasantly surprised. I open two bottles and hand her one. She takes a sip, and I'm jealous of the bottle.

"So, if you grew up here, where are your parents, if you don't mind me asking? Do they live somewhere else?"

I look down at the coffee table and think how I'm going to answer these questions. Anyone who knows me knows where my parents are. My silence must have been the cue that I don't want to talk about it.

"I'm sorry. I didn't mean to..."

"It's okay," I smile. "My mom died a long time ago, and my Dad lives with my brother Nick."

"I'm sorry," she says and touches my hand.

"It's okay. It was a *really* long time ago." I am desperate to change the subject. Turning on my side, I face her. "Tell me about Alex. What's his story?"

She rolls her eyes. "Alex is spoiled by our parents. They gave him everything he wanted as a child, which made him turn into a bratty adult. They paid for him to go school, which he wasted, and when he tried going back home after dropping out, my Dad said he needed to straighten up."

She shrugs. "Alex was pissed. He's never been told no by them. So he calls me up, gives me a sob story, and moves here with me."

She twirls another piece of her hair between her fingers.

"I don't know what he plans on doing in Wyoming. Hell, I don't even know what I am doing here." She blushes.

"Well," I rub her knuckles with my thumb again, "I'm glad you are."

And then we are lips and tongues and taste all over again. She surprises me by pushing me back onto the couch, swinging her leg out. It knocks over a bottle of beer.

"Oops!" she giggles. "Sorry!"

I tell her not to worry and pull her onto me. Kissing deeply, I wrap my arms around her, and she has her fingers in my hair. I feel myself harden again, and she pulls away. Inches from my mouth, she pants, "I'm sorry; I really don't know what has gotten into me." She sits up. "I'm not the type of girl who goes to a stranger's house and does this."

"Addison, I have no idea what is going on here. I feel..." I pause. "You make me feel so good."

I narrow my eyes, and my voice lowers. "I've got to be honest, today wasn't the first time I've seen you and *wanted* you."

She looks surprised, so I continue. "A few days ago I was at Zeke's with Jeremiah, and you came in with your brother." She smiles, probably remembering now where she'd seen Jeremiah before.

"I was in the aisle, and I couldn't take my eyes off of you. I stood there like an idiot, and your brother caught me staring."

She covers her face and blushes. "Blaine! You should have approached me then."

I pull her down onto me, closer, kissing passionately. A loud beeping disturbs our intimate moment, and I realize I've burned the lasagna. Getting up quickly, I carefully place her on the couch and run into the kitchen. She sits back and smiles at me while I pull the smoking pan out of the oven and put it into the sink.

"Yeah, so you can add to the *About Blaine info* that I'm not that great of a chef." I smirk and toss the oven mitts on the island.

"I can see that!" She giggles and crosses her legs in front of her.

"I can make a mean sandwich if you're interested."

"That sounds great, thank you."

We eat, side by side. The fire in the fireplace is crackling and warm, and it feels good against my skin after a rainy afternoon. I finish my roast beef sandwich first, and grab another beer since someone gorgeous knocked mine over.

"What do you have planned for tomorrow?" she asks, sitting up and adjusting her t-shirt.

I think about what I have planned, and get immediately distracted just looking at her.

"Nothing, actually. Jeremiah is usually off on Thursdays, and I just hang around the farm." I decide I'm taking this moment to ask to her come back tomorrow. "Would you like to go riding tomorrow, if it doesn't rain again?"

She beams. "I would love to!"

But I want her to stay. Does she want to stay?

"Addison?" I pause. "I want you to stay tonight."

She looks around as if I'm asking her to sleep on the sofa. That, or she's unsure about my offer. All of a sudden I feel vulnerable, like a deer in the middle of an open field during hunting season with nowhere to run.

"Or I can drive you back to town, to your car." I quickly say to let her know I'm not against her leaving. Even though I don't want her to.

She gets up off the couch, still not saying anything. Walks around the coffee table, steps over the puddle of spilled beer, and right up to me. Reaching around my neck she pulls my head down and whispers in my ear, "I want to stay."

CHAPTER THREE

A beam of light is forcing itself into my eye, waking me up—where is it coming from? I just slightly open my eye, and the glimmer shoots me down, so I close it quickly. Where am I? Nothing in my bedroom glistens. I tilt my head back and open my eyes again. This time I realize where the light is coming from. It's peaking through the blinds, bouncing off a tiny diamond earring and hitting me straight on.

Addison.

I'm pulled into a shameless haze, remembering last night. Remembering the deep, passionate, and intense night we spent together. I can't even count how many times we had sex. The connection with this girl is unfathomable; I am at a loss for words.

I look down, and she's lying on my chest. Her long auburn hair is messy and all kinds of beautiful. Tousled strands here and there, across the pillow and down her naked back. I feel her soft hand on my chest, and she's breathing ever so quietly. I don't want to move; I want to lay here with her, just like this. Gently tracing my fingertips down her skin, I close my eyes and fall back into oblivion.

A familiar sound wakes me. Rex is outside barking at something.

Please Lord, not another animal for him to chase.

How did he get out? My hand reaches to where there was warmth earlier, but it's now gone.

She's not here. I am still naked from our intense midnight tryst. Reaching down to the floor, I find my pajama bottoms and pull them on.

Through the upstairs window I can see Rex outside, favouring his right paw and limping around. He looks okay, but he's sniffing around the fence line. I love this dog. I found him four years ago wandering on Porter Road. He was a few months old, malnourished and filthy. I asked around for a few weeks to see if anyone knew where he came from, but no one claimed him, so I kept him as my own. The typical man's best friend cliché. Yeah, that's Rex, hands down.

Walking down the stairs, I start to smell a most delicious scent. Bacon. Reaching the bottom on the staircase I can hear the grease popping and crackling in the pan. Then as quickly as the smell reached my nostrils, I forget about it.

Instead all my senses are peaked when I see the gorgeous creature standing at the screen door, naked except for one of my white t-shirts. Leaning against the wooden beam, her one leg tucked behind the other, she's resting her head on the frame. I could stand here all day and look at her.

What is this girl doing in Wyoming? Why is she in my kitchen?

My eyes drink up every inch of her, and I am intoxicated, over the limit and headed to the drunk tank. Rex makes his way up the steps, and she opens the door to let him in.

He is wagging his tail as he approaches me. "Hey boy, how are we feeling today?"

I scruff his ears with my hands.

"Good morning." She pleasantly smiles at me. "I hope you don't mind." Her hands stretch out the hem of my t-shirt.

"Not at all. You look better in it than I do," I smirk.

"I'm making breakfast—bacon and eggs okay?" She starts walking towards the large steel range.

"Mmm. It smells good." I sit on one of the stools at the island.

"Blaine?" She looks up at me. "I really enjoyed last night."

She's blushing, and I don't know why. I saw every inch of this woman, and she has nothing to be shy about. She's as close to perfection as humanly possible.

"I did too, Addison." I reach for her hand, and our fingers touch, sending tingles up my forearm.

We eat breakfast and talk about what seems to be a beautiful day in the making. No rain in sight, and the blue sky is the most exotic shade, almost the color of the ocean. I clear our dishes and place them in the sink. I'll get to them later.

She goes upstairs and is back down just as fast, wearing her pants and my black t-shirt again. Searching through her purse for something, she pulls out a hair band. Leaning her lovely neck back, I watch her pull her hair into a ponytail and then flip it around, securing it into a messy bun on the top of her head.

She catches me staring. "What?" she laughs and holds her hands up questionably.

"Nothin'," I grin, and lick my bottom lip. "Just happy you're here."

It's the truth, I am happy. I haven't felt like this...well, ever. I usually enjoy my bachelor status immensely. I don't have anyone to answer to, and I can see whatever girl I want to, whenever I want to. And I can stop myself from getting too deep, getting hurt...hurting her.

But this? Shit, I have no idea why I'm completely at her mercy. Judge, jury, and executioner. I'm out for the count.

"You look eager, Ms. Cole." I say walking towards her. "I bet you can't wait to get out there and go riding. Am I right?"

She hooks each of her index fingers in a belt loop on my jeans and pulls herself into me. "Yes, I really want to go riding," she teases, and bats her long lashes.

Through the giant wooden doors of the barn, the smell of hay and grain flow through my nostrils. I love this smell; I grew up in this scent, and I couldn't imagine anything else.

"When you rode, what was your style? Do you prefer western or English? I have both." I point to the tack room door.

"Actually, I was hoping to ride bareback. I like to feel the horse move. It's more natural." She smiles and shrugs her shoulders.

Oh, fuck.

I inhale and flash back to my daydream of her riding, bareback, sexy and free. I give her the biggest smile, all teeth, white and ear to ear.

I grab my western saddle off its rack, a black leather Billy Cook. I grab a black saddle pad and Mischief's bridle from the hook.

"Both Arabs are great rides. Cylas or Roman," I say.

She thinks about her options for a moment.

"Cylas. The white one." she decides and clasps her hands together like she's about to say a prayer.

I grab his bridle too, sling my saddle over my shoulder, and we head out to the horses in the pasture. The horses are scattered around the field, and making a clicking noise with my mouth, I call out to them.

"Come on, boys."

Roman whinnies at us, and Cylas trots over to the gate.

"I can't get over how beautiful they are, Blaine." She holds on to the steel gate, looking out at the horses like a little kid waiting in line for a pony ride at the fair.

Mischief and Cylas are both bridled, and while I'm adjusting the saddle strap, I hear Addison talking to Cylas.

"Good boy," she says calmly. "What a beautiful boy."

She runs her hands through his white mane and, with reigns in one hand, she flings herself up on his back. She's smiling at me as I'm sure I'm gaping like crazy, and she giggles.

"It's like riding a bike; you never forget!" she says matter-of-factly and holds the black leather reigns with one hand while placing her other on her hip.

"Let's see what you've got, miss!" And I lift myself up into the saddle using the stirrup, much less gracefully.

Mischief takes the lead, like usual. He's a confident beast, strong and in many ways, just like me.

"So, have you decided how long you'll be in Wyoming?" I ask, realizing we've been silent for quite some time.

"Actually, I was thinking of applying for a nursing job at the hospital. I like Sheridan...so far."

"Mmm, nurses' scrubs, eh?" I envision her, and the thought makes me have to adjust myself in my saddle.

She laughs. "Yes, I think it's about time I get a job. Maybe Alex will get inspired and do the same." She shakes her head, probably thinking of her brother and his carefree lifestyle.

I don't know where it comes from, but I find myself offering him a job.

"I could use a hand around here. I know Jer wouldn't mind some extra help, too."

She grins and looks surprised. "Really? Well, I doubt he has any clue about farms. I don't know how much help he would be."

"I'd like to meet him; maybe he can come out for a beer," I suggest, unsure of why I even want to meet him. The last time I saw him, he looked like no one I could give a shit about.

"Okay, I'll call him when we get back to the house." She clicks with the side of her mouth and Cylas responds. They trot ahead of me, and she turns back to look at me, her eyes alight and so very blue.

I squeeze my legs around Mischief's girth. "Come on!"

And we're off, closely on their heels. In the open field, I am beside her. Neck and neck, our horses like two drag cars ready to take the competing pink slip. She looks so happy, cantering, free and beautiful. Not a care in the world.

She reaches up and pulls the hair band out of her messy bun. The red tendrils fall and whip in the wind. In this moment, there is nowhere else I want to be. We run faster, and it's hard to focus on where I'm going. I can't stop looking at the fire flowing beside me. Red on white and beautiful. With her legs wrapped around Cylas, they look like they were made for each other, two separate moulds that have finally connected and became one.

As if on cue, something spooks the horses, and they both jump to the side. A flock of birds fly out of the grass and scatter in the blue sky.

"Whoa, whoa, whoa, boy!" I try to calm Mischief; he's snorting and breathing heavily. I see Cylas to my right, but no Addison. I frantically look around, "Addison? Addison!"

I see her lying in the grass a few feet behind the horses. I jump down off my horse and run over to her. To my amazement, she's laughing.

She's holding her hands over her heart, and I lean down to help her get to her feet.

"Addison, are you okay?!" I reach for her face.

"Yes! I'm okay! I fell; he didn't throw me." She looks at over at Cylas, who is calmly eating some grass.

"Holy shit, I thought...I don't know what I thought," I say, running my hands through my hair.

She puts her hands in mine, and I pull her into my body.

"I'm okay, Blaine. Really. It's not the first time I've fallen off a horse, and it probably won't be the last." She is trying to make me feel better.

I felt such panic when I saw her motionless for a second, and I had an incredible urge to wrap her in my arms and never let her go.

"Are you okay to ride back? We can walk if you want to." I brush off some dirt on her arm with my hand.

"Yeah, I'm fine. Let's go!" She's eager, and I can't believe this woman standing in front of me. She's fearless.

Helping her up on Cylas' back, I can't resist running my hand over her behind and down her leg.

"Ready?" I look up at her, and she leans down to kiss me.

Easy boy, I tell myself, feeling the excitement build in my jeans.

"Now try and keep up this time, cowboy." She's making fun of me, pulling the reigns to turn Cylas around.

I get up on Mischief in one swift, and I must say, impressive move and give him a small kick to get moving. We walk back the rest of the way, side by side, as I want to keep her close.

"So what kind of nursing do you want to do?" I ask her as we reach the gate to the corral.

"I'd like to work in the NICU actually, with preemies and newborns with special medical needs." She pulls her hair over her right shoulder so it cascades down her chest.

"My brother was born at twenty-eight weeks gestation. My mother almost lost him." She looks sad. "I was five when he was born, and although I don't remember much, I do remember my father's fear and the panic when Alex came into the world."

Maybe that's why they gave him everything, I thought to myself—for fear of losing him.

"In school it was the field that interested me the most, and although it can be hard at times, I think it would be so rewarding saving a tiny life, holding something so small in my hands..."

She stops talking, and I realize she's looking at me. My face gives me away. I look...distraught? Sad? Some sort of emotion that I'm not ready to talk about.

"Blaine? Are you okay?" she snaps me back.

"Yeah, sorry. I think that's wonderful, Addison. You would make a great nurse; I really think you should apply." I smile at her reassuringly.

***

The horses are grazing in the pasture, and I take all the tack to put it back in the barn. Addison stays behind, running her hand along Roman's mane. He must have felt left out, as he came right up to the fence looking for attention.

Closing the tack room door behind me, I see she's now standing in the doorway of the barn. She has a look on her face; I'm not sure how to read it, but it sparks my curiosity. I stop walking and decide to test the water.

I run my hand over my abdomen, and lift my t-shirt to wipe the beads of sweat off my forehead with the hem, giving her full view of my sculpted body. She drops her jaw, and I grin immensely, biting my own lip this time, and narrowing my eyes.

"Mr. Blackstock, what exactly are you doing?" she asks and starts to saunter over to me, hands clasped behind her back. Her gaze is penetrating.

"I have *no* idea what you're talking about, ma'am." I roll my eyes to the roof and snicker. I know exactly what I'm trying to do.

When she reaches me, she puts her hands on my chest and runs her fingers down my body. Looking up at me intently, she smiles and blushes just a little.

Unsure of why there is still space between us, I put my hands on her waist and pull her into me. I find myself leaning down to kiss her under her earlobe, placing small kisses along her neck, under her chin and up the other side of her face. I hear her groan, and inhale deeply.

Brushing my lips gently against hers, I want to draw out this as long as I can, savouring each and every second, and every inch of her beauty.

Her hands are holding the hem of my shirt, and I lift my arms, giving her the okay to pull it off of me. She leans in to kiss my chest, and I throw my head back with anticipation.

Now my hands are in her hair, finding their way down her neck, over her shoulders and then lifting the borrowed t-shirt off her body. Her breasts are beautiful; no, they're exquisite. Fitting in my hands perfectly, I caress her.

One would think that like in the movies, all cowboys have their way with women in piles of hay all the time. But not me; this was a first. We find ourselves on a freshly opened bale, making love, her body on top of mine. The same legs that were just wrapped around Cylas, controlling his movements, were now wrapped around me, completely owning my body.

I inhale deeply, and she gasps when my final thrust sends us both into a screeching climax together. She leans down on me, her hair on my chest and her hands gripping my arms tightly.

It dawns on me, while we are laying entangled in our post love-making, that we did not use protection.

Ugh, stupid move, Blaine.

"Shit." I start to speak. "We didn't use...anything." I nod my head down towards my still hard erection.

"Oh..." She closes her eyes and covers her face. "I'm on the pill. I am so sorry; I really should have said something last night." Opening her eyes again, she looks up at me. "I usually don't do this type of thing, and I'm really surprised at myself for it." She looks embarrassed. "I haven't been with anyone in a very long time."

I don't want to know the specifics of another man getting to feel her in the way I just have, so I wave my hand in the air and hug her tightly.

"I'm all good, too—just so you know." I half smile and pull her closer to me, kissing her lips.

Eventually I let her go, and she lifts off of my chest. "I should really call my brother. Although he doesn't worry, he is probably wondering where I am." She sits, collecting her clothing.

I watch her dress, still lying on the open and now strewn everywhere bale of hay...Even though it's poking painfully into my body.

Just days ago I stood in Zeke's, undressing her with my eyes, not knowing the extent of the beauty in front of me. And now here I am watching her without the worry of getting caught. Just having been inside her, feeling her during the most vulnerable state, and I am putty. A feeling so unfamiliar to me, yet I don't push it away.

Back inside the house Addison calls her brother.

"Hey, Alex." She pauses. "Yes, I know. I'm sorry; I'm fine." She listens to whatever it is he's saying and glances at me, smiling. "Just give him a scoop in his dish, and please make sure you let him out a few times before you leave."

I assume she's talking about her dog.

"Okay. And hey, Alex? Do you want to go for drinks later? There's someone I'd like you to meet." Smiling at me again, she's twisting a tendril of hair between her fingers.

To give her some privacy, I motion that I'm going upstairs, and she nods, still on the phone with her brother.

Upstairs I take off my pants. I didn't put my shirt back on after our moment in the barn, and I toss them both in the laundry hamper in the bathroom. I need to shower. I am all kinds of dirty, and I smirk at myself in the mirror.

I step in and let the water beat down on my head and run down my body. I lather the bar of soap in my hands and start to wash myself. When I get to my groin, I hesitate; I don't want to wash her off of me.

My hands are no comparison to hers. They are rough, and even though I know my own body, I'd rather her hands and other parts of her on me any day.

I turn off the shower, letting the remainder of the water trickle down the drain. Getting out, I towel-dry my messy hair and then my body. Taking the same towel, I wipe off the condensation on the mirror. I look at myself and notice that I need to shave.

Eh, I'll do it later, I tell myself. I dress in the usual jeans and t-shirt. I am so typical. But I like comfort and simplicity.

Downstairs, Addison is sitting on the couch, Rex happily standing between her legs looking overjoyed as she pets and scratches him all over.

"Hey," I say, and she looks up at me, still petting Rex.

"Hey yourself." She smiles and gives him one last scratch. "I thought I'd shower at home. So I'd have clothes to change into." She holds the hem of the black t-shirt out. "Would you mind driving me back to my car in town?"

As much as I don't want her to go, I want her to be comfortable and if that means taking her home, then I don't refuse.

"Yeah, of course. Do you want to get some lunch while we're in town?" I ask, completely hoping she doesn't plan on going home and staying there.

In town I pull up in front of Bean There. Feeling a tinge of...anxiety? I don't know, I look over at her and smile. I really don't want her to get out of this truck right now.

She leans over and places a gentle kiss on my lips. Closing my eyes, I get lost in her. Missing posters are put up to find me, but I hope no one ever does. After a far too short kiss, she pulls back and smiles. "I'll text you in a bit."

I smirk my sexiest grin at her and wink.

Shutting the door behind her, she pulls a set of keys from her green purse and walks up to...

No. Fucking. Way. A 1967? '68? Mustang Fastback. I think I'm having heart palpitations. That can't be her car; in no real world does a girl that beautiful drive a car almost equally appealing to the eye. I pictured her in some little hatchback, maybe a Golf or Prius. Not this insane gunmetal silver machine. The teenager in me pictures her sprawled on the hood, on the cover of a gear-head magazine, and I exhale slowly and loudly.

She gets in the car, waves at me through the open window and lets that baby roar away from me. Turning at the lights, she's gone.

I'm still sitting, truck idling, my foot on the clutch with intent to drive, but nothing is happening. I reel through the images in my head of the last day and a half. I almost pinch myself to see if it's all really happening. Letting out a loud sigh again, I check my rear view mirror and shift into first, then second, then third...

Pulling into Jeremiah's driveway, I see him in the yard, raking stones on the off the grass. He looks up and waves. I honk the horn and grin.

"What's up, buddy?" Jer puts his fist out to bump mine.

"Not much. Just seeing what you were up to." I really don't know why I'm here; I guess I wanted to see him. I didn't want to be alone with my thoughts after seeing Addison drive away.

"Okay, let's hear it." He motions his hand in a beckoning for information.

I know exactly what he wants to know, and I let out a sigh while raising one of my eyebrows.

"Hear what?" I ask coyly, kicking my shoe into the dirt, flinging a few of the stones he had just raked up.

"The girl, man. What was she doing at your house?" He pushes my shoulder with his hand and laughs.

I tell him about her and me meeting in Dr. Jenkins' office, and how I just felt like I couldn't leave without talking to her. "I know—totally unlike me." I trail off, looking around at anything but his eyes.

"Blaine?" He moves to catch my gaze, laughing at me. "Are you in love?" He holds his hand on his heart and snorts.

"Fuck it, I'm going..." I turn on my heel and start walking like a child. Guys don't get this defensive, so why the hell am I right now?

"Man, I was kidding. She's beautiful, and you're a lucky guy," Jeremiah calls from behind me.

I turn around and kick the dirt again.

"Jer, I don't know what's going on. I'm..." I sputter my lips and look at the sky. "I *really* like her."

Jer suggests I be cool and not scare her away with my intense and unfamiliar feelings. I agree with him, as I am still unsure about it myself so I don't want to overwhelm her with hearts and rainbows and chubby cherubs with their sights set right on my ass.

"We're meeting for lunch today. Do you wanna come by later for a fire? I think she's inviting her brother over. I might offer him a job to help us around the farm." I don't explain why; I just shrug my shoulders.

"Yeah, okay." He looks inquisitively at me. "Can I bring a date?"

Aside from the girl he took to prom in high school, I've never seen Jeremiah *date*. He's like me; he has little flings here and there but nothing serious. And he has never brought anyone over or introduced them to me.

"A date?" This time I shove his shoulder with my hand. "Who did you have in mind?"

"It's a secret. You'll see later, man," he jokes and stands the rake up against his garage door.

I have no clue who he could be referring to, and I don't ask any more questions. I'm intrigued, as I know pretty much every available woman around, and I can't think of who it could be.

Jer brings out two bottles of beer from the house, and we sit on the tailgate of my truck and drink, enjoying the sunshine. It feels good on my skin, warm and inviting, and I soak it in.

It makes me think of her, of her warm skin on mine; it was like silk in my hands. She didn't seem to mind my rough hands exploring her body or her face as I caressed her. She even kissed a callous on the inside of my hand...

Here we go, I'm submerged in my thoughts again. This time I'm inches from the bottom, ready to buckle under the pressure and implode in the darkness of the sea. Remembering I'm sitting beside Jeremiah, I collect my thoughts and compose myself.

Get a grip, Blackstock.

My phone buzzes, and when I pull it out of my jeans pocket, I see a text from Addison.

Hey, handsome. Hungry yet?

I inhale deeply and smile at the screen of my iPhone.

"I don't even have to ask, do I?" Jeremiah says, shaking his head.

"Nope!" I pat his shoulder, hop off the tailgate of my truck and put the phone back in my pocket.

"All right, bro. See ya later," he says, jumping off in the same motion, but landing on a large stone and wincing.

"Shit! Ouch!" He chuckles and hold his foot in his hands.

"Crybaby." I laugh and climb up into the truck and back out of the driveway.

Jer waves, picks up his rake and continues to move the stones from the grass again.

At the stop sign at the end of the road, I pull my phone out of my jeans again and open the messages to send my reply. **Starving. Where to, miss?**

I hit the button, and it makes a whoosh noise as it sends my text to her phone. Almost instantly I get a reply. **Lakes?**

Lakes is a big diner in town, well known for its extended menu, catering to all kinds of palates. Their pizza is actually the best in town; I remember my Dad took us boys there almost every Saturday night when we were kids. Large Hawaiian with extra green olives—my favourite.

Lakes. See ya in 15? I hit send again and hear the whoosh. I realize there is a car impatiently waiting behind me when I am startled by its horn, honking at me to move. I wave my hand out my window, flip the turn signal to go right, and check for traffic.

I pull into Lakes' large parking lot and see that Addison is already here. She's leaning against the fender of her car, looking too sexy to be legal. She's wearing a pair of frayed jean shorts and a well-fitted blue t-shirt. I find a parking spot near the back, away from everyone else.

"You look beautiful." I take her hand and kiss it lightly.

"Not too bad yourself." She gives me a wink and curls her fingers into my hand.

"Okay, where did you get this car? I almost died when you got into it earlier."

She blushes and turns to look at the car. "It was my Dad's, his first car."

"Well, you look sexy as hell in it." I grin, and she smiles innocently at me.

Lakes has a typical diner theme—white walls, retro-styled seating areas rimmed with metal edges. A large menu over the opening to the kitchen, where you can see some of the staff hastily cooking amidst the steam of the grills and fryers. It's usually busy at lunch here, so I'm surprised when we find a table so quickly.

"Hey, Blaine!" A happy voice greets me; it's Sadee, the girlfriend of one of my nephews. Nick's kid, Bobby.

"Hey there, Sadee. What's good today?" I motion to the menu board. She smiles at Addison and looks at me with an approving smirk. "Well, the special today is a bacon cheeseburger with any side. For $5.95."

I salivate at the thought and look at Addison. She's reading the large menu and then turns her eyes to Sadee. "I'll have that! With fries and a Coke, if you have it."

"And I'll have the exact same."

"Alright, guys, I'll be back with your drinks in a jiffy!" Sadee says, bouncing off, writing down our order in a little spiral notebook.

"What?" Addison says, and I realize I'm gazing at her. I clear my throat and adjust myself in the vinyl seat. Every time I look at her I see some new beautiful detail, like the small and very faint splash of freckles across her nose.

"Oh, nothing." I smile.

"Tell me about your family." She asks slowly, batting her long lashes over her big blue eyes. I look out the window and try to piece together how to explain the Blackstocks' to her.

"Well," I start, "My mom and dad met in elementary school—grew up here, too. Got married young, then she got pregnant with my brother Nick."

She reaches to hold my fingers with hers, and I squeeze them gently. The touch slows and races my heart all at the same time.

"Owen came long two years later. They lived at the ranch; it was my great grandfather's."

Sadee is back with our drinks. "Thanks, Sadee." I look up at her.

"No prob, guys. The food should be out soon!" And she's gone again.

"Sadee is my nephew's girlfriend." I tell Addison. "Bobby, he's Nick's oldest son."

"How much older are your brothers?"

"Nick is forty-five, and Owen will be 43 this fall."

I wonder if she's doing the calculations in her head.

"Yeah, my parents didn't plan on having me."

She's still holding my fingers, not breaking eye contact once.

Sadee is back and places our food in front of us. "Can I get you anything else?" she asks happily.

"I'm good if you are." Addison smiles at me and then up to Sadee.

"Yep, we're good. Thank you."

Sadee gives a thumbs up and goes to help clear a table with another young girl.

We talk more about her applying for a nursing job, her brother possibly working at my ranch, and even a little about Jeremiah. I tell her the story about Ivy breaking his toes, and she laughs.

"That's why he was waving that big stick like a mad man yesterday?"

I snort. "Yep, she can be a handful."

I tell her how Jer and I have been best friends our entire lives. He went through a dark time after his parents died, and having him work with me at the ranch really seemed to keep him busy and in better spirits.

"He's lucky to have a friend like you." she says, and I realize that it's the other way around. I'm lucky to have him.

Dipping the last of my fries into a glob of ketchup on my plate, I ask her, "How do you feel about having your brother over tonight? We could have a bonfire, maybe roast some marshmallows?" I raise one of my eyebrows and grin.

"Yeah! That would be fun." She bites a fry in half and grins back.

Sadee is back to clear our plates, and Addison pulls her phone out her purse.

"I'll text Alex, and make sure he's let Luca out."

Her phone makes a beeping noise, and she picks it up to read the message. Eyebrows raised, she starts typing in what I assume is a response.

"He's in. As long as there's beer." She rolls her beautiful blue eyes. When she sets her phone back on the table, I reach for her hand and kiss her knuckles, the stubble above my lip whispering across her skin.

CHAPTER FOUR

I stoke the fire with a long thick branch. It pops and crackles, sending little orange embers up into the sky, disappearing into the night. Music is playing from stereo and out the open windows in the truck.

Addison went home after lunch this afternoon; she said she had things to do and would be back tonight with her brother. I miss her. Two days, and I miss her. The sweet scent of her hair, the soft touch of her hands in mine, and her big eyes staring into my soul.

I sound like a Hallmark card for crying out loud. I'm entranced, watching the flames flick around, like hot, sharp tongues lashing at the night sky.

The sound of a truck engine drowns out the music briefly, and I look over to see Jeremiah pulling up. He parks in front of the garage.

"Hey! Buddy!" Jumping out, he runs around the back of his truck to open the passenger door. Two long and tan legs emerge, followed by a loud, "Buh-lay-aineeeee!"

The overdrawn use of my name makes me cringe, and I see whose mouth it's coming from.

Gwen Wolf.

Jer, are you fucking serious? Gwen Wolf? Buddy...

Trying not to make my annoyance apparent, I greet them. "Hey, guys. How's it going?"

She's walking up to me, stumbling slightly. Jer catches her, and she laughs obnoxiously.

Oh, shit—is she drunk?

I shoot Jeremiah a look to ask him what the hell he was thinking bringing her here like this.

He shrugs and mouths back, "Come on!"

"Blaine Blackstock." Gwen looks up at me with the biggest sloppy smile on her face. "Youuuuu...are an awful host! Why haven't you offered me a drink?"

One: you just got here.
Two: like you need any more to drink, sweetheart.
I frown. "What would you like, Gwen?" I am beyond annoyed.

She sits in a green lawn chair, crosses one leg over the other and calls Rex over to her side. He happily wags his tail and walks over to her, the limping almost gone.

"Gwen?" I repeat sharply.

"Oh, yes. Just a beer please." She manages to speak without slurring, and I shoot Jer daggers with my eyes.

He follows me inside and as soon as the door closes behind him, I whip around. "Gwen? You really brought her here? And like that?" I point my finger out the door.

"Buddy, really? You like Gwen. What's the big deal?" he asks, and I realize he really doesn't see why I'm irritated.

"Jer, she's drunk. And it's only seven o'clock! Addison and her brother are coming." I look over at the large clock on the wall. "And you better hope she doesn't make a fool out of herself." I scold him like he's a child, and I instantly feel bad about it.

"Oh, well! Excuse me!" He puts his hands up defensively and then reaches to open the fridge door.

"I'm sorry, Jer. I really like this girl. I can't explain why. I'm just..." I trail off, not sure what exactly I am trying to say.

"I get it, Blaine. I do." He smiles and pulls out a six-pack of beer cans. "She is sa-mokin' hot!"

I can't help but grin because of his expression—and also, I couldn't agree with him more.

"Man, you have no idea." I say, as I completely envision her naked body on top of mine, that wild red hair falling on my face and chest while she devours me.

He asks me what her story is, why she's in Wyoming and where she's staying. I tell him as much as she's told me, and that she plans on applying at the hospital for a nursing job. The thought makes me smile, and I wish she was here already.

Where is she anyway?

"We better get out to your...date." I smirk, grabbing some bottles of water. He grabs the beer cans, and we head back outside.

Gwen's still sitting in the lawn chair; Rex is nowhere to be seen, and Toby Keith is playing loudly over the speakers. Gwen's singing to herself. She looks up happily at Jer and me, and I start to feel bad about reacting so poorly when she showed up.

"Here you go, missy!" he says and hands her a can of beer.

"Thank you, kind sir!" She nods her head at him and giggles as she cracks the seam of the can, beer spilling out. She sucks the foam up quickly.

I pull my phone out of my pocket—no messages. Where is she? I decide to send her a text. *Hey you, just wondering when I'm going to get to see your beautiful face again :)*

And I hit send. Two, three, four, 10 minutes go by and still no response. Should I start to worry? I don't know how to go about these things. I don't know her brother's number, so it's not like I can text him. Wouldn't that be weird anyway?

Half an hour goes by since my text, and between Gwen, Jer and I we've finished the six-pack and are two cans into the next set.

Gwen tells us about the new plans her brother Jesse has for The Wolfbarrow, how he wants to expand to another town in Wyoming and possibly have her manage the new location.

"I don't know if I want to leave home, though." She smiles at the both of us and looks at me intently. "I'll miss everyone."

Around 9:30, I feel my phone vibrating. I quickly pull it out of my jeans and see it's a message from Addison. *Blaine, I'm so sorry. I had to go to Big Horn. I won't be able to make it tonight. I'll makeit up to you ;)*

Relieved she is okay, but disappointed I won't see her or spend the night with her, I type a response. *:(How will you make it up to me? What's in Big Horn?*

Jeremiah and Gwen are talking amongst themselves about what I think is her unrealistic choice of footwear. She's wearing strappy heels, not something you'd see on a farm, and he picks up her left foot to check out the shoe closer. She's laughing at him, and I look back at my phone, anticipating a salacious reply.

You'll just have to wait and see...My brother was there, I had to pick him up.

Can't wait ;) I hit send, lean back in my chair and grin up at the starry sky, then over to my tipsy company.

There is no way I am letting these two drive home in their condition. Their condition? My condition, too. I'm drunk.

After Addison's texts I hammer back five more cans of beer, making my personal count ten? Maybe eleven...or twelve; I can't remember.

Gwen passed out over half an hour ago, and Jer looks like's ready to follow suit.

"You guys are staying, bud," I manage to say without slurring.

I have four bedrooms, and these two are definitely not driving anywhere tonight.

"Yep. We are. Thanks, man." He reaches over to Gwen's arm and shakes her hand. "Hey, baby. Let's get you in bed."

I give him a raised eyebrow, and he shrugs his shoulders at my silent accusation, "What?"

Gwen doesn't wake up, and so he leans down to lift her into his arms. I laugh at him as he can't even stand on his own two feet.

"Let me." I push him aside, and he falls back into his lawn chair laughing. Gwen smells like lavender and Budweiser. She's softly snoring, and I try not to drop her as I step up onto the porch.

Upstairs I put her in one of the spare bedrooms, cover her with a blanket and close the door behind me. Jeremiah is making his way up the stairs, holding on to the banister, and slowly placing one foot in front of the other.

"Where is she?" he asks me, looking down the hallway at each door.

"In there, but you're not going in, bro. Try to be a gentleman." I point to the closed wooden door and then back at him.

"Okay, *dad*. Thanks for a good night. We gotta do this again."

He leans down to take off his shoes and stumbles in to the adjacent bedroom, leaving the door open. I see him fall onto the creaky wrought-iron bed and sigh loudly—then burp even louder.

"Night, sunshine," I call back to him as I walk down the hall.

He laughs.

I make my way to my own bedroom, and take my clothes off. I set my phone on the night stand. No new texts. I curl my lip and pull on my pajama bottoms. My bed feels amazing. It must be the alcohol making my sense of touch more deep; the sheets are cool against my heated body.

My head sinks into my pillow, and I fall into a deep sleep. I dream of light blue dresses, flowing red hair, a beautiful body lying in a field, and long eyelashes against my chest. My dream feels so real. I can feel her heat beside me; I can touch her skin with my fingertips, and her lips are brushing my throat.

Mmm...Yes, baby.

She surprises me, disappearing into the darkness and suddenly I feel her mouth around me. I am hard as a rock, and her long, slow licks are sending star bursts into my eyelids. They fly open.

I'm not dreaming. I am not dreaming at all. I reach down to feel a head of hair bobbing between my legs. Pulling the blanket away, I am mortified.

"Gwen! What the fuck?!" I sit up as fast as I can, and she does too, wiping her mouth with the back of her hand.

"What the hell are you doing?" I say loudly, and then quickly lower my voice as I remember Jeremiah in the room two doors away.

"Don't act like you don't want it," she says in a husky voice. "You've wanted this for years!"

She trails her finger down her neck and between her breasts.

"Gwen. No. You're drunk. Go back to your own bed." I get out of my bed, hold my pants over lower-half, and I open the door, praying she leaves.

"Are you kidding me, Blaine?" she says angrily. "Fine. I'll go sleep with Jeremiah; at least he wants me!"

She sounds like a whiny brat, and the guilt I felt earlier tonight about not wanting her there is gone like the wind. I shut the door behind her, and I stand listening to make sure she actually walks away.

She does; I hear her whispering something to Jeremiah and then a creak of the old iron bed as she climbs in beside him. I turn the lock on my door and climb back into my bed. What the hell was that? I instinctively rub my hand over myself, my erection now gone.

Thank you. I think, looking up at the ceiling.

Ordinarily I would have been all over something like that. I would have grabbed that girl, thrown her down on the bed and kissed every inch of her, making her scream with anticipation before I drove myself in. She would have exploded around me, and in turn, I into her.

Maybe not with Gwen Wolf, but another girl I found attractive.

But I don't want anyone but Addison. I don't want to run my tongue down the throat and chest of anyone else but her. My erection is back, and I bury my face into my pillow, letting out a long groan of frustration.

Gwen...what am I going to do in the morning when I see you?

Act like it never happened probably. I'm not going down that road, and there's no way I'll let Jeremiah find out that the girl he brought to my house as his date just had my entire length in her mouth.

***

Rex barking outside my bedroom window wakes me up. I look at the alarm clock; it's 9:53 AM. I rub my hands on my face and sit up. I shouldn't drink like that. I'm only twenty-nine, but I'm not that young anymore. And hangovers have never appealed to me.

I toss my pajama bottoms into the hamper in the bathroom and turn the knob in the shower. Steam quickly fills the small room, and I breathe in deeply. Standing under the shower head, I adjust the setting to massage and enjoy the rapid motion pulsating down my neck and back. I just want to stand here all morning, wash this feeling out and the remainder of Gwen off. I close my eyes and wince at the memory of her wiping her mouth with her hand.

I am satisfied with my cleanliness and turn off the shower. Stepping out, I wrap a towel around my waist and decide it's time to shave the scruff off of my face. I lather the cream and use my hands to apply it to my face. I shave it all off, and when I rinse my face with water, I look up to see quite a handsome man staring back at me.

And where is she to see you looking this good, Blackstock?

I wish she was here. I wish she had been with me all night and this morning in the shower and in my arms right now.

When I'm dried off, I put on a pair of stained blue jeans and a black t-shirt. No point in dressing nicely today; there's a lot of work to do around the ranch, and I've been putting off painting the chicken coop for a few weeks.

Downstairs I hear the radio playing some hip hop music and a girl's voice trying to quickly repeat the lyrics in the chorus of the song. Jeremiah is dancing like a fool in front of the range, trying to sing along with her and very obviously not knowing the words at all.

When the song ends, I speak up. "Encore!" I yell and clap my hands together.

They both turn, and Jer bows graciously at my applause.

Gwen gets off the stool. "Morning, Blaine. How are you today?"

MEADOWLARKS

I know what you're doing, young lady, and it's not going to happen!

"Hey ya, Gwen. I'm great, thank you. How did you two sleep?" I grab a piece of toast from a plate on the island and shove it into my mouth, chewing down obnoxiously at her.

Jeremiah wraps his arms around her waist and plants a kiss on her cheek. She smirks and shoves her behind into his lap and then breaks free from his grasp.

He winks at me, and I can't help but smile back.

You better not play games with him, Gwen. So help me.

"We have a lot to do today, eh?" he asks, noticing my grubby clothes.

"Yeah, gotta get that coop painted. I've slacked big time." I slap my hands and rub them together quickly, hoping my insinuation gives Gwen the hint that we will be busy and she should probably go.

"I'm gonna drive Gwen back to her house, but I'll be back in twenty."

He's a mind reader.

"Okay, see ya. Gwen, have a nice day." I smile at them both, put my hat on my head and tip the brim down at her.

"Bye, Blaine." She looks like she's going to pout, turns on her heel and follows Jer out the door. I wave at him as he closes the door behind them. Grabbing my work boots, I slap my hand on my thigh and call to Rex.

"C'mon, boy!" He gets up from his giant pillow, and we go outside.

***

I may be one hell of a rancher, but I'm a horrible painter. I think I have more red on my hands than I do on the coop. Thankful, that's why I have Jer around—for things like this. He takes pride in his work, and I am always satisfied with the tasks he completes.

My phone buzzes, and I grab a rag to wipe my hands before pulling it out of my pocket.

My truck kicked the bucket. It won't turn over. I'm by Lander's. Come get me?

I laugh. I knew this was going to happen someday. That old Chevy should have died years ago. It was older than we were; it belonged to Jer's dad, and I think that was the reason why he couldn't bring himself to part with it.

Sure enough, Jer is sitting on the tailgate waiting for me with a big frown on his face. I pull in behind his truck and turn off the ignition.

"Hey buddy! Do you need me to call triple A?" I joke, and he gives me the finger.

"So, what happened?" I ask as I walk up to the front of the truck. The hood is already up, so I examine the engine, checking out the usual suspects.

"Don't know," he says and scratches his head. "I dropped Gwen off, pulled on to the street, and it just died. I had no power at all."

I laugh, as I doubt there's been any power in this old thing in a very long time.

"I hate to say it bud, but I think it's time for a new one."

I kick the bumper of his truck with the toe of my boot.

"Hey, now; I'm sure we can fix her!" he says, rubbing his hand over the spot I just kicked.

I sigh and lower the hood, letting it fall it makes a loud bang.

"Jer, if it's..." I trail off and look him in the eyes. "If it's about the money, I can help you out."

I don't pay him with buttons and marbles, but I know how much he does make, and he can't really afford to buy a new truck.

"No, Blaine! You aren't giving me a loan. I can afford a payment...I think." It looks like he's doing a mental calculation in his head.

After some pondering, he decides to take a look at a few new trucks. He surprises me when he asks me to pull into Moorehead's Dodge.

"Dodge? *Really?*" I snort. I've always been a Ford man, and I haven't really given a second glance to anything else. We slowly drive along a lineup of blues, reds, greys and blacks.

"Stop!" He puts his hand on the lever to get out. I stop, and he jumps down, briskly walking over to a white 2500 extended cab.

Not too bad, I think to myself. I can picture him flying down the dirt road in the truck with nothing behind him but a dust cloud.

"Well, howdy, fellas!" a deep voice from behind us says. "I see you are checking out this fine piece" A bald and burly man in a striped dress shirt pats the bed of the truck with his hand.

"Yes, sir; can you tell me about it?" Jeremiah quickly shakes his hand and goes back to eyeing up the truck.

The salesman, who mentions his name is Bruce, explains the mileage, horsepower, exhaust and the usual bells and whistles.

Jeremiah is like a kid at Christmas, and I can see he's sold already. "Can we take it for a spin?" He's beaming like he already owns it.

"You sure can, young fella. Just gotta ask your friend here to move that big black monstrosity parked behind us!" he jokes, pointing his thumb back at me and my Ford.

I snort. *Okay, Dodge man...*

I jump in and fire it up. His smile quickly fades, and I rev the engine while I drive away, parking in a spot close to the dealership entrance.

Bruce insists on coming along for the test drive, but since he made a joke at my Ford's expense, I ride shotgun and he sits in the back. I won't admit it front of him, but this Dodge is a nice ride.

It's a diesel—sounds almost like mine, just with a quieter rumble. Jeremiah is still elated, and we drive down Walker Street, turning onto the interstate. It's time to let this baby fly.

I can see over my shoulder that Bruce is shifting in his seat, probably regretting coming for the ride.

"Well, how does it feel?" Our windows are down, and the wind is blowing in so loudly I need to yell so Jeremiah can hear me.

"Oh, baby!" he says, not taking his eyes off the road. "Bruce, buddy! Where do I sign?" He taps his hands on the steering wheel like they're a set of drums.

Bruce pales and forces a smile with a furrowed brow.

Back at the dealership, Bruce is going over the loan details with Jeremiah. I stand outside, leaning against my truck, and they go inside to wheel and deal.

I cross my arms on my chest and lift my head up letting the warm sun fill my face. A soft rumble catches my attention, and I look over to see a grey Mustang turning the corner, driving up the street.

I stand up. I'm excited to see the vision behind the wheel. It's her, but she's not alone. It looks like Alex in the passenger seat, and they look like they're arguing. I watch closely as they pass by the car lot, not noticing me at all. I pull my phone out of my pocket and send her a text. **Hey beautiful. How are you today? I missed you last night. My bed felt so empty.**

Even thought it briefly wasn't, no thanks to Gwen. I wait for her response, but it doesn't come.

Jeremiah comes outside and jumps in the air like Rocky on top of the steps in Philadelphia. I lift my hand up to high-five and congratulate him on his new purchase.

I am so happy for him; he needs something more reliable and definitely something better looking than that old red Chevy.

He tells me how Bruce offered to upgrade his exhaust system and add a pair of chrome stacks to the bed for an additional charge. Jer of course agreed to it, telling me they would be installed in a few days. He has already called his insurance company to have the new truck put on his policy and the Chev taken off. We'll have to have it towed it back to his house.

I wonder what he's going to do with it. I doubt he will sell it, or crush it. He'll probably park it in the yard, and that's where it'll stay.

"Ready to get to work?" I smile and open the door of my truck.

"Yeah, buddy! Let's go!" He spins the key ring around his finger and punches the air like he's hit a home run.

On the drive back to the ranch, I have my phone in the cradle, and it rings. Without looking at the caller, I push the button my steering wheel to answer.

"Hello?" I say, turning onto Porter Road.

"Blaine, hey! It's Addison."

"Hey, you! How's it going?" I'm surprised, but happy that she's called me.

Following in Jeremiah's dust cloud, I am about three minutes from my house.

"I'm good. Sorry I didn't call or text earlier. I've been...busy." There is hesitation in her voice, but why?

"It's okay, darlin'. I was wondering when I was going to hear your voice again."

"My brother has been a handful, and I'm almost ready to put him on a flight back to Maine," she explains, her sweet voice sounding slightly annoyed. I can hear someone in the background talking, and then she sighs. "I gotta go; I'm sorry. Can I see you later tonight?"

As if it's even a question. "Of course. I seem to recall you have some making up to do?"

I smile, hoping she can tell in my voice that I'm excited.

"Oh, yes. *That I do.*"

And just like that, our short and sweet conversation is over.

I wonder what her brother has gotten into, why they were arguing in her car, and whether or not I should have offered to help her. Pulling up in front of the garage, I shift into park and turn off the engine.

If u need anything, I'm here. I send her a quick text. She responds with a simple ***thank you.***

Jeremiah and I finish painting the chicken coop much faster as a pair than I would have on my own. And we used less paint too, I'm sure.

Next, we busy ourselves by mucking out the stalls in the barn and laying down fresh straw for the animals. Ivy's calf is getting so big; he's wandering around with the other cattle, and she's lying down basking in the afternoon sun.

"Hey, we haven't named him yet," I say, pointing at the calf.

"Yeah, you're right. How about..." Jer ponders while tapping his finger on his chin. "Thor!"

I laugh. "Thor? Really?"

I think about it more and picture the strong hero from the comics. "Yeah, okay. Thor it is."

We'll give him some time to grow and then see what mere mortals try to conquer him in the ring. The thought makes me grin; I know the kind of money I can make from having a prize bull that no man can keep a leather grip on.

At 5:30 PM, we finish up.

"Feel like grabbing a bite?" I ask him as he brushes the dirt off his pants.

"Actually, I'm meeting Gwen at The Wolfbarrow for supper," he says, stretching his arms up in the air and yawning. "Aren't you meeting up with that fiery redhead anyway?"

I scratch the stubble already starting to grow on my jaw.

"Yeah, I hope so. She was busy today, so we'll see."

He leaves, very happily I must say, in his new truck, and I go inside to shower again.

Maybe it's something about the water, the warmth, I don't know what. I just love being in the shower, the feel of the water flowing over me. It's so calming and makes any troubles funnel down the drain.

I shampoo my hair, scrubbing my scalp with my nails. My eyes are tightly closed. Leaning in to rinse off, I feel hands on my back.

Not again...

I whip around, peeking out from one eyelid as the foam trickles down my face. I am thrilled when I see that it's not Gwen, but *her*. The sexy, sexy Addison.

My Addison. Completely naked and standing in my shower.

"I hope you don't mind. I let myself in." She smiles and bites her bottom lip. Saying nothing I put my hands on her face and pull her into a deep kiss. She tastes heavenly, and I'm intoxicated again. She wraps her arms around my neck, and we kiss deeper, if it's even possible. I'm the first to break away, and I kiss and suck across her cheek and down her neck.

"I missed you today," she says, breathing heavily.

I run my tongue along her shoulder and breathe. "I missed you, too."

We aren't in the shower long, just enough to rinse my hair, as I need to get her into my bed. I pick her up and set her down gently, kissing still. She sits back, leaving only her feet dangling off the bed. I climb on top of her, the water dripping off of me and falling on her beautiful skin.

I kiss down her throat, down her chest, spending time with each of her breasts. She breathes heavily and caresses the back of my head with her hand.

She lets out a tiny giggle when my lips brush against her hip, and I smile. "Ticklish, are we?"

"Mmm," she breathes.

I continue my journey south, and she invites me in. I tease and taste her, making every second last.

After she climaxes, I kiss the inside of her thighs, and she quivers at my touch. I climb back up her body and brush her nose with mine.

"Mmm." She moans again, eyes closed like she's trying to focus hard on something and not let it go.

"I've been wanting to do this to you all day," I whisper and kiss the side of her mouth.

She grips tighter on my arms and pulls me into her. "Make love to me, Blaine."

And with those five words, I do. We move at a slow but deep and intense pace, bodies in motion together, like waves slowly lapping the sand on a beach. Her arms are around mine, her chin on my shoulder, and I am holding her hair in my hand, pulling ever so gently.

She erupts again, throwing her head back into the bed. I kiss her throat and find my release. I can't see anything but her full lips slightly parted and her long lashes almost touching her cheeks.

I move so I'm lying beside her, my lips against her shoulder. She holds her hands on her chest, over her heart, breathing deeply, "Well..." She turns to look at me. "I should come over unannounced more often."

CHAPTER FIVE

The alarm clock displays 7:14 on its LCD screen.

"You hungry?" I take her hand in mine and kiss her thumb and each finger.

"Mmm, yes, I am," she says with a raised, perfectly shaped eyebrow.

I fire up the barbeque on the porch and let it heat up, grabbing some steaks wrapped in brown butcher's paper from the fridge. I put them on a plate. A few potatoes should be good too, and I grab them, making a slit with a knife and wrapping them in foil.

Back outside, Addison is sitting on the bench that's suspended with chains from the roof of the porch, something my dad made for my mom when Nick and Owen were little. I realize she's brought Luca when I see him and Rex wandering around, sniffing each other and barking at the cattle.

"I hope you don't mind that I brought him. I didn't want to leave him at home with my brother." She looks lovingly at her dog.

"I'm happy you did. Rex hasn't been getting much attention lately. Maybe he needs a buddy." I smile and flip the steaks onto the grill with a pair of metal tongs.

We sit on the porch and eat, sipping lemonade from mason jars. What does *The Ritz* have on this place? Addison finishes her steak before I do, and I smirk, thinking I can thank myself for giving her an appetite after our workout.

"Mmm, that was so good. Thank you," she says, quietly sucking sauce off her finger.

"You are most welcome." I take long sip of the cool lemonade.

We sit and watch the dogs play for a while after we've finished eating. Rex is fully recovered and is running around like he usually does, but this time he's got a friend to show off for.

The horses are grazing in the field. Cylas is rolling around in the dirt, getting that beautiful white coat of his filthy.

"Look at him," she says, pointing to the dust cloud he's created. He stands and shakes off; even dirty, he's beautiful.

My phone rings. I pull it out of my pocket. "Hello?"

It's my brother, Nick.

"Hey, Blaine, how are you?" He's speaking in a low tone, almost a whisper.

"Good. What's up, Nick?" I'm curious as to why he's calling me.

"Dad's birthday is this weekend; did you remember? We were hoping to have a party for him on the ranch. It's his 70th, and even though he'll grumble at the idea, we have to have a party or something for him."

Nick's obviously speaking so quietly in fear that our dad is listening, knowing his aversion to attention and parties—hell, any type of celebration. I can see why Nick's being shady.

"Maria and Kelsey have been planning the details already so all we have do is show up." He laughs. "One of them will call you later to let you know when they'll be over to decorate."

I look over at Addison. She's sitting on the steps with her knees pulled up into her chest, arms wrapped around them, watching the dogs play.

"Okay, bro. Jer and I will get things tidied up for the girls." I nudge her with my elbow, and she smiles at me.

"Yeah...okay...yep, no problem. Bye."

I hang up, and turn to face her.

"So," I start to say, quickly rubbing my hands on my thighs. "My Dad's 70th is this Saturday. The party will be here, and I'd love it if you came." I flash her my all-American smile, knowing she won't be able to resist my offer.

"Well," she says and starts to blush. "Meeting the family already?"

I stand up off the step and walk a few feet before turning around to face her, still backing up slowly. "It's not like I can keep you confined to my bedroom, as much as I would love that idea."

I smirk, clasping my hands together behind my head.

She grabs a small stone from the dirt and tosses it at me.

"Oh, really! You just can't get enough of me, can you?" And she's hit the bull's-eye dead center.

"No, I can't." I wink at her and bend down to pet both the dogs. "It'll be a big party. Lots of people in town are friends with my dad. My sisters-in-law are coming tomorrow to start decorating."

"I would love to help them if they need it." She smiles, standing up to walk over to me.

I run my hand up the back of her naked leg; I'm still bent down from when I was petting the dogs. I lean in to kiss her thigh, and she gently puts her fingers through my hair and grips.

"If you keep doing that, I'll have no choice but to keep you in my bedroom."

With one swift move I get to my feet, and then sweep her off hers. She shrieks and laughs.

"That's all I want to do right now," I say, and I adjust my grip to hold her closer and tighter to my body. She leans in, trailing her fingertips along my bicep, kissing my collarbone. When we get upstairs, we lose ourselves all over again in white sheets, salty sweat and sweet rhythm.

***

All I can hear is the sound of our breathing and the crickets chirping out the open bedroom window. It's a cool May night, and with all the heat pouring off this bed, the open window and breeze are very welcome.

"I can't stay." Her words open my eyes, and I look over to her and stick out my bottom lip.

"No?" I ask, wrapping my arms tightly around her, not wanting to let her leave this spot.

"I have to get back home and make sure Alex is there."

I wonder if she's going to tell me what's going on with him.

"He got caught for public intoxication in Big Horn, and I had to pick him up from the police station." She rubs her eyes with her fingers and sighs. "His attitude lately has been horrible, but he won't go back to Maine." Rolling on to her stomach, she nuzzles her head on my chest and kisses my heated skin.

"Wow, I didn't realize," I reply. "Maybe a farm job is what could straighten him out, and then at least you would know where he is." I run my fingers along her spine, the sheet only covering her behind and legs.

"Yeah, I really think so," she agrees, nodding her head. And our embrace is over as she sits up to get out of bed, her long hair unruly, and tendrils wisp on the small of her back. It's dark, but enough moonlight graces us through the window that I can watch her dress. She pulls on plain white cotton panties. Aware I'm watching her, she turns around and bends over to pick up her cotton summer dress.

"Do that again and you're not going anywhere." I groan and feel myself start to harden beneath the soft white sheet.

Her bra and dress are on now, and she climbs back on the bed, over top of me, straddling me. I pull her face down to meet mine and we kiss. I don't want her to go.

I breathe heavily in her ear. "I...I..." I don't know what I'm trying to say; I'm just full of passion and heat. All my blood left my body hours ago and is located centrally in one region alone.

"Me, too," she says, as if she knows what words are trying to escape my lips.

I have a very restful sleep, even though I'm in bed alone.

She sent me a text when she got home, letting me know she was there safely and to wish me a good sleep. Wish granted, I've been doused in slumber dust, and nothing will wake me. I left the window open all night, and the heat of the morning pours in the room, the sun warming my bed. I wake up, stretching as if I'd had a glorious circuit session—well, actually I did. I can't help but smile. I haven't been this happy in a very long time; only having physical connections with women and nothing emotional gets tiring. Addison stimulates me in more than just one way; she's like no one I've ever met, and I thank myself for working up the nerve to talk to her in Dr. Jenkins' office.

In the kitchen I pour food into Rex's bowl; the round pebbles clink the metal dish, and his ears perk up. I make myself thick toast slathered in chunky peanut butter, the only type I like.

My iPhone is sitting on the island, and I pick it up to send her a text.

Good morning, beautiful. How did you sleep?

I lick peanut butter off my thumb and shove the last piece of toast in my mouth. Jeremiah should be here soon; it's almost eight in the morning. I dress, put on my work boots and hat and head outside, ready to face another beautiful day in Wyoming. Just then, I get a reply from her.

Oh, I slept very well, thank you. Although I'm really tired this morning. Can't think of why...

I smirk; she's sarcastic and funny and beautiful, a perfect bundle all tied up with a big red bow. I could go on all day with reasons why she's still tired and then give examples why she'd be suffering from exhaustion well into next week.

Jeremiah pulls in the driveway, still with his stupid "Awe yeah, look at this white hot truck" look on his face. I wave at him, and he parks his truck next to mine in front of the garage.

It's only five minutes into our work day, and Jer is gushing about his evening with Gwen. They ate at The Wolfbarrow (go figure) then went for a walk by Johnson's Creek. His big toothy smile is so obviously telling me that either he made it to her house, or she to his.

"Yeahhhhhh, I stayed at her house." He grips his shovel and flexes his hips up and down like he's about to hump life into the wooden shaft of the round mouth.

A deep bellied laugh escapes my mouth as I dig deep into a hole with my shovel, piling the dirt off to one side. A memory of Gwen under my sheets and me in her mouth flashes across my eyes, and I quickly bury the vision in the hole I'm currently digging.

"She wants me to start going to the gym with her," he laughs, patting his small, yet growing beer belly. "I have no idea why!"

We laugh together, and I wipe my brow from the sweat starting to bead under my dirty blond hair. It's either from the fact that I've thought about the Gwen incident, or I'm digging feverishly trying to focus on anything except the conversation we're having.

Should I tell him about what she did? No, I can't. He's too happy right now. Instead, I tell him about Nick's call and that Maria and Kelsey are coming later tonight to start decorating.

He plans to cut the grass and trim the hedges today. I'll clean up around the barn, coop, garage and house. We'll have this place ready to go for the girls by this afternoon, I hope.

By noon, we've both worked up a hearty appetite and head into the house to make some sandwiches for lunch. The two plates from dinner last night are still in the sink.

"Have some company last night?" He smiles and turns on the water in the sink.

"I did," I answer, nodding my head but giving no further detail to our night. "I'm hoping she'll come tomorrow and meet everyone."

The hours pass, and we've accomplished quite a bit around the farm.

At exactly 2:30, Owen's wife Kelsey calls.

"Hi, Blaine. Did Nick talk to you about tomorrow?"

Kelsey and I haven't always seen eye to eye. Maria and I get along great, and it bothers me that Kelsey can't be as nice of a person. But I suppose she makes my brother happy, and that's all that matters.

"Yeah, he called. Jer and I have cleaned up, and you guys can come over anytime."

"Okay, great. Thank you. Your father has no idea; we really want him to enjoy himself. I've invited over fifty people!" she says, sounding very proud of herself. I'm sure it's going to be quite the event as any celebration in our family usually is.

Birthday parties are always over the top; my niece and nephews are terribly spoiled. My dad dotes on them. They say the love you have for your grandchildren is different than that of your own kids. Well, they hit the nail on the head with that saying, because the way he is with them—I would have killed for that kind of attention growing up.

We finish our conversation, she giving me a few items to check off a list before their arrival later tonight. I have to mow the side lawn for extra parking, even set up sticks with bright orange ribbon (if I have it), setting a parameter for the cars, and move the barbeque from the porch to the front of the house.

Jer is riding the mower behind the house, and I go back to find him, letting him know he needs to pay extra attention to the side lawn, per Kelsey's orders.

At 5:00 I take a look around, and I think we're done.

"Thank you for everything today; the place really looks good," I say to Jeremiah.

"Anytime, man. It'll be fun. Your old man will be pissed, no doubt, but after a while, he'll probably have a good time."

He knows my dad almost as well as I do. He was scolded and sent home numerous times when we were kids, getting into things we shouldn't have. One time my dad caught us shooting squirrels out of the trees in the field with slingshots, and I thought he was going to turn them on us, shooting rocks at our heels while we bolted back up to the house with our tails between our legs.

Nick and Owen were already teenagers when I was born, so having a youngster again, and doing it alone without his wife, changed him, I guess. He was moody, had very little patience, and by the time I turned eighteen, he had enough of the farm life and left me here.

I rarely talk about things that happened when I was growing up; I try and push them down into the dark part of my mind—but every now and then, they rear their ugly heads, and I go back.

***

"Blaine Blackstock! Get back in his house right now!" His voice was barrelling through the door frame. "Boy, do not make me come out and get you!"

I'm hiding in a big tree, thankful when I see Owen come outside and not my Daddy.

"Blaine? Where are you?" He's looking for me. It takes him all of three seconds to find my secret spot, and I giggle at him. "Get down here. Dad's mad. Come inside, please."

He reaches his hands up to me, and without hesitation, I jump down into his arms. I love my big brothers; I feel safe when they're around, like they really love me.

I'm five, and my Daddy is mad that I wet my bed. He rips the sheets off, throws them in a pile and stomps back downstairs.

Standing in my room, I really don't know what to do. I pick up the paper air plane off the floor. Nicky made it for me, and it can really fly!

I frown, crumple the air plane up and throw it in the garbage. Why is Daddy always mad at me? He doesn't yell at Nicky or Owen like he does at me.

In the hallway there is a closet full of sheets and blankets and pillow cases. I want to climb in where no one can find me. But knowing it would make my Daddy angry, I don't dare.

Instead I find a sheet, a blue one with little moons on it, and a quilt—Mommy's quilt.

Making a bed is harder than it looks. The springy corners on the sheet are hard to figure out, but I make it okay, I guess.

I lay down and over myself in the quilt. I can hear my Daddy downstairs snoring with the TV on some sports channel.

"Blaine? Buddy, are you asleep?" Nicky is at the side of my bed. "Are you okay? I saw the sheets. Don't worry about it, little guy." And he scruffs my hair with his hand.

"Thanks, Nicky." I pout, turn on my side, and fall fast asleep.

***

At this moment, I just want Addison here in my arms. Instead, Kelsey and Maria show up, not alone but with a small entourage of other women who completely go into party-mode and decorate my farm. A giant canvas banner is tied and draped over the front of the garage. It has "Happy 70th Bennett!" in big blue letters on it. Maria hands me a big shopping bag full of streamers and balloons to put inside until tomorrow morning.

"Blaine, the place really looks great!" she beams.

"Yep," I say looking around. "And I hope the weather stays this nice, too."

They party crew doesn't leave until almost nine o'clock. Once inside, I sprawl on the couch, place my hat over my face and drift off briefly until my phone starts buzzing.

Guess what? Addison's text message reads.

I wanted to wait until I heard back before I told you, but I applied for that nursing job. They called today and I got it!

I call her; I need to hear her voice.

"Hey! I just sent you a text." I can hear in her voice that she must be smiling.

"Yeah, I got it. Congratulations; I'm so happy for you." And of course, happy for myself, too.

"Thanks! I start training next week. I'll be shadowing another RN." She's so excited, and I smile because I'm thrilled now that she's really staying.

"I want to see you...*badly*," I say in a husky voice.

"Oh, really? *How badly*?" She's teasing, me and with just her words, I start to harden.

Instinctively I rub my hand over the zipper of my jeans but quickly stop, knowing I will get too carried away if I continue.

"Can I come over?" I ask.

"You better."

Town is quiet, so I make it to her house quicker than expected and pull into a space in the visitor's parking section of her complex. A small stone walkway leads up to her door, and she has flowers of all kinds planted in small gardens on either side of the path.

There's a ceramic malamute, about a foot tall, with a little "Welcome" sign dangling from its mouth by the entrance. As I reach the door to knock, she flings it open.

There isn't even a second to open my mouth to speak before her arms are around my neck. I pull her against my body and we kiss deeply. An onlooker would think I was just released from jail or back from overseas by the way we are mauling one another.

We've only been apart for a day, and I'm like a junkie who finally got his fix; she's my morphine. What is it about her that has me so high? Is it crazy that I would do almost anything for this girl that I haven't even known for a week? Most likely, but I don't care—not right now, anyway.

Her condo is just as small inside as it looks outside. A little kitchen, with enough room for the basics and a small round tables with two chairs.

"Want something to drink? I have coffee, tea, milk, juice." Opening the fridge, she stands back displaying its contents like a model on *The Price is Right*.

"I'd love a coffee, thank you."

She places a steaming mug on the dark wooden coffee table in front of me. It's black; she remembered, and I smile.

"So, beautiful..." I reach over and trail my finger on her shoulder. "We only have a few days before you start work. We will have to make good use of that time."

She drops her jaw like I've said something offensive.

"You are insatiable!"

"No, *you* are irresistible," I say, leaning in to kiss her neck.

My stubble must tickle her because she recoils but giggles.

"My girlfriends back in Maine would die if they saw the sexy cowboy I've got on my couch. You sir, are the irresistible one."

The compliment makes me smile.

Let's see how far I can play this.

I unbutton my shirt a little and sit back so it opens up, showing some of my chest. I take a sip of coffee and adjust myself so I'm leaning into the couch in a seductive position.

She looks away, pretending she doesn't notice and smiles a little before taking a sip from her glass of water.

"What exactly are you doing over there?" She doesn't look over but points her finger at me and twirls it around in a circle.

I don't respond, just unbutton my shirt completely and pull it to the side so my abs, belly button and the small trail of hair down into my jeans is showing. She mouths the words, "Oh, shit." She smiles and covers her face with her hands.

"Anything wrong, Addison?" I quietly ask with a smirk, and then take another sip of my coffee.

"Oh, no. Everything is great!" She smiles sarcastically, quickly glances at me and opens the small drawer in the coffee table.

Pulling out a white bottle, she puts her long beautiful legs up on the table and squirts pink lotion into her hands.

You're kidding me. You don't know what you're getting yourself into, my dear.

Slowly and sensually she rubs it into her skin, and I know at that moment I'm the cliché weak male; I've lost the battle. I sit and watch her for a good two or three minutes; she's really drawing this out, massaging her thighs and calves.

When she starts to travel up her legs even higher, she lifts the hem of her skirt, and I can't take it anymore. I take the bottle from her hands, toss it on the floor and pull her on top of me. She laughs a truly beautiful laugh, and I do, too.

"You totally caved!" she says, very much pleased with herself. She looks so happy in this moment, so young and carefree, so beautiful. I don't think she knows how amazing she really is.

"Why are you here?" I ask, and she looks bewildered.

"What? What do you mean?" She sits back.

"I mean, why are you in my arms and not with someone else? How are you not taken, or married, or whatever by now.

You are..." And suddenly, I don't have the words to express myself. "I just feel so lucky to have you in my arms."

She looks totally surprised, as if no one has ever told her how wonderful she is.

"Blaine, I..." She blushes. "I'm happy to be in them. You came along at the perfect moment. I really didn't think I was going to feel like this about someone—ever."

My shirt is still open, and she's running her hands inside of it, my body reacting to her soft touch.

"You are a great guy, Blaine. And so dashing!" She smirks and squeezes each of my cheeks like an over-affectionate grandmother.

I suddenly realize Alex isn't there, and I'm not about to get naked if he's upstairs or something.

"Ugh, where's your brother?"

"Oh, he's out. And better be behaving himself," she says, rolling her eyes.

"Good." I smile and raise an eyebrow. "Where's your bedroom?"

***

Catching my breath in her bed, I look around at her walls. There are a few photos of who I assume are family members or friends, and a big framed piece by the mirror with the words "To the world you may just be one person, but to one person you may be the world" hand-painted on it. How very true; in this moment she's the only thing in my world.

"Did you make that?" I ask, pointing at the quote.

"I took some art classes after I finished nursing school. It was either hang that piece or the one with the naked male model I painted." She grins, and I can't tell if she's joking or not.

"My dad's birthday tomorrow...Do you still want to come?" I turn so I'm facing her.

"Yeah, of course. If it's still okay. Can I bring anything?"

"I think they've got it all covered." I remember I need to pick up from stuff from Maria's list tomorrow morning.

We stop talking, and I hear her quietly breathing; she must have fallen asleep.

"Addison?" I ask softly, pushing her hair off her face.

"Mmm?" she makes a small sound but doesn't awaken.

"Nothing. Go to sleep, beautiful girl." I tenderly kiss her nose.

"Mmm..." she makes the noise again. "Love you." And she says it so softly I almost don't hear it. Did I hear it? *Damn...*

I eventually fall asleep too. Her alarm clock shows 3:53 when I open my eyes, needing to use the bathroom. Getting out of bed as slowly and quietly as I can, I try not to wake the sleeping angel—*who just told me she loved me.*

Flicking the bathroom light on, I'm momentarily blinded by the four bright bulbs above the vanity. My eyes still adjusting, I look at myself in the mirror, still playing those two words over and over in my head.

"*Love you.*" I mouth the words and rub my eyes, then rake my hands through my hair.

Something makes a noise downstairs, and I turn around, remembering Luca was lying at the foot of the bed when I left her bedroom. I wonder to what could be down there.

Tiptoeing down the carpeted steps, I peek into the darkness and see light coming from the refrigerator door. Alex is standing there, holding it open, and drinking straight from the juice carton. I clear my throat, and he turns, still drinking. Some juice trickles down his face.

"Ugh, hey," I start to say. "I'm Blaine."

He swallows the last of the juice in his mouth loudly and wipes his mouth with his sleeve.

"Hey, man. Addy told me about you." He points up towards the ceiling, "She sleeping?"

I nod that she is, and he looks relieved.

"Good, I don't need a lecture at four AM." He stretches to look at the clock on the microwave. "Juice?" he holds the carton out to me.

"No, thanks." I kindly decline and wave my hand at the carton.

He sits down at the small table in the kitchen and pushes the opposite chair out with his foot. "Sit down and tell me about yourself, Blaine."

I'm a little surprised that her brother wants to have a heart-to-heart with me at this hour while she's sleeping upstairs. But I sit down anyway, and when I do, I realize I'm only wearing boxers. Fantastic.

I must make some type of embarrassed expression because Alex starts shaking his finger at me. "Heyyyy, I knew I recognized you! You're the guy from that animal food place who was staring at Addy the other day!"

Oh, fuck. Here we go.

He thumps his fist on the table like he's proud of himself for making the connection. He is smirking, and I feel stupid that I've let this little shit make me feel this way.

"Ha, yeah." I laugh. "What can I say? She's remarkable."

"Well, be good to her. She doesn't need another asshole to treat her like shit." This time he's not smiling; he's serious. And I almost want to tell him to grow a pair and start acting like a man, to stop sponging off his sister, but I don't.

Wanting to change the subject, I take the moment of silence to offer him a job. "Addison tells me you might be interested in a job. I have a ranch, and I'm looking for another guy to help out a few days a week."

He doesn't say anything, but his eyes tell me he looks interested.

"My friend Jeremiah is there five days a week now. We work the farm and fields, tend to the animals and things like that."

Still not saying anything, I'm compelled, and slightly irritated, to give more detail. "Something like eight AM to 4 or 5 PM. I could start you at fifteen bucks an hour."

That was enough to seal the deal; he smiles and extends his hand for me to shake it.

"Sign me up, although I have no fucking clue about farm animals. Do I have to shovel shit and stuff?"

I try not to roll my eyes at him.

"Well yeah, there's that. But it's more about maintenance than shovelling shit...*and stuff.*" I smirk.

"Okay, man. Thanks. I could really use the money," he says, looking around him. "Maybe get my own place, ya know?"

Yeah, buddy, I know.

He needs to get his act together, and if doing this will help his sister, I don't mind putting up with him five days a week.

"Okay. Well, if you're up for it, Addison is coming out tomorrow for my father's birthday party. You're welcome to join her, you know, take a look at the place before your first day. Oh, and by the way—when would you be able to start?"

"Yeah, okay. I'll come. I have nothing else to do tomorrow. How's Monday? I like to sleep in on Sundays...do you expect me to work Sundays?"

He is *really* irritating, and I have to think about how much I care about his sister to push the annoyance away.

"Well, the occasional Sunday, yeah. There are rodeos and events that some of the animals and myself participate in. Sometimes they're on a Sunday."

"Rodeo?! You're like, a real fuckin' cowboy, huh?"

The annoyance is back, and I have to look away, exhaling slowly.

"It would seem." It's all I can muster, and I stand up; I have to get away from this kid. "I'm gonna go back to sleep now..." I point upstairs and say goodnight.

"Yeah, okay. Night, bro." He stays sitting at the table, tipping the juice carton up to get every last drop.

Addison hasn't moved since I left the bed, but Luca has. He's now lying where I was, very comfortably, too. He looks at me like he's thinking, "You don't expect me to move, do you?"

I sigh. *Great, some competition.*

I gently tap my hand on my leg and whisper, "Come on, Luca," trying to entice him to move. He does, slowly stretching before hopping off the end of the bed. I climb in beside her, pull her as close as I can and nuzzle the back of her neck. I fall asleep to the smell of green apple shampoo and a hint of dog.

Addison was up before me, like usual, and cooked a delicious breakfast of French toast with freshly ground coffee. I didn't mention anything about her sleepy admission of love, and she didn't say it again, so I'm pretty sure it wasn't something she knew she was saying.

I have to get to Lander's, and I apologize for dining and dashing, "I'm sorry, but I gotta get going. I have a bunch of things to pick up for the party."

She briefly pouts but then smiles and tells me it is okay.

"Thank you for breakfast."

"Be sure to fill out a comment card on your way out, handsome," she jokes, wrapping her arms around me and kissing my cheek.

"See you this afternoon," I say and kiss her nose, slipping on my shoes and heading out the door.

Lander's is swamped, which is no surprise for a Saturday morning. It looks like the same kids that were outside earlier in the week selling baked goods are back, so this time when I leave with my groceries, I buy two dozen butter tarts, lemon bars and some other cookie-ball things rolled in coconut.

"Thank you very much!" One of the kids' mothers touches my arm. "Let me carry these to your vehicle for you."

I very obviously see her wink at another mom, and I almost laugh out loud.

She follows me closely to my truck and thanks me again when she hands me the treats.

I grin and tip my hat, and she actually fans herself with her hand.

"Ma'am," I say with all the country boy charm I can muster.

"Oh, call me Chelsea!" She flutters her lashes.

Okay, stop toying with the poor woman, you dick.

I close the back door and open the driver's to get in.

"Chelsea." I smile at her, then pull out of the parking lot.

CHAPTER SIX

Someone tore into that bag of balloons and streamers and threw it up all over my farm. Or at least that's what it looks like. I am astonished when I pull into my driveway and see the party crew has lost their minds and gone completely overboard with decorations.

My dad is going to have a fit, and I can actually picture him trying to push the pretend brake pedal in my brother's car so he doesn't have to pull into the yard. (You know, that pedal that you push when you're the passenger riding with an erratic driver, and they take a corner too fast or don't stop quickly enough.)

"Ho-ly shit..." I don't disguise my expression, and Kelsey looks extremely displeased that I haven't thrown myself down worshipping their creativity and suggest they start a party planning business. Maria just laughs and says, "Well, you only turn seventy once!"

I agree, but wow...

Jer is already here, too, and has the barbeque area all set up.

"Hey, Jer! Thanks for all your help, Maria couldn't stop talking about everything you've done this morning." I slap his back, happy to see him.

"Yeah, she can really crack that whip," he jokes and turns around when Gwen walks out of my house, putting her arm around his neck.

"Hi, Blaine. Lookin' good this morning."

Is she actually doing this right now? Right in front of Jeremiah? What happened to the happy, bouncy girl who would just hug me and get it over with? I can't deal with this woman scorned bullshit.

I ignore her statement and smile my pearly whites. "Gwen! So good to see you." I overdo it a tad but just can't help myself.

Addison and her brother show up right around four PM, and she looks breathtaking. Like the day I first saw her, she's wearing a light blue dress. The top clings to her chest, accentuating her lovely breasts and delicious curves. The rest flows down wider and ends with a lacy hem just above her knees. Her long curls are pulled back into a ponytail, swept over her shoulder. She looks like she just walked out of a New England country club, not a condo in Sheridan, Wyoming.

"I might have to take you into the barn and find a mound of hay, missy, "I whisper in her ear and twirl her around with my hand. "You look gorgeous."

She blushes and kisses my cheek.

More and more guests arrive. I do the good son thing and mingle with everyone. I get many compliments on how well I've kept the ranch, and I tell them I couldn't have done it without Jeremiah.

Nick must have notified Maria that they were on their way, because she starts clapping her hands to draw everyone's attention.

"The guest of honour is on the way!" she calls out.

Five minutes later, Nick's black Cadillac pulls in the driveway, and it takes everything in me not to burst, as I can see my father through the windshield looking around, pissed off and clearly cursing at everything he sees.

"Happy birthday, Bennett!"

Everyone almost on cue shouts joyously as he gets out of the car, and I can see in the minute before he opened his door that he composed himself. He is now smiling and thanking people as they approach him.

I don't rush over; I wait until he's close enough, and I walk up to him.

"Happy Birthday, Dad." I extend my hand, expecting him to shake it.

"Blaine. Did you do all this?"

He doesn't shake it, and I drop my arm to my side, disappointed.

"No, the girls did, Dad. I think it looks pretty good."

Ignoring me, it takes him all of two seconds to notice Addison standing beside me, and it's like a switch gets flipped.

"Well, who might we have here?" he questions.

She extends her hand.

"Hi, Mr. Blackstock. I'm Blaine's friend, Addison. Happy birthday!"

He takes her hand in his and pats the top with his other. "You are lovely, and thank you. Ignore that sign, too," he says, pointing to the big banner. "It should say twenty-five with 45 years of experience."

And he winks, still holding her hand.

"Bennett! Bennett! Come sit over here, will you?" Patricia Pattison, the store manager at Lander's, waves and beckons my Dad over.

He turns to go, but not before placing his hand on my shoulder as he passes.

"Keep her close, Blaine, my boy. One's like that don't come around often."

And I don't say a word. I just nod at him, then look over at Addison and smile.

There are only fifteen or so people left by eight o'clock, and most of them have been drinking far too much. In fact, someone threw up at the base of the giant oak tree beside the garage.

My father has also had his fair share, and I glance over at Nick, who is obviously thinking the same thing but just shrugs his shoulders.

Yeah, Maria is right; you only turn seventy once.

Jeremiah and Owen start a fire in the pit, and we all pull our chairs around closely. Alex and Bobby, my nephew, have been gone for a few hours. They took my Gator for a rip, and we can hear them every now and then in the distance *yahoo-ing* and laughing.

I go inside to get a sweatshirt for Addison; she looks cold but probably won't ask me for anything. When I drape the blue hoodie around her shoulders, she looks up and smiles at me.

"Thank you."

My dad is telling some story from when he was in school and bought his first truck, some old Ford that he ended up driving into a tree on a stormy night. He wasn't hurt, but the truck was totalled.

He moved on to another tale about making out with Clara (he can't recall her last name) before he dated my mother. They were caught behind the school with his hand in her shirt. He's very proud of himself as he recalls the account, and he finishes another bottle of beer.

Louie, the now-retired butcher from Lander's is still here. He went to school with dad, and he loudly belly-laughs when he remembers the Clara incident as well. It must have been quite the scandal. We all laugh aloud, too.

"Yeah, Clara. She was a nice girl. But nothing compared to my Nicola..." My Dad sighs.

And my laughter stops.

He looks down at his hands, picking dirt or something out of his fingernail.

"God rest her soul." Louie nods his head and takes a swig of his beer.

I look down at my hands too, not sure what to say or do. When I look up, my father is staring at me, and I feel like a fish in a barrel.

"Blaine. Did I thank you yet, for all the decorations?" He's not smiling; actually, he has no expression at all.

"Yeah, Dad, you did. Thank you, but like I said earlier, the girls put it all together."

I feel five again, and I want to wrap myself in my Mom's quilt.

"Right, yes, you did say that. Thank you Maria, Kels." He tips his bottle at each of them, and they both smile.

"Happy Birthday, Dad," they say in unison.

He directs his gaze on Addison. *Here we go...*

"Young lady, tell me about yourself." He puts her on the spot, and everyone around the fire is looking at her.

She surprises me when she responds right away. "Well, I'm new to Wyoming. My brother and I moved here from Maine. I'm actually starting a nursing position at the hospital this week."

"Ooohhh!" Kelsey squeals and claps her hands. "You might get to work with Johnny; he's my brother's son, a nurse there, too!"

Addison smiles. "Which unit is he in? I'm hoping for the NICU, but for the first few months I'll be in emergency."

"Oh, I'm not sure. I think he works in palliative care—you know, with *the old folks*," she says, blocking her mouth so my father doesn't see her words. He clearly hears them and roars.

"Kels, you stop making fun of this old man, you hear? You'll be sitting' here someday too, and your twins will make a big ol' banner for you."

Conversations change here and there, and after people get driven home by DD's, only Nick, Maria, Jeremiah, Gwen, Addison, Alex and Bobby, me and Dad are left. Bobby is gushing about the ride with Alex, and they both dramatically re-enact almost tipping the side-by-side over while cornering sharply.

"Sorry, Uncle Blaine. We were trying to be careful." Bobby realizes I don't look amused.

"Uh huh." I don't say anything else, but I do grin at him, and he relaxes.

"Oh, Bobby, don't worry about him. He got into enough trouble when he was your age, too. Why do you think I went grey so early?" Dad snorts. "You know there was a time when these two little shits," he says, pointing at Jeremiah and me, "stole a cow from the Wilson's farm and tied it to the flagpole at school."

Jeremiah and I laugh, remembering.

Addison looks up and gapes at me. "Blaine!" she says astonishingly.

I shrug and grin.

Dad goes to open another bottle, and Nick leans in. "Dad, I think you've had enough. You don't want to be up all night." He moves to take the bottle, and Dad turns so he can't reach it.

"Now, listen here, Nicholas Blackstock. You aren't touching my beer, ya hear?"

Everybody knows that any parent means business when they use your first and last name together.

"I'm fine anyway, just enjoying my birthday with my family," Dad continues. "What's the harm in that?"

"Nothing, Dad." Nick looks annoyed but knows when to argue with him and when not to. It's all about picking your battles—or so I've heard.

"Blaine, does this young lady know about your bull riding?"

I hadn't mentioned it, so she nudges my arm with her elbow. "You didn't tell me you ride those bulls!"

"Well, yeah, but not for long anyway," I snort. "Only a few seconds." I wink at her.

"Addison, Blaine's actually really good. You should come to a show!" Jer backs me up.

Thanks, buddy.

"He's not *good*, Jeremiah. He's one of the best. Isn't that right?" Dad forms a gun with his index finger and thumb, points it at me, winks and makes a shooting noise with his mouth.

Trying not to act surprised, I'm actually dumbfounded. I don't understand why my father is acting like this. It must be because he's drinking. He's never bragged about me. Ever.

We talk a little more about the rodeo business, and Nick tells Dad it's time to go. He's finally complacent and gets up out of the lawn chair to leave.

"Goodbye, my dear. It was a pleasure," he says to Addison. "Make sure Blaine brings you around some time; you are very welcome in my home." And by his home, he means Nick and Maria's house.

"Thank you, Mr. Blackstock. I hope you had a good birthday." She leans in to hug him, and he hugs her back.

"Goodnight, my son." he says to me. I don't get a hug, but again, a pat on the shoulder. Hey, at least it's something.

"Night, Dad." It's all I can muster right now; I'm still organizing and filing the events of tonight in different folders in my mind.

"Blaine." Nick nods his head to the side, motioning me to come talk privately with him.

"What's up?" I ask when we turn the corner of the house, away from everyone.

"We can't let him drink like that, huh? I haven't heard him like that in years! I'm really sorry about what Louie said too."

I know exactly what he's about to say.

"When he said about God resting Mom's soul, I thought Dad was going to flip."

He puts both hands on each of my shoulders, like a coach to his player in the bottom of the ninth. "Listen, we buried this a long time ago, right? You don't ever let that old man get the best of you."

I can't look at him in the eye, and I feel myself getting emotional, so I break away from his grip. "Nick, I know. I don't want to do this, not right now."

"Blaine, I'm serious," he says and kicks the grass with his boot. "I wish you could have grown up with the father that we did. But things happen for a reason, and I couldn't imagine life without you."

His eyes are watering, and I feel my face starting to flush with anger.

"Nick, I'm fine, really. I've dealt with all this before. It's done and buried, and thank you for being such a good big brother."

I think hugging him might shut him up. So I do, and it does.

Thank you, Lord.

We say our goodbyes, and Addison stands beside me, waving as they pull out onto the road.

"Mmm." She nuzzles into my chest. "You smell so good."

I hold her tightly and kiss her forehead. "Sorry about tonight."

"Sorry for what?" She leans back to look at me. "Sorry for not mentioning you're this extreme bull rider, and I should worry about you coming into the hospital on a stretcher some day?"

She sticks out her tongue at me and kisses my chin.

"Well, yeah. That." I laugh "It's not that bad. And I make good money doing it, too."

"I started to picture you when he told me, and I almost had to excuse myself because the thought of you was so...so...hot!" She bites her lip and trails her index finger on my collarbone and down my chest.

"Addison, keep it up; I dare you." I grin the biggest, most salacious smile I can, and we kiss.

Jeremiah is playing his guitar, some old Willie Nelson song I can't remember the words to and Gwen and Alex are making up some other lyrics like typical drunk people do.

"Want some water?" I ask her, getting up to grab a few bottles from the house.

"Yes, please." She zips the hoodie and shoves her hands into the pockets. She sits down beside Jeremiah, bopping her head to his new rendition of the song.

There aren't any bottles in the fridge, but I keep a few cases in the pantry. I go in to grab some, and the door shuts behind me. Pulling the string for the light that's dangling above my head, I see that Gwen is standing in front of me, looking like a lion ready to take down a gazelle.

"Gwen, what the hell are you doing? Not this shit again, so help m--."

She doesn't let me finish, just puts her fingers over my mouth and tells me to shush.

"No, listen to me right now." I grab her by the wrist and shove her hand from my face. "This has got to stop. I have no interest in you. Why are you doing this?"

"Are you kidding me? You've wanted me for years; I know it."

Here comes the same old song and dance again. I try and get by her, but she holds her arms out to either side. "Gwen, get out of my house. Now."

She doesn't move, so I grab her hands and move her out of my way. Opening the door, I'm relieved to be out. A mixture of claustrophobia and potential assault have me choking for air.

"Go to hell, Blackstock. You can't handle this anyway." She's pulling at the hem of her skirt. "Go fuck your pretty little ginger." She points at the outside door.

Like it's a blur of slow motion, I turn to see Addison standing there, eyes wide. For the first time since I've met her, they're empty and grey.

Gwen stomps by me, intentionally nudging Addison with her shoulder on her way out, and slams the door. Addison's gaze doesn't change, and it's like she didn't even notice Gwen at all.

"*Addy.*" I use Alex's nickname for her. "That..." I point out the door. "She just came in the pantry."

"It's okay." She smiles a tiny half smile, and takes off my hoodie, gently placing it on the floor. "I'm going to take my brother home now."

And just like that, she's gone, the wooden screen door clicking shut behind her.

I stand there like an idiot, not chasing after her, not saying anything, I'm just in shock, at both Gwen and her unbelievable actions and words, and at Addison just leaving. She wouldn't even listen to my explanation.

I can hear Jeremiah calling after her. "Addison? Everything okay?"

She doesn't answer him.

"Don't worry about her, Jer," Gwen says and then raises her voice louder. "Guess she needs to find some other guy. Maybe one without daddy issues. Go find a nice doctor now, sweetie!"

And that's all it takes; I am out the door like a bat out of hell. "Gwen, get your fuckin' ass outta here *right now*."

She stares at me, mouth open.

Addison's tail lights are all that's left of her now.

"Blaine, what the hell just happened?" Jeremiah is completely bewildered. His night just went from a scene from *The Great Outdoors* to *Carrie* in about two seconds.

"Jeremiah, get her out of here. And don't bring her back."

I'm livid, and I feel a pang of guilt for talking to him like that, but I can't stand the sight of that bitch standing next to him.

"Blaine, really. You're throwing me out? Awe, and we were having such a good time." She's really pushing it now, but I don't say another word.

I slam the door behind me once I'm inside my house. I sink to the floor against the kitchen door. I can hear Jer trying to get information out of her, but she's not saying much. Just whining about how she must have said something she didn't think was wrong but "that girl" took it poorly, and I freaked out over nothing.

His truck rumbles to life, and soon the sound is in the distance...then it's gone.

What is the protocol for something like this? Is Addison my girlfriend? Do I go after her? Do I get an old boom box and stand outside her window blaring music? I have no idea.

All I do know is that the only thing I've ever really cared about just walked out of my house and had the coldest look in her eyes when she did it.

I decide to send her a text.

I'm so sorry, I don't know what she was trying to do. Nothing happened.

Tick, tick, tick. The clock is the only sound in my head. No new message alerts chime in.

I don't know what to say...she's just crazy and she's gone.

Still nothing. I am wearing down a trail from pacing, and I don't care. Maybe the floor will cave in, and I'll fall into a black hole. It's now two in the morning.

Please just let me know you're home safely...Please.

It is 2:05, and I'm in my truck heading to her condo. I can't sleep; I don't want to sleep. I just need to know she's okay. Her car is in the parking lot, so I run up to her door, almost tripping through her flowerbeds.

Knocking...knocking...

Please open the door, baby.

Nothing. I knock again, and Alex opens, "She's not in here, bro."

I'm puzzled. "Where is she?"

He points to her car.

I don't knock on the car window; I just open the door and slide into the seat beside her. She's looking straight head, hands neatly folded in her lap. I can tell she's been crying.

"Addison?" I reach to put my hand on her leg, and she moves it away from me nervously.

She sniffles her nose. "Blaine, I think this was a mistake. You should go. I'm no good for you."

"What?! Are you kidding me? No. I'm not leaving. I want to talk to you, please." I turn my body so I'm facing her, but she still doesn't look at me. "Please, baby."

I move some hair out of her face and tuck it behind her ear. "Nothing happened with her. She cornered me. And I got the hell out of there."

"I believe you." She sniffles again. Reaching into her purse, she pulls out a little package of tissues and wipes her eyes and nose. "I don't even know why I'm crying," she laughs. "I'm not your girlfriend, anyway. Thank you for inviting me, but you should go."

She still won't look at me, and I can't take it anymore. I turn her face with my hand, gently making her look at me. Her eyes aren't empty anymore; they're sad, and my stomach does flip flops.

"I...I think I've fallen in love with you. Please don't cry."

She blinks like I've said something totally unbelievable. "What did she mean by you having *daddy issues*?" She wipes another tear from her cheek.

Didn't she hear me? I think I just told her I loved her, and she wants to know about the ramblings of an insane drunk woman? I inhale and figure now is as good of a time as ever.

I hold my breath and look out the windshield at the brick wall in front of the car. "My mother died having me, and my father has always resented me for it." I can feel my skin going cold and my heartbeat slowing. "When I turned eighteen, he figured I could handle it on my own and left me at the ranch alone. He's always been...distant."

There. It's out, but I still can't breathe, and she doesn't say a single word. I have never actually said the words out loud; everyone in my life already knew anyway, so this was a lot harder than I thought.

It overwhelms me, and I need to get out of the car. I open the door and step out into the cool May night. I run my hands through my hair a few times and then slowly down my face. I'm exhausted; this has been the longest day of my life, and I just want it to be over.

Her door shuts, and she walks over to me. She hasn't said anything since she asked that question. She just takes my hand and motions me to follow her.

Walking towards my truck, she stops and puts my hand on her cheek. "Take me to your house, please."

I think I'm too tired to drive, "Addison," I say, handing her the keys, "can you drive?"

She looks surprised but takes them, and we get in. I feel so emotionally drained that I don't even mind when she stalls the truck backing it out of the parking space. Twice.

I am a little embarrassed that I'm acting like I've lost it and should be in a padded room somewhere secure.

"I'm sorry, Blaine. I had no idea." Her soft voice snaps me out of it, and I clear my throat.

"I'm sorry, too. I have never told that to anyone before." I reach to hold her hand and she takes mine and kisses it.

"Never told anyone what happened to your mom? Or never told a woman that you loved her?" She has the smallest smile in the corner of her beautiful mouth.

"Both," I say and exhale, as I feel I've held my breath that entire time.

At home my mood lifts a bit when Rex greets us happily at the door, like he's excited we're both here. I know I am, too.

Upstairs we stand by the end of my bed and she slowly undresses me, button by button, unbuckling my belt and then my jeans. I'm left in only my boxers and socks, and she starts to slide the straps of her dress off. I take her hands and put them down at her sides. I want to do this.

My hands slowly pull her dress down, exposing her breasts and lace bra. I can see through the lace, and I lean down to kiss the top of each breast. By the time the dress reaches her waist, I let go, and it falls to the floor, a light blue pool at her feet.

She's wearing matching lace panties to go with the bra. I sweep her up into my arms, and she pulls her hair band out, letting it fall over my shoulder and all around.

As gently as I can, I lay her on the bed and climb on top of her. We haven't spoken since we were in the truck. It makes this moment feel a million times more concentrated, and even though my body wants to rush, I'm holding on to every second as long as I can.

"Blaine, I love you, too," she whispers in my ear, tenderly sucking on my earlobe.

"I know," I whisper back and kiss her neck, her throat, her chest and belly. All the anticipation from today, the drama from tonight and the painful admission just a little while ago has turned into Mount Vesuvius. The moment I enter her, I'm ready to explode, but I don't, forcing myself not to be selfish and give her everything I have.

I love her. I want to spend the rest of my life loving her. I only want to smell her sweet scent and taste her sweet lips and kiss her soft skin.

MEADOWLARKS

She starts to move faster under me as she's getting close to hitting her peak. She's breathing heavily, and her mouth is open; her head is turned to the side. I put my arms on either side of her head so I'm holding myself up with my elbows, and she kisses my wrist. I erupt and bury my head into her neck and hair.

CHAPTER SEVEN

It's Tuesday morning when Addison starts her first nursing shift. We used Sunday and Monday to recover from the events after my dad's 70th. I haven't spoken much to Jeremiah, other than to give him the last two days off. I know it's not his fault Gwen acted like she did, but I don't want to get into it with him over her, not right now. I need to recoup from everything and start feeling normal again.

Addison's wearing light pink scrubs, her hair pulled back into a pony tail and the sight of her makes me excited.

"What are you staring at?" She elbows me as she walks by to grab a bottle of water out of the fridge.

"Clothes that are about to be on the floor if you don't get out that door, little miss." I cross my arms and give her a sexy glare. I'm not even close to kidding, and she knows it.

"Don't work too hard today. I'll call you on my break to let you know how it's going." Picking up her purse from the island, she waves goodbye quickly and is gone.

Alex shows up promptly at eight AM, driving Addison's car. I took her home yesterday to pick up clothes for work and her car.

"How's it going, Blaine?" He shuts the car door and shakes my extended hand.

"Good, Alex. How'd you get her to lend you her car?" I ask quizzically.

"Well, if it wasn't for this job, she wouldn't have. And she made me vow to be here on time." He looks around. "So, what do you have planned for me today?" He kicks the dirt with his boot, and I'm impressed to see he's actually prepared for work.

I explain my plan for today—cleaning out the stalls in the bar, all twelve of them, fixing the hinge on one of the doors and splitting some firewood. He looks like he's ready to dart back into the car and speed off.

But instead he quickly rubs his hands together like he's trying to start a fire. "Let's get started!" He's eager, and we get to work. Alex is a very talkative guy, which I don't mind, considering he doesn't stop moving while he's yapping.

He talks a bit about how boring Wyoming is and Maine, aside from the scenery, wasn't all that exciting either. Some girls he dated in high school were mentioned, as well as his heavy partying in college which lead to him flunking out and ended up here. I smile and nod at most things he talks about; he's not his usual cocky self, and it's a nice change. I only stop moving when he brings up his sister, and I realize I wasn't paying attention until I hear her name.

"So Addy ditched that fucker and moved here," he says.

"Sorry," I say and shake my head. "What?"

"The guy, Jacob?" He's not sure what part I've missed. "Her ex?"

He's still trying to get me to clue in, but I'm blank. "Ah, don't worry about it. Just some asshole back home." He waves his hand in the air and goes back to spreading out a bale of fresh hay with a rake.

"What did he do to her?" I don't continue what I was doing; I want to know, and I feel like a dick for not listening in the first place.

"Well," he says, moving hay around, "he pretended to give her some nice life. Then cheated on her with one of her friends, in Addy's bed. She caught them, and he beat the shit out of her for coming home early."

What the fuck did he just say?

I flush, from surprise, from anger—no, pure rage. I can't imagine someone putting their hands on her, and the image makes me sick to my stomach.

"Holy shit, Alex. What did he do to her? Is he in jail?" I'm livid.

"Gave her a black eye, bruises everywhere..." He goes quiet, closing his eyes like he's picturing her beaten body. "She was in the hospital for three days. Our mom never left her hospital bed."

My feet are starting to grow roots, I'm sure; I still haven't moved except to pick my mouth up off the ground.

"And what about the guy?" I ask.

"He got probation. The slut he cheated with said Addy attacked them, and he came to their defence. She got a restraining order against him, but it wasn't enough. He still tried to see her, so..." He trails off, looking around. "*Green Acres* is hopefully far enough away."

I'm reeling. I want to hop on a flight to Maine and show this guy, Jacob, how it feels to end up in a hospital bed. I comb my hands through my hair and flash to Saturday night when Addison stood in the doorway silently watching Gwen unravel.

And it all makes sense, the look in her eyes, the emptiness and the fact that she didn't say or do anything. She was afraid to; was she afraid of me? I shudder at the thought, and I could crawl out of my own skin.

"I can't believe she didn't tell me. That motherf---" I put my hands on my hips and stare down at the wheelbarrow full of hay.

"Do you really blame her, bro?" Alex asks. "How would she?" He exhales. "*'Oh hi, nice to meet you. Please be good to me because my last boyfriend put me in the ICU.*' Come on, man."

He shrugs, and I understand why she didn't.

We don't talk about it again, and I let out all my anger and aggressively wield the axe to chop firewood. We take load after load in the side-by-side and, by 4:30, we have accumulated a nice sized pile.

"Good work today, Alex," I say, trying to catch my breath as we load the last of the wood. "Addison is coming home for dinner; you're more than welcome to stay as well. I was planning on barbequing some—"

Suddenly, Alex cuts me off. "Addison is coming *home*?"

I smirk when I realize what I had said. But, actually, it sounds really nice, and she's here enough that it could be—*home*, that is. But since we've only actually known each other less than two weeks, it seems a tad rushed.

"You know what I mean." I toss a chunk of bark at him. "Get in; you can drive back to the house." The sun is still blazing, but it's not hot. It's about sixty-five degrees, and I wish the weather would always be this nice. It makes hard work outdoors not seem as gruelling anyway.

"Where's the other guy that's usually here? Your friend Jeremiah?" Alex turns a corner sharply.

"Whoa!" we both exclaim at the same time.

"He's off today," I answer. "You'll work together tomorrow."

I really should call Jeremiah, maybe even go to his house to see him. There's never been more than a day of silence between us, and who knows what the Pantry Predator has been filling his head with. I smirk at myself, amused at my new nickname for Gwen, even though I know I won't ever say it out loud.

Does this mean we won't have those nights at The Wolfbarrow anymore? Just sitting, eating ribs, watching whatever is on the flat screen, without any drama at all? I really hope not; it's almost a tradition with Jer, and I'm not ready to let it die.

"Addison asked me to come and pick her up," Alex says, holding his cell phone up and then shoving it into his back pocket.

"You want me to? We can take the truck." I nod towards the garage.

"Hell, yeah! Let's go!" We jump in and head toward the hospital.

She's standing outside of the main entrance, and with her is an older woman, also in nursing scrubs, but she's wearing a white triangle-shaped hat, like nurses years ago used to. The other woman is smoking a cigarette and puts it out in a tall metal canister once we pull up to the curb.

"Hey!" Alex leans out the window, smacking his hands on the door.

She says something to the other nurse, who smiles and heads back inside. "I didn't expect you to come get me, Blaine!"

And I'm a little hurt; did she not want me to? After all, she sent Alex the text to pick her up, not me.

"We are done for the day, and I need to go to Lander's for a few things anyway." I try and make an excuse, even though neither of those things are the reason why I'm sitting here idling in front of the hospital.

"Are you going to make me sit in the back?" She reaches in the window and punches Alex's arm with a huge grin on her face.

"Alright, alright." He gets out to let her in.

"Hey, handsome." She pulls her messenger bag off her shoulder and slides into the center to kiss my cheek. I guess she is happy to see me; I tell myself to stop over-analyzing things.

"So? How did it go?" I pull out onto the street and head toward the grocery store. She tells us how the morning started slowly, but then there was a small accident on the interstate that kept her busy the rest of the day.

"No one was seriously hurt, thankfully. Just bumps and bruises, one broken leg." She's talking so fast, and I'm happy she's had a good day, but listening to her speak about bruises makes me think of her bruised and battered. I reach across the seat to hold her hand.

Alex stays for dinner. I barbeque some chicken, roast zucchini, carrots and asparagus, and we sit outside at the picnic table, enjoying the last of the day. The sun sets, and Addison insists on clearing the table. She pushes me back down with her hands on my shoulders and kisses the side of my neck.

"You two worked hard today. Please let me take the dishes in."

How can I resist those lips and that sweet voice?

"I'm gonna get going. I have...a hot date." Alex holds his phone in his hand and smirks.

"You need a ride back into town?" I offer. I don't really want to, but it would give Addison and I some alone time.

"Ummm..." he says, leaning back and taking a swig of his beer. "Addy! Can I borrow the car?"

She answers him from inside the kitchen. "For what?"

Rolling his eyes, he chugs the last from the bottle and stands up, burping.

"To go back to town. Or are you planning on coming home tonight?" He is heading into the house, and I stay sitting at the picnic table, taking a drink of my own beer.

I can hear them talking quietly, and I try not to eavesdrop. Okay, I lie. If I could possess bionic ears I would, but I'm only able to make out some words like "Drinking. Driving. Excuses. Maine. Becca."

Becca? I wonder who she is.

They come back outside, Addison in front of him, looking irritated but smiling at me.

"Blaine, it was a pretty cool day. Thanks." Alex extends his hand to shake mine, and when we're done, he pulls away to scruff the top of her head with his hand. She ducks out of the way and slaps at his chest with her hand.

"Get going before I change my mind!" They both laugh, and with a wave, he's gone.

"Whatever are we going to do now?" She smirks and climbs on to the picnic table, sitting right in front of me. I am between her legs as she holds my face to kiss me.

"You're too much; you know that, right?"

Our lips lock, passionately, lapping tongues together. I've needed this all day.

"You've been so quiet; are you okay?" she asks me.

I guess I have been pretty quiet, but one has to be when Alex spends most of the time doing all the talking. And I've learned so much today; I'm still flipping through note cards in my head.

It is dark now, only the last of the sun is left, a warm copper line touching the tops of the trees in the distance. I put my index fingers in the waistband of her light pink scrubs, running them along her hips. I look up at her and grin. We don't say anything, but I know it's okay to continue when she lifts her behind up a little, and I slowly pull them down, revealing white cotton panties and her beautiful bare legs.

I take off each of her shoes and toss the pants on the ground beside them. Running my hands up and down her legs, like a man clinking his knife and fork together, bib around his neck, ready to devour a delicious meal. Slowly spreading her legs, I kiss and nibble the insides of each soft thigh.

She leans back and breathes heavily, and I have my dessert, right there on the picnic table. When she stops crying out with wonderful ache, I lift my head just as the last of the suns trail on the trees are gone. We're in complete darkness now.

"I missed you." I kiss her left calf and pull her down so she's sitting on my lap.

***

Lying in bed we stare at each other, not saying anything. I'm getting lost in big blue eyes, and I don't know what she's got her gaze fixed on; but whatever it is, she smiles.

"What's Maine like?" I ask, coyly. I really want to come right out and tell her I know what that guy did to her, but I don't want to ruin this beautiful moment.

"It's beautiful. My parents live in Bangor, not too far from the ocean," she says with her eyes closed, like she's envisioning her old home. She looks so happy, I decide not to pry into anything else about the place. But she continues...

"It just got old. Some people I was surrounding myself weren't who I thought they were, and I knew if I wanted a better life, I had to leave."

Should I ask? Is she going to keep going?

"People like who?" I swallow a gulp of imaginary liquid courage and wait for the response.

"No one in particular. I still talk to my girlfriends; the ones I was closest with in high school are great women. I miss them very much." She pouts a little, and I can see she really does have great friends that she longs for.

"My best friend Riley is hilarious," she says, giggling, "That girl will do anything! She's fearless and has always been there for me." She turns to lay on her back, looking up at wooden beams supporting the white ceiling.

"She got pregnant near the end of high school and has a son, Isaac. He's eight now. Cutest kid ever." She's beaming, and I smile because—well, because she is.

"That must have been hard, having a baby so young." I kiss her naked shoulder.

"Yeah, it was at first. Her parents flipped out at the time, but as soon as that baby boy was born, it was like they couldn't have been happier."

"Do you want kids?" I surprise even myself with the question.

"Well, at one time, I thought I did. But thankfully the person was wrong for me, and I'm happy not to be tied to him in any way."

She's got to be talking about Jacob, the cheating woman-beater. I scowl at the thought of him. "I think we all have one or two of those in our past." I try to lighten the conversation, really regretting asking about Maine in the first place.

"I know Alex told you about Jacob and Becca." She turns back onto her side and stares at me. "He told me when we were in the kitchen. I wish he didn't..." She covers face with her hands and sighs deeply.

"Why wouldn't you want me to know? I thought all the blood drained out of my body when he told me." I pull her into me. "I can't believe someone hurt you, Addy."

She starts to sniffle, and I know she's crying.

"I'm sorry, baby; I didn't mean to get you upset. I shouldn't have..." I stop talking. I just want to hold her and not let her go, not let her be sad or in pain or anything like that.

"Everything happens for a reason, but it was the worst thing I have ever been through. In the end I was stronger because of it." She hold up her arms and examines them. "No scars, nothing permanent. Bumps and bruises heal."

She isn't crying anymore and smiles a half smile. I'm sure she's trying to make me feel better.

Sure, skin heals...

"I love you, beautiful girl." I kiss her hair.

"I love you, handsome man."

And we fall into a deep sleep, entwined in a warm embrace.

***

Three weeks ago by, and Addison has spent almost every night at the house. Luca is even here most days which Rex seems to really be happy about.

I ended up going to Jeremiah's, and we sat on his porch, talking everything out. I told him all about Gwen, everything she did, including what happened in my bed. He was angry; for a moment I think it's with me, but he explains that he knew she wasn't right for him and that he hasn't seen her in over a week.

I apologize for any problems between us, and we clink bottles, vowing to never let a crazy girl get between us again. We talk about Addison and her new job, her brother and his new job, and Jeremiah seems happy to have another helping hand on the ranch.

Since that day a lot of work has been done at home, we're preparing for a busy rodeo season.

Addison is busy at work. She's started on a night shift rotation, so there are times when we don't get to see each other. I miss her a lot.

It's been so different having a woman actually staying at the house. There hasn't been a feminine touch to that place since my mother died, and it feels warm and inviting now. There are even flowers in a vase on the dining room table from Addison's little flower beds at her condo.

"I told Alex everything we need done before Thursday night," Jeremiah says, closing the lid on the large tack box. I help him lift it into the front of the black trailer.

This weekend is the first rodeo of the season for me in the Mountain States Circuit, and Addison got the time off from work, so the four of us are travelling the one hundred and fifty miles to Cody together.

"Getting nervous, old man?" he jokes, clicking the big steel door shut.

"Nope," I lie.

Anytime I think about lowering myself down onto a two-thousand pound ticking time bomb I tense, but when I'm actually in the moment, my mind is clear. You have to push every fear out of your mind or your body will give you away, and the bull will feed off of it. Like he's not pissed off enough already.

"Everything okay, love?" I ask Addison. She's been quiet all afternoon.

"Yeah, I'm good, babe. Just trying to make sure I've got everything." She kisses me and slides on her flip flops.

The drive to Cody takes a little longer than expected, as we stop twice for bathroom breaks. Pulling into gates at the event, I can see Addison and Alex in awe. To Jer and I this is normal, something we've done many times. I forget that we're travelling with newbies.

Everything about the rodeo has been pre-planned well in advance, and we pull into our designated area. We walk around for a while, looking at some horses, and I talk to some familiar faces I've seen over the years. Introducing Addison as my girlfriend, I can see they all approve by the grins on their faces—grins that quickly fade to friendly smiles, as many of them are also standing with their wives or girlfriends, and a few get that "excuse me!" glare.

She is a beautiful sight, I can't deny it, and I'm not going to get jealous over the looks from others.

If I were a kid again, she would be the shiny medal I won at the championship baseball game. I would proudly wear her around my neck, showing her off to all my friends.

Since we're sharing a hotel suite with Jer and Alex, we are respectful and somehow manage to keep our hands from tearing our clothes off when we get into bed.

Alex snores, which keeps me awake, and everyone else is sleeping soundly. I sneak outside and sit in a wooden lounging chair by the front entrance. I slouch down to lean up and watch the night sky. Hours pass, I don't know how many.

A few guys stumble by, helping each other walk in to the rotating glass doors. They're laughing and singing an old country song way out of tune.

"Can't sleep?" Jeremiah surprises me by pulling over a chair to sit beside me.

"Nope. How could you with that racket?" I snort and then turn to face him. "I'm nervous, Jer."

He looks at me, like he's unsure of how to respond.

"I just feel..." I look up at the sky and close my eyes. "Scared."

"You've done tons of these, Blaine." He tries to sound reassuring and shrugs his shoulders. He's probably trying to understand my fear, but can't really relate since he's never actually sat astride a bull in a chute before. This will be the first of many for me this year; I've got to get a grip.

I don't get much sleep, but I wake up before everyone else. I shower, shave and dress—jeans, boots, a black button up shirt with long sleeves, and my black Resistol hat. After everyone wakes up, we have a hearty breakfast of omelettes, back bacon and thick toast, courtesy of room service.

"My, *oh my*. I don't know if I should let you walk out in public like this." Addison straightens the collar on my shirt and wipes lint off my shoulders.

"Oh no?" I grin.

"No, but I guess I have to." She pretends to pout and kisses me, telling me it's for good luck.

She stands with Alex while Jer and I get everything prepared. It will be the first time she's seen a bull-riding event, and I know she's nervous for me. Some crew have taken Del Mar, my bull, to the chute where he will wait, very irritably, I'm sure.

"What's the matter, baby?" I cup her face in my hands, searching for something in her eyes.

"Nothing," she smiles, an attempt to stop me from seeing the worry in her face.

"I'll be fine, I promise. It's over in the blink of an eye. The worst that's happened is I've got a bruised ass for a few days." I laugh and pull her closer into me. "Thankfully I've got my own nurse at home."

We kiss, and I can feel her body relax in my arms. I am nervous, but I don't dare let it show, especially not in front of her.

Anything can happen in the few seconds when the gate is opened. I've seen it firsthand, bodies flying through the air, landing poorly, and bones broken. Bulls can and will turn if you don't get out of there as fast as possible. Two years ago a guy was gored in his thigh by a bull. Thankfully, it wasn't life-threatening, but it sure was deep enough that he was rushed to the hospital.

The bull's anxious, and I hold on to the steel rails while I slowly lower myself down on him. He pounds the dirt, and one of the flankmen smiles at me encouragingly. Del Mar tenses, and I slide my gloved hand around the braided leather, ready for the ride of my life. I've only ever lasted seven seconds on Del Mar—the longest seven seconds of my life, mind you—but my time's too short to be anything to brag about.

I'm quickly introduced, and in the seconds before we're released, a calm washes over me. I pray to God to keep me safe, keep Del Mar away from me when our bond is broken, and that I come out victorious—and alive.

I slowly exhale through pursed lips; it's time. He jolts forward, and I lift up, holding myself one-handed as tightly as I can and trying to stay dead-center.

Seconds are seconds. They go by too fast and for the regular onlooker, it's over quickly. But for the person on the back of a hurricane in the form of an animal, it's more like slow motion. He whips and thrusts, and I inhale until my lungs can't hold anymore. Everything starts to blur—and I go black.

CHAPTER EIGHT

When I turn eight my brothers make me a birthday cake that has green, red and yellow icing all over it. It says, "Happy Birthday, B" in shaky writing made of colored sugar. Dad doesn't sing along with them wishing me a happy birthday, but he sits at the table smiling. When the song ends, they tell me to blow out the candles, and I do.

I wish...I wish for...

I don't know what to wish for. What do eight year olds usually want? Dirt bikes, BB guns? I already had all those because my older brothers got them for presents on their birthdays.

I don't make a wish; instead I open my eyes and blow out the eight white candles. Smoke slowly lingers up toward the ceiling and disappears in the wooden beams.

"Here ya go, my boy." Dad pushes a big box across the table; it's wrapped in black paper with *"Happy Birthday!"* written in bright neon colors printed all over it. I tear it open. Inside the box is a baseball glove and a hard white ball.

Looking at my dad and brothers, I say, "Thank you." I smile, slide my small hand into the leather glove. It's smooth and smells like oil.

"I thought you could practise this fall and maybe join the team at school in the spring. I even picked myself up a glove so we can toss the ball together."

I don't stop smiling, even though I'm really surprised my Dad just said that to me. He was going to play catch with me? I feel emotional, like I probably could cry at any moment, but swallow it down hard and fast not letting them see me.

Owen can't stay long as he works early and needs to get home. Nick, Dad and I head outside to play. Aside from Owen leaving too early, this was the best birthday I've ever had.

We toss the white ball, now streaked with green grass stains from all the times I missed catching it. It's dark when I go to bed. Nick's gone home and Dad tucks me in.

"It's hard to believe it's been eight years already, Blaine. Happy Birthday, my son." He pats my forearm with his big rough hand and sighs.

"Thank you for the presents, Daddy." I roll onto my side. He clicks the lamp on my nightstand off, and the room goes dark. The only things I can see are the little plastic glow-in-the-dark stars and moons glued to my ceiling.

"Good night." He leaves, and I fall asleep to the faint sound of the television downstairs.

***

I feel a familiar tingle on my face, but I can't think of what it is. I must be really tired because I can't open my eyes and see what's going on. Softly and slowly, something presses down and scrapes down my jaw and chin.

Then a cool dampness wipes the same places where the scraping was. Is someone shaving my face? That's exactly what it feels like, but I still can't open my eyes to see. Why would someone be doing this to me while I'm sleeping? Better yet, who is doing it to me? I don't know who would be in my bed shaving my face.

There's a faint low beeping sound, and occasionally I hear soft voices speaking, but I can't make out what they're saying.

I fall asleep again and dream about one of the girls I dated in school. Beth, with long brown hair and green eyes. She was short and really cute. She caught my eye one day at school while she played her violin on stage while two other girls sang.

Jeremiah elbowed me. "Cara sounds like a drowning cat, but Melanie is pretty good!"

I smile and agree, but I'm not paying attention to either of them. I can't stop staring at Beth and her graceful arm moving back and forth, her small chin resting on the copper wood of the instrument.

John Clapman has a party when his parents take a trip to Nashville without him or his older sister. Beth is there, and we spend almost the whole night making out on a long lawn chair. When we aren't making out, we're drinking beer from cans, listening to loud music and laughing with our friends.

She's the first girl to let me touch her breasts. Any other girl I liked would only kiss me, but Beth let me slide my hand right up her shirt at John's party that night.

That's where it started, and I thought it was the best two months of my life—until she came to school one day crying because her family was moving to Montana.

I never saw her again, even though we promised to talk on the phone all the time. I used the same locker all through high school, and even on the very last day, her name with a little heart beside it was still written in black Sharpie on the inside of the metal door. Any girl I dated after her would snort or roll their eyes at the black ink, but I didn't care.

***

It's dark and quiet when my eyes lazily open, just enough for me to see little lights on a machine that blink at the same time as a low beep. I swallow, and my mouth tastes horrible. My throat feels like sandpaper, and my saliva is painful to ingest.

I can open my eyes a little wider to see I'm alone in this room. Am I in the hospital? I can lift my arm a little and see an IV in my hand with a clear tube coming from it. It runs up past my shoulder and is hooked up to a stand letting out tiny drips every few seconds.

Why am I in the hospital? What happened to me?

I open my mouth to speak, but nothing comes out but air. I am so stiff, but I manage to turn my head to look for one of those call buttons, the ones that alert the nurses that someone in the room needs assistance. I see it; it's pinned to the bed above my head with a metal clamp, and I try to reach with my left arm. It's painful. I'm so achy, but I manage to press the red button and wait for something to happen.

Nothing does immediately, but within a few seconds, a short woman rushes in the door. She's muttering something to herself in a soft voice. She smiles at me while she quickly looks in my eyes with a small light and checks out the beeping machine with the little flashing lights on it.

"Welcome back, Mr. Blackstock. I'm Gloria. I'm going to get the doctor for you, okay?"

I try to speak again but still can't.

"Shhh, it's okay. You're just fine; I'll be right back." She quickly scurries out, and by the time I clear my throat, she's back with a man in dark blue scrubs.

"Hello, Blaine. I'm Dr. Tyler." He pulls the stethoscope from around his neck, holds it in his hands and asks me, "Do you know why you're in the hospital?" He leans in, putting each end in his ears and places the cold round piece on my chest.

"You had an accident, Blaine. Do you remember?"

I shake my head.

"You were thrown from your bull in a rodeo here in Cody. You had some minor trauma, something like a concussion, so we kept you to watch your brain activity."

I am able to open my eyes all the way now, and they're wide with anxiety.

"Wh---" I swear at myself because I still can't get the words out of my mouth. "What...hap...happened?" I manage and exhale deeply.

"Well, from what I've been told, you held on for a while. They don't know whether you were thrown or if you let go, but when you landed, you were knocked out." I can't remember it happening, but he sounds like he knows what he's talking about, and his expression is very serious. "You've been here for four days. Your family has been, too; they just left a few hours ago."

My family? I'm mad for not waking up sooner to see them. They must be so worried.

"I'm going to call right now, okay, Mr. Blackstock?" Gloria touches my hand, the one without the IV in it. She smiles and then leaves. I reach up slowly with my left hand, touching my face.

"Did someone shave my face?" I thought I dreamed it but my skin is smooth and soft, so it must have been real.

"Yes, we thought it wouldn't hurt. The young lady said you wouldn't want to wake up looking like Grizzly Adams." He chuckles and writes down something on a paper attached to a metal clipboard with BLACKSTOCK, B. Room 294 written on a white sticker across the back.

"What young lady?" I ask. Maria or Kelsey wouldn't care if I had stubble or not. And they're not really *young*...

He stops writing and looks at me. "I believe her name is Addison. Or Madison, something like that. Very pretty, with red hair?"

He is looking for any type of expression on my face, and when it's apparent I have no clue who he's talking about, he puts the clipboard to his hip and tells me he'll be right back.

A few hours go by, and there's no more talk of the redheaded girl Dr. Tyler mentioned, just a few random questions by Gloria about what year it was, the month, who the president is and my birth date.

"Two thousand and eleven. May. Obama. September 25th, 1981." I proudly say with a smile.

"Close; it's June. Your family is on their way to see you. Do you feel like you could take a shower?" Her question makes me feel normal again, and I tell her I would love one.

She and a guy in green scrubs and a white t-shirt help me out of bed and into a wheelchair.

The guy, introducing himself as Peter, wheels me out of my room and into the brightly lit hallway. Passing a few doors we come to one that says "Shower" and has a tag with "Vacant" on one side. Peter turns it so it says "Occupied" and opens the door.

Inside the room there is small counter to the left, a plastic chair to the right and a shower, with no curtain, in the middle.

"I don't think you'd want me to stay in here with ya, but I have to make sure you can stand before I leave, okay?" He helps me stand, and I feel strong enough that I'm sure I'll manage on my own.

"Thanks." I'm not even embarrassed when the gown I'm wearing falls open at the back exposing my backside to him; I'm sure this kid has seen everything working in a place like this.

He turns on the shower for me, telling me to take my time and use the call button if I need any help at all.

Closing the door behind him I look at myself in the large mirror above the counter. I look like hell. My hair is a mess and aside from my face being clean shaven, I don't look like myself at all. I let the green striped gown fall to the floor. When I do, it reveals two large, yellowing bruises. One is on my ribs; I lift my arm to see the rest—it's huge. The other is down by my hip, smaller but just as colorful.

The small room is filling with steam as I step carefully into the shower. The water pressure is horrible compared to my shower at home, more like a spritz than a spray. I lather some shampoo from the tiny bottle I took from the counter and rub it through my hair. My fingers graze a lump on the left side of my head, and I wince when I touch it. I remember Dr. Tyler saying I had some sort of concussion; this is where I must have hit my head.

I'm starting to feel better after my shower, and I wrap a white towel around my waist. It's scratchy, but it will do. I don't put the gown back on, and I open the door and walk right by the wheelchair. I need to get it together so I can get out of this place and back home.

A few women standing at the nurse's station see me coming and very obviously check me out. I smirk. One turns and nonchalantly clears her throat, acting like she's not eyeballing me at all.

When I walk through the door to my room, I see Nick, Owen, Maria, Kelsey and my father standing there. They gasp, and Maria rushes over to hug me.

"Blaine! We were so worried. You have no idea how scared we all were!"

I hug her back with one arm, avoiding my sore side, the other holding the towel around my waist.

"I'm okay. I don't remember what happened. The doc told me though."

She lets me go to stand back beside my brothers.

"We brought you some clothes, honey," Kelsey says, and I'm surprised because she's never regarded me like that, ever. "Jeremiah got together a bag for you; he's been worried sick, too."

Jer had packed me jeans, socks, boxers and a white t-shirt—the guy does know me well. I ask for some privacy while I dress; my dad is the last to leave the room.

"Happy you're okay, my boy." He hesitates. "Thought we almost lost you." He closes the door behind him.

Gloria comes back in first. "Dr. Tyler said you can have some Tylenol for the headache I'm sure you have. He will be back in a few hours to assess you, okay? He might even let you go home soon." I take the two small red pills and swallow the cool water she hands me from the little paper cup.

"Thank you, Gloria." I smile at her. "Who was the girl who shaved me?"

She looks up, puzzled. "Dr. Tyler said you don't remember her? Well..." She's looking around, seemingly searching for a way to explain it to me. "She arrived with two other men when the ambulance brought you here. She was very distraught, said she was your girlfriend and kept telling you how much she loved you." She looks sad, and I look like I don't have a clue.

"Things like this sometimes happens, Mr. Blackstock. Memories come back most of the time. You weren't seriously injured and didn't suffer any internal bleeding, just a little bit of swelling."

She's smiling but still looks sad. "Maybe your family can speak with you about everything and you'll start to piece it together."

When everyone comes back in the room, Jeremiah is with them. "Buddy! Holy fuck, man!" he exclaims. He looks over at my dad. "Sorry, Mr. B."

My father grins and shrugs his shoulders.

"We were freaking out! You held on for 7.3 seconds, man! But then...you let go." Jeremiah goes white. "You looked like a rag doll."

"The doctor told me what happened, but I don't remember any of it." I feel frustrated, and I hold my hands up, shaking my head. "Who is Addison?"

And every person in the room holds their breath at the same time.

"What?" I look around at all the faces, staring at me with wide eyes.

"*What?*" Jeremiah looks at Nick, then Owen, then back to me. "Who's Addison? She's your girl, that's who. Are you joking right now?"

Jer looks almost angry, but I don't think it's at me—at least I hope not.

"Blaine didn't remember her when Dr. Tyler mentioned her, so that's why we asked you not to bring her, Jer," Nick chimes in. "We didn't want to upset her. I'm sure it'll all come back with time." He looks reassuringly at Jeremiah, who doesn't seem to believe Nick's hopefulness.

"Bro. I don't know what to say." He's upset and puts his head in his hands. "Hell, I'm just so happy you're alive."

Dr. Tyler comes in and explains what my latest test results have to say. "All signs show he's going to be okay. He can go home maybe tomorrow, as long as someone is able to stay with him for a few days."

"I'll stay. I'm there every day anyway," Jeremiah says to the doctor, who nods and smiles. "What about his memory, Doc? He doesn't remember...certain things."

He looks at me. "Well, things like this can happen from a bump on the head. Nine times out of ten the memories come back within a few days. He does not have amnesia," Dr. Tyler explains to my family, who all look relieved.

I'm released the next day, and the drive home takes no time at all. I go with Jeremiah in some big beefy Dodge.

"Is this a rental?"

"Umm. No. I bought it; you came with me."

"Sorry, man. I'm trying' to figure all this out." I put my head in my hands and groan. How can I lose weeks of my life? How can I get it back?

Jeremiah pats my shoulder. "We'll deal with it as it comes."

Rex is frantic when I get out of the truck. I've never seen him more excited; he probably thought I was never coming back. I slowly lay down on the couch inside, kicking my shoes off. They land with a thud on the wood floor.

"Want anything?"

"Naw, I'm okay. Thanks for everything, Jer." I smile and reach for the remote to turn the TV on.

That night I sleep peacefully and dream about a beautiful woman. I can't see her face, but she's sitting on my porch, swinging on the bench. I just stand there in the door way watching her. She is looking out into the field, but there's nothing there but trees.

She's humming a song, and the bench is moving in rhythm with her sad melody. When I wake up the dream is very much in the front of my mind, and I think about it all morning. But I don't mention it to Jeremiah.

***

The next week is painfully boring. He refuses to let me do much of anything; I'm surprised he leaves me alone when I need to use the bathroom. He does all the cooking, and cleaning—well, as much cleaning as a single guy does.

"Your appointment is at 11:30 today. I'll drive you and then bring you home." Jer looks at his watch, then pulls out his cell phone to send a message to someone. Whoever it is sends a reply which doesn't make him smile, but he does seem to relax a little.

"Who was that?" I ask, and he shoves it back into his pocket.

"Nobody. Let's go!" He motions with his hand, and I put my shoes on. I miss driving. I really miss driving my own truck and doing things for myself. I do like having Jer around, thought. It would be lonely if he was gone. The feeling of being alone makes me cold, and I push it away.

Dr. Lloyd, my family doctor, assesses me and gives me a thumbs up. I'm all good. Finally! My goose egg is gone for the most part, and with all the resting I've been ordered to do, my body no longer aches. Even the bruises are almost gone, a faint yellow color now.

"Wanna get some lunch?" I ask Jeremiah. "I don't know about you, but I'm starving." Of course. I know the answer before he even says it. Jer's always hungry.

"Where do you want to go?" I suggest The Wolfbarrow, and he looks at me like I've grown a second head.

"You sure?"

Why wouldn't I be sure? We go there all the time.

"Okay," he relents. "Let's go." He puts the truck in reverse, and we back out of the parking lot. Idling at the lights, waiting for the red to change to green, I see a silver Mustang pull up beside us.

Damn. Nice car. I look down into the driver's window. Jer's truck is lifted like mine, so I can't see anything but a pair of women's legs disappearing beneath the steering wheel.

Mmm, even better. I smirk. The light turns green and we drive ahead. The Mustang turns right and is gone.

Seconds later his phone beeps, and he ignores it.

"You going to get that?" I ask, reaching for the phone, but he snatches it away before I can touch it.

"Can't text and drive, bro. Better to be safe than sorry!" And he shoves it into his pocket, scolding me for suggesting something so stupid.

The Wolfbarrow is busy, but we're able find a table and sit. Some new waitress takes our order. She's gorgeous. She's got black hair, cut really short but very feminine. I usually go for girls with long hair, but this one has a body to die for and a face to match. We order, and I keep feeling like he's glaring at me.

"What!?" I kick his shin with my shoe under the table. "Did you even see her? Or are you too busy texting...whoever. You haven't put that thing down since we got here."

He snorts.

"Yeah, I saw her, she's pretty. And she's Jesse's new girlfriend, so don't go getting any ideas."

Oh, well. I'm not the type to move in on another man's girlfriend, but it doesn't mean I can't appreciate her beauty. I roll my eyes at him, and take a big rib off my plate, ripping the meat off the bone with my teeth.

When he leaves to use the bathroom, he forgets his phone on the table. I can't resist, so I pick it up, sliding the screen with my finger to unlock it I open up the messages.

The most recent set of texts is open, so I take a quick look at the bathroom door and start reading.

He's OK today, not in any pain.

That's great!

Yep. Sorry about everything. I still feel awful.

I know, me too. I still can't believe this happened.

Shit. We all just gotta pray he starts to remember.

I have been praying. Every night and every morning.

Well our prayers for him to be alive were heard loud and clear.

Thank you, I really appreciate it.

No worries Addy. Please try and stay positive.

I will. I love him too much not to be.

Hey, his appointment is today. You sure you won't be there right?

Hi, yes I'm sure. I don't work until later anyway.

I know it will be hard, but we need to take it slow, ya know?

I know.

I'll call you later and tell you how it went.

K thanks.

"Shit." He stands at the table, arms crossed, and I don't know if he's mad at himself for leaving the phone unattended or at me for reading it.

"I want to see her, Jer. Please." I can feel tears starting to well in my eyes. "Get me out of here." Standing up to walk out, I'm beyond frustrated. Why did this happen to me? I have a girl who is in love with me somewhere out there, and she's in agony. I can't bear it; I cover my face with my hands in anger, desperate to remember what I had and what I hopefully haven't lost.

"I'll take you home, and then we'll talk about it, okay?"

I agree and climb into his truck. At home we talk about her. He tells me how we met, how I first saw her at Zeke's and drooled like a St. Bernard. How she was always here, and we were in love. He talked about her brother working for me, too, and that the car I saw today was hers. I don't speak; I just sit in the chair at the dining room table and listen.

After a while his phone beeps again, and he leaves the room to answer it. I lay my head down on the wooden table top and cover it with my arms.

Please Lord, let me remember her. I pray up to the heavens, desperate to reminisce.

When I raise my head I notice a vase of dying flowers on the table in front of my face. A tiny white petal drops onto the table, and I inhale sharply.

Like a projector screen dropping down in front of my eyes, it all comes back, memories flying into my mind. Zeke's, the dog treats, her hair, and her blue dress. I'm reeling.

Spilled beer, her giggles, dad's birthday, Gwen, her tears.

Everything is there; everything is back, and when Jeremiah walks back in the room, I'm almost catatonic.

"Holy shit, Blaine! What's wrong?" He rushes over and sits beside me.

"I remember, Jer. I remember everything." I see myself sitting on Del Mar's back inside the chute, the flankman smiling at me.

I stand up so fast my chair falls over, and I head into the kitchen to find my keys.

"Blaine, she's at work. You can't just..."

I glare at him, even though I don't mean to.

"Okay, okay." He puts his hands up like he's surrendering.

"You're right; I can't just run in there. What times does she get off?" My stomach is doing flip flops, and I'm feeling all kinds of strange emotions that I can seem to get a grip on.

He looks at the big clock on the wall. "In two hours."

Two agonizing hours I have to wait.

"I'm gonna call her, Blaine. I want to tell her, let her decide what she wants to do. She's been through a lot." He takes out his phone, looks at me sympathetically and goes outside.

I don't wait for him to come back in and tell me what she says. I know she will want to see me—if she really loves me, she will, anyway. I run upstairs to shower and redress. Even though what I already had on was fine, I want to look my best, like it's my prom or something. I'm nervously buckling my belt and pulling my shirt over my head.

"Bud?" he calls from the bottom of the stairs. "She's going to come over when she's done work. So I'm going to head out, okay?"

I come down the steps and sit on a stool at the island in the kitchen. "Thanks, Jer." What would I do without this guy? I really don't know. He gives me a one-armed hug before he leaves, and I sit with anticipation for the next ninety minutes.

I can't stay inside and wait, so I sit, very impatiently on the porch steps. Her car pulls into the driveway, and my heart starts racing. It feels like the first time I've ever seen her.

When she steps out, I stand up, wiping my sweaty palms on my jeans. She looks tired—beautiful, but tired—and is still wearing work clothes. I can't say I'm not disappointed when she doesn't run up and jump in my arms. She just slowly walks through the grass over to me and smiles.

"Hi, Blaine," she says, inhaling deeply like it's the last breath she'll ever take. "How are you?"

How am I? I'm beyond confused. I was expecting fireworks or something, not this cold feeling washing over me.

"Baby," I start to say, and she looks away, at anything but me, it seems. I reach out and touch her crossed arms, "Please. I'm so, so sorry. I..."

I'm getting frustrated; why won't she touch me?

"Over the past week and a half," she says, speaking as quietly as she can, very calmly, staring at her shoes, "I've had nothing but time. Time to think about everything I had and everything that I lost."

"But you didn't lose me," I burst. "Addy, I don't know why it happened. But it's all back now, I love you. Please." I try to touch her again, and this time, she backs up two steps. I can feel all my blood leave my body and pool at my feet.

"Blaine, I realized that I love you more than I thought, and it frightened me. Watching you fall...and everything after was torture." She starts to cry. The tears roll down her face, and she laughs while trying to wipe them away, but they just keep coming.

"I don't want to go through that again. My God..." She places her hands on her face. "You could have been killed. You hit your head hard enough to forget me, and I just lost it."

This time I don't care if she tries to get away. I grab her and wrap her in my arms as tight as I can. She's sobbing, and I can't stand it. "I won't do it again, baby. For you. I won't ever ride a bull again. Please." I promise and rock her gently in my arms.

We stand there forever, and she finally stops crying. "I don't want you to stop doing something you love."

Is she serious? I love her! I love her more than that—can't she see?

"Addy, you mean more to me than anything. I would do anything humanly possible for you." I squeeze tighter and then take her up into my arms, into the house and up to bed.

"Jeremiah's gone, and I can't be alone. You have to stay. Doctor's orders." I raise an eyebrow as I set her down on the bed.

She half smiles and pulls her ponytail so it hangs over her shoulder. I sit on the bed beside her, and we talk about everything that happened. She said she was in the hospital for the first two days, she couldn't leave. I told her I remembered someone shaving my face.

"I knew when you woke up you wouldn't want to have grown a beard." She laughs and crosses her legs.

"I had to go back to work, and I didn't want to leave you. Jeremiah and your family told me to go, that they would be there with you and call me if anything happened." She clears her throat and then reaches down to pull of her shoes.

"They were so kind to me. When Nick called to tell me what happened when you woke up... He said I shouldn't come."

I think she's going to start crying again, so I pull her close to me, kissing her hair.

"I knew he was right, and I was so happy you were okay. But I was devastated at the same time."

I pull her over so her legs are wrapped around me, sitting on me, and we're face to face. I kiss her mouth, her cheek, all the way down her neck. When I pull her shirt off, I kiss her shoulder and chest. The clasp at her back opens with my touch, and her bra falls down, exposing her breasts. I kiss each of them, savouring all of her.

Once we are completely undressed and in bed, she rolls over so she's facing away from me, and I lift her leg so I can slowly enter her. She gasps, and I kiss her back. In this position I can reach around and caress her breasts while we make love.

Tenderly I pull her chin so her face turns up, and I kiss her mouth deeply. I can feel myself reaching my peak, and I try to hold out as she hasn't not yet climaxed.

"Come on, baby," I whisper in her ear. It sends her over the edge; her muscles tighten around me, and I pull her closer, our bodies heaving together.

CHAPTER NINE

Over the next few weeks we discuss more about our plans for the future. I tell her I want her to move in, and she's a little hesitant.

"I don't know if Alex can afford the condo on his own," she says.

I don't push, just think of a way to make it happen. While she's at work I talk to Jeremiah about asking her to live with me; he thinks it's a good idea, too. Then he suggests something I didn't even think of.

"Well, I could rent him one of the bedrooms at my place."

Hmm...That might just work.

When Addison comes over after work I tell her about what Jer suggested. She smiles, agreeing that it's a good idea and that Alex will probably go for it.

One week later we're at her rented condo, loading what few possessions she has into my truck and Alex's into Jeremiah's.

"I'm a little nervous that you two will be living together. I hope it doesn't turn into a frat house over there." She laughs and pokes Jeremiah's shoulder.

"Hey, now. I think we'll be fine as long as there's beer in the fridge—right, Alex?" He smirks.

Addison closes the door once everything is out. I bend down to pick up the ceramic malamute with the welcome sign, and she smiles. I kiss her and we head to our home.

***

August is a profitable month for the ranch; between the hay and cattle sales, I'm well into the red. During the last week before the end of the month, Alex, Addison and I fly to Maine so they can visit their parents, and I can finally meet them. They both make fun of me when I seem nervous about flying, which I have never done before. Once we are in the air, I feel much better. I have a window seat, so I marvel at the beauty of God's creation.

Their parents meet us at the airport. Addison is a spitting image of her mother, who doesn't look old enough to have two children in their twenties. Her father is very tall, stocky, and I'm a little intimidated.

"My babies!" Their mother beams and takes them both in her arms. Their dad extends his hand to me.

"You must be Blaine. It's a pleasure."

I say the same and call him Mr. Cole; he quickly corrects me, telling him to call him Richard. I'm not used to addressing my elders by their first names, especially not the father of the woman I'm in love with on our first meeting.

"Dad." Alex hugs his father, who embraces him back. I can tell he really does love his son. Momentarily I wish I had that with my own father.

"Mom, this is Blaine. Blaine, my mom Lillian." She hugs me and then holds me out so she can get a look at all of me.

"Addy, you weren't wrong when you said he was handsome!"

I blush, and I'm thankful I wore a baseball cap so when I look down, no one can see my face.

We climb in to their brand new Escalade, and I feel totally out of place, like some lost puppy Addison found on her way home from school.

Her parents' house is about thirty minutes from the airport, and we drive through a beautiful landscape to get there. The houses along the street keep getting bigger and bigger as the numbers on the mailboxes get higher. We turn into a driveway, through an open gate, and I look at Addison like she's forgotten to mention something to me.

Their house is enormous, to say the least, with huge vaulted peaks, big white pillars and a massive brick chimney on the one side. We park outside a four-car garage, and I hope my jaw hasn't been on the floor of their too-clean Cadillac this whole time. Flowerbeds line the walkway, and the driveway, too.

The inside of the house is just as I expected, straight from the pages of a magazine, very clean and flowers everywhere. The walls are white, and the floors are a very dark rustic wood.

"Make yourself at home, Blaine. We have a room upstairs all for you, too!" Lillian beams and motions up the large staircase.

"Thank you very much." I smile and start carrying our luggage up the black wooden steps of the huge staircase in the middle of the room. Addison shows me her bedroom, still decorated as if she never left. Posters are on the walls, a few ribbons and trophies on a little shelf above her desk. A large canopied bed in the center of the room, trimmed with light purples and pinks.

"It's very...girly." I smirk and place her bags on the bed.

"Yeah, well, I *am* a girl! And I haven't slept in this room since I was like, eighteen." She laughs and takes my hand to show me where I'll be sleeping.

Across the hall is Alex's room; he's in flopped on his bed with one foot on the ground tapping loudly to the heavy music coming from his stereo.

The bedroom she leads me to, is just as big as hers. The bed in the center is covered in a blanket that's creamy white with dark blue flowers printed all over it. I drop my bag, the only one I brought, compared to Alex and Addy's combined six.

"So, listen here, Mr. Blackstock. I better not catch you sneaking into my room in the middle of the night." She kisses me, and I wrap my arms around her, wanting to climb on that flowered bed and make love to her.

"My dad sleeps with a gun under the bed." She winks, and I can't tell if she's joking... I hope she's joking.

Her parents take us out to dinner. The restaurant is huge, almost as big as their house is, and decorated about as nicely, too. In my jeans, boots, and button-up shirt, I know I'm sticking out like a sore thumb next to everyone else in town. Her parents are dressed immaculately, and even Alex is wearing dress pants and a tie. Addison, is wearing a gorgeous black dress, accentuating her body, and for the first time I see her in heels. She's almost as tall as me in them, and I imagine her lying on the bed, her beautiful legs up and a black heel resting over each of my shoulders. I know where my mind is headed, and I shift to adjust myself in my chair.

Dinner is salmon. Smoked salmon boursin, to be exact. I have to read it a few times and listen to the others order it before I can pronounce it myself. What is it with rich people anyway? Why can't they just say "salmon and cheese'?

It's delicious, and I'm disappointed when I realize that the only plateful I got served is considered the main course. How do these people not starve to death on so little food? To make myself seem more out of place, I'm drinking a draft beer, and they're all sipping from glasses of wine.

Addison is sitting across from me with her brother, and I have her parents on either side of me. She keeps looking at me seductively, and I think she's enjoying her little game because she knows I can't react while I'm sandwiched between Richard and Lillian.

Dessert is some sort of pastry, filled with cheesecake and deep fried. With a scoop of ice cream on top, drizzled with caramel, it looks too good to eat. And looking at it more closely I notice it's not just drizzle; it's drizzle spelling out the word *Enjoy!*

Jeremiah would laugh if he saw me sitting in front of a plate like this. I'm almost tempted to take a picture with my phone and send it to him…but I don't.

Alex is talking to his parents about everything he's been doing on the ranch, and they are very impressed with him. I glance at Addison, who is watching me. She dips her finger into the cheesecake and slowly puts it into her mouth.

Fuck…I'm going to die. Her father has a gun under his bed, but all I want to do is jump over this table and throw those heels over my shoulders…Yep, I'm going to die.

I remember the game she played the first night I spent at her house, with the pink lotion on her legs. And I remember that two can play at this game.

Game on, baby. I raise my eyebrow at her suggestive finger licking, look away, and nonchalantly undo the top button on my shirt. She smirks and sits up in her chair, talking to her mother, trying her best not to look at me.

"So Addy tells me you were in an accident. How long have you been riding those animals?" Richard turns and looks at me.

"Well, since I was nineteen. And this was the first time I've been seriously hurt." I look at Addison, who is still talking to her mom. "And it scared me enough that I don't want to risk it again. I'll stick to my horse."

"It's a shame, really. It's a magnificent experience, I'm sure, but you're right that it's dangerous..." says Richard. "Especially when you have loved ones watching you." He looks lovingly at his daughter, and she smiles at him sweetly. I'm assuming she didn't mention by bought with temporary amnesia because he doesn't bring it up, and I don't either.

It's getting late, and Richard and Lillian tell us they're going home but we three should stay out and enjoy the night.

"Show him how we have fun in Maine, Addy!" Lillian gives her daughter a kiss on the cheek, and Richard shakes my hand. They leave, and we sit back down at the table, discussing what to do next. Alex suggests a club, which I am not really interested in, and Addison turns her lip in disgust at the idea.

"How about we go to *THE Club*—and maybe I can get the girls to come out!" She almost squeals and has an ear-to-ear smile. I can see she's excited about the idea.

"Girls like who? *Riley?*" Alex raises his eyebrow quizzically.

"Yeah, Riley. And maybe a few others. Why do you care anyway? You're not going to stick around once we're there!" She elbows him in the ribs, and he acts like he's hurt.

Six text messages later, she's heard back from "her girls", and I'm almost dreading what's next. The man at the podium in the lobby calls a cab for us, and we wait under the canopied entrance for it to come.

On the way to *The Club*, she tells me nothing about what I'm about to endure. Alex sits in the front, and I figure it's a safe time to tease her a little, considering how worked up she had me during dessert. I undo another button, showing off my pectoral muscles and what little chest hair I have. I shift in my seat so my knees are touching the back of the chair in front of me and I rub my hand slowly across my abdomen.

"Mmm. Dinner was good, wasn't it?" I smile at her with salacious, hooded eyes.

She keeps her poker face well.

"Dessert was better," she replies and puts the same finger that had the cheesecake on it back it her mouth, biting down with her front teeth.

Damn it, she's good.

Thankfully the cab ride is short, as I was two seconds away from tearing her dress off and ordering the driver and Alex to get out of the car. The Club is just that—a country club with rolling green hills for golfing.

This should be interesting. I'm pleasantly surprised when we're inside, and I see that it's not full of middle aged people in khakis and polo shirts with argyle sweaters tied around their shoulders. Instead I see people our age; well, Alex's age, most likely, dancing and conversing around a large bar in the middle of the room. Alex sees people he must know because he leaves us and walks over to them, hugging and shaking their hands. He says something to them and points in our direction; they all look over.

Yeah, that's right. Say hello to the country bumpkin. I smirk and Addison and I walk hand in hand over to another side of the bar to order drinks.

"I'll have a beer," I say loudly to the too-tanned guy in the too-tight golf shirt.

"And I'll have a margarita!" Addison leans in, placing her order. He nods and gets to work on our drinks.

"Cole!" Someone shouts her name, and we both turn to see four girls straight from a magazine standing in a line, walking toward us. I'd say something like a Victoria's Secret magazine, not because they're dressed in lingerie but because they're all hot enough to be featured in the catalogue.

"Hey, girls!" Addison exclaims in a voice I've never heard her use before; it's high pitched and very excited. They swarm around her, all hugging and bouncing at the same time, and I step back before I'm knocked over by a huge leather purse.

"Ladies, this is Blaine." She turns and holds her hand out, like a curator does to a feature at a museum. They gape, and I can't resist grinning my best smile. It's one I've only been using to get Addy excited, but why not? I figure. When in Rome—or, Maine.

"Addison Cole, you failed to mention how *hot* of a cowboy he is!" says one of the girls, a beautifully tall woman with black hair and deep brown eyes.

"Blaine." I extend my hand to her, and she grabs it.

"Riley. I've heard *so much* about you!"

Ah, so this is the infamous best friend.

"And I've heard a lot about you, too. It's a pleasure." I pull my hand back, and the other three brunette girls all introduce themselves in turn. Camille, Zoe, and Leah.

Addison hasn't seen her friends in a long time, so I lean in to tell her I'm going to check the place out. I softly trail the tips of my fingers down her spine and stop right before I reach her behind. I kiss her earlobe and bite down gently. I'm making sure the girls don't see what I'm doing, but they see her blush, and I know I'm the one doing all the teasing now.

The men's bathroom is as big as my bedroom in Wyoming. Every surface is dark marble, and glass basins serving as sinks sit on top of the counters with polished silver faucets. When I'm finished, I wash my hands and pick up a white hand towel to dry them off.

"So, who are you supposed to be?" a voice asks from the doorway, taking me by surprise. I thought I was alone. I look up and see a guy standing there. He's wearing jeans, a white shirt, black jacket and a tie.

"Sorry?" I ask. I have no idea why someone would be asking me who I was—not in the bathroom in Maine, anyway.

"I said, w*ho are you supposed to be?*"

Like he thinks I really am sorry for not hearing him the first time. "I heard you. I'm Blaine, and who are you?" I toss the towel into a tall basket and walk toward him. Now I want to know what's going on.

"So you're the new one, eh? Looks like she's downgraded to redneck in my opinion."

He's still standing in the doorway, looking cocky, and I can feel my chest tighten.

"I don't know who you think I am, *friend*. I'd like it if you got out of my way." I start to walk by him, and he puts his hand out in front of my face, planting it on the wooden frame, stopping me. Okay, that's it.

"Listen, you fuck..." I glare at him, and he just looks back, smiling like a weasel.

"No, you listen, *friend*. My Addy will come to her senses and come back to me, so I'd suggest--"

That's all it takes. Next thing I know I've got him up against the door, my right arm across his chest under his chin, and my left arm cocked back ready to strike.

"Listen to me clearly. I know who you are, *Jacob*, and I know what you did to her," I hiss through clenched teeth.

He's not smiling anymore, and I lean in closely. "Next time you want a fight, I'll show you how it's done, you fuckin' coward."

"Blaine! Ohhhh, shit!" Alex rushes in, and when I look over at him, Jacob swings at me but misses. Alex gets close enough and throws his first up, punching Jacob under his chin, sending him back into the wall. He slides down, and his shoes slip on the marble floor as he tries to get on his feet.

"Alex, you punk! You'll regret this." Alex knees him in the groin so hard Jacob falls on the floor, holding himself, coughing and swearing at the both of us.

"Stay away from my sister, you piece of shit. I swear to God if you come near her again..." Alex is seething, and I have to stop him from kicking the squirming pile of garbage on the bathroom floor.

"She'll just fuck you like she fucked me, redneck!" Jacob laughs.

I turn, giving him a swift but forceful kick to the stomach, and now Alex is the one holding me back from pounding the shit out of him.

The electricity is charging through me as Alex and I furiously make our way outside for some air. I can't believe what just happened. When we get out into the cool Maine night, Alex shakes my shoulders with his hands, then steps back and pulls his tie off, shoving it into his pocket.

"Holy shit, bro! What the fuck was that?" He's half laughing, half in shock.

"He's lucky we didn't kill him. Holy shit, Alex!" I'm spinning and tell him I need a drink.

Jacob must have composed himself and left because no one is acting like a scene from *Fight Club* just took place in the men's bathroom. Addison isn't by the bar anymore, and for a moment, I anxiously look for her.

"There she is!" Alex reads my mind and points through the crowd on to the dance floor. She's dancing with her friends, laughing and singing along to the song. She looks so happy and so beautiful. I am relieved she's okay and hope that she doesn't know Jacob was just here. Alex and I treat ourselves to three shots of Jack Daniels each.

"Yee-ouch!" Alex throws his head back and shudders after the third shot.

Three songs later the girls all walk over to us, giggling to each other. Addison wraps her arms around my neck and kisses me. "Baby! Mmm, have you been drinking whiskey?" She pulls back, examining my face.

"Yes, ma'am." I wink and kiss her quickly. As if the moment couldn't get any more perfect, a song comes on that I finally recognize, and I pull her behind me on to the dance floor.

During the chorus of *Drunk on You*, I twirl her with my hand. She leans her back into my chest, and I hold her hands in mine, across her front. The moment doesn't last long enough, and a fast-paced Lady Gaga song comes on. I smile and start to walk off the tile floor.

She pouts. "Not going to stay for this one?"

The other girls start to surround her.

"She's all yours, ladies." I grin and walk back over to the bar where Alex is talking with two young girls, and I have two more shots of J.D.

The girls all say their goodbyes. We leave for Wyoming tomorrow afternoon, and they're all hugging and kissing cheeks.

"We are going to miss you so much, Cole!" Riley has tears in her eyes, and she hugs Addison tightly. "You take care of my girl, Blaine."

I smile and nod, telling her I have every intention of doing just that.

"I think I'm gonna hang around a bit longer with my favourite ladies." Alex drapes his arms on Riley and Zoe's shoulders, and they laugh. "I'll be home later." He winks, and they all wave while we leave The Club, my arm protectively around her waist.

In the cab back to her parents' house she's quiet, probably thinking about how she'll miss her friends, I guess. I hope she didn't see Jacob, but I'm sure she would have said something if she did.

"Did you have a good night?" I lean over and kiss her shoulder.

She looks and me and smiles. "I did; thank you for coming. They all loved you!"

"Well, I'm not surprised really," I smirk. "Who can resist this?" I wave my hand down my body, showcasing it like an exhibit, and she throws her head back and laughs.

"You're too much, and I love you."

"I love you more." I take her hand in mine and kiss her knuckles.

Her parents must be in bed because when we arrive, the house is in darkness except for a small lamp on a table right as soon as you walk in the door. She skips out of her heels, and I pull my boots off. Then I walk over to her and lean her back to kiss her deeply. She quietly giggles, and I feel myself start to harden. I wouldn't disrespect her parents by sleeping with her in their home, but I'm starting to feel like a rule breaker. I stand her back up, our foreheads touching and our eyes closed.

"I want you, Blaine. So badly right now." She breathes, and my body responds. We kiss again, and all of my taste buds explode like they're little cherry bombs thrown into a fire. She tastes like lime, coconut and tequila. And, of course, her natural sweetness.

"Addison, we can't." I look upstairs, and she pouts. My insides are clawing at me and it takes every fibre of my being to go upstairs and simply kiss her goodnight in her doorway before heading to my own temporary bedroom.

I sleep in my boxers; well, I don't sleep, actually. I just lie there, staring at the white ceiling, watching the dark blades of the fan above my head slowly spinning.

The last time I remember looking at the ticking clock on the nightstand beside the bed, the hands show 3:19.

CHAPTER TEN

I feel her sitting on the bed, running her soft fingers on my cheek. "Wakey, wakey, handsome." She quietly beckons me out of my slumber.

"Hey, baby." I am groggy, really regretting drinking last night, especially tossing back all that Jack Daniels. "What time is it?"

I see the clock shows 8:05. Falling back down on the bed, I cover my face with my arm, not wanting to get out of this comfort.

"Have you heard from Alex?" she asks, scrolling with her thumb on the screen of her phone.

"No, I thought he was coming home last night." I wonder where he is.

"Hey, girl, it's me. Do you know what time my brother went home last night? He isn't here, and I'm a little worried. Call me." She ends the call and looks down at me with a smile. "Hungry?"

I am starving. Actually, I'm ravenous, and the thought of breakfast gets me up and out of bed.

"Mom's making a feast; let's go!" She pulls my arm, and then steps back to eye me from head to toe. "Well, get dressed first. Then come down." With a kiss she leaves the room, closing the door behind her.

When I get downstairs Richard and Lillian are sitting at the round white table in their kitchen. "Good morning!" Lillian says melodically. I smile and say the same to them.

"Hope you kids weren't out too late!" Richard looks at me over his newspaper and smiles.

"No, sir. We had a good time; thank you again for dinner," I say politely and sit down beside Lillian, reaching for the pitcher of orange juice.

Addison comes into the kitchen, pulling her phone out of the pocket of her jeans. "Riley! Hey…Are you kidding me?" She looks at the three of us, smiles and quickly walks back out of the room. I can hear her whispering and giggling, and then she's back.

"Mom, this looks delicious!" She sits down beside her father, kissing his cheek and piling a scoop of scrambled eggs on her square plate. I wonder what Riley said to her, and I look at her quizzically, but she gives nothing away.

We talk about going to see the ocean today, before we leave for the airport.

It's just after 9:30 when Alex walks through the door, still wearing the clothes he had on last night, looking very dishevelled.

"Hey guys. Mom, Dad...Blaine." He doesn't even get his shoes off before Addison pulls his arms and wisps him up the staircase.

"Whoa, slow down! My feet aren't exactly on speaking terms with my brain yet...What's up with you?" he yells in surprise but goes along with her.

What is going on? I'm so confused and really tempted to follow them up there, but if she wanted me to know, I'm sure she'd tell me.

Richard just looks at me again, this time before sipping from his coffee mug, "Kids," he says and shrugs his shoulders.

I smirk and thank Lillian for a delicious breakfast. She smiles and tells me I'm more than welcome.

"I'm so happy that Addison has someone so kind." She trails off, looking out the window, probably thinking about sitting at her daughter's side while after she was beaten by that animal.

I shudder at the recollection, then grin quickly to myself as I remember Alex and me giving him a taste of his own poison last night in the bathroom at The Club.

The ocean is everything I expected it to be and so much more. You can't only smell the salt but taste it in the air, too. The spray feels amazing, and Addy and I walk along the beach hand in hand.

"So, are you going to tell me what's going on with Alex?" I swing her arm up high and spin her around.

She laughs. "Well, you're not going to believe it, but when Riley called me back, she said Alex didn't come home because he was with her."

I don't see the big deal until she raises her eyebrows and widens her eyes.

Ohhh! Light bulb! "Really?"

"Well, he always had a crush on her. You know, older sister's best friend and all," she says and picks up a stone, throwing it into the water. "I think it was just a one-time thing anyway."

We walk a little longer. I could stay there all day with her, but knowing we have a flight in four hours, we head back to her parents' house.

***

Touching down in Wyoming feels good; I'm happy to be home. Jeremiah picks us up from the airport. He tells me all about the whole lot of nothing that has happened in the three days we were gone. He stayed at the ranch to take care of the dogs and the rest of the animals, enjoying not having to work over the weekend, I'm sure.

When we get home, Addison and Alex hop out of the truck. I lean over, double-checking they've shut their doors behind them.

"Jer?" I flick a small piece of straw off my jeans. "I need you to come with me somewhere."

"Where? What's up?" He looks at me puzzled.

"I want you to help me pick out a ring."

And the puzzling look is gone, replaced by a little bit of surprise and a big smile. "Bro, wow. I don't know the first thing about rings...But I'll come for sure." He shakes my hand, and I smile.

I knew I wanted to marry her months ago, before my accident. With each passing day, it's made more clearly that she's the only woman I want.

The next day while she's off at work, we give Alex some excuse about having to go into town for an appointment and leave him piling wood at the farm.

"You know, Jer, I never thought I'd be doing this." I look over at him and smile. "I'm glad you're coming with me."

We pull up in front of the jewellery store; walking in, I'm sure we look like the odd couple. A blonde dressed immaculately in black skirt and silk shirt greets us, asking if we would like some help.

"Yes, ma'am. I'm looking for a ring, for my girlfriend." I blush.

"An engagement ring? We have beautiful pieces right over here!" she says and guides us toward a large glass display. The stones are twinkling as we approach them, lit up like sparklers.

"Do you know what kind of ring you're looking for? The stone, clarity?" I'm sure she can clearly see she's lost me. I have no idea about rings, and I realize I don't even know what size Addison's finger is.

"Well, what would do *you* like?" I ask her, since Jeremiah is no help at all—he's across the room flirting with another associate. A woman is probably a better choice for assistance.

"Me? Well..." She scans the rings while holding onto the large string of pearls around her neck, even though I'm sure she's looked at them hundreds of times, she takes her time examining each one.

"This one." She reaches down to unlock the door and slides it open, pulling out a glittering platinum ring. A large square diamond in the center, with three more tiny diamonds on either side.

"This is a classic beauty any woman would love to have." She starts going on about the clarity, setting—and, of course, the price.

I don't care what the cost is. It's perfect, and I can just see it on Addison's beautiful finger. I ask the blonde to put the ring on; I think her hands are about the same size. The ring fits. After all, we can always get it sized if it's too big or small, right? After she hands me my credit card back, I carefully tuck the box into my breast pocket and exhale slowly.

Jeremiah and I have lunch in town (not at The Wolfbarrow) then head back home to finish work. Not knowing how or when I'm going to ask her to marry me, I tuck the little box into a shoe box in our closet. The likelihood of her finding it is almost impossible—well, I hope so, anyway.

***

It's the middle of September, my 30th birthday only a week away. Thirty. Damn, time really does fly. So much has happened my three decades on earth. Most of it happened this past year, and I wouldn't change any of it. No, I'm wrong; I'd change a few things, like my accident. But Addison always says everything happens for a reason, and I know she's right.

"What do you want to do for your birthday?" she asks me over dinner, taking a bite of chicken from her salad.

"Well, I don't know. Definitely not something crazy like my Dad's 70th!" I snort and remember the insanity of the planning, decorating and then the tragic ending to the night.

"I was thinking of just having a nice dinner with your family and the boys," she says, referring to roommates Jeremiah and Alex, who seem to be making their living arrangement really work. They have become good friends.

"That'd be nice, baby." I smile and shovel a heaping forkful of chicken and Caesar salad into my own mouth, smiling with packed cheeks.

"Mmm, isn't that a sexy sight!" She laughs and raises one eyebrow. "You have a little..." She points at the corner of her own mouth, hinting at me that I've got something on my face.

"Let me," she says and leans across the table, pushing our plates out of the way. Then she reaches me, she slowly licks salad dressing from the corner of my mouth.

I instantly forget about food and pull her right across the wooden table top. She squeals, and I sit her down on my lap.

"You're everything to me, you know that?" I say as I kiss her nose.

"I know. And you're okay in my books, too." She laughs and runs her fingers tenderly through my hair, looking at her hand while it's moving.

I want to ask her right there at the table to marry me and make me even happier than I am now, if it's possible at this moment. But the ring it still in the closet, hidden away for safe keeping.

"Want to watch a movie?" she asks.

I'm surprised and smile. "You want to watch a movie after what you just did to my face? I can think of other things to do instead..." I trail off, kissing her neck gently.

"Blaine! Please? There's one coming on at eight o'clock. Remember that one I told you about a few days ago?"

Of course I don't and feel like an ass.

"Oh, yeah. Right. Sorry." I am sorry but don't tell her I really don't remember.

The movie is playing on a regular channel, so it has commercials every ten minutes or so. One commercial break shows a local news channel segment, reporting coverage from a rodeo earlier today in Casper. I don't say anything, and neither does she. We haven't talked about rodeos or even been to one since what happened in July.

They show a clip of a young woman weaving through barrels on a buckskin. A few more shots flash on the screen of cowboys on broncos and then one of a man thrown from a bull. And without warning for the viewer's discretion, they play another clip. Mine.

It's me and Del Mar leaping from the gate with the heading "July in Cody: Sheridan circuit rider Blaine Blackstock thrown from bull and almost killed."

I see it for the first time, and Addison gasps, covering her face; it's not the first time she's had to witness it. They play it fast, seconds of me hanging on, Del Mar bucking and kicking, and then I'm airborne. Like Jeremiah said, it looked like a rag doll.

I shudder watching myself land, and the camera quickly turns to Del Mar who is running around frantically away from me. Then, they replay it in slow motion, just in case we missed it the first time; they want all the details clearly embedded in your mind.

I'm wide-eyed watching myself fall again. I see me land, I'm on my left side (that explains the bruises), and then *thud*! My head whips down, smacking the ground. I instinctively reach up and touch where the bump once was.

I am in too much shock to notice that Addison isn't sitting beside me anymore. "Addy?" I call her name, but she doesn't answer. Getting up, I see the kitchen door open and I rush out, see her sitting on the steps. She's got her arms wrapped around Luca who is sitting beside her, panting.

"Baby? You okay?" And I already know the answer; she's not. Frankly, neither am I. You know sometimes in your dream you see yourself from a different point of view, watch yourself from above? Well, that's exactly what this news clip was like—a slow, agonizing dream that thankfully ended without me waking up thrashing and sweaty.

"I'm okay. I just couldn't watch that. Not again." She looks up at me. She isn't crying but it looks like she could at any minute. She lets go of Luca, and he jumps off the step, runs over to the fence to howl at the cattle. I don't say anything; I just sit down beside her and pull her close to me.

CHAPTER ELEVEN

"Good morning, birthday boy!" She climbs on top of me, kissing my mouth, and I conclude that this is one of the best ways to wake up, ever.

"Thank you. Good morning." I smile and squint from the bright sun filling the room.

"I have a present for you! Well, the first present of the day, anyway." She grins, and I look at her like she's up to no good. I'm dead wrong; she's up to good all right. The mind-blowing type of good—the best actually.

She disappears beneath the sheets and takes me into her mouth, as deep as she can. I actually think I feel my heart stop.

"Baby, holy sh---" My mouth may be open but nothing else is coming out except groans.

Jeremiah calls to wish me a happy birthday, as well as both of my brothers. Addison has planned a big family dinner tonight. She promises it will be low-key, no streamers or balloons or giant banners.

Around noon Jeremiah and Alex arrive to pick me up, not telling me where they're taking me. Addison just winks and tells me to enjoy myself. She's staying home to arrange dinner, and I admit I'm really excited to find out what the boys have planned for me.

Evan's Extreme Pay & Play is displayed on a giant billboard as we turn down a dirt road. The kid in me is freaking out.

"No way!" I almost start clapping with excitement. "Are you serious, buddy?!" I reach over and shake Jeremiah's shoulder aggressively; he just laughs, and Alex grabs my shoulders from behind me.

"Got your pacemaker ready, old man?!"

Evan's is an outdoor park full of trails, mud and fast and loud all-terrain vehicles. We go into the large building; most of it is covered in camouflage paint and has deer and moose heads mounted all over the walls.

We are welcomed by two young guys, Brad and Mike, according to their name tags. They ask us if we've ever driven any of the vehicles they have here, and we all snort because of course we have. They explain the rules and safety precautions of the park.

We sign waivers basically saying that they've used all measures of safety, and we agree that if anything happens it's our own fault and we won't sue the pants off them. I scribble my name down, eager to have some fun.

I pick a bright blue ATV, Jeremiah and Alex choosing yellow and red. We are completely decked out in gear, helmets on, and Brad quickly explains the trails and how they all end up back at the main building, so we can't get ourselves lost. He also tells us that we each have radios embedded in our helmets so we can communicate with each other and call for help if needed.

We rip through the trails; I take the lead, being the birthday boy, after all. I feel free and young again. This is just what I've needed, especially on my 30th birthday.

Three hours later we are back in front of the building. We're splattered with mud, adrenaline still pumping through us, and we can't stop talking about how much fun we just had.

"Thank you, guys. That was crazy!" I say excitedly.

All the way home, we laugh and talk about our ride and replay the entire three hours to Addison when we get back to the farm. She laughs when we tell her about Alex getting stuck in the mud and us getting sprayed while he floored it trying to get out.

"Dinner will be ready in about an hour," she tells us. "Everyone should be here soon!"

She is excited. It smells so good in the house, and I'm salivating at both her and the food she's cooking for dinner. She's wearing tight jeans and a pale pink sleeveless top with a lacy back, showing her beautiful skin.

"What if I'm hungry *now?*" I whisper to her, raising an eyebrow.

"Get up there and change, mister." She scolds me playfully and smacks my ass when I turn to walk away from her.

Oh, this girl is going to be the death of me.

We all shower; the guys use the guest bedrooms to clean themselves up, and we all sit on the porch together drinking beer. The family shows up at exactly 7 PM.

"Happy Birthday, Uncle Blaine!" Casey, my niece, hugs me.

"Thanks, sweetie!" I spin her around, and she laughs.

"Happy Birthday, my boy." My Dad actually hugs me, and I feel like the wind has been knocked out of me. I know that my brothers are shocked too by the looks on their faces. Maria actually gasps and covers her mouth. Is she going to cry?

"Thank you, Dad." I hug him back, not wanting to let him go. Why has it taken him thirty years to hug me? I think I'm going to start crying and let him go, clearing my throat. I realize everyone is quiet and staring at the two of us.

"What?" My father notices all the jaws on the floor, too. "Can't a man hug his own son on his birthday?"

He shakes his head like he's got no idea why they're surprised and goes to sit on the couch.

I exhale deeply, and Owen gives me a big hug, "I've waited a long time to see something like that."

"Me, too, buddy. Me, too," I say, and I hug him back.

Addison overdoes herself completely. She's made lasagna, a little jab at me I'm sure, since I burned one during my first attempt to feed her. She's also got garlic bread, salads, meatballs and some cheesy artichoke dip. Everyone raves about her cooking abilities.

Jeremiah, Alex and I tell everyone about our playtime at Evan's. My nephews make me promise to take them there some day, and Kelsey snorts, "We'll see about that!"

But Maria shoots her a look, and she smiles. "Okay, okay. As long as you're careful."

I chuckle to myself. *Thanks, Maria.*

My Dad has been chatting Addison up all evening, asking her all about her parents, what they do for a living, if they'll ever come and visit Wyoming. He says he would love to meet them and show them some country hospitality. I smile at him.

Is this the father that Nick and Owen had? The one that disappeared when I was born and was never seen again? Until tonight, that is. I silently pray that this continues; I would really like having my Dad around again.

We're all ready to unbutton our pants, having eaten so much at dinner.

"Are we going to have some cake?" Casey sits up in her chair, eagerly tugging on Addison's hand.

"Why, yes we are, sweetie! Would you like to help me bring it out?"

Casey leaps off her chair and runs into the kitchen.

"I hope everyone likes cheesecake." She winks at me, and I smirk, remembering the last time we had cheesecake, her tantalizing removal of it off her finger.

Casey brings out two plates at a time, a wedge of cheesecake for everyone, with cherries on top and red drizzle all around the white plates. I'm the only one without any and Casey sits down, smiling ear to ear at me and giggling to herself.

What's she up to?

Addison finally comes out, holding a plate with a single white candle burning. She's holding her hand in front of it so it doesn't blow out before it reaches me.

She places the plate down on my place mat, leans down and kisses my cheek. She whispers, "Happy Birthday. I love you." into my ear, and I smile.

"Blow it out, Uncle Blaine!" Casey can't contain herself, so I lean in to blow...but suddenly stop. My heart slows down to almost barely beating, then flips back and starts hammering out of my chest.

"*Marry Me?*" is written in the red drizzle, just like the dessert at the fancy restaurant in Maine. I look across the table. She's now sitting in her chair with a half smile on her face, and I'm speechless.

"Blaine? Everything okay?" Maria asks, sounding worried. "Blaine?"

She's trying to snap me out of it, but I'm in too deep. I'm caught, and Addison is reeling me in. I don't say anything else; I keep my eyes locked on her face and I blow out my candle.

Now she's not smiling anymore. She looks unsure because I haven't said anything, so I get up and walk over to her. I turn her chair sideways and kneel down in front of her.

"Oh, my Lord!" Maria realizes what was on my plate, and there is a huge commotion at the table. "Addy, you're the sweetest little thing! Blaine you better say something!"

Addy does before I can. "Well? Aren't you going to answer me?"

"You first." I reach down and pull the tiny box out of my pocket, opening it up to her wide blue eyes. The silence is deafening.

She inhales at the open box, but no sound comes out of her mouth. "Blaine...I...I...yes!"

She hugs me so tightly I'm almost winded, and I float out of my shoes, straight out of the house.

"The drizzle! Look at the drizzle everyone!" Maria holds up my plate, the cheesecake slice slowly sliding downwards; she's holding it up like it should be framed or something.

"Does anyone have a camera? We are not missing out on capturing this memory!"

Everyone around the table congratulates us and jokes how truly in sync we must be to have proposed to each other on the same day, without knowing the other was going to do it, too.

"Baby, you're unbelievable. You never stop surprising me. I love you so much." I tenderly kiss her cheek, my stubble tickling her soft skin, and she giggles.

"I love you, too. And this ring! Blaine, it's beautiful. Thank you." She holds out her hand for me to slide it on her finger—perfect fit.

"I asked your parents for their permission when we were in Maine." I can tell it surprises her.

"When? Where was I?"

"Well, when Alex finally came home after his *sleepover.*" I nod my head toward Alex and wink. He grins back at me. "Your dad didn't even seem surprised, but your mom almost started crying."

"Well," my dad interrupts, "we've got to celebrate a little more now that the birthday boy is engaged!" He stands up and puts his hands on my shoulders.

"I'll get some glasses!" Maria bounces all too happily into the kitchen, and Casey follows right behind her. "I wanna help!"

I didn't think to buy champagne, but we do have wine, so I pour some in each glass. Fruit juice is for the kids, and the older boys sneer at their parents when they get passed by with the wine bottle.

"Thank you for coming to this delicious dinner that my beautiful *fiancée* has made for us." I hold up my glass and smile. "Also for being part of this special moment."

"Cheers!" Everyone raises their glasses and begin to clink with each extended arm around the table. If anyone had of told me that on my 30th birthday, my father would really hug me for the first time, and my beautiful girlfriend would propose marriage when I had every intention of asking her instead, I would have told them they were crazy. Certifiable, even.

I feel like a giant puzzle, with a thousand tiny pieces scattered everywhere and only the outside trim put together. I realize that was me only a few months ago, and now I'm finally being completed, filled in; the full picture is almost clear.

Maria and Kelsey swarm Addison, asking her when she plans on going dress shopping, who her bridesmaids will be, and where she wants to get married.

She looks at me. "I think Blaine and I have a lot of planning to do." She's kindly telling them she has no idea and that everything will be up to the two of us...I think.

"Well, we are here, sweetie. Anything you need, you ask!" And they both hug her tightly. "We've got a lot of connections!"

Jeremiah slides his chair closer to mine. "Looks like the ring was a hit."

He takes a chug of his wine, and in my happy moment, I have a twinge of sadness for him. I wish he could feel as happy I was right now.

"You'll be my best man, obviously..."

He cuts me off. "Yeah, of course! And you know what that puts me in charge of?"

"Bachelor party!" Alex chimes in.

He's all too excited, and they high five across the table. Nick and Owen both grin, and I swear I see Kelsey momentarily lose her eyeballs in the back of her head.

By the time everyone starts to leave, it's almost midnight. The three girls have discussed having lunch this week and roped Addison in to visiting a bridal show in Cheyenne next month. I'm glad they came, but I'm happier to see them go; I finally have the love of my life all to myself.

I fully expect her to kiss me or hug me or anything when the door closes, but she doesn't. She starts filling the dish washer with plates and cutlery.

"Everything okay, babe?" I ask her, and she opens the top rack, putting cups and mugs on the wires.

"Of course. I'm just really tired."

I walk over and stop her from doing anything else. We hug, and I lift her chin up to kiss her lips. "I love you. You have made me the happiest man in the world tonight. Do you know that?"

"I love you, too, so very much." She smiles at me affectionately and holds my face in her hands. Then they start to travel down my neck to my chest, unbuttoning my shirt.

"I thought you said you were tired."

I lift her up so she's in my arms, her legs wrapped around my waist, and I carry her upstairs. She nuzzles into my neck and kisses me every time I take a step.

When we get to the bedroom, she jumps out of my arms and starts slowly walking away from me, backwards.

"Where is your hat, cowboy?" she asks in a quiet voice. She bites her lip and goes into the bathroom; before she closes the door, she slowly starts lifting her shirt off her beautiful body. "Go and get your hat, put it on the bedpost and strip."

Yes, ma'am!

I hear the click of the door closing before it registers that she's shut it on me. I am hard as a rock, and she hasn't even really touched me yet. I run downstairs, grab my hat, and I'm back in less than twenty seconds. I actually slide across the wooden floor on my socks, just like Tom Cruise (except I don't have a broom) because I'm in such a fluster to undress.

I toss everything in a pile at the end of the bed and climb in, staying on top of the covers. I lay down and very impatiently as I wait for her to emerge from the bathroom.

When she does, it takes every single strand of my existence not to spontaneously combust, or jump out of bed and take her right there in the doorway, or both. I control myself, slow my breathing and obvious excitement as much as I can, but I am raging, and she can clearly see how badly I want her.

"Excuse me, sir. I really hope you don't mind if I borrow this." She picks my hat from off the bedpost and places it on her head. Aside from her smile and the hat, she's only wearing a pair of black lace panties and my belt, the leather one with the giant golden and silver buckle with a bull on it. It's synched much further than the last notch and is hanging slightly on an angle around her hips. Her long hair is pulled down over her shoulders, covering her breasts, but the curls are parted just enough to see some of her warm flesh.

Her saunter tantalizes me as she slowly climbs on to the bed and then on top of me. Tipping the hat down, so her eyes are barely visible, she grinds herself into me, rubbing against my stone hard length.

"You're going to make me explode!" I reach up to grab her, and she quickly pushes my hands down.

"Oh no, baby. Not yet." She puts my hands on her thighs, and I start to slowly rub them to the same rhythm as her movements against me.

Her slow and sensual torture is building and building my need for her, and I'm not sure how much more I can take. She unfastens the belt, and lets it fall behind her across my legs.

"Do you like these?" she asks playfully and holds my hands, travelling them up her thighs and on to her hips, putting my thumbs into the top of her panties.

"Mmm. Yes, ma'am, I do. Very much." I lick my bottom lip and close my eyes.

"Rip them off," she commands, and my eyes fly open.

I am not one to disobey an order, especially when it comes from someone so beautiful, so I do. I rip the lace in two swift tugs, and she throws them on the floor, next to my pile of clothes.

The slow agony ends when she lowers herself on to me and picks up speed. I reach up and caress her breasts; she pulls her hair to one side over her shoulders, and I pull her down so her breast is in my mouth. I suck and bite it gently. She starts moving faster and faster, and I know I'm seconds away.

"Baby..." I breathe, and it doesn't slow her down. She sits back up and leans back holding herself up with her hands resting on my thighs. My hat falls of her head as she throws it back, and she sits up straight, pulling her hair up with her fingers and letting it fall all around her face and shoulders.

Boom. I'm done, in every sense of the word. I just can't hold on any longer, and as soon as I start to heave, she does, too. She falls on me, chest to abdomen she rests her head under my neck. I'm still inside of her, feeling her pulsate around me.

"Oh...my...oh..." I feel her warm breath rapidly blow across my chest. I feel like I've run a marathon, and I was only laying there. Her heart is thumping out of her chest right into mine. I wrap my arms around her, running my fingers through her hair and gripping gently. I pull so her face looks up, and I kiss her.

"That was...wow."

"I have one more present for you." She sits up and carefully climbs off of me, walking naked into the closet. She comes back with a small blue gift bag. "Happy birthday"

I look at her. "Another present? You have given me more today than I ever expected." I don't want or need anything else in my life; as long as I have her, I'm golden.

Inside the bag is something heavy wrapped in white tissue paper; I open it, and a large silver buckle falls into my hand. It's a stunningly made western-style piece with an ornate B in the center, surrounded by small horses running and rearing up and a large bull with horns. In the top corner are three flying birds.

I trace my finger around each detail, and I stop at the corner. "The birds?" I ask.

She smiles. "Meadowlarks."

I remember our first ride, when the meadowlarks flew out of the ground and spooked the horses.

"I love it, baby. Thank you."

***

Addison has come back from the bridal show with Maria and Kelsey, and bags, of what I'm told is *swag,* are piled on the island in the kitchen. She's reeling about her day and about all the vendors, dresses and tiny details she's managed to jot down in a small white binder.

"Come look at these with me!" She opens a thick magazine and flips to a section about tuxes. "What style of suit do you think you would want to wear?" She scans each image and flips the pages too quickly for me to actually see what they're wearing.

It's been over a month since our engagement, and I really haven't given any thought to what I want to wear on our wedding day.

"Did you find a dress you like?" I ask. I already know her answer is no; what woman finds *the dress* the first time she goes looking at them?

"I saw a few I like, but nothing really stood out. I like simple things. I don't want something big and flashy." She closes the magazine with a loud thud. "Maria and Kelsey love big and flashy. They kept handing me hangers with ball gowns attached, big shoulders..." she winces, "not my style."

"We could always just get married like this!" I laugh and point at myself in my jeans and button-up shirt.

"You know...I like that idea."

And I don't know if she's joking or not. "You do?"

"Yes, I love it! You are most comfortable in jeans, and I like simple dresses." She grins. "Besides, I can't really picture you in one of these suits!"

She holds up the magazine and tosses it into a bag of swag. "Let's get married here, surrounded by friends and family." She wraps her arms around my neck. "You wear your boots, and I'll wear my flip flops. How does that sound?"

"It sounds like I'm going to marry the woman of my dreams." I smile and sweep my lips against hers. Then I kiss down her cheek and neck.

"Mmm. Have you thought about a day yet?"

She breathes. "I was thinking in May. The day we met?"

One year since I asked her for coffee, one year since she agreed, and one year since I first felt her lips on mine. On that day next year, it will be another first kiss, as husband and wife.

I can't sleep. The moonlight pools in, illuminating the room, and I count all the knots in the wooden beams on the ceiling. Twenty-seven. An angel is sleeping next to me; softly her chest rises and falls as she breathes. I gently brush her hair off her forehead and kiss it. As I lay there watching her sleep, I feel a cold tingle in my skin, a fear washing over me like a wave.

I don't know what I would ever do if I lost her, just like my dad lost my mother. The thought terrifies me, and I almost can't bear it. Morning comes, but I don't think I slept at all.

"Good morning," she says sleepily and stretches like she's had a very restful night. I know she has since I witnessed all of it.

"Good morning, my love." I kiss her forehead again in the same spot as only a few hours ago. "Ugh. I don't want to work today!" She pouts, looking at the alarm clock.

"I'm on twelve hour shifts this week. I told you, right?" She rolls over onto her stomach and frowns at me.

"You told me." I stick my bottom lip out and throw my arm and leg over her. "But how can you go to work when you're trapped at home?" I laugh, and she reaches down under the sheets, gripping me gently.

"I think I can persuade you to move, one way or another."

"You shouldn't start things you can't finish, my dear." I thrust my hips, and she moves her hand faster. I close my eyes and let out a heavy sigh. Rolling over on to my back, she's off her stomach quickly and between my legs.

"Baby," I breathe, and she takes all of me into her mouth. I don't think my head can get any deeper into the pillow. Addison devours me, soft and hard all at the same time. I'm like a cracked window, and the slightest blow is going to shatter me at any minute.

Her eye contact and slow sensual grip makes the pleasure more than I can take. I release, her hand running over my abdomen and gripping the base of my length.

"I can't...Oh, fuck!" I can't handle any more, and she slowly squeezes the last ripple of orgasm out of me. I'm still deep in my pillow with my eyes glued shut. Before I can say or do anything, she climbs off the bed, and I hear her turn the shower on.

I'm not going to let her leave without me giving that intensity right back to her. I don't care if she'll be late for work. I slow my breathing and sit up; my head is dazed, but I stand and walk into the bathroom.

She's in the shower, her beautiful body showcased by the glass surrounding her like she's a doll in a box. The sound of the shower door opening gives me away, and she turns, grinning.

You know those shampoo commercials with hot models standing underneath waterfalls? That's exactly how she looks at this very moment, her hair soaked and wild. The water is trailing down her body, running over her breasts like little rivers. I almost forget why I'm in there, but once my eyes travel below her belly button, I remember.

"Your turn." I raise an eyebrow and smirk.

"I have to go to work, Blaine!"

Is she actually refusing me? Her hand on my chest almost pushing me out of the shower tells me exactly that.

"Do you really think you can do something like that to me, and I'm not going to want you in the same way?"

"I like teasing you; isn't that obvious?" She smiles and squirts some shampoo into her hand. "Besides, it'll give you something to think about all day, and when I get home, you can have me any way you want." She's lathering now, the little rivers now streams of tiny bubbles flowing down her chest, stomach and down the place I want to be the most right now.

I'm standing as close to her as I can, my erection sliding in between her legs but not inside of her.

"Blaine!"

And that's all I let her say, all she can say because I grab her behind and lift her up, sliding into her. She moans, and I lean her against the glass wall. We make love with the water flowing over us, and I get lost in her waterfall.

Jer and Alex arrive for work, and I try not to let my obvious grin give away my good mood. Jer smirks at me, knowing exactly why I'm amused. I'm sure Alex knows, too, but is ignoring it, considering it was with his sister.

"Well, today's the big day!" I tell them, turning the handle of the trailer and pushing the wide door open.

"Did you say your goodbyes?" Alex smiles and pats my back.

We're taking twelve cattle and Del Mar to an auction. I've thought long and hard about it, and Addison and her happiness mean more to me than a few adrenaline-charged seconds of uncertainty. Besides, there are other ways of making money as a rodeo cowboy.

"I did. Thank you for your concern." I joke and pretend to pout.

The auction is just on the outskirts of Buffalo, and since Addison is working until 7:30, we have all day to spend there. Within four hours, I've sold all the cattle, bringing in a nice profit.

Del Mar is placed in a box stall, assigned a number, and when it is announced, bidders from left, right and center raise their cards and start a bidding frenzy. Alex drops his jaw when a man in a big white Stetson interrupts the auctioneer and calls out a bid for twenty-seven thousand dollars. No one outbids him.

"Sold! To number 3139. Thank you, sir!"

After the auction house takes their twenty percent, the older man at the desk hands me my money, and I smile.

"Thank you, sir. Have a good day." I tip my hat and turn to the guys. "What's the plan now, boys?"

I slap the stack of cash in my hand, fold it up and put it in to my pocket.

"Beer?" Alex suggests with a smile. Beer is always a good suggestion in my book.

"Beer." Jer and I say in unison.

The auction house happens to be located in a busy part of town, so we don't even have to drive to find a good place for a drink. One of the staff members tells us there's a place one street over, and we head off on foot.

Mazey's is a lot like Lakes, a diner, but this one is complete with a bar. Liquor bottles line the shelves behind the counter, displaying all the options they have for their patrons. We sit on green stools rimmed with steel at the counter. Only four other people are here, all older men sitting at a table drinking coffee.

MEADOWLARKS

"Three Buds, please," Jer asks the waitress kindly, and she smiles. Turning her back to get the bottles, he nods in her direction and raises both eyebrows suggestively. He's like a horny teenager; I think living with Alex has made him worse in that aspect.

"Well thank you, *Lucy.*" Reading her name tag, he tips his hat at her, and she blushes.

"Anything else for you boys?" she asks.

"We're good. Thank you." I answer her before Jer can say something else. She smiles and walks into the kitchen.

He elbows me. "What?"

"Nothin'." I smirk.

Jer and Alex have two more beer each, but I stop at one since I'll be driving home. Jer has managed to charm Lucy into giving him her number, which she scrawls down on a white square napkin.

"You have a good day now, darlin'." He folds the napkin up neatly and puts it into his pocket.

I pay for the beer, and Jeremiah gives her a twenty dollar tip on top of the tab. He walks out of the diner backwards, smiling at her, and he almost falls when he trips over his own feet.

Alex and I laugh hysterically at him, and Lucy giggles. He graciously bows, laughs at himself and tips his hat to her. "Ma'am."

"I thought I was going to fall on my face!" He laughs deeply once we're back at the stockyards and climbing into my truck. "We're not going home now, are we?" He almost looks like a kid, had a good day and now doesn't want it to end.

Maybe he'll fall asleep on the way home.

"How was work, baby?" The best part of any day is seeing her walk through the door. The dogs both run up to her, and she bends down to give them affection.

"Hello, my boys! Did you miss me?" Luca licks her cheek, and she giggles.

"So, what do I get to do to you if I've missed you too?" I grin and cross my arms.

"Mmm, well, what exactly do you want?" When she gets close enough, I grab her and pull her into me. I want her, and that's all.

We sit on the couch, and I pull her legs up on my lap. Pulling off each shoe and sock, I rub her feet.

"Mmm, that feels so good." She closes her eyes and sighs deeply.

"I sold Del Mar today."

She opens them. "Did you?"

"Along with twelve others. Made a good profit, too." I kiss each toe slowly, my stubble tickling her skin.

She pulls her foot away. "That tickles! Well, I'm happy if you're happy. Whatever you decide to do." She smiles.

"I was also thinking about Thanksgiving," I mention.

"Yeah, I guess we should talk about what we are going to do this year." She crawls over to me and lies down, her head in my lap. "What were you thinking?"

I've only ever spent holidays with my family, my dad, brothers and their wives and kids, never a girlfriend, or anyone remotely close to that. "Well, I don't know. What does your family do for the holidays?"

She's quiet for a while. "I don't know if I can take any time off work to fly to Maine again."

"Well, we could fly your parents here." I surprise myself, even though I actually wouldn't mind seeing Richard and Lillian again. Addison hasn't since we were last on the East Coast, and I'm sure she wants to talk about the wedding with her parents since they heard about the engagement over the phone.

"I would love to see them, baby! That would be so nice." She kisses my thigh and rubs her hand over my shin.

At least this will give our families times to get to know one another before we get married. I realize how much time I spend thinking about the wedding, and I wonder if all guys think about it this much. I guess I'm just preparing for the inevitable? No, that sounds bad. I just want everything to be perfect for her; after all this is her world, and I'm just living in it.

CHAPTER TWELVE

"Let's all bow our heads and give thanks." My dad stands at the head of the long harvest table in my dining room. "Father, we thank you for today, a day where we are blessed to be surrounded by family and this wonderful meal. We thank you for uniting the Blackstock and Cole families and most importantly for your son, our Saviour, Jesus Christ. Amen."

"Amen!" We all open our eyes and smile while filling up our plates. Almost every inch of the table is covered with turkey and ham, potatoes, corn, beans, stuffing, cranberries and other little dishes I haven't yet figured out but am excited to try.

"This is just perfect!" Lillian beams and clutches her daughter's hand from across the table. She almost looks like she's going to cry but shakes her head, smiling, like she's pushing the emotion away.

After dinner I feel like someone is going to have to roll me out of the room; I've never eaten so much in my life. I finished almost an entire pumpkin pie myself, not to mention the two helpings of trifle that Lillian made. Layers of strawberry, sponge cake and custard are all deliciously flowing through my veins.

The kids are playing a bowling game on the Wii in the living room, and Lillian is telling Maria and Kelsey all about Maine. They're both wide-eyed and completely captivated.

"Have you two decided where you're having the wedding?" Richard asks while sipping coffee from a small white mug.

"We're going to get married here!" Addison smiles and holds my hand.

"A nice country wedding—are there any other kinds?" My dad chuckles, and Richard smirks. Two different worlds are sitting at my long wooden table, two worlds about to become one, and it's going so well I'm afraid it's too good to be true. Something's gotta give—isn't that what they say?

"Dad, we should get going. It's getting late." Maria puts her hands on my dad's shoulders and leans in, making sure he's heard her.

"Well, if you say so." He stands and puts his hand out. Richard stands as well and shakes his extended kindness.

"Lil and I are very happy to be a part of this day. Safe drive home, now."

I load the dishwasher and turn it on; the quiet flow of water sprinkling is all that fills the house. The Coles went to bed after everyone else left, and Addison and I have finished cleaning up. We're both beat, and I'm still full to the brim from dinner.

"Want to know what I'm thankful for?" she asks, smiling at me later, while we're lying in bed face to face.

I nod.

"I'm thankful for foxes on midnight adventures into barns, and dogs with bionic hearing." She smiles.

We kiss and fall asleep, tangled in each other's arms.

***

"Blaine, it's snowing!" She stands at the bedroom window, barefoot and smiling back at me over her shoulder. She looks so sweet and innocent, big green eyes looking out the window like it's the first time she's ever seen snow before.

I smile, putting my hands behind my head and lay in the warm bed watching her. "You know, we're going to have to get you a car that you can drive safely in the winter."

As much as I like seeing her in that muscle car, it's rear-wheel drive and not something I'm comfortable having her drive in the snow with.

"I'm not getting rid of my car."

"I wasn't saying that. I just think you should drive something safer in the snow. That's all."

She's standing in front of me now, arms crossed against her chest and giving me a raised brow.

"What do you have in mind? Do I really need another car? Can't I just get snow tires or something?" She's really sexy when she's being difficult.

"Come here." I push the blanket down my body, stopping it right above my pubic bone.

"If I come over there you will distract me," she states with her arms still crossed, brow still raised.

I know I'll get my way if I play dirty. She does it to me all the time, so what can I say? I lead by example, and I kick the blankets right off of me, exposing my naked body. Naked and fully erect, I hope I'm not *too* distracting.

Even after all this time I can still make her jaw drop, just as she can mine.

"Like I said, *come here*," I growl, slowly and as salaciously as I possibly can, enunciating each and every word like I'm trying to seduce my own request.

She slowly pulls my t-shirt up and off her beautiful body. My eyes wander down her flesh, drinking in every inch of her.

When she finally climbs on to the bed, I don't give her the chance to get away, I flip her over and pin her down with my hands on her wrists, my knee between her legs.

"You are the most beautiful thing I've ever seen. I love you so much." I kiss her lips, her neck, chest and stomach. When I let go of her wrists, she runs her fingers through my hair, pulling gently.

"I love you more," she breathes and moans when I trail my tongue along her hip.

***

I lazily sleep in on Christmas morning. Every year I wake up alone, make toast and wander around outside with Rex doing odd jobs around the house. My brothers always invite me over, and I always decline, telling them I'm not into the present thing and maybe next year I'll make it over. Next year I never do, but I always send a card to each of them with money inside for each of the kids. They always call to thank me and tell me what they plan on buying with the cash. But by not going for the present thing, I also miss out on Christmas dinner.

Jeremiah and I usually go into town and get beer and some sort of conciliation prize of a meal for people without family. At The Wolfbarrow Jesse has his cook whip up ham, potatoes and all the fixings, even plum pudding for dessert.

This year I wake up to the smell of bacon frying, French toast crisping and fresh coffee being brewed. I tip-toe down the stairs, holding on to the banister like a little boy trying to sneak a peek of Santa putting presents under my tree. Addison and I put up our tree three weeks ago; we picked out the tallest one we could fine, over eight feet, I think. It's trimmed with silver beads, all different shades of blue ornaments, and a beautiful antique angel with real feather wings on the top, in place of a star. At the base is a large white piece of fabric, which I was told is a tree skirt by the snobby cashier while we checked out with our decorations.

She must have heard me get out of bed, because when I walk into the living room, she has breakfast sitting on the coffee table, two white plates heaped with food still steaming.

It's snowing, so it's not very bright out, and all the lights in the house are off except for the twinkling white strands around the tree—six strands to be exact, which all had to be circled around just right. The dogs are lying on the floor in front of the fireplace. They don't get up when they see me, but they perk up their ears, and Addison looks over.

"Merry Christmas, beautiful." I smile and sit down beside her. She wraps her arms around my neck; I put mine around her waist and we kiss. It's our first Christmas together, the first of many, I pray, and maybe someday we will have kids to share this beautiful morning with.

"Merry Christmas! I hope you're hungry." She flips on the TV, choosing a satellite radio channel called *Country Christmas*. Alison Krauss and Alan Jackson sing their song about angels crying while we quietly eat breakfast.

I'm not sure if it's the atmosphere, the song and the story they're singing about, or the fact that I'm not alone today, but I can't eat. I feel my eyes start to water and I get up from the couch. Walking toward the door, I open it, staring outside into the cold.

"Blaine, are you okay?" she asks.

I'm not okay, but I don't want her to see that I'm upset. In this moment I feel so vulnerable, like a child; part of me just wants to cry out for my mother. A woman I never knew, but a woman who loved me so much that she died giving me life.

When I was growing up Christmas was never warm like those commercials you see on TV during the entire month of December, or like what other kids grow up with. Mine was cold—a few presents under a sad little tree. It wasn't even the lack of boxes or bows; it was the warmth that was missing. It was a little boy in pajamas getting presents but not the hugs from the parents after he goes crazy with excitement over his new R/C truck.

"Blaine? You're scaring me, babe!" She steps in front of me, trying to catch my lost gaze. It's cold, and she pushes me back in the house, closing the door behind her.

"I'm sorry. I'm okay. That song just made me..."

"It's okay; don't be sorry." She hugs me, kissing me under my ear. "Can we talk about why you're upset?" She sits down and pats the leather cushion on the couch for me to sit beside her.

"I don't know what to say. I just felt so emotional all of a sudden." I feel stupid, so I stop, shaking my head and covering my face with my hands.

"Don't cover your face; talk to me."

"Everything is perfect. Breakfast, the tree, even those damn dogs." I point at them, sleeping in the same spots they were in when I came downstairs.

"So what's the matter?" She looks worried, and I need to find the words to ease her mind.

"I haven't ever had this before." I hold my hands out, palms up, looking at everything around me. "Christmas was never like this."

She hugs me again, squeezing tightly like she's afraid I'm going to lose it and leave the couch again.

"I'm okay, really," I tell her. "I'm sorry to upset you."

She doesn't believe me and makes me talk. I tell her about when I was younger, how my dad was cold, that this was my house but it didn't feel like a home. That is, not until she came into my life, moved in and put those flowers in a vase on my table.

"He was always on me about something. Keeping oil in my truck, not letting the gas gauge get below half." I smirk and flash back to being seventeen. "I ran out once, on the side of the road. He flipped out, and I didn't think I was going to ever hear the end of it."

She narrows her eyes, taking everything I'm saying in, but not saying anything herself.

"I just felt like...nothing I did was ever fucking good enough for him."

"Blaine. Do you ever think that maybe losing his wife was devastating but having to raise a little boy basically on his own was even harder?" she asks quietly. After a moment's pause, she continues. "I think your father loves you very much, even though he couldn't express it to you by telling you." She stops and inhales deeply. "Maybe he was always on you because that's the only way he knew how to express love after he lost her."

I stop breathing. No, that can't be right. It doesn't make sense—does it? I'm reeling through every moment I spent with him as a child. The weekend he took us three boys fishing, I couldn't get the worm on the hook properly, and he snatched it from me, grumbling to himself and handing it back when he managed to put it on with one hand. Then the time we went to Lake's for pizza, and I started choking on a piece of pineapple; he lost it, and we left the restaurant, not finishing the pizza. Now that I think about it, the look on his face wasn't anger—it was worry.

I start breathing again. I can't believe I'm thirty years old, and I've just realized for the first time in my life that my dad really does love me.

"Baby, I'm sorry," Addison says. "We can stop talking about it if you want."

"It's okay. I'm okay. Thank you; it all makes sense now." I'm wide eyed and piecing it all together. I look down at her. "Thank you for everything, for all of this, and for making me see clearly."

I feel the urge to call my father and tell him I love him, to wish him a Merry Christmas. I decide that I will later, after presents, I need to get out of my funk and start enjoying this day with my beloved. This revelation was the best gift I could have asked for, and I finally feel at peace.

We sit cross-legged on my mom's quilt on the floor. I slide over a large box wrapped in gold paper. She rips it open, smiling and when she opens it. She has to stand to pull out her gift. I know she likes bareback, but I wanted her to have her own saddle, too.

"Blaine, it's beautiful! Thank you." She lifts out the black leather Billy Cook and traces her fingertips around the detail in the leather.

AB is engraved in the horn. "This part is my favourite." she smiles. "Here you go!" She sits back down and holds her hands clasped together under her chin in anticipation.

I tear open the paper, and inside the slim box are two tickets for a trip to Texas. My eyes fly to meet hers.

"Texas!" I'm elated. Aside from Maine, I've only ever visited three states around Wyoming: Nebraska, South Dakota and Colorado. Texas is a dream.

"Thank you! When do we go?" I'm not sure if she can tell if I'm excited or not, so my voice raises a little, and I blush.

"Well, I booked time off in March so we can spend a whole week. Can you wait that long or should I call the hosp--"

I cut her off by pulling her onto my lap and kissing her, tongues twisting, tasting and softly lapping. I could kiss her all day. "I can wait to go anywhere, as long as it's with you."

We call everyone to wish them a Merry Christmas. When I call Jeremiah I'm surprised when it sounds like I haven't woken him up. Alex didn't fly home to Maine; instead he stayed at Jer's. They even cut down their own Charlie Brown tree, bachelor-style.

The plan this year is for us all to drive to Nick's for Christmas dinner, including Jeremiah and Alex, who I'm sure have exchanged cases of beer as gifts.

My sisters-in-law go all out for everything, obviously, so I'm the only one not gaping when we pull into their driveway and see all the Christmas crap everywhere. I'm willing to bet that you can see their house from space with all the lights strung everywhere.

"Merry Christmas, everyone!" Maria rushes out of the kitchen with a tray full of glasses with eggnog. It's sprinkled with nutmeg and smells amazing.

"Is there rum in this?" I say, holding up my glass inspecting it. I might just need some booze to help me through tonight.

"Now, Blaine, of course there isn't." She winks ever so obviously and asks—no, tells—Nick to take our coats and hang them in the closet. Everything is different when it's her house we're in and not mine; she's got full reign here.

"Well, there's the lovely Addison. Merry Christmas, my dear." My dad grabs her hand and holds it, smiling at us as he then shakes my hand.

"Merry Christmas, Mr. Blackstock. How are you doing?" She leans in to give him a hug.

"Now, now, none of that Mr. Blackstock nonsense. Call me Bennett."

Dinner is as filling as I expected, and Maria has packaged up two large plastic containers full of leftovers for Jeremiah and Alex to take back home with them.

"Thank you!" Alex grins widely when she hands him his. He pulls it away from me when I try to peek at what she's put inside. "Don't think so, bro!"

On the drive over, I decided that I'm not going to say anything to anyone about my revelation earlier today. I want to keep this joyous feeling all to myself for now. When we get ready to leave I hug my dad

"Bye, Dad. Merry Christmas."

"You too, son. You make sure drive careful now; the roads could be slippery."

And I hear the comment in a different light than I would have yesterday. He's not ordering me; he's truly hoping I listen to him and take care on the way home.

Our first Christmas together was both emotionally fulfilling and draining. Come to think of it, almost everything since I met her has been. Is this what living is really like? Was I just going on day by day before, not truly experiencing life?

CHAPTER THIRTEEN

We don't have much of a winter, so when March hits, you can feel the difference in the air. Spring is coming. March also only leaves just over two months until I stand with my brothers (including Jeremiah in that regard) and wait for the most beautiful woman on earth to walk down an aisle and marry me.

Our trip to Texas is in three days, and Addison has our bags packed already. And by bags, I mean my single suitcase and her three—not including a carry-on.

"What?" She giggles and uses all her weight to heave the largest suitcase off the bed. It slams down on the floor loudly.

"Need some help?" I smirk.

"I've got it, thank you. I hope we don't forget anything!"

I look around at the bedroom. All the drawers are pulled out, and there are hangers all over the floor in the walk-in closet. "I think you got it all."

She smiles and walks over to push all the wooden drawers back in.

"Ouch!" she cries out as she pinches her finger and puts it into her mouth.

"You okay?" I take her hand and kiss her finger.

"Yes, thank you." She pouts and puts her arms around my neck. "I can't wait to get away for a while."

She's been working a lot since she started in the fall. Most shifts are twelve hours long, and at least one week out of the month, she's strictly on nights so we don't see much of each other. When she comes home at eight in the morning, she stays awake for a little while, trying to spend at least some time with me before I have to get to work. Next month she starts full time in the NICU, and even though it may mean I see her less, I know that's what her dream is. I'm not going to stand in her way.

I'm not as nervous during the flight as I was on my first, when we went to Maine. I have a window seat again, but since our plane left at ten at night, we fly in complete darkness. We arrive in Dallas just after three-thirty in the morning. Our cab ride from Dallas International to the *Hilton Anatole* takes roughly twenty minutes.

"Reservations for Cole, please." Addison smiles and hands the older man at the front desk her credit card.

"Thank you, Ms. Cole. Welcome to Dallas; here are your room keys." He smiles and hands her an envelope with two plastic cards. "Benjamin will help you with your bags." He motions with his hand, and a man around my age in a suit comes out of nowhere to pick up all three pieces of Addison's luggage. Looking at me, I think he's trying to figure out how he's going to add mine to the pile.

"I got this one, buddy." I hold my own and take one of hers, freeing a hand for him.

He smiles. "Thanks. The elevators are over here." He points and starts walking. Benjamin opens the door to our room and sets the luggage down, asking if there is anything else he can do for us.

"No, I think we're good. Thanks." I hand him a tip; he smiles and thanks me.

"Wow, this is beautiful!" Addison flops down backwards on the bed and laughs.

"It's the most beautiful thing I've seen." I'm not talking about the room.

"So do you want to pull an all-nighter or sleep for a few hours?" She smiles, pulling her shoes off and tossing them by the large loveseat.

"Well, what exactly does an all-nighter entail?" I grin.

"If we don't sleep, we will miss part of the day!"

She starts unzipping a bag and pulls out a long t-shirt. She undresses and pulls it on before I can take my boots off.

We sleep for five hours. When I wake up, she's still sleeping with her head on my chest, exactly where it was when we fell asleep. I breathe in the scent of green apples from her hair; it's so much longer now than it was when we met. It flows halfway down her back, and with her working all the time, I rarely see it down. She has to keep it pulled back and out of the way while she's at the hospital.

"Addy," I whisper softly, not wanting to get out of bed. But if we miss out on all the things she has planned for us, she'll be disappointed. "Wake up, my love." I hug her tightly, and she starts to stir.

"Hi." She smiles, looking up at me through sleepy eyes, slowly batting her long lashes.

The room is full of the smell of maple and cinnamon. Room service has brought us a delicious breakfast of French toast, scrambled eggs and sausage. We sit crossed-legged together on the bed watching the Dallas morning news. It looks like today will be a good day to be a tourist.

Our first stop is to a car rental shop; we choose a nice black Ford Taurus.

"Wanna drive?" I smile, and Addison grabs the key from my open hand. First stop: Fort Worth Stockyards.

"I could get used to driving a car like this!" She floors the pedal and beams while she's gripping the steering wheel. She looks good in this car.

Since I couldn't convince her to let me get her another car to drive in the winter, I had insisted she take my truck when she needed to, and we parked her Mustang in the garage.

"Why don't we get you one when we get home?" I smile and reach over to gently rub her thigh. Slowly sliding up her skirt, my rough palm trails along her soft skin. Tingles shoot through my fingertips, and I close my eyes.

Time really does fly when you're having fun; whoever first coined that phrase was bang-on. Five days pass, and we visit almost every possible attraction that we can in the big and beautiful Lone Star state.

Back in Dallas, our last stop before going to the hotel is the JFK Memorial. Encased in two large square walls is a simple black plaque with John Fitzgerald Kennedy embossed in gold. A mere two hundred yards from where we stood, JFK's life ended. We do the typical sightseer thing and take a photo of ourselves standing at the memorial. We've filled three memory cards during our visit.

Since my accident last summer, when I couldn't remember the love of my life, there hadn't been any pictures of her around that I could look at to possibly spark a memory. We've since rectified that, and our home is full of framed love, hanging on the walls where there wasn't any images before.

After my mom died, my dad took down all the pictures. I'd only seen a few of her in photo albums that he kept in the closet in his bedroom. It's like he didn't want to share her with anyone, so taking down her pictures would keep her all to himself.

Now my mother's portrait is placed in a large frame on the mantel of the stone fireplace. She was young and beautiful; she looked like an angel even before she actually became one. Her long blonde hair is flowing down her back as she stands in the bluest water I've ever seen, looking over her shoulder and smiling out of bright blue eyes at whoever took the picture—my dad, I'm sure.

"Where do you want to go for dinner tonight?" Back in our hotel room, Addison is changing out of her pale yellow cotton dress and into a sleek black one with an open back. It's clinging to her body like it's painted on, and I'm salivating.

"Do we have to go out to eat?" I grin, and she tosses the yellow dress at me.

"We do. This is our last night here, get dressed!"

I am a creature of habit, so I put on another pair of jeans, a cleaner pair than what I'm wearing now. I also choose a white t-shirt underneath a dark blue button up shirt, a leather belt with the buckle that she bought me for my birthday, and my boots.

"Mmm, so handsome." She adjusts my collar and kisses me deeply. She's in those sexy black heels again so she doesn't even have to lean up much to reach my lips. Her eyes are blazing blue, and I wonder what she's thinking about.

"What's with that look?" I narrow my eyes quizzically.

"Oh, nothing at all. Just thinking about how hot you look. I don't think you even realize it."

If she keeps this up, we won't make it to dinner, and we'll probably miss our flight in the morning too. I grin my sexiest smile, and I feel her pulse quicken as I tenderly kiss her neck and throat.

"Let's go, baby," I breathe.

Texas was just what I needed, but I'm happy to be back home. The one downfall is that Addison has to go right back to work.

When I pick her up after work she's standing outside with Ruth, the older nurse who she shadowed for her training. Ruth's still wearing her triangular white nurse's hat, and she puffs away on her cigarette.

Turning the corner to park right in front of the building, I can now see she's not only standing with Ruth but also a guy in blue scrubs. They're talking, and he puts his hand on Addison's elbow. I narrow my eyes, watching him touch her. When she hears my truck pull up, she turns and smiles. His hand drops from her arm, and for a moment I'm glad I have tinted windows. I wouldn't want her to see the daggers I was shooting him from my glare.

They say something to her, and she smiles, turning to walk to the truck. I lean over and open her door from the inside.

"Hey you!" She leans in to kiss my cheek.

"Hi," I say. I want to say something else, like, "Who the hell is that guy touching you?", but I don't. If this is what jealousy feels like, I don't like it at all. I trust her completely, but I'm a man, and I know exactly how we think. I try to ask without actually asking.

"How's Ruth?" I've never asked how she is before, so I try to be nonchalant about it.

"Umm, she's good. She's actually retiring this summer, just gave her notice last week."

"Well, that's good for her. How long has she worked there anyway?"

"Over thirty years. That was Reid. He's going to be shadowing Ruth in her last few months." She's too good; she could tell I wanted to ask but didn't have the guts.

"Oh, yeah. I guess it'll take a lot of people to fill her shoes then, eh?" I avoid his name like the plague. Something about him rubs me the wrong way.

She doesn't say anything but smirks at me, shakes her head and looks out the window as we drive home. We have a late dinner. I managed to make lasagna before I picked her up. This time, I didn't burn it—granted, I didn't have her sexy body distracting me this time. She eats two plates full and drinks three glasses of wine. Letting out a small burp, she covers her mouth and laughs.

"Excuse me! Oh, my goodness." She blushes, and I laugh because I've never heard her do that before.

"In some countries they say that's a compliment of eating a good meal." I take it as a compliment anyway.

"I didn't eat all day; I didn't get a chance to sit down once. This is exactly what I needed. Thank you. It was so good!" She stands to take our plates, and when she walks around the table to my side, I wrap my arms around her waist and hug her.

"I miss you." I breathe her in. She smells like rubbing alcohol, latex gloves and soap, and Addison. "I might just have to get you pregnant so I can have you home more."

She tenses, and I look up at her. "What?"

"Nothing," she smiles. "I just love you. And I miss you, too." Leaning down to kiss me, she runs her fingers through my hair. "I want to have babies with you, too. Let's get married first, though." She rubs her stomach and laughs. "I don't want to be a pregnant bride."

She takes our plates and glasses into the kitchen, and I hear her phone ring.

"Hello? ... Hey, you! ... Are you serious? Don't tease me, Riley...Okay, call me when you have all the details!" She almost bounces back into the dining room.

"That was Riley! She said she's bringing the girls here and throwing me a bachelorette/birthday party next month!" She pulls her hair out of a pony tail and scruffs it with her fingers. The curls fall all around her face and down her shoulders. "Can't wait to get wild, baby!" She bites her lip and winks at me.

"Oh, really! Just what does Riley have planned?" My interest is extremely peaked now, even though part of me knows it involves drinking and half naked men.

She sits on my lap, pulling her hair over one shoulder. "I don't know, probably a nice quiet dinner, you know. Nothing special." She looks around the room at everything but me and tries not to smile.

"I highly doubt that. It's okay though, I'm sure you'll have fun..." My turn. "I can't wait for my bachelor party" I continue. "I think I overheard the boys talking about tassels...or was it thongs?" I grin and throw my head back laughing.

She drops her jaw and pulls my face into hers, our noses touching. "I don't care what you look at, as long as you come home to me." She smiles and kisses my lips softly.

"Right back at ya, baby." I wink and kiss her deeply.

I watch her fall asleep. She turns over, facing away from me and hugs her pillow. I roll onto my back and count the twenty-seven knots again. I'm restless, and I don't know why. I can't remember what time I eventually fall asleep. When I do, I dream about her.

Long red hair blowing in the wind and big blue eyes gazing through long lashes, pink cheeks blushing from whatever the lips on her ear just said to her. She's smiling. She's now lying in a field with long grass; when she reaches for the hands outstretched to pull her up, she laughs and grabs them. They pull her up to her feet. The arms that wrap around her and spin her in the long grass aren't mine, nor were the lips that were whispering in her ear. I watch her as they walk hand in hand through the field.

"Ahh!" I sit up, panting. My eyes fly over to where she's lying, still sleeping and holding on to her pillow. I run my hand through my hair, still trying to catch my breath.

"*Reid.*" I hiss and fall back into bed, closing my eyes tightly, trying to crush the vision of them out of my head.

I have no chance to getting to sleep now that I'm whirling from my dream. Why would I even dream something like that? The thought of another man with her makes my stomach turn, and I almost can't bear it. Watching her smile and laugh and look at someone else in that way, with those eyes, is painful. I shake my head, wishing I could erase it like an Etch-A-Sketch, but have no such luck.

As soon as daylight breaks, I dress and go outside, starting work early, wanting to get his hands off her body and out of my mind. Nothing about this feels good. I feel awful about getting out of bed without saying anything, leaving her sleeping alone.

I hear a tapping on the upstairs window. I drop the wheelbarrow and look up; she's standing in the window in her t-shirt, smiling at me. I smile back hastily, pick up the wheelbarrow and push it toward the barn. I can't get over how childish I'm being, yet I can't stop myself. It's not like it's her fault that I dreamed about the two of them, and it's for sure not like it really happened. So why am I pouting? Maybe this is my guilty conscience finally making an appearance and telling me to fess up about Gwen all those months ago, sneaking into my bed and blowing my...*mind*. Pushing the wheelbarrow up by the handles, I flip it over in frustration. I can't tell her, not now, not after all this time.

"Blaine, is everything okay?" She's standing in the doorway of the barn in her light pink scrubs, my favourite ones.

"Yep, it's all good." I smile, using every cell in my body to push that sickening dream out of my mind and get over my stupid temper tantrum.

"You haven't woken up before me in a long time. I'm running late, though; can you drive me to work?" I didn't even notice she had her bag and purse in her hand.

"These are my favourite on you." I tip her chin to kiss her lips, tasting her sweetness and feeling like the biggest asshole on the planet for feeling like I did about something she didn't even do.

When I pull up to the curb to drop her off, Reid's out there. What the fuck? Is he waiting for her? I inhale deeply and force a smile, thanking myself for wearing sunglasses, so she can't see my eyes blazing.

Blaine, get a grip!

"Have a good day, my love!" She kisses me quickly, rubs her hand along my thigh and reaches my zipper. "Think of me all day, and when I get home, I'll give you a big kiss." She gently squeezes around my growing erection. "*Everywhere.*"

I want to beg her not to get out of the truck, not just because she's got me worked up and I want to pull her on to my lap to make love to her, but because I *will* think of her all day—her and that asshole standing there in his blue scrubs. I turn up my lip at the sight of him through the dark glass, my chin over her shoulder as she hugs me goodbye.

"I love you, Ms. Cole."

She smiles, telling me she loves me too, and gets out. My nostrils flare when I see his elation as she walks up to greet him. They walk in the big glass sliding doors together.

"Everything will be just fine as long as you keep your hands to yourself, Reid," I say in the quiet rumble of the cab of my truck. Saying his name puts a bad taste in my mouth.

The drive home usually doesn't take this long, but I feel like I'm going at a slug's pace so I don't have to pull into the driveway and see Jeremiah and Alex. In the beginning, I wasn't bothered at all by guys staring at her; they did it almost everywhere we went. Hell, I was proud to be with her and wanted to show her off like a trophy. I think it's the fact that he touched her. Even though I know in a job like hers there's always physical contact—but not the way his fingers were on her skin.

"I hope you're ready for the best bachelor party of your life!" I'm not even out of the truck before Alex jogs over, cupping his hands on either side of his mouth to make sure I hear him yelling.

I'm still in a shitty mood, but surprisingly, what he says makes me laugh. "Yeah? What do you have planned? We aren't going to Vegas, are we?" I slam the door of the truck, and we walk over to the barn where Jer is filing buckets with feed.

"So, what am I in for?" I ask Jeremiah.

"You know we can't tell you. Besides, if I did, you would probably say no." He grins and shrugs. "Well, the *old* Blaine wouldn't but this one would." He points to me and smirks.

"I didn't go anywhere," I say. "Let's hear it!" I grab a handful of grain and throw it at him; he ducks and laughs.

"Can't. Sorry. You'll just have to wait until Friday night." He's not going to give me any details; Jeremiah is pretty good at keeping secrets, and if he wants me to have a good time, he'll keep his lips sealed until I find out when it's actually happening.

Since I'm not getting any more information out of either of them, I change the subject from my stag party to Addison's doe.

"Riley called." I don't even finish, and Alex perks up at the mention of her name. "She's coming to Sheridan and taking Addison out."

"Oh, *is she?*" He pretends not to show he's anxious, but it's oozing from his pores. Jer and I both joke and get him going about his feelings for Riley, and he spills about their time together last year during our visit to Maine.

After lunch my phone rings. "Hello?" I answer.

"Hey, baby." It's Addison. She clears her throat. "I'm not feeling well; I've thrown up twice. Can you come get me?"

"Yes, of course. I'll be right there."

"Are you sure? Ruth offered to drive me home if you can't."

Why couldn't I? "I'll be there in ten minutes."

When we got home, she took a long bath and now is lying in bed, under three blankets.

"I think I've got the flu," she whimpers. Even when she's sick, she looks beautiful.

"Go to sleep." I brush a lock of hair from her face. "I will stay with you."

"No, I'm okay. You can go back out to work; I promise I'll text you if I need something." She smiles and closes her eyes.

"She okay?" Alex asks while loading boards in his arms for the new fence. "She never gets sick."

Considering she works in a hospital, I'm surprised it's taken this long for her to catch a cold or the flu. Suddenly, like someone said it but no one heard a word, the three of us all look at each other, knowing exactly what the other is thinking.

"Bro, is she pregnant?" Alex almost looks scared. And for a moment, I feel my knees get weak.

"No, she would tell me..." I hope she would; besides, she's on the pill. I remind myself to Google the effectiveness of that tiny capsule she takes every morning.

If she is, then it's something we will tell everyone together. I change the subject and try to get some work done. The fencing is so old that we've needed to replace it for years. Having a third person really helps, so we're able to get it done faster. The ground has thawed, so we can bore holes for the new posts, and by five PM, we're all exhausted.

"Ready to call it a day?" I take my baseball cap off and wipe the beads of sweat from my brow.

"Sounds good to me. C'mon, Alex; let's get going." Jer shakes my hand and rests the shaft of the shovel over his shoulder. "See ya tomorrow, buddy."

Addison hasn't messaged me, so I quietly open the door to the house, hoping she's still sleeping. I pull off my boots and set them down gently. Rex barks at the door.

"Shh! Boys, come on." I open it and let them both in. Luca heads right for the living room and flops down in front of the warm hearth.

The old wooden stairs creak a little when I try to tread lightly up them, and when I get to the bedroom, I can see she's still asleep.

She must be really sick; she's snoring softly, and I can't help but smile. Her hair is an absolute mess, and when she stirs, she rolls on to her side and breathes heavily with her mouth wide open. Now *that* is sexy. I grin, trying to keep myself from laughing.

Closing the bathroom door behind me quietly, I turn the shower on and pile my dirty clothes into the wicker laundry hamper. I exhale deeply and stand under the heat, pressing my hands against the tile in front of me. I lean so the water beats down the back of my neck. After I wash, I turn the knobs off and step out. I dry my hair quickly with a towel and then wrap it around my waist. I wipe off the fog on the mirror above the sink and lather my face with shaving cream. While I'm rinsing off my face, I turn to see her coming into the bathroom. She squints from the light and blocks it with her hand.

"Hey, you. How are you feeling?"

She looks rough and stumbles a little. I quickly reach out and catch her. "Whoa! Baby, are you okay?"

"I'm okay, and turn around! I don't want you to see me like this." she sleepily giggles.

"Oh, believe me; I've seen it all." I clear my throat and laugh. "I even heard a little snoring earlier."

"No, you didn't! I don't snore. I'm a lady." She pulls from my arms and sits down on the toilet. "See!" She pretends to curtsey while she's sitting, and I can't help but laugh out loud.

"Quite the lady. I'm glad to see your sense of humour is back. You must be feeling a little bit better."

I pull the towel from around my waist and toss it on the counter. I walk right by her while she's still sitting there, I'm completely naked. And even though she's a hot mess, she's still *her* and I'm slowly hardening.

"I'm not feeling well enough for that!" she yells from the bathroom and leans to close the door behind me.

I put on a pair of pajama bottoms and climb into bed. When she comes out I pull the blankets on her side back so she can get in.

"Thank you." She smiles and lies down, and I cover her up all the way to her chin. I get under the enormous pile and try to get close to her. "Blaine, no! You can't. I don't want to get you sick."

"Anything you have I would have caught by now anyway. I would risk it just to be close to you." I pull her into me and kiss her hair. "I love you."

"Mmm. Back at ya, handsome." She nuzzles into my chest and kisses my heated skin.

"You know, your brother thought you might be pregnant."

Silence.

"Ha, he would think that, wouldn't he? I'm not though, baby. I took a test at work before you came to get me." She looks up; her big eyes are more grey than blue. "Besides, you know I would tell you if I was."

"I know. He was just being Alex. He got really excited when I told him Riley was coming."

She chuckles a little. "He's got it bad. He just won't admit it. Too bad I don't think Riley would ever give him a *real* chance."

We sleep in each other's arms. I wake up sweating from the heat of being under all the blankets and being against her hot flesh. I slowly lift her so I can get out of bed, laying her back down gently. She mumbles something I don't understand and smiles sweetly in her sleep. Her cheeks have a little color; hopefully she's almost kicked this bug. I call the hospital to tell them she won't be in, which they fully expected, since she left early after throwing up.

It's Thursday, so Jeremiah and Alex are both off. I want to stay around the house in case she needs something, so it looks like an uneventful day for me. I tidy up the kitchen, putting away the clean dishes from the dishwasher. Collecting all the laundry, I do a few loads and watch some TV while I wait for the washer to finish.

Addison has been sleeping almost all day. When she wakes up, she's going to be starving, and I have no idea what she'll want. Chicken noodle soup, maybe? I open my laptop and Google a recipe, since I was unsuccessful in finding a can in the pantry. When I find everything I'll need, I set it all on the island in the kitchen and smile, pleased with myself for having such a great idea. I exhale loudly and cross my fingers that I can pull it off.

"Mmm, something smells good."

I am startled and sit up. I must have fallen asleep on the couch, waiting for the soup. "Hey, you." I hold out my arms to her, and she sits on my lap, wrapping her arms around my neck. "You look so much better. How do you feel?"

"Much better. Thank you for taking care of me." She touches my nose with hers and smiles. "Did you make chicken noodle soup from scratch?"

"I did! You seem surprised," I snort. "Hungry?"

She sits with her legs crossed on the couch, covered by my mom's quilt, blowing the steam from the bowl in her hands.

My phone buzzes.

How's Addison feeling? Are you still up for tomorrow?

I reply to Jeremiah's text. **She's better. I'll let you know, I don't want to leave her if she's sick.**

K. Talk to you in the morning, bro! He sends back.

"How is it?" I put the phone on the coffee table and turn to face her.

"It's delicious. Old family recipe?" She smiles.

"Google." I laugh.

I don't hear it ring, but she does. "My phone. Can you bring me my purse, babe?" She looks around for it and points to the small wooden table by the front door.

When she pulls it from her purse, she narrows her eyes and presses a few buttons, then holds it up to her ear.

"Alex, hey. Yeah, rude, considering I've been sick!" She looks at me and rolls her eyes. "I know; I didn't forget.

Okay...See you later." She hangs up and puts her phone down next to mine.

I raise my eyebrows, waiting for her to tell me what that was all about.

She does. "He texted me about tomorrow night, making sure I'm not going to keep you at home because I'm sick."

"Well, I'm not going to leave you here alone while you're sick."

This time she rolls her eyes at me. "I'm feeling much better. Please, don't not go because of me. You're only going to have one bachelor party, you know."

I grin and pull her hand up to my lips, kissing her knuckles. "Well, for now..." I look at her and smile; she drops her jaw in astonishment.

"Well then, when I'm at *my* party, I'll have to keep an eye open for my next husband!" Picking up her bowl of soup from the coffee table, she takes a mouthful, then points her spoon at me with narrowed eyes.

I love this woman beyond words. She's everything I could ever want, even when she's dishevelled in PJ's with her hair piled on her head in a messy bun. She's perfect.

By the next morning she's back to her normal self, up and out of bed before me, showered without me and downstairs making breakfast.

"Mornin'." I smile when I reach the bottom of the stairs.

"Mmm! Good morning! I'm in a huge rush; sorry but I have to go." Since we haven't pulled her car out of the garage where it was stored for the winter, she grabs my keys off the hook by the door. "Can I take the truck, or do you need it today?"

"Nope, go ahead. See you tonight." I wrap my arms around her, inhaling her sweet scent, and kiss her goodbye.

"Love you!" She smiles and heads out the door.

"Love you."

Jeremiah and Alex pull into the yard about five minutes after she leaves for work. They both almost hop out and skip over to the porch where I'm standing drinking a cup of black coffee.

"Are you ready for tonight?!" I don't know whether Alex is asking me a question or making a statement. He's beaming ear to ear.

"I'm starting to get nervous considering the two of you look like kids who are about to touch their first pair." I hold my hands up to my chest, circling in a motion to resemble breasts, and I laugh. "Where are you taking me?"

"Can't say, sorry." Jer is stone-faced serious, with a slight smirk in the corner of his mouth. Wherever it is, I know I'll probably have a good time.

"Let's get to work, make this a short day!" I take the last sip of coffee and set the mug down on the wooden step of the porch. "Come on, boys!" I whistle to Rex and Luca, who get up from laying on the grass and follow us out into the field.

"I was thinking of buying Addison a new car; do you think she would mind?" I ask Alex.

"If you're offering, I'll take one, too!" He laughs.

"Nice try. Want to go into town?"

Jer slices into the ground with the mouth of his shovel, pushing down with his boot. "Yeah, I bet Bruce--"

I cut him off. "No Dodges." I smirk.

The three of us wipe the dirt off our clothes and pile in Jeremiah's truck; Alex leans over the front seat from the back and cranks the music. We fly down the dirt road and sing our hearts out to Jason Aldean's song—how fitting. Usually I turn the tunes down when the pavement begins, but not today. We drive down the street with the bass thumping and the windows down.

When we approach a stop light, we pull up beside another truck with two pretty girls in it. Alex leans out his window, serenading them, slapping his hands on the doors to the beat, and the girls giggle at each other. When the light turns green the driver, a beautiful blonde, floors her black Chevy, and the sound of them laughing is louder than the music flowing out of my truck.

"Catch them!" Alex yells like he's a captain of a pirate ship after some sweet booty.

Why not? I think to myself, and Jer floors it, quickly shifting into second gear. We are on a long stretch of street with no other cars around. It takes about four seconds to catch the girls in the Chev; we pull up beside them, and the guys go crazy. The passenger, another blonde with very curly hair, blows a kiss, and Jer holds his hands over his heart dramatically. She laughs.

At the next light, we're stopped beside them again. "Where you boys headed?" the driver asks, biting her bottom lip.

"Wherever you're going, baby!" Alex shouts from the backseat. They laugh, and when the light turns green, we all fully expect them to drive straight again. She pretends to, but turns right at the last minute, and we can hear them yahoo-ing and cat-calling as they drive away.

"Awe, damn." Alex pouts.

When we arrive at the Ford dealership, Derek, who I usually do business with, walks out of the big sliding doors with his arms open.

"Mr. Blackstock! Where is that big bad truck of yours?" he says, obviously noticing I arrived in the competition.

"My girlfriend has it today, but I'm actually looking for a car for her."

"Oh, very nice! Let me guess; she's a Mustang girl!" He's good.

"You should see the 'Stang she's got now! Sixty-seven Fastback, bro," Alex pipes up as he climbs out of the Dodge.

Derek doesn't say anything, just puts his hand on my shoulder and walks me over to a long line of cars. They're all freshly washed and sparkling in the sun. He stops in front of a Fiesta, and I curl my lip. I can't picture her in that.

"We like the new Taurus. An SHO would be even better."

Derek's eyes light up. "We have twelve right over there. Let's go check 'em out!"

I trail my fingertips along the hood and fender of the Taurus. This is the one. Black and sleek just like my truck, a matching pair.

"I'll take it."

Alex gapes, and I grin.

At Derek's desk, I sign all the paperwork, writing Addison's name as the title owner.

"Our current promotion also gives her two years of free oil changes and a $300 gas card!"

"Even better! Thanks, Derek." I lean over his desk and shake his hand.

"Always a pleasure, Mr. Blackstock."

Alex is sitting in her new car when I get outside. He's almost drooling.

"Jealous?" I smirk.

"You know, my birthday is coming up soon." He laughs and gets out of the car. "She's gonna freak!"

And for a second, I'm nervous. Freak? Freak good, or freak bad? I decide to text her. **When is your lunch break today?**

She replies. **In about 30 min. What's up, babe?**

I don't text back. The guys are going to The Wolfbarrow for lunch, and since it's one of the last places I want to be, I drive over to the hospital to surprise Addison. While I sit in the parking lot for a few minutes, trying to think of how to tell her I just bought her a car, I see Reid get out of a Lexus SUV parked one car over. I narrow my eyes watching him. He looks like a snake; something about him crawls under my skin, like poison, and I shudder remembering the dream I had about him and Addison.

I have the car engine off, but my window is down and I can hear him talking when he pulls out his cell phone and makes a call.

"Yeah, you got it all right? I told you to get some extra just in case...Hell, yeah. Buddy, it's gonna be good!" He looks around and must see no one because he keeps talking. "Whatever, man. She's worth it. Fuck, you should see the ass on this girl." Then he catches a glimpse of someone coming out of the hospital doors. "Shit, call you later."

"Hey, there she is!" He jams the phone in his pocket and opens his arms widely.

My heart stops, and I freeze. It's her; it's Addy. She smiles and walks right into his arms, embracing him. I don't know whether I want to rip the steering wheel off, or puke. I'm gripping it tightly enough that my knuckles are going white, and I feel sick to my stomach.

I swallow the bile that's starting to rise in my throat. They're talking now, but I can't hear what they're saying. He hugs her again, and I feel the top of my head blow off, steam filling the interior of her new car.

I slowly get out of the car and shut the door. I don't say anything, but she sees me coming over his shoulder.

"Blaine! Hey, baby!"

I am deaf. I have tunnel vision, and I don't even see her anymore. Reid sees me.

"Oh, hey man. How's—"

One punch, and I knock him on his fucking ass. I'm heated, and seething.

"Blaine! Oh, my God!" Now I see her; she's at his side, helping him sit up. He touches his mouth and sees the blood on his fingers.

In a small and brief moment of clarity, I hold up the black key fob and click the lock button. It sounds the horn on the Taurus, and she looks over at it.

"This is for you," I say, my voice clipped and fuelled with anger. I toss the key down onto the black pavement and start walking away. I can hear her calling for me, but I keep going.

I know my truck is parked here somewhere, but I'm so fucking angry that I can't see straight enough to drive. The only thing powering me is my rage and complete despondency.

I wouldn't believe it if someone told me it was going to happen, but seemingly out of nowhere, that same Chevy with the two blondes from earlier pulls up beside me.

"Hey, cowboy! Where you off to?" The curly haired passenger smiles at me and pops the pink gum in her glossy-lipped mouth.

"Blaine!" I can still hear Addison calling me—which means she hasn't left his side, because she's definitely not standing beside mine right now.

"The Wolfbarrow. On Blair Street," I answer the girls. "Want to take me?" I raise a salacious brow and, without a word, the blonde opens the door. I slide in beside her and don't give the parking lot of the hospital another look.

They're both asking me a million questions on the ten-minute drive: who I am, where I live, who the other two guys were in the truck I was in earlier, why I was walking down the sidewalk. They're the usual questions, but they're all compacted into one bubblegum-enhanced sentence. I regret my decision to get in the truck with them about three minutes down the road when a song comes on the radio about saving horses and riding cowboys. They both scream that "this is their jam!", and I have to look out the window and laugh; I think if I did it in their faces, they might just cry.

At The Wolfbarrow, they park next to Jeremiah's truck.

"Shall we, ladies?" I motion my hand to the front door, and they both beam.

Hell, it's only 3:40 in the afternoon, and I've just had my heart broken, so why not get drunk with my two best friends and two random girls that just picked me up off the side of the road?

Inside, I order us some drinks. "Jess! Three shots of J.D. for me and these two lovely ladies." I snap my fingers, feeling like an ass, and as shocked as Jesse looks, he still grabs a bottle and starts pouring.

I don't even have to introduce the girls; Jer and Alex know exactly who they are.

"Boys, this is..." And I realize I have no clue what their names are. *Oops.*

"Jennifer!" the driver blurts out. She holds out her hand, and Jer kisses it.

"I'm Madison!"

Hearing the other girl's name almost makes my knees buckle. Alex half glares at me and half smiles at her.

"Hi there, *Madison*." He enunciates her name and grins. "That was some nice driving today, girls."

They both giggle. "Can you excuse us for a sec?" Madison says, and they hold hands, bouncing into the bathroom.

"Don't." I hold my hand up to Alex, his mouth open ready to start the interrogation. "Let's start this bachelor party now, shall we?" I grab a shot glass off the tray in Jesse's hand before he can even place them down on the table. I sling it back and wince as it burns its way down my throat.

"Blackstock. You okay buddy?" Jesse pats my shoulder and looks questionably at Jeremiah and Alex for an answer as to why I've just walked in, snapping my fingers, with two blondes on my arm.

"I'm all good, Jess. Thank you." I tip the other shot glass at him and slug it back, quickly followed by the third. "Five more, please." He doesn't question me and goes back to the bar.

"Listen, I don't want to hear anything from either of you," I tell the boys. "You were all excited about this night; let's get it going now!" I slap the table with my hands, looking back and forth between the astonished eyes staring at me.

"Blaine..."

"Nope, Jer. Don't even ask." I hold my hand up again.

Alex pulls his phone out of his jeans pocket and narrows his eyes at me.

"What?"

"Addy said you punched a guy she works with? What the fuck, man?"

"Did she happen to mention that he was all over her before I punched him?" I clear my throat and puff my chest out like I'm ready to take a hit. I know I elaborated a tad about the details, but I don't correct myself.

"Buddy...Damn." Jer refills his glass of beer from the pitcher on the table.

Alex holds his phone up to me. "She wants to talk to you."

My good friend Jack Daniels is surging through me, and my head is screaming at me not to take the phone from his hand and talk to her. But my heart—what's left of it, anyway—gives my head the double middle finger.

I grab the phone and walk away from the table, just in time for the blondes, Jennifer and Madison, to return from powdering their noses or whatever.

"Hello." I sicken myself at how cold I sound.

"Blaine, what's going on?"

"I hope you like your car. I'm going out with the boys."

She's quiet for a few seconds, and I'm not sure if it's the loud music in the bar or if I even really hear her crying.

"I know you are. And I love the car; thank you." She inhales deeply. "Please be careful, and come home safely. Okay?"

I fight the urge to mutter a sarcastic remark about her calling it 'home', but I don't. I am already acting like the biggest dick on earth.

"Addy, I—" I breathe and pound my fist down on a table beside me. I don't say anything else, just hang up the phone and toss it back at Alex. "Let's get this started, yes?" I take a shot and slam the glass down on the table.

I hear a familiar voice from behind me, and when I turn around, Gwen is staring at me with a look I've definitely seen before.

"Hey, Jeremiah, Alex. *Blaine*. How are you?" She looks me up and down, and for the first time in my life, I actually feel myself give in to her sexuality.

"Gwen, how are *you*?" I ask, pulling my belt buckle down a little with my hand, the same buckle Addison gave me for my birthday. Her eyes travel down my chest and to my buckle—or around the area, anyway.

"Jer! It's so good to see you again." She snaps out of her daze and almost jumps in his lap, completely ignoring Jennifer and Madison standing there. She's trying to get me jealous like she's always done in the past.

"Hey, baby." He nuzzles her hair with his nose. Jennifer purses her lip and elbows Madison, who looks equally annoyed. "I've missed you. Hey, what are your plans tonight?"

She looks at the ceiling momentarily and then smiles.

"Nothing, why? What are we up to?" She's already included herself, it seems.

"Well, it's Blaine's bachelor party." He says it like he's almost questioning me, if he should still call it that or not. I nod and smile. "So we're taking him to Cody. We could use a DD." He raises a brow, and she almost looks hurt.

"Just using me for a chauffeur, huh?" And then she changes her tune. "Well, it could be fun, I guess." She winks at me, and I smirk right back.

I've forgotten that Alex has been sitting here witnessing all of this, and I feel embarrassed. I look at him, and he shrugs. "Whatever, bro."

Is that him saying it's okay? Or that he doesn't care what I do because his sister is done with me? I hand him a shot and pick up one for myself.

"To tonight!" We clink our tiny glasses, and I finally get a smile out of him. "To Cody!" We all cheer, and I feel like I want to crawl into a dark hole and die.

I think I nod off and on during the drive to Cody. I'm sitting in the front with Jeremiah driving and Gwen sandwiched between us in the middle. Alex is sitting between his blonde playthings in the back.

"Blaine?" Gwen nudges my arm, but I have my head turned, and I close my eyes pretending to be sleeping.

"Leave him. He'll need to re-energize for tonight!" Jer taps the steering wheel just like he did during the test drive of this very same truck.

I feel my phone vibrating and adjust myself to pull it from my pocket. I swipe the screen with my finger and see three text messages from Addison.

You hung up on me?
I love you so much. Please, baby. Answer me.

I won't bother you for the rest of the night. Just come home to me.

I shove it back in my pocket just as Gwen starts to bounce in her seat. "Welcome to Cody, ladies and gents!" She turns around, and all three girls squeal at the same time, deafening me.

I wince and shoot Jer a "What are we doing?" look; he just smiles and shrugs. Jer's GPS instructs him to drive eight miles and turn left, then another three miles and turn right. We reach our destination and pull into the parking lot of huge of a building with 5 *O'CLOCK SOMEWHERE* displayed in big blue neon block letters. I gape.

"Blaine Blackstock, are you ready?" Jer smacks my knee with his hand, and I grin. "Let's go ladies! And Alex." He laughs.

The bouncing blondes, Jennifer and Madison, aren't quiet one bit while they eye up every single guy wearing a cowboy hat or boots waiting in the line outside. Hell, I think someone with even a leather belt on would stand a chance of getting into their pants tonight.

"Ladies, control yourselves!" Gwen snaps; like she's anyone to talk about self-control.

Our wait in line doesn't take long at all, and we're in the bar within minutes. It's western-themed but overdone with all the strobe lights and spinning rainbow-colored balls that send streams of light all over. The bar is located in the center of the room; it's huge, with at least ten bartenders trying to fill the orders of at least a hundred thirsty patrons.

I'm not a dancer, but the music is starting to make me want to move my body. I find myself nodding my head to the beat, and Jennifer grabs my arm.

"Dance with me, handsome!"

I stare wide-eyed at her, trying to get over that she just used the same term of endearment that Addison calls me.

"Soon, darlin'. I need a drink first!" I smile and try not to hurt her feelings, but she pouts her glossy lips anyway. "What would you like?"

She yells something, but it's so loud I can't hear. I feel hands on my shoulders from behind me. It's Alex.

"This is a one-time thing, bro. What happens in Cody stays in Cody; got it?"

I look at him quizzically.

"Yeah, that's right." He looks seriously at me. "You have fun, and then go home to my sister and explain yourself, okay?" He pushes me in the direction of the bar and orders us two shots of Jack Daniels each.

The last time Alex and I drank this together at a bar, we had just beaten the crap out of that piece of shit, Jacob. The thought makes me smile, and we clink our plastic shot cups of alcohol together, tip our heads back and let the poison stream down our throats.

Gwen has managed to pull Jeremiah onto the big black dance floor. I have never seen him dance, and I have to admit that he's pretty hilarious. I don't know where he got some of those moves from, though; I tilt my head to the side and watch him hop on one foot while pulling his other bent leg back and forth. Gwen laughs and bounces with her hands around his neck. Why did she have to turn into such a crazy bitch? She makes him so happy.

"Dance now?" Jennifer is back and pulling on my belt. Her cold fingers touch my skin and I flinch. Madison grabs Alex's hands, and they both pull us out onto the black sparkling tile.

The song isn't country, but it's not bad, and I feel myself starting to move. Jennifer stands behind me, running her hands all over my chest and squeezing my pectorals. I grab her hands and pull her in front of me, pulling her body close to mine. She has one thigh between my legs and is grinding herself against me. My body responds, and I feel myself start to harden. *Shit.*

I pull back, and she doesn't even notice. She keeps convulsing slowly to the rhythm. When she opens her eyes, she notices me and grabs me again.

"Damn, cowboy. You're so hot!"

I don't answer, just give her a small grin. It's enough to make her close her eyes and throw her arms around me, crushing me. The J.D. has taken over, and I feel totally out of control. My blood is sizzling, and my skin feels hot to the touch. She spins around and bends over, pushing her behind right into my groin. I unconsciously hold her hips and thrust. She squeals, and I bite my bottom lip, wanting to slam myself deep inside her, glossy lips, popping bubblegum and all. I'm disgusted with myself, but I'm too far gone to care.

When I look up slowly from Jennifer's back, my eyes meet Gwen's, and they're blazing. She isn't dancing with Jeremiah anymore; I don't even see him around her. She walks through the crowd of people and grabs Jennifer's hands, pulling her away from me and not even giving her a second look.

"Hey! Bitch..." I hear Jennifer whine, but she quickly finds another guy and starts grinding him instead.

Gwen's eyes don't leave mine. The song changes to something slower and more sexual, rougher. She puts her hand on my chest and places one of mine on her lower back, her t-shirt tied in a knot to the side so her stomach and back are bare.

I can't make out all the words, but I can tell the song is about a guy getting hurt and taking out his fury on another girl by fucking her senseless—*Only for tonight*, the lyrics moan. It's enough to send me off the deep end, and I find my other hand deep in Gwen's hair, gripping tightly and pulling her face up to mine.

We slowly move our bodies together, and I can feel her hot breath on my lips. Her eyes aren't blazing anymore; they're glistening, raw and wanting. I push hard against her, and either she's ready to burst from her longing, or my belt buckle hurt her. *Both, I hope.*

I'm drunk, but I'm also sober enough to remember what she did to me in my bed last year. How she crept in like thief in the night and wrapped those pouty lips around me, and how she seductively wiped her mouth afterwards. I'm getting heated by looking at her hot mouth—until she says something.

"Told you," she breathes heavily.

I lean in to her ear; my lips graze her skin. "Told me what?"

Her hand runs down my chest and down into my jeans, gripping my growing erection. "Told you she wasn't good for you." And she squeezes me tightly, gazing with wide eyes.

I blink and pull back. Her hand comes out of my jeans, and she looks surprised.

"You..." I point at her, raise an eyebrow and ever-so-slowly lick my bottom lip. "*Fuck you.*"

She groans and grabs me, holding herself against me again. "*Exactly.* That's right, Blackstock. I'm all yours."

Gwen is the epitome of why I've never had a relationship last. Anyone I've ever been with has been just like her. She's completely raw and sexual, which drives me crazy, but that's where it ends. Her eyes have never been passionate or emotional. She's empty.

"I'm outta here." I start to back up and stumble into a few people dancing. I hold my hand up to apologize, but I don't even think they notice me. I have to find Jeremiah.

When I do find him, he's sitting in a booth with his arm around a pretty girl with jet black hair.

"I've gotta go." My voice sounds panicked.

"You okay? What's up?"

"I gotta go home, Jer." I look at the ceiling, wanting to scream out at how disgusted I am with myself. I just want to be at home in my bed, with Addison.

"Sit down and relax, buddy. We'll go home soon." He lifts up his beer bottle and nods it at me. I sit down on the vinyl seat and put my head in my hands.

"You need a drink!" the black haired girl shouts. I lift my head, and she's blurry.

"I've got one right here!" It's Gwen. She's at the table with two drinks in her hands. She flops down beside me and hands me a pink drink in a martini glass. "Drink up, *big* boy!"

Jeremiah doesn't seem bothered that she's even in the booth; he's in deep with the other girl.

"Blaine is getting married soon. We need to show him what he's gonna be missing!" Gwen holds up her drink and elbows me. "Drink!"

I inhale deeply, but I take the glass and pull the straw out, tossing it on the table. The glass is rimmed with green sugar crystals, and Gwen traces her finger along my glass and licks her finger off seductively.

I toss back the drink in a few chugs. It's far too sweet, and I wonder if there's any alcohol in it at all. Alex and Madison join us at the booth. I have no clue where Jennifer is, and I don't really give a shit either.

"Bro, you look wrecked!" Alex laughs and points at me.

I grin back. I'm starting to feel better, and now I don't want to go home just yet.

"What do you guys do?" the black haired girl asks in a high-pitched tone, talking over the loud music.

Gwen takes the reigns of the conversation, explaining about each of us and what we do. She spends the most time talking about herself, of course, and not much about Alex at all.

The night turns into a blur, a blur of flashing lights and beams of color. I feel like I'm spinning in the booth, like I'm on one of those rides at a carnival that you spin around in by turning a large wheel in the center.

CHAPTER FOURTEEN

I remember Alex and Jeremiah helping me walk, though I'm not sure to where. I remember being in a cab and then an elevator. Now I feel like I'm laying on a carpet or some plush surface, and I'm falling into the black. The buzzing around me is deafening. I try to open my eyes, but I'm in a fog. I can't even move my body. The commotion is becoming more clearly now.

"Blaine? Blaine! Baby, please wake up!" Someone is shaking me, warm hands on my face, and she's hysterical. "What did you give him?!"

"I...I...I don't know! We were just having fun!"

"Gwen, so help me, tell me what you gave him!" I can make out Jeremiah's voice.

"Fuck, I don't know. I think it was *E*."

My shirt opens, and I feel warm skin against my chest and soft hands on me.

Mmm. It feels good.

"Oh, my God. Baby! Come back to me." She sounds more controlled now, but I can feel her panic. "Get her out of here, Jeremiah!"

I hear more commotion, then a door open and close, and now it's quiet.

"Blaine, my love. Please wake up."

I groan and clear my throat. I hear Addison inhale quickly, and the fog starts to clear a little.

"You." I smile and peek out slightly with one eye. My body is tingling, and my head is full of pressure.

"Sweetheart, you're okay. I'm here." She hugs me; some of her hair falls on my face, and I breathe in her familiar scent. It's the smell of home, and I know I'm safe in her arms.

"Can you get up?" she asks softly.

"Mmm, no. Let's stay down here." I grin and close my eyes, trying to pull her on top of me.

"I think you need to go to the hospital. You were drugged."

Jeremiah comes back in the room, and I hear her tell him to call 9-1-1. What seems like only a few seconds go by, and two paramedics are at my side. They're asking a bunch of questions, which I don't have the answers to, and flashing small lights in my eyes.

"We'll take him in and pump his stomach," one guy says, and I feel a tightness on my arm from what I assume is a blood pressure cuff.

"Thank you, guys. Can I ride with him?"

"Of course, ma'am."

I'm loaded into an ambulance. The interior lights are dimmed a little once we start driving, and when I adjust my eyes, I see Addison sitting on the bench beside the gurney I'm strapped to.

"Hi, beautiful."

She has tears in her eyes; they pool at her lashes and start rolling down her cheeks. She begins to sob. "Blaine...I...I."

I try to reach to wipe her tears, but I can't move my arms. "Do you like your car?" I look at her, feel like I could cry, too, but nothing is coming out. I am full of emotion, but I can't express any of it.

She laughs, and wipes her tears. "I love it. Thank you."

"I'm sorry I didn't text you back."

She shakes her head like she's dismissing my apology. "I'm just happy you're okay." She brushes my hair off my forehead. "I love you so much."

I manage to mouth the words back to her before I close my eyes and fall into the dark again.

"Mrs. Blackstock? Hi, I'm Doctor Sheldon." A woman's soft voice speaks.

"I'm Addison. How much did he ingest?" I hear Addison say.

"Seems as if it was only one tablet, but he had a lot of alcohol in his system."

I open my eyes and swallow loudly. They both turn and look at me. Addison has wide, worried eyes, but she smiles. The last time I woke up in a hospital, I had no idea who she was, so I'm relieved when her beautiful face is the first thing I see. Her smile warms me.

"Mr. Blackstock. You had quite a night, I heard. We had to pump your stomach, but you're going to be just fine. Luckily, you have a nurse to take you home and care for you." She smiles and looks at her watch. "He can go home in a few hours; we just want to keep an eye on him since he just woke up."

"Thank you, Doctor Sheldon."

She smiles and leaves the room, closing the curtain behind her. Through Addison's half-open hoodie, I can see she's wearing one of my John Deere t-shirts. Her hair is up in a messy bun, and she's wearing jogging pants. She looks beautifully unkempt, and I reach for her hand.

"You're gorgeous, Addy." I smile.

She sits down on the bed and takes my hand, holding it with both of hers. My hand tingles from her warm touch.

"I'm sorry about what happened with Reid."

I stop smiling.

"I thought he was a friend; I was wrong." She looks away, and I try to sit up.

I pull her closer to me; she almost hesitates but then leans in. "After you walked away and I was making sure you didn't break his face, he tried to kiss me."

I inhale deeply and clench my teeth so hard it almost hurts. Her eyes are wide and glossy, and she starts to cry again.

"I told him to stop and that I didn't like him like that. I love *you*. I'm marrying *you*." She sniffles, and I can reach up this time to wipe a tear.

"I'm sorry I walked away. I'm even sorrier about everything that happened since then." I trail off not wanting to talk about any of it, because I'm sickened at myself.

"Alex told me; you didn't do anything. You were hurt and upset, I understand."

I shake my head; she's wrong. "Addy, I just wanted to..." I stop before I tell her how badly I wanted to drink myself into a stupor and fuck other women on a dance floor in a bar.

"I wasn't myself." Or maybe I was. Maybe the person I was before she came into my life is the real me, and the person she got to know is all a facade.

"No, we're not going to talk about it," Addy says. "You're okay, and I'm here now. I just want to take you home." She rolls up her sleeves and rubs her eyes with her hands. "That is if you want to come home with me."

"Where else would I want to be?" I'm starting to feel better now that all the toxins were either pumped out or have been absorbed. "I just want you." I pull her closer until she's almost right on top of me.

"Blaine!" She giggles. "Not here!"

"Why else would they have these curtains?" I smile and hold her face in my hands. "I love you, Addison Cole. I love you so much."

We talk for another hour or so, and Doctor Sheldon comes back to release me. I thank her immensely for everything.

Addison drove her new car to Cody; it's in visitor's parking, glistening under the morning sun. She holds up the key fob and pushes a button to unlock the doors. I wince when I think about how it's the same key that was in my hand yesterday before I threw it at her.

Our drive home is quiet. I sleep off and on, and the clock on the dash reads almost ten when we drive under the Blackstock banner across the driveway.

Rex and Luca get up from laying on the porch and run to greet us as we pull in to park beside my truck.

"There's my boys." I pet them both, and Luca does the big howling noise he makes when he's excited. "Missed you too, Luca."

"They slept at the foot of the bed last night." She smiles, but it's a sad smile. "I think they wondered where you were."

"Well, my side of the bed won't be empty ever again." I pull her into an embrace and kiss her neck. She moans softly and kisses my collarbone. "I want you," I breathe.

We shower together. The steam is invigorating, and I feel tired and recharged all at once.

My mouth travels down her body, kissing and licking gently. She has one hand in my hair, pulling gently, and the other is against the glass. Her stomach heaves in and out when she climaxes, and I kiss between her legs and look up at her. Her head is thrown back and her mouth wide open; when she looks down at me, her eyes are so deep they're almost midnight blue. I suck and kiss inch by inch up her body until I'm standing, and I kiss her lips as hard as I can. Our tongues wrapped in each other, we don't even breathe.

I pull one of her legs up, and hold it against my hip. She puts one hand on my shoulder, and the other caresses her breast while she looks at me intensely. I almost orgasm right there on the spot, but I restrain myself and ease into her. Her body is heated and responds to me like it's been waiting eagerly. Our stare doesn't break, and I thrust deeper and harder, biting my bottom lip to keep myself from roaring.

Over and over I push and pull, deeper until I can't go any further. She starts to unravel around me, and I push as far as I can. Her body is pulsating, and she screams out.

"Baby! Oh! Please...Ahh!"

The words are like a spark to dynamite, and I hold her against me as I shatter and grip her thigh tightly. My knees feel weak, and I almost buckle before letting her leg go and pushing against the tile wall to steady myself.

"You okay?" She breathes, her chest heaving and eyes still heated.

"Mmm. I'm more than okay." I grin, breathing heavily. "Ready for bed?"

"I start night shifts tonight." She pouts. "So, if we go to bed, you have to promise to let me sleep...eventually." She narrows her eyes and smiles.

"I promise." I hold my hand over my heart, unsure if I'm going to keep my oath, and kiss her forehead. I break my promise, and once I have her on our bed, I pull her on top of me and guide myself into her again. Afterwards, we lie in bed, panting. The bed feels so soft and warm against my skin.

"What do you want for your birthday?" I ask.

She smiles and closes her eyes. "Just you."

"Wish granted." I kiss her cheek softly, and she drifts off to sleep. My phone vibrates on the nightstand beside the bed and I carefully roll over to look at it.

Hey buddy. I want to talk to you, I hope u are OK. It's from Jeremiah.

Come over, we'll talk. I reply.

I need to hear from Jeremiah about what exactly happened and why I ended up in a hospital. I draw the blinds, and the room darkens. I dress quietly and close the bedroom door behind me so she's not disturbed.

Fifteen minutes later, while I'm sitting on the tailgate of my truck, drinking coffee out of the biggest mug I could find, Jeremiah pulls in and parks behind me.

"Hey, man." He walks up slowly, looking like a kid who just broke a window and is scared of what his dad is going say to him. "How are ya feeling?"

"I'm good, actually. Feeling much better." I take a sip from the mug. "Coffee?"

"No thanks, I've had like, ten this morning already." He laughs nervously. "Shit, man. I'm sorry about everything."

"It's not your fault, and I don't blame you for any of it." I feel awful that he blames himself. "You did everything I wanted to do."

"Pfft. *Gwen*." He hops up and sits beside me on the tailgate. "She's nuts, man. I finally got it outta her that she bought pills from a bouncer there. That's what she gave you."

I laugh and shake my head. That woman is a fucking trip.

"I guess 'cause you had so much to drink, it hit you hard. It just turned her into a bigger lunatic." He chuckles and rubs his face with his hand.

"How did I get to a hotel?"

"We left the bar and took a cab to the hotel. I already had reservations there but only ever planned for the three of us guys."

"Oh, right. The blondes."

"Yeah, well, once we got you into the room, you blacked out and we didn't know what do to. Alex called his sister. But we should have just called an ambulance first."

I already knew the rest. Addison told me while I was still in the hospital. Alex called and woke her up; she drove to Cody and rushed to the hotel.

"Did Addison tell you what she did to Gwen?" He smirks.

My blank look tells him that she didn't.

"After the paramedics loaded you into the elevator, there wasn't enough room for her too. So, she was going to take the stairs. Gwen was standing in the hallway, and Addison walked up to her and slapped her across the face." He bursts with laughter.

"What!" I'm flabbergasted, and I can't help but laugh, too. "What did Gwen do?"

"She didn't say anything, just stood here holding her cheek."

"I'm sorry I missed it." I finish my coffee and set the mug on the bed of the truck. The thought of Addison so aggressive and defensive makes me a little hot.

"Addison stood right in her face and told her to stay away from you. Let me tell you—it was a very quiet drive home."

We sat in silence for a few moments.

"So, hey, she likes the car." I smile.

"Good; I'm glad. And if she didn't, I'm sure her brother would happily take it off your hands." He laughs.

"Her birthday is in a few weeks. Riley and her other friends from Maine are coming."

"Oh yeah, Alex is excited about that one."

We decide to take the rest of today off and work a little longer tomorrow to get the fencing finally finished. When he leaves, I make myself another coffee and check on Addison. She's still sleeping. I decide to do something I haven't done in months; I'm going to go for a ride today. Hard to believe I haven't in so long, but I don't feel like I have the time these days.

Mischief comes right over to the gate when he sees me standing there with his saddle and bridle. He opens his mouth, and I put the cold steel bit in and the leather straps up and over his ears, pulling his forelock out and smoothing it down. After I synch the girth, I grab the leather horn and pull myself up on to his back.

"Let's go, boy." I pat his neck, and my legs give him a squeeze. We walk along the finished portion of the new fence line. Meadowlarks fly out of the grass in the distance, and I remember my first night with Addison.

She was so beautiful, riding high and free; even when she ended up on the ground, she was still smiling and happy. When I think about everything I've put her through since then, I feel sick. How is this woman still with me? How has she agreed to stand at my side and become my wife?

Here and now in this field, I make a vow to myself to never let anything happen to jeopardize our love again, as long as I have a breath in my body.

Mischief starts to get antsy. I know exactly what he wants, and I know I need it, too. I turn him so we're facing the house; it's a small dot in the distance, so we've got a nice long stretch to go. I give him a squeeze and click with the side of my mouth. His body responds, and we lift off the ground. The only sounds I hear are the wind whipping by my body and his galloping hooves rhythmically thumping on the ground. He's running so fast that I'm barely moving in my saddle at all.

I pull his reigns to slow him to a canter as we start to approach the fence. The other horses hear him and start to whinny; he starts to get excited and jumps around, snorting feverishly.

"Heyyyyyy. Easy, boy." I pull the reigns and try to calm him down, but he's still anxious when we get close to the gate. I jump down and pull his saddle off. When I open the gate, I take his bridle off and give his behind a slap. He whinnies to the other horses and takes off toward them, kicking his back legs up. I haven't seen him like that in a long time, so I stand and watch, leaning my arms on the steel gate and resting my chin on top of them.

"Hey, handsome." I feel her hands on my back before I hear her voice. "That was quite a show."

I turn around so my back is against the gate, and she wraps her arms around my waist to hug me. She inhales deeply and sighs. "I woke up and looked outside. I saw you coming up the field; I couldn't believe how fast you were going!"

"What can I say?" I smirk and kiss her forehead. "I'm not too bad."

She touches my neck softly and gently traces her finger down my chest, opening two buttons. She leans in to kiss me.

"Addy," I breathe.

"You are the most beautiful man I've ever seen," she says to me. "I still get butterflies when I see you. Do you know that?" She blushes and kisses my chest again.

I tip her face up with my fingers under her chin and brush my lips against hers. Quickly, I grab her behind and pull her up so her legs are wrapped around my waist, her arms around my neck. I sit down on the top of the picnic table and she puts her hands on my face to kiss me deeply. Slipping my hands up the back of her shirt, I feel her warm skin and pull her closer, kissing deeper and tasting her sweetness. She pulls her lips off mine, our foreheads and noses still against each other, only letting enough space between our mouths to let the breeze cool our warm breath.

"I want to feel you inside of me," she whispers and kisses me again, not giving me a moment to respond, even though I probably can't even speak right now. "Baby, please."

She breaks our kiss again and pulls her shirt off her body in one swift move. She's not wearing a bra, and she pulls my head down to her perfect breasts, moaning softly while I kiss and suck on each of them. I kiss back up her chest and neck feverishly. Lifting her up, I stand and almost fall when I try to lay her down on the grass. We both laugh,

"You okay?" she asks and kisses my cheek.

Leaning back on my knees I quickly undo my jeans and pull my t-shirt off my head—not as stylishly as she did, but just as fast. I lean down and kiss her stomach, running my tongue along her waist from hip to hip just above the elastic of her pajama shorts. I pull them down slowly, and she lifts up for me to take them off. Her long hair is spread on the grass all around her head, the sky reflecting down off her big blue eyes, and she almost doesn't look real, with her glowing perfect skin.

At just the sight of her laying there I can't stand it. I lower my body on to hers, and she moans softly when I ease myself into her. She gasps and closes her eyes. I kiss her neck and softly bite her shoulder.

"Mmm...Faster baby, harder."

I do just that, faster and harder, like early this morning when we were in the shower. I dig my nails into the grass beside her head, holding on as much as I can, as I slam in and out of her as hard as I can. I pull out, leaving just my tip inside, and she moans while running her hands through her red hair. She's looking up and biting her bottom lip; I slowly move back in and thrust hard at the last moment. Her eyes widen and blaze and her mouth forms a perfect O.

Out there, on the grass, in the middle of my yard with no one around, I have the most raw and passionate sex of my life with the most beautiful creature on the planet. She comes undone like a canister of confetti being shot off by a gun, and her squeezing and pulsing grips my insides. I release, digging deeper into the earth.

"See that one?" She giggles and points up to a cloud formation.

"Yeah?"

"It looks like Luca!"

"Yeah..." I cock my head to the side, analyzing from not much of a different angle. "It kinda does."

She turns on her side, her body only covered by my t-shirt, and lays her head on my outstretched arm.

"Have you thought about what song you want to dance to for our first one together?"

I look at her and smile. I really don't care what song plays. It could be thrash metal for all I care; all that matters is that she's in my arms. My face must show that I don't have a clue, so she giggles.

"I'm sure we'll come up with something!"

The sisters-in-law graciously offered their decorating services; they've been very secretive about the details, keeping a giant black binder full of paper, scraps of fabric and who knows what else. Whenever they call Addison, or she calls them, she looks at me and smiles innocently, and then leaves the room. Women.

"You need to get back to bed, miss."

She pouts. "I know."

I lift her chin up to kiss me. "I'm going to town to get a few things, but I'll be back to make dinner when you wake up, kay?"

"Thank you; love you."

"Love you."

Lander's is usually a bustling place on Saturday's, but today is unusually quiet. There's not even any kids outside selling baked goods with their cougar mothers. In the veggie aisle, I pick out a few good sweet potatoes and put them into my basket. One rolls out of my hand, and when I bend down to pick it up, I see a pair of women's shoes standing in front of me.

When I stand, I meet green eyes and a stone-cold face with no emotion.

"Hello, Blaine."

"Gwen." I toss the dropped potato in a nearby plastic trash can and select a new one, placing it carefully in my basket with the rest.

"How are you?"

"I'm great; thanks for asking." I can't even look at her. The girl that I saw almost every day in school as a kid, and then frequently at her brother's bar in the last few years, is now an angry and unpredictable woman. Disparaged. Part of me wants to toss something at her, hoping when she goes to catch it, I can make a run for the exit. The other part of me has no idea what to do.

"Listen, I—" she quietly starts to speak.

I put my hand up to stop her. "Gwen, I have no interest in anything you want to say." Turning my back to walk away, she grabs my arm, and I shiver, giving her a glare.

"Sorry." She recoils. "I just wanted to say that I'm sorry for what happened in Cody." She looks around, either making sure no one is near us within earshot or she can't look me in the eye. "I'm moving to Casper. Jesse got everything started on the new bar there, so I'm leaving in a week."

I try to not let my elation spill out of my skin, but I smile kindly anyway.

"Good for you, Gwen. Best of luck."

"Thanks, Blaine. I guess I'll see ya around."

I nod, hoping that I don't see her in a very long time. I can do without the drama, the drugging and the green eyes that try and infiltrate me every time I see them.

She turns and heads toward the sliding doors. She doesn't purchase anything, which means she must have followed me into the store just to talk. Or corner me in the frozen foods section. Who knows?

I make it to the travel agency thirty minutes before it closes.

Martina Sanford is Jeremiah's aunt and the owner/operator of San Martina's Travel, a big white building which doubles as her business in the bottom and her apartment on the top floor.

"Blaine Blackstock, I've been wondering when I was going to get a call from you!"

"Ms. Sanford, how are you doing?"

She leans in and kisses my cheek, holding my shoulders she stands back and looks at me. "Jeremiah tells me you're getting married! I still remember when the pair of you would come in here after school and look at all my brochures, talking about all the places you wanted to visit."

"Yeah." I smile and look at the wooden shelving unit holding the same type of brochures today, just updated and quite a few more than I remember. "Well, it's time I take one of those trips."

"Come, sit!" She walks behind her large mahogany desk and turns the screen of her desktop computer on. "Where were you thinking? We have some wonderful promotions right now for a few countries in Europe!"

I'm not sure where we should go on our honeymoon. Addison has mentioned a few times about wanting to take a trip to somewhere tropical, so I look over at the brochures again, scanning for palm trees and crisp blue water.

"I was thinking somewhere warm and tropical."

She smiles and pulls out a large catalogue. It thuds on the desk, and she flips through pages, humming to herself.

"My parents went to the British Virgin Islands on their honeymoon..." I trail off, thinking of how happy they must have been. When Martina finds the right page in the big travel book, she turns it around so it faces me. I'm looking at the bluest water I've ever seen; that's where the picture of my mother was taken, just has to be. I trail my fingers over the pictures, thinking of her walking in the ocean, young and beautiful.

"The BVI are gorgeous! Great choice, Blaine."

It's a hard decision, but I manage to choose a resort in Tortola with breathtaking photos of their beaches, palm trees, and big white and red villas. The suites have almost panoramic ocean views. I managed to sneak our passports out of the house just after Addison fell asleep again.

When Martina opened Addison's up to put the information into her computer, she smiled and looked up at me. "She's quite the beauty."

"She is." I smile and almost blush. Sometimes I look at her, while she's sleeping or when we're watching TV and she laughs at something funny, and I can't believe she's mine. That she'll be my wife, and I'll get to look at her every day for the rest of my life.

"Okay, we're all set!" She hands me the passports back, along with my credit card and all the travel information we'll need. "Is this going to be a surprise?"

"I hope so! She's good at getting info out of me though."

She pulls a large manila envelope out of a drawer. "Here. Put everything in this and hide it somewhere you'll remember and where she won't find it!" She rubs her hands together sneakily.

"Thank you for everything, Ms. Sanford." I look at the clock on the desk; it's almost 6:30. "And sorry for keeping you past close."

"No need to apologize; anything for you. You know that! Congratulations again; you're going to make a wonderful husband."

I smile and take my envelope, praying she's right.

All the lights are on in the house when I get home, so I leave the travel package under the seat in the truck. I'll bring it in the house after she's left for work.

"Hey, baby!" She smiles, towel-drying her hair, wearing only the bottom of her scrubs and a bra. Instantly I'm sad that she has to leave. Sleeping alone is something I valued before but now I hate the thought of.

"Hi, my love. Sorry I'm late; did you eat?" I kiss her and put the grocery bag down on the island in the kitchen. "I was going to make dinner, but I lost track of time."

"I made a sandwich." She sticks out her bottom lip. "What were you going to make?"

"Steak, sweet potatoes..." I pull the potatoes out of the bag.

"Awe. Tomorrow?" She smoothed her damp hair with her fingers and quickly pulls it into a messy bun, securing it with an elastic.

I smile and nod, not thinking about dinner anymore.

"I know that look, and it's not gonna happen!" She shakes her finger at me and backs up slowly toward the staircase leading upstairs. "Blaine!" She giggles.

I don't say anything. I just grin and start unbuttoning my shirt slowly, knowing well what impact it has on her.

She reaches the stairs, turns and bolts up them. Taking two at a time, laughing so spirited, I run after her, almost tripping on the first step. I make it to the top just after she runs into our bedroom and closes the door behind her.

She doesn't lock it. When I walk in the room she's standing beside the bed with one hand wrapped around the post on the end of the bed.

"You..." She points and smiles. "I have to work in half an hour!"

"*So?*"

"So? You are going to make me late!"

What does she expect from me? Wearing no shirt and being that beautiful will make anyone late for work.

She grabs her top from the bed and pulls it on, covering her body, and I pout.

"Meanie."

She rolls her eyes and walks over to kiss me. "Love you."

I kiss her deeply, tasting her sweetness and a hint of peppermint from mouthwash. I lift her shirt at the hem and gently touch her waist with the back of my fingers.

She pulls back from my touch and laughs. "I love you, too. See you in the morning."

CHAPTER FIFTEEN

Riley and the girls' flight is arriving in three hours, and Addison hasn't stopped moving once this morning. She's cleaned almost every surface in the house, freshening and tidying for our guests. She's even put Jer, Alex and me to work outside, adding to our list of jobs every half hour or so.

"So, when does the Queen and her posse arrive?" Jer scoffs, tossing chopped wood into the wheelbarrow.

Alex shoots him a dirty look. "Riley."

Jer raises his eyebrows and grins. "Oh, yes, I'm so sorry. *Queen Riley.*"

Alex doesn't say anything, just wields the axe, ripping a piece of wood apart, straight through the middle. I point my thumb in his direction and mouth the words "What's up with him?" to Jeremiah.

He shrugs his shoulders and has a look like he doesn't have a clue on his face.

"Babe!" Addison calls from the porch. "I'm going to the airport now."

"Okay." I walk over from the garage and take her hands. She leans down to kiss me. "Drive carefully."

She climbs into her car and honks the horn as she pulls out on the road, driving slowly so she doesn't create a big dust cloud behind her.

"I'm not feeling so good, bro." Alex rubs his stomach. "Mind if I go home?"

He's been acting weird lately, so I want to know what's up. "Everything okay?" I ask.

"Yeah, just must have ate something bad." He kicks the dirt with his boot and puts his hands on his hips. "I'll work later tomorrow to make up the time."

"Don't worry about it. Go home and feel better." I pat his shoulder and call Jer over so he can take Alex home.

"What's going on with him?" I ask Jeremiah when he comes back after dropping Alex off. "He's been weird."

"He hasn't said anything to me. Though we don't talk about feelings and stuff when we're at home knitting," he jokes and throws more wood into the wheelbarrow.

I have a feeling it has something to do with Riley, judging by the way he said her name earlier, but I don't know what it could be. They got along well in Maine, obviously, so I don't know. "Are you knitting my wedding gift?" I laugh and throw the axe down, splitting a log.

He chuckles and wipes his brow. "So, these girls..."

I know what he's going to ask before he gets a chance.

"Gorgeous." I grin, and he smirks.

"You know I've been working on this." He slaps his stomach, which now that he mentions it has shrunk, probably since Gwen told him he should start hitting the gym.

"Light beer?" I joke, and he laughs. "I'll be over before dinner, so I'll pick up something on the way."

Since Addison hasn't seen her friends since our trip to Maine, I thought I should give them time to visit. I'll hang out with the boys, in the peace and quiet with beer and wings.

We finish with the firewood and all the other little things on our Honey-Do list just as Addison's Taurus pull in the driveway and parks. I can't make out much through the tint, but when all four doors open, I know the gang's all here.

Zoe, Camille and Leah get out of the back, all in heels with big sunglasses and even bigger purses. The trunk pops and Leah opens it. It looks like it was ready to burst at the seams with bags, suitcases and more bags. Jer and I start walking over to help them carry the four wardrobes they've packed for their four-day vacation.

Addison gets out of her seat, and when she looks at me, she's got an expression on her face that I can't read. She smiles softly and swings her purse over her shoulder, grabbing a bag from the trunk. The passenger door opens, and Riley gets out.

I smile when I see her, and she waves and walks to the back of the car where the others are standing, obviously waiting for us to get their luggage.

Addison closes the trunk, and I can see now what the look on her face was about. Riley is standing there, stunning in a pink summer dress, her long hair spilling over her shoulders, and her hands holding the basketball in her stomach. She's pregnant.

"Blaine! We're so glad to see you!" Zoe beams, and Camille hugs me. They quickly turn to Jeremiah, who needs to get it together and pick his jaw up from the dirt.

"Hey, ladies." I grin. "Hey, baby." I kiss Addison on the cheek and grab four large bags to take in the house.

"Hi, Blaine; how are you?" Riley smiles sweetly.

"I'm good, thanks. You're obviously doing well; I had no idea you were expecting..."

"Neither did I!" Addison shoots her a blazing glare and narrowed her eyes.

"Well!" She smiles and holds her hands up. "I wanted to surprise everyone."

"Congratulations, Riley." I smile nervously, as I'm not sure why Addison seems angry about it.

"Okay, Auntie Addy, let's go see your farmhouse!" She giggles, and it takes everything in me not to drop the bags I'm overloaded with.

Auntie Addy...Auntie. Alex. *Shit.*

As soon as I drop the bags in the hallway at the top of the stairs, Jeremiah pushes me into my bedroom and shuts the door.

"What the..." He's buzzing.

"I had no idea either." I sweep my hands through my hair. "Do you think Alex even knows?" I wonder if maybe that was why he has been moody lately.

"If he doesn't, he's going to real soon."

I'm surprised Riley didn't even tell Addison before she came, or that one of the other three hadn't let the cat out of the bag.

Addison comes in the room, and starts to close the door behind her. I can see the other girls laughing and talking to themselves as they turn the other bedrooms into their temporary suites for the weekend.

"Jer, my brother didn't say anything to you?" She is flushed.

"Nothing! We're as surprised as you."

She walks over and sits on a chair by the window, running her hands on her jeans. "I'm standing there waiting for them at baggage claim, and Riley walks out, all smiles. I almost fell over."

Jer leans against the door, the girls still on the other side loudly clicking their heels on the wooden floor.

"The girls were getting their bags, and she just came out and told me the baby is Alex's. She wanted to surprise me, but he already knows." She half smiles. "He's going to be a dad."

"Well! What am I missing in here?" The door flies open, and Riley walks in, beaming from ear to ear. "I'm sorry," she says to Jeremiah, "I didn't introduce myself outside. I'm Riley."

Jeremiah shakes her hand, loosely, like he's afraid if he gets to close he'll impregnate her, too. "Jeremiah, ma'am."

"Oh, you're too cute!" She looks at me. "Blaine, your house is lovely. Thank you for having us here."

"You're all welcome anytime, Riley." I smile, trying not to stare at her Baby Cole-bump. "Did you get everything in the rooms okay?"

"We did, thank you." She reaches her arm out. "Cole! Let's go look at the animals!"

Addison smiles and takes her hand, as they walk out of the room she turns her head and sticks out her tongue at me. I smile and shake my head. *City girls.*

Addison took Riley, Zoe, Leah and Camille on their first farm tour. The four of them took a few steps on the grass in their heels and quickly traded them for flip flops.

They are now all seated around the dining room table, drinking wine, laughing and talking so loudly that they didn't even notice me standing in the doorway.

"Blaine!" Zoe pouted. "You're not leaving us, are you? And where did your friend go?" She blushes.

"I am," I say, smiling. "Jeremiah and I are going to his house. You ladies have a good night." To give them some country hospitality, I even tip my hat before leaving the room and grin to Jeremiah, who's standing in the kitchen. Suddenly, we hear them all giggle and whisper something.

"You better be careful those charms don't get us some permanent house guests!" Addison whispers while she follows me out to the door.

I kiss her. "Have a good night, Ms. Cole." I wink and bite my bottom lip, trailing my finger down her chest. She looks to see if Jer is witnessing this; he isn't. He's outside on the porch, and so she runs her hand down my chest.

"You drive me crazy," she says, and she teases me by leaning in slowly like she's going to kiss me but backs up at the last minute and winks before turning around and sauntering into the dining room.

In town, we pick up beer, a few cases since we're not sure what kind of night we're going to have with *Baby Daddy*, and a whole mess of wings.

At Jer's house, we're both surprised to see Alex sitting outside at the picnic table by himself, staring off into the field. He turns when he hears the diesel engine and waves at the truck. "Hey, guys!"

I look at Jeremiah with a raised brow and then back to Alex, unsure of how to start the "So. Holy shit, you're going to be a dad" conversation. I open the back door and lift out two cases of beer, bumping it shut behind me with my hip.

"So, guess you got the news, huh!" He's strangely happy, which is nice surprise. "And you came prepared to fuckin' party." He eyes the cases, probably doing an intellectual calculation of how many it'll take to get him drunk.

"Alex, are you okay?"

He scoffs, waving his hand in the air and my question away. "I'm fine."

"Why didn't you say anything about Riley?"

"Well..." He pauses, taps his finger on his chin. "I was in a little bit of this thing they call *denial*. Then I was angry for a while, didn't really wanna talk about it."

I drop the beer on the porch. "How long have you known?"

He does more calculations. "Since...December? January? I can't remember."

"Man, we live together, and you didn't even tell me!" Jeremiah says like he's totally offended not knowing the secret.

"Well, sorry, man. Hey, how did Addy take it?"

I shake my head. "She was shocked, *is* shocked. But we're both happy for Riley—for the both of you."

Alex opens the case and takes out a bottle, using his shirt to help him twist off the cap. "Everything happens for a reason; that's what my Mom always says." He shrugs and takes a long drink from the brown bottle.

We sit at the picnic table, eating wings and drinking beer. As the sun sets, we build a fire and pull lawn chairs around it, feeling the warmth and talking about everything except for the baby. The fire crackles, and Alex repeatedly stokes it with a long stick, chewing on his nails between sips of beer.

"So, I think I'm gonna ask her to marry me."

Jeremiah and I look at each other, then Alex, who looks back and forth at us, expectantly. "*Well?*"

"Well..." I start, inhaling deeply. "You should do whatever you think is right. You two really need to talk though."

"You live thousands of miles apart. You gotta find out where you're going to live, you know, all that kinda stuff." Jeremiah tries to sound like he knows what he's talking about.

My phone buzzes, and I pull it out of my jeans.

"Who is it? Is it Addy?" Alex tosses a log into the flame, and it sends embers flying up into the air.

Hi handsome. Just wanted to tell you I love you. How's Alex?

He's OK. Happy, actually. I love you.

Good. I was worried.

Miss me?

You have no idea. Riley went to bed, Zoe Cam and Leah are a little drunk.

And what about you?

Well, I'm missing you. Badly ;)

A 5 min drive is about a 20 min run. If you keep teasing me I'll have to come home.

Stay. Have fun, make sure Alex doesn't overdo it.

:(

I'm going to bed soon. I'll think of you ;) Goodnight, my love.

K, that's it. I'm coming home.

Blaine!

Love you

"Welcome back!" Alex flicks a bottle cap at me when I put my phone back in my pocket and look up from my private daydream. "Well, what are they doing?"
"They're going to bed."

"Oh." He seems disappointed, maybe because there wasn't anything mentioned about Riley. "Let's get some tunes going!" He jumps up and runs into the house. Minutes later, two big windows open, and music starts thumping from the living room. We all sit around the fire, singing to the music and drinking beer like we're teens having a good time.

I haven't been drunk since my botched bachelor party in Cody. I think I've sworn off hard liquor. I'll stick to beer, and I pull another out of the cooler, twisting off the cap.

I have no idea what time it is when we pass out. When I wake up, the sun is just rising, and the fire is nothing but smouldering ash now. Jer is still asleep, curled in his chair like a giant baby, but Alex is nowhere to be seen.

"Alex?" I call out, and Jer stirs but doesn't wake up. My head is pounding, and my body aches when I get up from sleeping in the chair. "Alex?" I call him again, no response.

Staggering into the house, I need to use the bathroom badly. When I open the door I find Alex, passed out on the bathroom floor, one hand around the base of the toilet. I kick his shoe with mine. "Alex, wake up." He grumbles something incoherent.

"Buddy, wake up. I gotta use the toilet."

"Man...Just go." He attempts to sit and wipes drool from his cheek.

"No, get out. Come on; get up!" I help him stand, and he braces himself on the counter top. Trying to adjust his eyes, he looks at himself in the mirror.

"You're such an idiot," he says, either to himself or to me.

"What?"

"Nothin'. Where's Jer?"

"Outside sleeping." I nod at the door. "I don't need help.

His good mood from last night is gone, and the little jerk that I saw at Zeke's and met in Addison's small kitchen is back. *Wonderful.* He leaves, and I slam the door behind him.

I wash my hands, and when I start to dry them, I hear the music start to thump again. The bass rattles some frames on the wall; they're dusty old shadowboxes with dried flowers. I'm sure they're from Jer's moms gardens. She would turn in her grave if she saw how he let them get overgrown. The flowers eventually died, and Jer didn't seem to care; after all, his parents were dead, too.

The house isn't falling apart, but it is dusty and hasn't changed much in years. I really should take some time and help him around here instead of my house all the time, especially after everything he's done for me. And in this moment, I feel like an ass for never thinking of it until now.

"Bro!" Alex, or *Dr. Jekyll,* as I'm close to calling him with all his mood changes, calls from the kitchen. "Breakfast of champions!"

The toaster pops up, and he drops two waffles on a plate and slides it down the counter to me. I shrug, grab syrup from the fridge, douse them with sweet maple goodness and devour everything on my plate in about five forkfuls.

"Thanks," I manage to say with a mouthful of waffle.

"No problemo." He slides two more frozen waffles into the toaster and pushes the lever down. "Well, good morning, sweetheart!" he says to Jer, who has just joined us.

"Mornin'." Jer looks about as good as we do, and walks even worse. "I hurt. Everywhere."

I laugh, and he sits down at the kitchen table, holding his head in his hands. "Getting' too old for this shit, eh?" I joke and scoop coffee grounds into the coffee maker on the counter.

Alex grabs the remote for the stereo off the counter and turns down the music. The toaster pops, and he puts a plate on the counter, piling two waffles on.

"Here ya go, old man." He slides it toward Jeremiah who grumbles and stands up to get his breakfast. "So, what's the plan for today guys?"

"Can we wake up first?" Jer groans.

The coffee is percolating, and it smells amazing, exactly what I need to get it together. Jer covers his waffles with even more syrup than I did and eats them like a sandwich. Syrup's running down his fingers, but he doesn't even bother to stop it, just lets it pour down on his plate.

"Jer! You're making a mess." Alex scolds him, and I can't help but laugh at how domesticated they've become with each other. Definitely the odd couple.

The coffee finishes dripping, and I pour a steaming cup of "I have a hangover and I need to wake the hell up" and walk outside to sit on the porch. The sun is up and blazing already; it looks like it's going to be a good day. The clock on my phone says it is 8:34 AM, so I call Addison, hoping she's awake.

"Good morning," she answers, and I can hear the smile in her voice.

"Hi, baby."

"Mmm, you sound groggy. Have a late night, did we?"

"Little bit." I clear my throat. "What are you up to?"

"Well, the girls want to go out for breakfast so we're going to Lake's. Wanna meet us there?"

I take a big sip of black gold. "Umm, yeah. Okay."

"And bring those two—let's get this over with." She's clearly talking about the pregnancy bombshell.

"Kay, see you soon. Love you."

"I love you. And I missed you, very, *very* much last night."

This girl is going to be the demise of me. I feel myself start to get anxious with just her words.

"Addy, you're gonna get yourself in trouble. Lake's has big bathroom stalls, you know."

"I know." She laughs. "Bye!"

"Bye."

Hands slap my shoulders, and Alex almost jumps from behind me. How does he go from sleeping on the bathroom floor to perky and upbeat in five minutes? Must be his age; I guess I used to be like that too. And that thought makes me feel old. I finish my coffee and take the mug back in the house.

"Get cleaned up; we're going to Lake's for breakfast."

Jeremiah looks anything but enthused.

"With the girls." I add. And he smiles, gets up and heads into the bathroom. The shower starts, and he's in and out in minutes, ready to go.

The efficient staff at Lake's pushes two tables together to accommodate all of us. The girls are already there by the time we arrive, scanning the massive breakfast menu.

"Hey, boys!" Riley waves to us when we walk in, like we wouldn't notice them all sitting there. Alex lights up and goes to sit between her and Addison. When he does, Riley gives him a kiss on the cheek, and he whispers something in her ear.

Since the only two seats are either between Zoe and Leah or at the end of the table, I don't get a chance to pick as Jeremiah swiftly sits beside the two girls and puts his arms on their shoulders.

"Ladies, how are we today?" He's got his game face on. "You're all looking lovely this morning."

They giggle.

"Jeremiah, behave yourself." Addison narrows her eyes playfully. "You be nice to my girls."

"That's *exactly* what I am doing, thank you!" He's on a roll today, and we haven't even ordered yet.

I haven't seen Addison since last night when I left the house. She's got her hair down, my favourite way. It's falling over her shoulders in long perfect curls, and she's wearing a sexy blue dress with a low neckline which lets me see her...*Oh, Lord*...chest.

Come to think of it, I think it's the same one she was wearing the first time I saw her at Zeke's. As everyone makes conversation around the connected tables, I watch her while she peruses the menu, her eyes trailing along the words, and her long lashes batting gently. She catches my gaze and smiles at me.

"Love you," she quietly mouths the words to me.

"I love you," I whisper back.

Sadee is our server again, and she lights up when she sees us. "Hi, everyone! So good to see you!"

"Hey, Sadee, how's it going?" I smile and introduce the faces she doesn't recognize, the four women at the table looking very out of place.

"It's great! Has everyone had the chance to look at the menu?" She eagerly looks at us, pen and spiral notebook ready.

"I think so!" Addison smiles, looking around, and everyone nods.

I order a hearty omelette filled with red peppers and onions, shredded cheese, spinach and ham. I add on thick toast and diced potatoes on the side—and, of course, black coffee. When Sadee places it on the table in front of me, I nearly salivate, the steam from the eggs wafting into the air and right into my nostrils. This beats frozen waffles hands down any day.

All the girls order pancakes. I guess I didn't pay attention when they ordered because what comes out on the plates don't look like any pancake I've ever seen. They're stacked and oozing strawberry sauce, covered with a mound of whipped cream and blueberries sprinkled around the base of the pile.

I've finished my omelette in record time, and when I take a piece of toast to slather jam on, I feel someone watching me. Her blue eyes are blazing, and she's got a devilish grin on her pretty face.

What is she up to now?

A finger slowly dips into the whipped cream on her plate, and she closes her eyes and puts it into her mouth, tormenting me while she sucks the sweetness from her fingertip. When she opens her eyes, she smirks, and I narrow my stare. She knows how to get me going.

I guess a stall in the bathroom will have to do because I don't think I can let her out of here without being inside of her first. We are completely oblivious to everything and everyone around us; it's like a blur of noise and colors just whipping by, and we're in our own private moment.

"Addison?" No one is paying attention but her. "Can I talk to you outside for a sec?"

She smirks and wipes her mouth with a napkin. "Of course."

"Where are you going?" Riley calls after her.

"I'll be right back!" She smiles and follows me out the door, and the little bell dings when we leave. "Everything okay?" she asks once we're in the parking lot.

I take her hand and lead her to the side of my truck, facing away from the building, with nothing but trees around the back.

"No, it's not okay," I say sternly, trying to not smile and to shield my face from her as we walk.

"Babe? What's wrong?"

I push her up against the side of my truck, putting a hand on the glass window on each side of her head.

"Listen here, *little miss*." I narrow my eyes. "You can't just tease a man like that in a room full of people and not expect him to—"

She cuts me off by throwing her arms around me and pulling me into a deep kiss. I move my whole body closer to hers and press the hard ridge in my jeans against her. She moans quietly, and I tongue her deeper. I'm not sure how long we're standing there, devouring one another completely. I lift her leg so it's resting on my hip and I push against her, desperate to be inside.

"Baby," she breathes.

"I told you this was gonna happen." I kiss her neck and shoulder, only stopping long enough to let each word out. Her skin is soft and sweet; I pull down the strap of her dress and gently bite her shoulder.

"I can't stand it anymore. *Please*, baby."

I apologize to myself and the rage that's building in my pants, and I pull away from her slowly. Her eyes are closed, and she's breathing heavily, her chest rising and falling rapidly. Composing myself, I pull her strap back up with my finger and smooth her hair over her shoulders.

"You aren't the only one who can tease around here," I smirk, and she drops her jaw.

"You. Are...So mean!" She pouts and runs her hands through her hair, turning around to look in the reflection of the dark windows, checking to make sure it doesn't look like she's just been ravaged—well, almost ravaged, anyway.

I chuckle, very proud of myself for getting her worked up, and not giving in and tearing off her panties to make love to her right here in the parking lot of Lake's. And for not having an orgasm myself just from grinding against her beautiful body.

I kiss her softly. "Are you able to walk back in there now, or should I carry you?"

"I can walk, thank you very much. You know, you're gonna get it later!"

"Mmm, I hope so." I smirk, anticipating tonight. Maybe she'll wear my hat again...

CHAPTER SIXTEEN

It's in the early afternoon when we get back to the ranch. The girls talked about going riding, and Addison asked me if that was okay with me. I told her of course I didn't mind, what's mine is hers and besides, I think it would be fun to go out and see these city girls in a saddle.

Riley and Alex stay behind. He grabs a blanket from the house and lays it on the ground for her to sit on. We all know they need time to talk, so we're gone for what feels like a few good hours. Addison and Leah are gracefully riding Cylas and Roman. Leah actually rode with her in Maine, and she was quite enthused about showing off her skills. Zoe and Camille are each riding a horse for the first time today.

Jeremiah pulled out all the stops to play the best cowboy he could for the girls, wearing his hat and boots, even chaps. I laughed to myself when he walked out of the barn with them on. The girls all but fanned themselves at the sight of him, and he's now beaming while he's explaining all about Wyoming. I'm sure he's made some of it up, but they are eating it up like candy.

"Well, looks like you had fun," Riley shouts over to us once we reach the gate, shielding the sun from her eyes with her hands. She's sitting on the blanket with her legs stretched out, wearing a long strapless dress. She looks beautiful, and Alex is laying down with his head on her lap. The sight of them makes me smile. I look over at Addison who looks like she's about to cry; she smiles and waves at them.

"Riley, Alex! You guys missed all the fun!" Leah says melodically as she pulls the saddle off Roman and slings it over her arm like a pro.

"Oh, yeah? I'm sorry I missed out on walking bow-legged for the rest of the day!" Riley laughs and points to Camille and Zoe who are walking slowly like they've ridden on a barrel for hours.

"Oh, shut up, Riley!" Zoe laughs and bends down to wipe the horse hair off the back of her jeans. "It was worth it." She grins at Jeremiah, who is *Cheshire Cat*-smiling right back at her.

Addison's birthday is in four days, and tonight the girls are taking her out for a birthday/bachelorette celebration. I overheard a few random words like reservations, booze, singles, and chaps. Which only tells me two things: dinner and strippers. It will be a typical bachelorette party, I'm sure; the girls have been very secretive otherwise.

Jer and I bathe the horses and feed all the animals after our long ride. Alex is in the house with everyone else. He's been almost attached to Riley since she showed up, doting on her left, right and center. They actually look very happy together, and I hope everything works out for them.

"Alex took me aside earlier and asked me if Riley could stay with us until the baby is born," Jer says while he fills a water bucket with the garden hose.

I had no idea she wanted to stay in Wyoming. "Really? Wow..."

"Yeah. I said it was okay. I guess he'll be able to save some money to get a place of his own this way."

"Jer, you sure? I mean, she's not due until when? June?" I try and remember the date she told us. June the fourth, I think it is.

He shrugs. "It's a big house, needs life in it again."

"What's she gonna do about her son?"

"He said since her parents are flying in for the wedding, they'll bring him then and he'll stay." He fills another bucket with the hose.

Addison is in our bedroom getting dressed. When I walk in and close the door behind me, I have to lean against it because my knees almost buckle. She's standing in front of the mirror that's on top of the long wooden dresser, smoothing her hair with her hands. Her long red curls are flowing down her back, one side pinned back by a small silver comb with pearls on it. She's wearing a white cotton dress that ends mid-thigh, and it's completely strapless. A thin leather belt deliciously sits around her waist, and she's got the brown Dan Post cowboy boots I bought for her on.

"Do you really think I'm going to let you out of the house now?" I slowly walk over to her with my hands on my hips.

"Oh? This old thang?" She pulls the hem of the dress up to one side, showing even more skin than she already is. My heart starts to race at the sight, and I narrow my eyes at her.

"I miss you."

She leans over the dresser and looks closely at her reflection as she applies mascara to her long lashes. "I know, baby. I miss you, too."

"No." I sweep her hair from her back and stand behind her, leaning in to slowly kiss her shoulder. "I mean, I *miss* you."

"Mmm. Mr. Blackstock, are you trying to seduce me?" she asks in a low, raw voice.

I don't say anything back. I just trail my hands down her body, down to her bare legs and back up, lifting her dress with my fingertips. She's still leaning over the dresser; she's put the makeup down and is holding herself up with her palms flat on the wood. I can hear her breathing slowly but heavily, and she's got her chin resting on her shoulder to look back at me. Her white lace panties are barely covering anything, and I run my fingers up the back of her legs, over her behind and around her waist.

"Blaine, I..." She breathes. "You're going make me..."

She stands, and I turn her around and hold her hands together, putting them on my chest, over my heart.

"I love you, Addy."

She kisses me, her hands in my hair, then holding my face. "I love you, too. So very much."

I exhale deeply, and she leans her forehead on my chin. "When I get home, you better be awake." She looks up and me and grins.

"Or else."

And I don't even need to know what *or else* could entail; she makes it sound so intriguing I'm actually considering falling asleep.

"Cole! You are fucking hot!" Riley beams when we walk into the kitchen; I even see Jeremiah widen his eyes at the sight of her.

"Blaine, are you sure about this?" Riley asks.

I smile. "Have fun! She's only gonna get one of these things."

Riley is wearing another long strapless dress, her tan skin glowing either from the sun she got today or the pregnancy. Both, I'm sure.

Leah, Zoe and Camille are all wearing brightly colored cocktail dresses. They look like they should be endorsing bubblegum or Rodeo Drive or extras in another *Legally Blonde* movie. I can just see the local girls' faces when these five walk in, a high-end motley crew indeed.

"Bye, handsome." Riley kisses Alex's cheek, and he blushes. "Behave now, boys!"

I almost tell them to do the same, but I know they will. Well, Riley and Addison will without a doubt. The other three? Well, let's just say it wouldn't surprise me if they lassoed their first cowboy tonight. *Look out, men of Sheridan.*

Jer, Alex and I play some poker and drink some beer. A baseball game is playing on the TV for background noise.

"She's having a girl," Alex mumbles, looking down at his cards, and his forehead wrinkles. "Two pair! Ha!" He tosses his winning cards downs and laughs.

"Wow! Congratulations, man." I toss my cards, too, pouting on the inside that I thought I had the game won with my two kings.

"Awe, yeah!" He wraps his arms around the stacks of blue, white and red chips and pulls them into his small pile.

"I mean about the baby." *What a moron.* I roll my eyes.

"Oh, yeah. Thanks, man." He grabs our cards and starts shuffling them. "Jer said she could move in for a while until I get my...*our* own place."

"She's planning on living here for good?" I ask as I feel a little twinge of jealousy as I think of Riley spending all her time with Addison; between that and work means even less time for me.

"Well, maybe not forever. But she thinks this would be a good place to raise a kid." He shrugs and deals the cards out to each of us. "Plus, she can sell real estate anywhere."

"What about her son? What about his dad?" Jeremiah asks and tosses a card down, wanting to be dealt another.

"He's some dickhead deadbeat, never been around the kid." Alex curls his lip like he's disgusted by the thought of him.

It's almost midnight when Alex's phone buzzes. He answers it quickly. "Riley? Hello?"

I crack another beer and take a sip, curious as to why she's calling. I haven't heard from Addison all night.

"You're okay, though? Do you need to go to the hospital?"

Jeremiah and I both sit up in our seats and stare at him, waiting for him to tell us what's going on.

"Okay...yeah of course...twenty minutes. Bye."

"What's going on? She okay?" Jer plays with some poker chips in his hands nervously.

"Yeah, she's just not feeling well. She wants me to pick her up at some club. And I'm the only one here who hasn't been drinking."

I'm surprised and relieved when Alex tells us they're at the karaoke bar in town and not some strip joint. When we pull into the parking lot, the music is thumping out of the building. Some awkward voice is almost screeching a *Stones* song, and we all chuckle to one another and open the door to the bar.

The inside is just like the bar in Cody, except it less western-themed and more flashing lights. There's a big stage at the front with some scrawny kid up there who, judging by the group of kids cheering him on from a table near the stage and his Birthday Boy t-shirt, just turned twenty-one. The butchering of *Painted Black* ends, and Jeremiah is the first to spot the girls.

"Over there!" he calls out.

They're sitting together at a round table, all colorful and clapping kindly for the birthday boy, who stumbles over a chair while walking past them.

Poor kid. I smirk.

Alex finds Riley and bends down beside her, holding her hand. She smiles, and I can read her lips that she tells him she's okay. When I get closer, I realize I don't see Addison anywhere.

"Where's Addy?" I pull a chair up and sit beside Leah.

"Oh, she's in the bathroom. She'll be out in a sec!" She grins like she's up to something mischievous and casually sips on her pink drink.

"You okay, Riley?"

"Yeah. Thanks, Blaine. I just felt a little light-headed." She fans her face with her hand. "I think it was all the lights."

Soft music starts to play, a guitar and a violin, and my eyes trail up to the stage. A beautiful voice starts singing, and I'm frozen.

Cowboy take me away...

How have I not ever heard her sing like this before? My hands are tingling, I have goose bumps on my arms, and I can't believe what I'm hearing.

She's smiling, slowly swaying back and forth and tapping her fingers on her thigh with the hand that's not holding the microphone.

I'm so captivated I don't even notice that Leah crept up there with her and was singing in the background. All the kids at the birthday table are gaping, completely blown away, probably like everyone else in here. Riley is sitting back in her chair, a huge smile on her face, like she's witnessed this before. She seems thrilled to finally see her best friend open herself up and sing in front of people.

Addison gazes at me throughout the song. I don't even think I've been able to blink. She's a siren, singing to me, seducing me with her melodic chorus of adoration.

The song ends, but I don't notice until I hear everyone clapping. People are whistling, and every guy at the birthday table is standing and cheering.

"Yeah, Addy!" Alex puts his hands around his mouth and shouts loudly over the crowd.

I get up and walk over to the stage. She stands at the edge and smiles down at me.

"Hi." She grins.

"Hi, yourself." I run my hands up over the leather of her boots, up her bare skin and pull her down into my arms. "You're amazing."

"Right back at ya." She wraps her arms around my neck and leans down to kiss me. I completely forget that we're in a bar full of people, until I hear the cheering pick up again.

"Go, buddy!" someone yells.

"She's smokin'!" says another.

"Cowboy! Take *ME* away too!" a woman shouts, and I turn to smile. I slowly lower her back to the floor, back to earth from our short ride in the clouds, and she blushes and heads back to the table.

"Addy that was so crazy!" Zoe says excitedly and leans in to hug her when she sits down.

"You know that was all for you, right?" Leah elbows me. "Riley's fine."

I look at Riley, and she smirks.

"Thank you. I love you." I take Addison's hand in mine and lift it up to kiss her soft skin.

"So, what are you going to serenade me with?" She smiles and the girls all laugh.

"Oh, no. The cab of my truck and the shower are the only two places you'll ever hear me sing." I hold my hands up with declination and shake my head.

Addison doesn't sing again, but Leah and Jeremiah attempt a *Johnny* and *June* song, quite successfully, I think. Everyone cheers and applauds when they stand holding their hands together up in the air.

We sit and listen to a few more singers. The birthday table all get on stage (with the exception of the Birthday Boy), and they sing him some song about big asses that I've never heard of. A few staff members have to help to drunk kids off the stage, and we all clap and whistle for them.

Oh, to be 21 again.

The moonlight is pouring into the open window, the cool night breeze slowly crawling into the room, down the wall and across the floor. It makes its way up the bed and over our bodies.

We are laying in bed face to face, our arms over the covers with our fingers interlocked, talking about the day and how much we enjoyed it.

"I didn't know you could sing like that." I smile and close my eyes, remembering how she stood on that stage and captivated the whole room. No flash, no smoke machines or pyrotechnics—just a beautiful girl in a white dress singing a song to the man she loves.

"Well..." She blushes. "It's not something I brag about. My mom always said I should be a singer, but my heart is in medicine."

I lift her hand up to my lips and kiss it gently.

"I'm glad you liked it." She smiles. "It describes how I feel about you perfectly."

She moves closer, her warm body against mine, and she feels the stubble on my jaw with her fingers. "You're the best thing that's ever happened to me, Blaine."

I kiss the side of her mouth. "I love you."

"I didn't think I could feel this way again." Her eyes start to water. "Or have someone love me like this."

"Baby, don't cry." I frown and wipe a lone tear falling down her cheek. "You deserve the world; I want to give you everything."

"After Jacob," she sniffles, "I didn't feel like I was worth anything."

I inhale deeply at the thought of him, the sickening pit in my stomach when I picture him hitting her over and over again. I wince and close my eyes, exhaling.

"Addy…" I breathe.

"I know what you did in Maine. Alex told me."

"He did?" I am surprised. When did he tell her?

"He told me after you proposed to me."

"That piece of shit is lucky I didn't kill him." I inhale again, thinking of how satisfying it was driving my boot into his gutless body. "We don't have to think about him again, baby."

She kisses me. Her soft lips are warm, and she tastes like lime and tequila again. Margaritas. "I can't wait to marry you," she breathes in between heated kisses.

Taking her hand, I lift it over her head, and she rolls onto her back. I climb on top, parting her legs with my knee and resting between them. She moans softly as I kiss her face gently, lowering further and further down her body, her fingers still intertwined in mine. We make love deeply, passionately, completely raw. It feels like it's been so long since I've touched her, so long since I've felt her lips on me and her body around me, squeezing me. I'm lost in her hotness.

I have to grip the headboard and she runs her hands down my chest, her thumbs rolling over each of my abdominal muscles as my body thrusts and contracts. Like the rolling of a wave, I'm a fluid motion.

I hold on to the wooden board as hard as I can and growl loudly as she comes undone underneath me, crying out for me, calling my name. Her gaze and clenched muscles cause me to explode, and I crush my eyes closed as tight as I can, rippling out my gratification.

I fall onto the bed beside her, our chests rising and falling together, catching our breath. I smile and put my hands behind my pillow, resting my head in them.

"Shit."

"Mmm hmm," she hums and turns on her side to lay her head on my chest, my heart thundering under my skin.

Not a moment later, we hear our house guests cat-calling and yelling from their rooms. The sounds of them slapping the wooden floors with their hands makes me laugh out loud explicitly.

Addison buries her face in my chest out of embarrassment. "I forgot they were here!"

"You *ride* that cowboy!" one of them shouts, and I can't tell which one.

"Goodnight, girls!" she yells back, completely mortified.

The next morning is exactly as we both expect—completely obvious smirks and giggles from all four of them the moment our feet touch the bottom step leading into the kitchen.

"Good morning, *ladies*." I smile, trying my hardest not to bow; I'm sure Addison wouldn't be too impressed. "How did we all sleep last night?" I decide to stick to cheeky remarks. Yeah, that'll make less of an impact, I'm sure.

"Oh, we slept just fine..." Camille grins, but Addison cuts her off before she can elaborate in more detail.

"Okay, okay! That's enough!"

"What? Did I say something wrong?" Camille puts her hands on her hips and smiles at the others. "Or was I *too loud?*"

They all burst into laughter, Addison included, and she's gone from peachy blush to crimson in two seconds flat.

I finish filling my mug with coffee and sneak outside, quietly calling the dogs to follow me out.

"Hey! Where are you going?" One of them calls after me through the screen door.

"Off to work. Have a good day, ladies!" I chuckle, and I'm glad I'm not the one left in there getting interrogated left, right and center. *Sorry, baby.*

Tonight all the girls are going back to Maine, even Riley, though she'll be back in a few days with whatever belongings she can fly with and her son, Isaac. She told Addison she was going to wait to have him come out with her parents for our wedding, but she later changed her mind. I hope Alex is ready for all of this.

"Bye! I'm going to miss you all so much!" Addison hugs each of them tightly, all the ooh's and sobs between each embrace. I stand there looking out of place, not sure what I'm supposed to do during their goodbyes.

"See you in a few weeks! I can't believe you're getting married, Addy!" Leah starts to tear.

"Oh, Leah! Relax." Riley rolls her eyes and leans in to hug Addison, sandwiching her belly in between them. "See you soon, babe!"

Addison leans into me, her head on my shoulder as we watch them walk into the entry for their gate. I've got to say: I'll miss the liveliness and laughter while they're gone, but it'll be nice to get back to some peace and quiet...and no audience to cheer us on.

She falls asleep on the drive home from the airport.

"Baby, we're home." I lean in and unbuckle her seat belt and lift her into my arms to carry her inside.

"Mmm. I can walk." She groggily tries to stand, giggling softly when she stumbles on the steps of the porch.

"Clearly!"

"Hey, now." She smirks, and when we get upstairs, she pulls off her jogging pants and climbs into bed. She's out like a pretty little light.

CHAPTER SEVENTEEN

Today is April twenty-fourth. Today is also Addison's 27th birthday. I woke up extra early this morning to make her breakfast: omelettes, French toast and sausage.

"Mmm, that smells so good!" She says, standing standing at the bottom of the stairs, jogging pants on, and rubbing her eyes sleepily.

"Hey! You're supposed to stay in bed for this!"

She walks over to the island and sits down on a stool.

"Happy birthday, my love." I walk over and turn her stool so I'm standing in between her legs.

"Awe, thank you! This looks so yummy." She scans the counter top and picks a piece of red pepper out of the omelet, putting it into her mouth.

"Eat up; I have a big day planned for you." I'm so eager I could burst.

All the signs on the drive give my surprise away that I'm taking her to Yellowstone. I remember coming here when I was a kid. My school did a day trip here, and I remember back then how much fun it was. Not much has changed; we wander around the vast landscape, mesmerized by geysers and waterfalls.

Addison's mom calls her during lunch to wish her a happy birthday, and she almost starts crying at something her mother says.

"I know, Mom! Yes, I promise. Okay, love you too." She beams and when the call ends, she wraps her arms around me, breathing me into her. "I love you so much."

"I love you." I squeeze her tightly. "How's your mom and dad?"

"Oh, well she found out about Riley and the baby." She smiles. "She said she wished she knew earlier. I'm surprised she didn't find out sooner, but they're both excited to become grandparents."

"What's that look about?" I ask her, trying to determine what her expression means.

"Oh, nothing."

"Umm, yes. Something."

"She just thought I would be the first to have kids." She shrugs. "Whatever happens, happens."

I'm starting to wonder if she does actually want to have children someday, but today isn't the day to talk about it.

I change the subject. "Are you ready to go?"

I hold her hand and pull her toward the parking lot. "I have another surprise."

This time there aren't any signs that can foil my plans, and when we pull into the driveway of a big ranch, she looks over at me and narrows her eyes.

"What are we doing here?"

"Well, you'll have to wait and see." I'm not giving anything away.

I park the truck in front of a massive garage, right next to an even bigger house with giant pillars and windows everywhere. It's kind of like the Coles home in Maine, but more...Wyoming.

"Blaine! You're right on time! And this must be Addison. I've heard so much about you, my dear!"

"Addy, this is Lynn. She was my Mom's best friend. This is her place."

Addison smiles and shakes her hand. "So nice to meet you!"

"You are just lovely, Addison." Lynn hugs her and winks at me over her shoulder. "He better be good to you, or you come and tell me!"

"Oh, I will!" Addison grins at me. "He's pretty good though."

She still has no idea why we're here; it can't be just to meet my Mother's friend.

"Well, let's go over and see the babies, shall we?" Lynn hooks her arm in mine and leads us behind the house, down past the fencing and into pasture through a large steel gate.

Addison gasps and covers her mouth with her hands. "Blaine!"

"Now, they're all still very green." Lynn takes her hand and they walk over to a mare standing with a little brown colt. "I've been working with them, enough to get them used to me. You can put halters on them all except that one." She points over in the distance to a smaller Appaloosa foal.

The mare stands beside her little one, keeping an eye on the new stranger, and the colt leans his neck close to Addison's hand and sniffs it. Lifting his top lip to her flat hand, he nibbles at the air.

"What a darling!"

"He's a warmblood, and he'll be a big boy when he's done growin'. At least seventeen hands!" Lynn says and slowly touches his mane. "I told Blaine that if you need any help at all, I'm just a phone call away."

It dawns on Addison, and she turns and looks at me, mouth open and eyes wide. "Wait...*what?!*"

I walk over and hold her hand. "Which one would you like?"

"Are you serious? I...I don't know what to say!"

"Well, it's a big decision! You'll have a lot to do, but with the right training, you'll have yourself a wonderful horse." Lynn smiles and starts walking over to a pair of twin foals with their mother.

"Baby, I can't believe this!" She's still bewildered. "How much is this going to cost?"

"What? Don't even worry about that. It's your birthday." I kiss her hand, and we follow Lynn.

After spending a little time with each of them, she wanders back over to the first colt, the brown warmblood.

"I really like this little guy." She bends over and slowly extends her hand to him again, this time with a bunch of green grass in it. He walks over to her and eats it right out of her hand.

"He seems to like you, too!" Lynn elbows me. "I'm so happy, Blaine. Your momma is, too; I know it." She says it quietly and looks up to the heavens, closing her eyes.

"Thank you, Lynn. This means so much to me." I hug her, and for a few seconds, it's like hugging my mom. At least, it's as close as hugging my mom that I can imagine. Since Lynn loved her, then she's got to be a part of her.

"I think he's the one, Blaine!"

"Good lookin' little guy, too," I say, smiling.

"Now all you have to do is think of a name for him!" Lynn rubs the face of the mare and scratches under her neck. She extends it and leans into Lynn's shoulder.

We make plans to pick the mare and colt up next week; the mare will just come along for safe travel from one home to another. I think Addison thanked and hugged Lynn at least fifty times before we left; she's a kid on cloud nine. Every time I look over at her on the drive back, she's grinning, looking out the window and singing softly to the music on the radio.

"I can't believe you bought me a horse! Thank you, baby." She reaches over and holds my hand.

"Anything for you." I kiss her fingers and hold her hand close to my heart.

Everyone has parked behind the house, so she's got no idea when we pull in what's waiting for her inside. Maria and Kelsey even had the lights off when we showed up so that she couldn't see inside the windows when we are walking up to the house.

"Surprise!"

Addison gasps and covers her face.

Alex, Jeremiah, both of my brothers, all their kids, my Dad, Ruth and two other of her friends from the hospital—and of course Maria and Kelsey—are all standing in the house when we walk in.

"You guys!" Addison starts to cry, fanning her eyes with her hands. She laughs and hugs Maria and Kelsey who are standing right in front. "Thank you!"

The sirloin steak, lobster tails, twice-baked potatoes, asparagus and cheese biscuits were all catered for her birthday. They had to find the extra leaves for the eighty year old table in my dining room; to accommodate the extra guests it's extended to twelve feet long.

"Blaine, you are so sweet!" Maria gushes when Addison tells her about me taking her to Lynn's.

I smile and cut my slab of steak.

"How is Lynn doing? I haven't seen her in ages." Dad perks up in his seat. "Still livin' in that big place by herself?"

"Yep. She's doing really well, Dad. You should go see her sometime." I shove steak into my mouth. It all but falls apart, and it tastes better than anything I've ever made. "She'd love it."

"You hear that, Nicholas?" He raises his voice to my brother who's sitting across the table. "You wanna take me out there sometime?"

"Of course, Dad." He smiles with a cheek full of food.

My dad got his license revoked about eight years ago when he had a *small episode*—that's what we call it when he's around—but the doctors said it was a T.I.A.: Transient Ischemic Attack.

I was still boggled until an older nurse at the time rolled her eyes and said, "A mini-stroke." So he's unable to drive himself anywhere. Thankfully he already lived with my brother at the time.

"Addison, how's the wedding planning coming along?" Dad turns to her, sitting right beside her across the table from me. "The girls don't talk about it when we're around."

Maria winks at Addison, and they smile without giving anything away. "It's going to be beautiful, Bennett. You'll just have to be patient!" Kelsey chimes in.

Casey bounces in her chair. "Uncle Blaine, I'm still gonna be your flower girl right?"

"Of course you are, sweetie!" Addison peeks around my Dad to see Casey's excited face. "How could we get married without a beautiful flower girl?"

Casey settles back down in her chair, beaming with happiness, and I'm sure full of anxiousness for her big flower girl debut.

"This is just...wow. Thank you all so much!" Addison gazes widely at the array of desserts placed on the table once everything else is cleared. Cheesecake, of course, and when she sees it she looks over to me and grins. There's also carrot cake with the creamiest frosting I've ever seen, and lemon bars sprinkled with powdered sugar.

Kelsey stands in the doorway behind Addison and grabs my attention. She nods her head toward the kitchen, and I stand up to follow her.

"This one is for her. We thought you should take it in." She holds up a small plate with a huge white cupcake on it, covered with small sugar flowers and pearls. It's almost too elegant to eat.

"Thank you, Kels." I smile, and she gives me a small but warm hug. When I get to the doorway, I light the single candle and everyone sings happy birthday to Addison. I take her hand and kiss it once I've set the small plate down on the table in front of her.

"Happy birthday, beautiful."

She sticks out her bottom lip. "Thank you."

"Happy birthday, old lady!" Alex, who has been pretty quiet all night, missing Riley, no doubt, shouts from the end of the table. She sticks out her tongue at him.

"Hardly!" Kelsey hisses, and he smirks at her. I chuckle to myself. I'd love to see her try to boss that kid around like she does with everyone else.

After dessert, Jeremiah and I start a fire outside. We pull all the lawn chairs around the growing heat, and all the birthday guests trail out of the house and sit down with some sort of spirit in their hand.

"Happy birthday, sweetheart." Ruth hugs Addison. "We've got to work early, so we're going to get going."

"Awe, thank you so much for coming!" She hugs Ruth and then the two others, Leanne and Olivia. "It meant so much to me!"

"Blaine, you're a darling. What a beautiful night." Ruth hugs me, too.

"Oh, that was all those two. No birthday is a small occasion around here." I smirk and point over to my sisters-in-law, who are sitting next to their husbands around the fire.

"Goodbye, ladies! Thank you for coming!" Maria shouts from her seat and smiles warmly.

After they've gone, I go inside to get myself a beer. My Dad follows me in.

"Blaine, come with me." He starts walking toward the staircase, and I follow him, wondering where he's about to take me. At the top of the stairs, he reaches up and pulls on a short rope, bringing down the large wooden set of stairs that leads up to the attic. It creaks as it comes down, as it hasn't been opened in years.

"Up there." He points. "There's a trunk, a big brown one. Open it and let me know what's in it."

I look at him questionably, but do as I'm told.

The attic is exactly as you'd expect—old, dusty, and warm. There are boxes upon boxes, old lamps and old chairs with torn seats or broken legs. In the corner by the only window to the outside is a large trunk. The locks aren't closed, and when I open it, the smell of mothballs and old linen trails into my nostrils.

"Okay, Dad, there's some sheets..." I lift things up here and there, trying to see what else there is to find. "Some books, a few boxes..."

"Is there a pink box?" he shouts from the bottom of the staircase.

"Umm..." I search and find it under a stack of old newspapers. "Yeah, one right here."

"Bring it to me, please."

I slowly back down the stairs and hand the box to my Dad. He carefully opens it, closing his eyes like he's praying. When he reaches in, his eyes open and they're full of tears. He clears his throat and composes himself, pulling out a small string of pearls.

"These are your mother's."

I stare at the delicate string of beautiful and imperfect pearls; they look so small and fragile in his old, worn hand.

"I want you to give them to your beautiful bride." He examines each bead and rolls them between his fingers. "Your mom wore these on our wedding day."

I feel myself starting to choke up. "Dad...Are you sure?"

"I'm sure, my boy. I'm sure." He looks up at me with glistening eyes. "That's what she would want."

"Thank you."

He passes me the pearls, almost hesitantly, as it's like he can feel her in those beads and doesn't want to let her go. I take them into my hands and then do something unexpected.

I hug my father. Not just some small embrace, but I fully engulf him in my arms. He seems surprised at first, but when I feel his body relax, he puts his arms around me, too.

"Thank you, Dad." I start to cry. "I'm sorry."

"You're sorry? Whatever are you sorry for?" He's still hugging me, and I'm quickly transformed into a small five year old boy again. I've just wet my bed, and this time he's not angry; he hugs me back and tells me it's okay, that it's nothing to be sorry for. This is what I've missed out on; this is what most kids get on a daily basis from their parents. This is all I've ever needed.

"I'm sorry Mom died." I choke on my tears. I can't control myself.

"Blaine!" He releases me and pushes me back from him, his hands on my shoulders. He looks terrified. "Please!"

I'm standing in front of him, a thirty year old man, wiping my tears and sobbing like a baby. I still have the pearls clutched tightly in my hand, like I'm the one afraid of letting them go now.

"She gave me *you*." He clears his throat again. "If it was between you or her, and she had a choice, you'd still be standing here in front of me today."

I sob.

"I'm the sorry one, Blaine. You deserved much more than I gave you."

"You gave me everything, Dad." I hug him once more, desperate to feel that warmth again.

We both compose ourselves, and I nervously start to laugh. I feel so much better; I've swallowed this down over and over again for my entire life. Finally I became too full and ready to overflow.

I put the pearls back into the box and close the lid. I put the box on my dresser for now; I'll give them to Addison later, when we're alone. We go back downstairs where everyone else is still sitting outside around the fire.

"Hey, there you are!" Addison leans up in her chair, and I bend down to kiss her cheek. "You okay?" I guess she can see the redness in my eyes.

"Yeah, I'm great." I smile and sit down beside her.

Alex has just told everyone about Riley, the baby, and their plans for her to move to Wyoming.

"Babies are truly a blessing. You're going to make a great father, Alex." Maria beams from her chair and looks lovingly at her own three children. "When are you two planning on having little ones?" she asks, looking over at Addy and me.

Addison smiles at her. "Whatever happens, happens."

It's her usual saying for things that life delivers. I'm really curious now, and I've decided that I can't hold off asking her why she doesn't seem eager to have children. Aren't most women at some point in their lives? I won't do it now, but when we're alone. No one mentions babies again during the rest of the night.

We say goodbye to everyone. My Dad shakes my hand and winks. I'm thankful he does because if we hug again, I'll probably wail some more.

"Thank you so much, girls. You're wonderful. I can't get over how lovely this night was." Addison calls over while they're each getting into their cars.

"Tired yet, birthday girl?" I ask, trailing my fingers down her spine and gently patting her backside.

"Exhausted," she breathes.

"Well, I better get you up to bed then." I smile and swiftly scoop her up in my arms. She laughs and kisses me deeply.

Upstairs in our bedroom I lay her down and she scoots to the middle of the bed.

"Take that dress off, please." I grin and she sits up, lifting the dress over her head, throwing it onto the floor. She lays back down against the pillows, only wearing her bra, panties and a small grin of her own.

I walk to the end of the bed and start to slowly unbutton my shirt. I shrug it off my arms and it falls on the floor. Next comes my signature white t-shirt; I lift it off my body even slower, letting her see me inch by inch. Once it's off my head, I narrow my eyes sensually at her. She chews on the corner of her lip and shifts in the bed. She's anxious, and I fucking love it.

"So, birthday girl, did you get enough presents today?" I bite my lip, too, and run my hand across my abdomen, slowly over each muscle.

"Definitely not," she breathes, her eyes blazing sapphire.

"Oh, no? Is there something else you want?" I ask huskily while unbuckling my belt. I ease the leather strap from the loops in my jeans.

She's panting now, and I'm trying my hardest just to keep myself controlled.

"Get up here, Blackstock," she commands, impatiently.

"Mmm mmm." I shake my head. "Not yet, darlin'."

I unbutton my jeans and pull them open; pushing them down, I'm left in my boxers. I climb over the end of the bed and crawl in between her legs. Her scent intoxicates me as I run my nose up her chest and into her neck. I kiss her soft skin gently, not touching her anywhere else. She's breathing heavily, lifting her body into mine.

"I want you so bad," she whispers in my ear and sucks my earlobe. I close my eyes and push my body down into her.

I'm going to try and draw this out as long as I possibly can. I lower myself down her body, slowly kissing every inch, pulling on the edge of her panties with my teeth and kissing from hip to hip.

"Blaine, I can't handle this!"

"Yes, you can." I inhale between kisses. And she grabs a handful of my hair in her hand, gripping tightly and breathing heavily. Her panties end up on the floor with her dress and my clothes. I lay down on my stomach and lift her knees up; she pulls them into her arms. I devour her right there, eating *my* piece of birthday cake, licking and pulling every tiny detail until she screams and shudders. Her knees fall, and her hands grip my hair again.

"Baby! Ahhhh!"

I withdraw my mouth, and her body even winces from my hot breath on her tender flesh. I take the same route back up her body, kissing her again, and she leans up to release the clasp on her bra, tossing it off. I have no idea where it ends up. I tower above her, holding myself up with my hands. She caresses my chest and holds my face with one hand.

We kiss, our tongues rolling all over the other, and I don't stop as I slowly pull off my boxers and ease my tip into her beckoning heat. Just the tip, though, and it drives her off the edge.

Her hips buck, wanting all of me. I give it to her, every inch and then some. I lay down on top of her, holding my weight up with one arm and the other gently squeezing her breast.

She bites my shoulder and digs her nails in my back. I know she's about to lose herself. I push in deeper and harder, and I feel her start to pulsate around me. The tightening grips me to the core, and we both orgasm at the same time.

A tangled mess of skin, sweat, heat, and bed sheets is all that's left in the aftermath. Panting, I lower myself down on her, still inside of her, and our bodies stay connected as one for just a little longer.

When I roll onto my side, I look at her beautiful face. She's looking at the ceiling and smiling.

"I have something else for you."

She looks at me like I'm crazy. "I don't know if I can handle anything else from you just yet."

"Okay, let's shower and then I'll give it to you."

She still looks unsure but smiles and agrees.

In the shower, I have to feel her again, and she doesn't resist me. She turns herself so her back is against me, and she places her hands on the tile of the shower wall. I pull her hair off her back, and it falls around her shoulder. I kiss her neck and back as I ease into her; this time I keep a slow pace, tenderly filling her over and over again.

When she unravels, she turns her head to the side and reaches behind mine to pull it down to kiss her lips. Breathing heavily into her mouth, I push the last inch in to her, and I can feel my knees start to buckle. I hold onto her hip tightly, and my body slowly comes down from its high.

***

"What's this?" she asks sweetly when I hand her the small pink box. She's sitting cross-legged on the messy bed with her wet hair wrapped in a towel.

"Open it."

She does and looks at me when she pulls out the string of pearls.

"They were my mom's." I clench my jaw, quickly pushing back my emotion. "My Dad wanted you to wear them on our wedding day."

"Blaine..." She breathes. "I don't know what to say. They're just...*beautiful*." They looked out of place in my Dad's hands, and even in mine. But they're just perfectly imperfect in hers.

I want to surge and tell her that he hugged me, and even though it would sound stupid to the most people, it was everything to me. But I don't tell her. I keep it to myself and smile.

The pearls go back into the box and she places it on the nightstand beside her side of the bed. Climbing into my arms, she hugs me. "Thank you for everything. I mean it—everything. I don't deserve all of this."

I look at her like she's insane. "You deserve everything, and I wish I could give it all to you."

"You've given me everything, and what have I given you?"

"Addison, don't be crazy. You're going to marry me." I decide now is the time. "You're going to be the mother of my children some day."

She looks away.

"Baby, why do you do that?"

"Do what?"

"Look away, or change the subject. Or shrug off the idea of having kids."

She inhales and leans her forehead into my shoulder. "I'm afraid."

"Afraid? Of what?" And I instantly think of my mother. "Because of what happened to my Mom?"

"No, of course not!" Her eyes are glistening with tears. "I've seen so much sadness, Blaine."

I feel awful for even asking; why would I do this on her birthday? "That doesn't happen to every baby, Addison."

"I know. I just remember Alex, and how scared my parents were." A tear spills from her eye, quickly followed by another. "I couldn't bear it."

"This is something we are in together. I want to have children with you; don't you want that with me?"

She burrows her head into me again. "I do want that. Of course I do."

"Well, it's a brave thing to admit your fears. Hell, think of how strong you are just by moving halfway across the country."

"Yeah..."

"Well, that was pretty gutsy in my book. You have more strength than you give yourself credit for."

"I love you so much, Blaine. So, *so* very much."

I lean back into the mattress and pull her down with me. She lays her head on my chest and trails her finger along my skin.

"I love you, beautiful. Happy birthday."

CHAPTER EIGHTEEN

Addison is back to work today. She's on six-day work weeks, twelve hour shifts, right up until our wedding. As much as I would love to, I don't interfere with her work. She loves it, and I love her. As much as I miss her, everything we sacrifice is worth it in the end.

On the home front, all the new fencing is complete, everything is spruced up, and the place looks amazing—better than it has in decades. I couldn't have done it without Jer or Alex.

The three of us are way back in the field on the side-by-side when my phone rings. I don't recognize the number, but I answer anyway.

"Hello?"

"Blaine? Oh, hello; it's Ruth. I'm calling from the hospital."

"Ruth? Hi; how are you?"

"Well, we need you to come down, please. Addison is okay, but—"

I panic. "What's going on?"

"Just come down, please. She's asked me to call."

"I'll be right there." I hang up the phone and turn to the guys.

"I gotta get back; Addy needs me." I jump in the side-by-side and quickly turn the key.

Alex drops his gloves and jumps in beside me. "What's happening?"

"I don't know. Ruth just called and said Addison needs me."

Jer hops in the back, and we race up toward the house.

I don't know how long it takes me to get to the hospital. I wasn't paying attention at all at thetime, just drove as fast as I could; worried about what I might be walking in to.

When I park in the visitor's lot I compose myself and walk quickly into the main entrance. "I'm looking for Addison Cole."

The receptionist at the desk smiles and tells me to wait a moment. She picks up her phone and dials a number, softly speaking into the receiver so I can't hear her.

"If you'll have a seat, sir. Someone will be right with you."

I can't read the expression on her face, and I don't say anything, I just turn around and sit down in an uncomfortable chair in a row of other uncomfortable looking chairs.

Minutes that seem like hours go by, and finally, I see the elevator doors open and Ruth step out with a man in a suit.

"Blaine, can you come with us, please?"

"Ruth, where's Addison?"

The man introduces himself as Peter O'Brien, the director of Human Resources. "Ms. Cole is upstairs in her unit. She's okay, we just had...an incident," he replies in a hushed voice.

We're in the elevator now.

"What kind of incident?" My skin is tightening, and my pulse is racing. Why can't they just spit it out?

"Blaine, do you remember Reid? He's a nurse here," Ruth says nervously.

"What about him?" I hiss. I start wondering if he's having me charged for knocking his ass out—is that why I'm here?

"He assaulted—"

I am faint, mush, tumbling. I'm death. "He...*what?*" I can't breathe.

"Blaine, please." Ruth motions to an office across the hall from the open elevator door. In the room Addison is sitting on a small sofa. Her eyes are bloodshot, and her face is puffy from crying.

"Addy, are you okay? What's going on?" I rush to her side and sit, grabbing for her hand.

"Mr...?" I didn't even notice the two cops in the room.

"Blackstock." I nod. "I'm Blaine."

"Mr. Blackstock. I'm Officer Herring." The older of the two introduces himself while holding a leather notebook in his hand, writing what I assume is my name down on the paper. "Ms. Cole was assaulted by a co-worker today. We have him in custody, thanks to Ruth here." He nods toward her and smiles softly.

"What did he do, Addy?" I choke out the words.

She wipes her eyes with a tissue and looks at me, and I don't know if I want to know. "Reid..." She winces when she says his name and looks down at the crumpled tissue, playing with it in her hands. "We just moved a patient into another room, and I was taking out some equipment when he locked the door. Trapped me."

"What?" I clench my jaw, feel like my thumping heart is going to explode.

Ruth pipes up when she sees Addison struggling to explain. "I knew it shouldn't take that long to bring out a C-PAP, so I went to find her. When I did, I saw through the glass that he was attacking her."

Addison inhales deeply, listening to what probably isn't the first recollection.

"My fingers just wouldn't work! I'm so sorry, Addison!" Ruth puts her head into her hands.

"Ruth! No! You saved me. Please don't cry." Addison stands to walk and hugs Ruth. That's when I notice her torn pants. She's holding onto one side to keep them from falling down.

"Addison." I breathe. "What happened?" I'm livid; I could choke the life out of Reid if I could get my hands on him. I thought what Jacob did was the worst I could imagine.

"Can I be alone with him for a minute please?"

"Of course, Ms. Cole. We'll be right outside." Officer Herring says, putting his notebook into his pocket, and they all leave the room.

She sits back down on the sofa again. "He kept saying how I was teasing him. But I wasn't! Baby, you know I wouldn't do that." She looks anxious and scared.

"Of course not. I know that." I take her hands into mine and hold them tightly.

"He pushed me down on to the bed. I tried so hard to fight him off." She pulls the hem of her destroyed pants open. "He tore my pants and..."

"And what?"

"He forced my legs open."

"Addison, did he rape you?"

She inhales deeply, and I can see a tiny bit of calm wash over her. "No, he didn't. Ruth got the door open in time, and she miraculously pushed him off of me."

"Oh, fuck." I flush. "Where is he now?" I search the room like I'm expecting him to be standing there. *Oh, how I wish he was right now.* "You're coming home; let's go." I stand and take her hand.

"I have to make sure I can first."

"What? No, let's go." I open the door and lead her out. "I'm taking her home."

"Addison, I'm so sorry about this. Please take as much time as you need." Peter frowns.

"Thank you, Mr. O'Brien. I'll be okay. I'm just so thankful for you, Ruth." She turns to Ruth and hugs her again.

"Ms. Cole, I'll be in touch in the morning. Okay?" Officer Herring hands her his card and offers a reassuring smile. "He's in custody right now. So please don't worry."

Outside I call Jeremiah, who's still at the house with Alex. "Jer, hey. Yeah, she's okay. Can you drive Alex into town to pick up her car? ...Okay, thanks."

I don't tell Jeremiah what happened because he'll tell Alex, and as much as I'd love to tag team this fucker with him like the last one, Addison doesn't need her brother and me ending up in jail next to the asshole. I narrow my eyes and clench my jaw when we pass the staff parking lot and I see his Lexus. I want to drive my truck over top of it.

"Baby, I'm okay. Really." She's somewhat smiling at me from across the cab of my truck. "I was just a little shaken."

"Addison, he could have—" I close my eyes, trying to smother the image. I remember my dream about him; I just knew he was trouble. I knew it. "I'm so sorry I left you that day. I walked away, and he could have done something to you then." I am sickened with myself for what could have been.

"No one knew what he was like, baby." She reaches over and takes my hand. "I know you're upset. Think about what I went through when Gwen tried to take advantage of you!"

I do remember, and for some reason, it brings some sort of clarity. "Yeah, but..."

"No "but"s. It's almost the same thing."

"We're just going to have to lock ourselves indoors from now on." I force out a smile.

"You can lock me up with you any day." She is starting to look like herself again, puffy eyes, torn scrubs and all.

When we get home, she takes a long hot bath, and I throw her clothes in to a garbage bag and toss them in the garage. I don't know if the cops will need them; they probably would have taken them if they did. Just to be sure, I'll keep them for now.

Alex flings open the screen door when he gets back to the house with her car. "Blaine, what is going on? Where is my sister?" He looks ready for a brawl, wide eyed, looking all around him.

"She's upstairs taking a bath. Sit down; I'll explain it all."

He sits, and I keep my end of the deal. I tell him what happened and it takes everything to keep him seated.

"What the fuck is wrong with people? Two fuckin' guys, Blaine. *TWO!*" He's talking about Jacob and Reid.

"I know." I sigh. "She tells me she's okay."

"Yeah, heard that before." He looks away and bangs his fist on the top of the wooden island.

"Alex?" She walks slowly down the last two steps of the staircase as we both turn around. You can see the sadness in her eyes, but she looks a little better. She's wearing her jogging pants and one of my t-shirts.

"I'm okay; I promise."

"Addy, I don't know what I would do if..." He gets off his stool and hugs her. She smiles at me over his shoulder.

"Nice to know I'm cared about."

"No one fucks with my big sister." He puffs his chest, and she smiles. "What's going to happen to him now?"

"Well, the police said that he'll be charged with assault." She sits down on a stool and turns to face the both of us. "Then it'll be up to a judge whether he's guilty or not. And if he gets time or who knows what."

"Guilty or not? I thought that woman from work caught him?"

"Ruth. She did, but who knows what story he'll tell." She rolls her eyes. "Either way, he's lost his job, and he's not allowed in the hospital unless he's brought in there for some emergency."

"He'll need the E.R. if I see him." I look at Alex and raise my eyebrow; he knows what I'm talking about. "Or the morgue."

"Listen, none of that. Okay? From either of you. I don't need you two in jail." She's good, knows us too well.

"I can't promise anything. Sorry," Alex says it, and I nod my head in agreement. I'm thinking the same exact thing.

She sighs, knowing there isn't any point to arguing with us, the two men who are ready to throw down for her any day, anytime, anywhere. She's loved more than she knows—or maybe she does know, and that's why she puts up with us.

Once Alex is convinced that she's okay and safe, he goes home. He takes the side-by-side down the dirt road so he doesn't have to call Jeremiah to pick him up.

We eat a small dinner, not talking about anything that happened today. Instead, she wants to talk about the wedding, which is a surprise since she's kept me in the dark for months. She hasn't even give me one slight detail except that it's happening here and the time I should be ready.

"The girls know a good baker for the cake. What flavour would you like?"

Of course Maria and Kelsey know a cake maker; they probably know a balloon and streamer maker, too. I bet they've got a Rolodex for party planning.

"Cheesecake?" I smirk, and she giggles. It's the most beautiful sound, and I haven't heard it all day. It warms my blood, and my heart finally recovers from the trauma of earlier and starts functioning again.

"What about carrot cake with cream cheese icing? Full of raisins and walnuts?"

She had me at cake; I just don't tell her. I'm a man. I don't care what kind it is; I'll eat it. "Sounds perfect."

"Okay! Carrot cake it is." She writes down in her wedding binder and quickly closes it when she notices I'm leaning over the table to take a peek at what's in there. So much for finding anything else out.

I yawn and sigh loudly.

"Tired?"

"Yeah, a little."

"Let's go to bed, babe." She reaches for my hand, and we head upstairs. Rex and Luca follow us up and lay on the floor at the foot of the bed. They say dogs can sense emotion; maybe they know something's up, and they want to be close to her.

She gets as close as she can to me, and I wrap my arms around her. I nuzzle into the back of her neck and breathe in the familiar scent of green apples. I can feel her body relax as she falls asleep.

I'm tired, but I can't sleep. I stare at the walls, the door, the ceiling, those twenty-seven knots again, the clock, the windows, my hand—anything to bore me enough to sleep. But it doesn't happen. I'm restless, and I try not to wake her up by fidgeting.

The last time I look at the clock, it's almost five in the morning. Great, I'm going to be dead on my feet in the morning for work. I hope the guys are ready to carry me around; I don't do well on fumes.

***

I'm awake when the sun rises; it was absolute torture all night long not being able to close my eyes and keep them shut.

I wanted to sleep so badly, but I just couldn't. My mind was racing, thinking about everything that's happened, everything that could happen in the future and how much I would lose it if she was hurt again.

The dogs whine at the door. I slowly climb out of bed, and they follow me downstairs so I can let them outside. I have to scold them when they bark at the other animals, even though they don't listen. I wonder why dogs do that; it's not like they're new cows, or chickens or horses. They're the same ones they see every day, yet they still have to howl at them.

Addison sleeps until almost two in the afternoon, which is very unlike her. She obviously needs it, and I even manage to keep Alex out of the house all morning. He kept wanting to go and check on her, even though I told him she was sleeping.

"Hi, guys." She smiles, holding four bottles of beer in her hands. "Thought you might wanna take a break."

"Hey, love. How are you feeling?" I walk over to her and kiss her warm cheek. It still has lines on it from lying on the pillow; she must have just woken up.

"Good, actually. I feel refreshed." She hands each of us a bottle and uses my t-shirt that she's wearing to crack the cap off hers. "So what are you up to?"

"Just tearing down part of this wall. It's starting to rot, and we need to replace it before it collapses." Jeremiah kicks the bottom of the rotted wood on a big section of one of the barn walls.

"Sounds like fun," she says. "Need any help?"

Alex drops his jaw, Jeremiah furrows his eyebrows, and I grin.

"You wanna help?"

"Well, yeah. So what?" She looks at all of us like it's the nineteenth century and she's telling us she wants to vote or something. "Mr. O'Brien called and asked how much time I wanted off. I said just a few days." She takes a sip and wipes a little bit off her mouth that escaped her lips.

The sight makes me harden slightly.

"So, I thought I could help around here and keep myself busy."

"Well, you could. Or..." I pull out my phone. "I could call Lynn and ask her if she can bring someone over today instead of waiting until the weekend."

Yeah, that worked. Rotted barn boards forgotten, she squeals in excitement. The idea of having her new little colt brings her eyes to life. "Really? Thank you, babe!"

Lynn loads up the mare and colt and is at the house within a few hours.

"He looks like he's grown so much in a week!" Addison holds her hands together under her chin in excitement as Lynn leads him off the trailer. The mare whinnies for him and stamps her hoof down.

"Oh, calm down there, Barbara. He'll be just fine without ya," Lynn calls into the trailer as if the mare can understand her. "Mares." She smirks and hands Addison the lead rope.

"Thank you so much! I love him already." She rubs his neck and her fingers flow through his mane. "Hi, my little guy."

In a sectioned off part of the pasture she leads her new colt around; he follows her almost like a dog. He's one of the calmest I've ever seen at this age, and I'm impressed with Lynn's progress. The other horses notice him right away, and they all end up standing at the fence that divides him from them. They whinny, and he perks up and whinnies back.

"Should I let him go?" she calls to me.

"Yeah, he'll be fine." I'm standing at the gate with the guys; she unclasps the lead rope and stands back to let him go. He trots over to the others, keeping his distance, but leaning in just close enough to smell them. Mischief rears, and it scares him. He turns and runs a few feet, then stops and looks back. He's not ready to be in with them yet. Maybe I'll put one of the other mares in there with him for now so he's not alone.

After we finish tearing as much wood out as we can, the guys go home, and Addison and I drive into town to Zeke's feed store. She's going to get her colt some new goodies; that's what she called them. My terms would be halter, brush, feed bucket—you know, all the things I already have around the farm. But she insists that he needs all brand new and all his own.

"Well, hey there, you two." Zeke's behind the counter, rolling coin when we walk in. "I haven't seen you in a while!"

"Hey, Zeke. How's it going?"

He ignores me.

"Ms. Cole, how's that big mally of yours? You haven't come in to get any treats lately."

I smirk and shake my head. This is the usual around other men; I'm nobody, and she's the only person in the room.

"Hi, Zeke. Luca's good." She smiles. "I know; I've been so busy with work."

"Well, what can I help you with today?"

"Blaine got me my own colt for my birthday!" She beams and wraps her arm around my waist.

Hmm, there ya go, Zeke, my friend. Eat your fuckin' heart out.

"Well, Blackstock. That was awful good of you."

"I'll need a new halter and lead rope..." She trails off and wanders down an aisle. I stand at the counter, and we both watch her.

"Never thought that was gonna happen, eh, buddy?" He taps my arm with the back of his hand.

"What?"

"That girl." He grins, and it makes me uncomfortable. "Remember that day? Oh, man. We were all gawkin' like horny kids."

"All right, all right." I cross my arms and refrain from telling him off.

She picks out royal blue everything, and I mean *everything*. Whatever a horse could possibly need at this stage in his life, she's put it all on the counter.

"Are you sure you got it all? I saw a few more shelves you didn't clear in there." I smirk as we climb into my truck.

"Hey! It's not that much." She turns and looks into the back seat at the bags. "Okay, maybe I went a little overboard. But I couldn't help it."

"Just think how much I'll spend when we have actual children to buy for."

I look over at her, and she smiles. "Should I get the boys to start building an addition to the house?"

"You just might have to do that!" She laughs and turns up the radio.

Her moods have been so good since the Reid incident. Too good, even. I'm afraid it all might collapse like a house of cards, and that this is a front she's putting up so I don't worry about how she's really feeling.

As it inches closer and closer to our wedding, Addison slowly transforms back into the girl I met almost a year ago. I was right about her enthusiasm being too good to be true, thought. She had a breakdown while we were in bed a few nights ago. I woke up to the sound of her sobbing, and I jumped up to turn on a light.

"Baby? What's the matter?" I held her in my arms and stroked her hair.

She melted into my body, her not saying anything was agonizing to me, but I knew she needed to just let go. Eventually she opened up and said she just felt like crying. She's been overwhelmed, and it just started flowing like a burst dam. Since that night, she's been wonderful. All the poison released from her body, and she's recovered in her own way, I guess.

Riley moved a few belongings to Wyoming; she's been staying with Alex and her son, Isaac, in Jeremiah's house. When she found out about what happened with Reid, she almost marched down to the jail herself.

"If I ever see that dick, I'll crush his balls." She held up her hand and tightly gripped the air. I think Jer, Alex and I all felt that one. "Cover your ears, baby," she says to her son.

Isaac smirked at his mother and covered his ears with his hands.

Addison went back to work after a week, and Ruth called to tell me she's been having great days. The Human Resources team would like her to talk to a counsellor, probably so she doesn't have a breakdown at work. She agreed and told me that she speaks to a kind woman at work.

She makes it an effort with her colt every night after work. She asks for my help sometimes, but other than when she asks, I don't interfere.

"Are you ever going to name him?" I joke while I bend down to pick up his hooves, checking each one.

"Well, yeah. I was thinking of a few names."

"Like what?"

"How about..." She stands back and looks at him, like she's done about a million times since his arrival. "Jax."

"Jax?"

"Yeah, he looks like a Jax."

I have no idea what a Jax looks like, but what my baby wants, my baby gets.

"Good, I'll get Lynn to start on his papers." This will be a little piece of ownership for Addison, which she'll probably frame and hang somewhere in the house proudly. "You'll need to think of a registration name for him too."

"Oh, really? It took me forever just to come up with three letters!"

"Well, you want to show him off someday, right?"

"Yeah." She smiles and hugs me.

I lean in and pick her up so she's lifted above my head. "Do you know how lucky I am to have you? You are everything to me."

She stares down at me with those big blue eyes, and her long red curls fall over my shoulders. "You are everything to me too, handsome."

"I finished my vows last night." I slowly stand her back on the ground, but she doesn't take her hands off me. She takes off my hat and puts it on her head, scruffs my unruly hair with her hand.

"You did? When?"

"You know what it does to me when you have that on," I tell her. This girl could convince me to rob a bank if all she was wearing was that Resistol.

"I know what *everything* does to you." She grins. "Tell me when!"

"Oh, right. When you were sleeping. I sat downstairs watching infomercials, and it all just flowed out." I try and sound like I knew what I was doing, when really what I had was a pad of paper full of gibberish and many spelling mistakes. I know what I want to say to her when we're standing hand-in-hand in front of God and all of our friends and family—that I love her—does there really need to be more than that?

"Well, I haven't finished mine yet. Still perfecting my masterpiece." She laughs and pushes my hat up off her forehead. "Blaine? Do you remember that day? Over there?" She nods toward the picnic table and starts slowly walking backwards.

"I remember." I follow her, narrowing my eyes and growing extremely hard.

"Well, good..." She unbuttons her blouse, and it falls open, showing her beautiful body. At that moment she turns and starts running, taking my hat off and holding it in her hands as she goes. I follow but can't catch her. Like a cat she climbs the steel gate and leaps over the other side, laughing the whole time.

"Come on, old man!"

Oh, she's really going to get it now.

I stop running and walk casually to the gate, opening it and closing it behind me. I look over at her and smile. This cat and mouse game we play keeps my blood thumping through me, and I love it. It's like the build-up to the best sex I've ever had, the anticipation of touch and taste and sparks.

She's standing by the picnic table now, shirt still unbuttoned and hat still in hand. I walk over and rake my hands through my hair. Then I pull off my t-shirt, throwing it over my shoulder, not breaking my gaze with hers. "Old man, huh?"

"Well..." She swallows and bites her lip.

"Well *what?*"

She knows she's lost this one. She drops my hat and almost knocks me over by jumping into my arms. We kiss, deeply and feverishly. I weave my fingers in her messy red hair and pull it down, forcing her face up. I suck and bite her neck.

"Ahhhh!"

"Mmm... What, baby?" I breathe.

"You drive me crazy!"

"Is that what you wrote in your vows?"

"Did you peek?" She giggles and kisses me again. We fall onto the ground, and she straddles my stomach, running her hands on my chest.

The sun blazes through the locks of her hair, igniting them, and she looks like she's ready to burst into flames. She sits up and unbuttons my jeans; I lift so she can pull them down, boxers, too. I am rock hard, and she grins when I break free from the clothing. I don't even notice when she takes off her own jeans; I think I was too busy being locked in her eyes.

When she eases on to me, I get a rush of tingles, and I have to lean my head back into the ground and close my eyes tightly. It feels like every time is our first time, and it's an indescribable sensation to be inside of her.

She rises and falls slowly, leans down to kiss me, and her hair falls in my face. She strokes my chest with her tongue, and I devour her shoulders and neck, high on my redheaded morphine again. I can't get enough.

CHAPTER NINETEEN

Three days. Three days until the *big day*. Maria, Kelsey, Riley and her son Isaac have been here from sunrise to sunset almost all week, whipping us guys into shape and getting the farm looking wedding-ready.

An enormous white tent arrives, and the crew it came with set it up to the right of the house. It has no sides but large towering peaks, like God had reached down and pinched a sheet on the ground, pulling it up toward the sky. Large beams on the inside keep the peaks up. It's amazing, and it's not even finished yet.

Day Two brings stacks upon stacks of wooden folding chairs and a trailer full of long tables. The guys and I set everything up with the direction of my relative party planners. Kelsey might as well have a whip in her hand. Maria tells her a few times to relax and reminds her that it's not her wedding.

"It's gotta be just right, Maria!" Kelsey whines.

"It will be. Just let the boys have their space." Maria winks at me, and I smile back. I want to stick my tongue out at Kelsey, who is almost pouting at this point.

Riley and Addison have gone into town to pick up their dresses, though I'm sure that's not all. When they return, they've got a truck full, just like I expected. Maria and Kelsey load bags into their arms and scurry into the house. I offer to help, of course, but I'm told not to look.

One of the bedrooms upstairs has been transformed into Wedding Central. The door stays closed, and I don't bother to look in. I'd probably be risking life and limb if Kelsey caught me.

Tonight everyone from Maine flies in—Mr. And Mrs. Cole, the girls, and Riley's parents. We have two vehicles to pick them all up at the airport from their 5:15 flight.

"Just look at this place, Richard!" Lillian gasps when she steps out from Addison's car and takes in all the wedding decor. "It's just breathtaking!"

Addison takes her parents into the house and she and her mother go upstairs to the room they'll be staying in.

"Now who is this beauty?" Richard stands at the fireplace and points at the photo of my mother.

"That's my mom." I smile, looking at her. I wish she was here for all of this, for her to tell me I'm going to be a good husband and she's proud of me.

"Lovely woman...Just lovely." Lillian walks up behind me and smiles warmly. "When are your brothers and father going to be here?"

I look at the clock on the wall. "In about an hour."

"Well, my dear. What can we do in the meantime?" She looks at Addison and crosses her arms on her chest. "Anything your dad and I can help with?"

"Actually, yes; come with me!" She grins and takes her parents by their hands, leading them outside.

Once Nick and Owen arrive with their kids and my Dad in tow, it's time for dinner. Because there are so many people in the house, we all eat outside, enjoying the beautiful evening. Jeremiah makes another fire, probably the thousandth one he's made over these years.

Isaac fits right in with the other kids, and they all run around the yard, playing in the massive tent. Kelsey gets after them a few times, like an uptight mother hen, or an anal perfectionist. Take your pick. My nephews Bobby and Alex take turns driving them around in the side-by-side when they get bored with the tent, which relaxes Kelsey.

Riley's parents, Ann and Clive, seem like very nice people. They're staying at Jer's for the duration of wedding. They are eagerly awaiting the arrival of their second grandchild, and even though they seem sad she's living out here now, they said they're happy as long as she's happy.

"Addison, you've got some catching up to do!" Ann grins, and Lillian nods happily in agreement. Richard shifts in his seat, probably uncomfortable with the talk of his daughter making babies.

"We do." She smiles and takes my hand in hers. "We're going have to put an addition on the house for all the children, right, babe?"

I smile, remembering our conversation about kids in the truck after the shopping spree at Zeke's. "That's right."

I squeeze her hand and rub her fingers with my thumb, envisioning all the practising we will have to do.

Tomorrow is the last day of details. Then it's all or nothing, and the day will be a blur, I'm sure of it. We both try and fall asleep after such a long day, but to no avail. We're wide awake.

"Are you ready for this, baby?" she whispers softly.

I turn on my side and look at her. "Of course I am. Are you?"

"Yes. I was just making sure." She's looking up at the ceiling and smiling.

"You're going to make the most beautiful bride; I can't wait to see you."

"This is our last night together you know."

"I know." I kiss her hand and she places it on my cheek, gently feeling my stubble.

I want to make love to her so badly, but the last time we had company, we gave them quite the vocal show. I press into her, my growing erection sliding against her heated skin, and she turns to look at me.

"My parents are across the hall!"

"So."

"So?"

I smirk. "There's no gun under your dad's bed this time."

"Blaine!" She whispers. "I can't be quiet when you touch me; you know that."

I grin. "Oh, I know. Let's have a shower then."

The sound of the water will hopefully drown out most of the noise. I just want to feel her; I don't care if we even have to go outside.

"Or we could go outside..." I slyly suggest.

"Shower. Let's go." She whips the sheet off and strips her t-shirt while skipping toward the bathroom.

I make sweet and deep love to my girlfriend for the last time tonight. She holds my hand against her mouth and bites down when she's splitting at the seams. Her soft moans are muffled by her clenched jaw and the water from the shower.

The next time I do this, it'll be with my wife. The thought drives me crazy, and even though she's unhinged, I thrust deeper and faster. Her eyes go wide, and she looks like she could scream. Her palm slaps the glass wall, and she ripples again. When I release, I feel light-headed and almost crumble to my feet.

The heat from the water and the electricity flowing in my veins is almost too much. Is it going to be like this every time? No one has ever made me feel like this; our connection is unlike any other I've experienced. I never want this to end.

I slowly lean down the tile, sitting under the shower head.

She slides down and sits with me. "Are you okay?" Her hands are holding my face, and I catch my breath.

"Yeah. I hope we were quiet enough."

"I think so. You sure you're okay?" She looks at me with concern in her eyes. "Do you want me to turn the shower off?"

I take her hands and hold them in mine, pulling her to sit on my lap, the water still rushing out like a waterfall down onto us.

"Do you feel it, too?"

"Feel what?"

"Feel like you could just...*explode*."

"When we're making love? Every time." She giggles and looks away from me and blushes. "After that time in the barn I had to seriously consider doing it again. My heart didn't stop racing."

I look surprised. "Really?"

"Blaine, I don't think you know what you do to me." She blushes again and wipes the water from her face. "After that day, when you punched Reid, I was devastated. Not only because I thought I lost the one person I loved most, but also because I couldn't imagine anyone else touching me like you do. Or making me feel like this."

"Let's go to bed, my love." I smile, and we somehow manage to get to our feet and out of the shower. We both fall asleep quickly. Tomorrow night she'll be in this bed alone, and I'll be at Jeremiah's.

Just as I expected, the entire day was a blur. By the afternoon, the guys and I were pretty much told to leave. All I was able to do was give Addison a quick kiss before Maria and Kelsey shoved me into the driver's seat of my truck and stood in the driveway to make sure I was actually going to leave.

"Hey, you," Addison calls my cell as I'm driving away. "I just wanted to tell you that I love you."

"I love you too, beautiful. I'll call you tonight."

"Okay, bye."

Jer, Alex, Dad, my brothers and I have some dinner and drinks. Dinner consists of wings, ribs and wedges, compliments of Jesse Wolf. Drinks are about three cases of beer. It should suffice for my last day as a free man—or so my brothers both tell me. Dad falls asleep on the couch after we eat, and we don't hear from him for the rest of the night.

I try not to drink too much, but I lost count after...a lot. Bottles are all over the ground under my lawn chair, and we're all sitting around Jer's biggest fire yet.

"Those feet gettin' cold yet?" Owen flicks a bottle cap at me and laughs.

I stretch out my feet and look at them. "Nope. They're nice and toasty."

"You're lucky, man. Girls like her don't come around too often," Nick chimes, in and Owen shakes his head in agreement. "Maria just loves her."

"That makes two of us." I smile and chug the remnants from beer number...well, more than ten, less than 20.

I promise myself not to pass out in the chair and sleep outside again; the last time I did, was stiff for hours—and not in the good way, either. When I know I've had enough, I stand up and stagger into the house. "G'night boys!" I call back to them and wave my hand in the air.

"You sure are a cheap date!" one of them, not sure who, calls back to me. They all laugh.

Dad is snoring loudly on the couch, and I pull off a quilt from the rocking chair and cover him with it. He smiles in his sleep, and it makes me smile too.

I find a bedroom, and flop down face-first on the bed. Not bothering to take off anything, I lay there as the room starts to slowly spin around me. Or the bed is spinning—I have no idea. I can feel my phone vibrating, and it takes me a few minutes to work it out of my pocket.

"Hi?" I groan.

"Blaine?"

"Ohhhh, it's you…" I growl.

"Who else would it be?"

"Well, you never know." I roll onto my back and laugh. "I've heard I'm not too bad on the eyes."

"Mmm. How much have you had to drink?"

"Oh, just a few." I hold up my fingers, trying to count.

Addison giggles in the phone.

"Do you have any idea just how fucking wonderful that sound is?" I breathe.

"What sound?"

I groan through each word. "Your. Sexy. Giggle."

She does it again, and I smile, my eyes closed like I'm ready for a daydream.

"You better get to sleep, Mr. Blackstock. You have a big day tomorrow."

"I'm in bed right now, ma'am."

"Oh, *are you*?"

I can hear the suggestive tone in her low voice, and my hand travels down my chest and ends up on my jeans.

I grip myself and whisper into the phone. "I wish you were here. I'm *so hard*."

"Remember it's only a twenty minute run." She quietly laughs and whispers. "Just how hard are you baby?"

"I'm built Ford tough." I laugh at myself and appreciate she probably doesn't get the reference.

"Well, whatever you are, you're mine. I'm in bed, too."

"Addison Cole, I want you here right now. I want that mouth around me."

She's quiet for a beat. "Give me ten minutes."

No way. I've actually convinced my own fiancée to sneak out of our house and come here to have sex with me on the night before or wedding. Ten minutes seems like an eternity. I fight the sleep, but it wins and I pass out.

She's a woman of her word. She wakes me up by doing exactly what I said I wanted her to do. She's got me engulfed in her mouth, and my hands search the dark room for her. When I feel her long hair, I grip tightly and push my hips up, deepening myself in her throat.

"Baby..." I breathe heavily. Just before I let go, she stops. My stomach is heaving like I'm a bottle full of baking soda and someone just shook me after dousing me with vinegar.

Quickly, she's on top of me, and in seconds, I'm inside of her. She cries out, and I grab her. Turning both of our bodies so I'm on top of her, I lift her shirt up and hungrily devour her beautiful chest.

"Get on your stomach," I groan and whip my shirt over my head. I slide out of her warmth, and she moans. Turning over onto her stomach, she lies flat, and I straddle her legs. I'm slowly easing myself back into her depths, pushing my pelvis down as much as I can into her backside. She buries her face in the mattress and loudly moans something incoherent.

"You like that, baby?" I thrust and almost blow my own mind.

"Yes!" she hisses, and I lean down so I'm right on top of her. I push in and pull out, over and over, kissing and biting the back of her shoulders and neck.

There's something about booze that puts a little rage in my bones. To put it as blunt as I possibly can: I just want to fuck her silly. Stupid, even. I want to tear the sheets and break the headboard. Sweat drips from my forehead and lands on her back, and I'm not even close to being done yet.

"You okay?" I try and catch my breath.

"Mmm, better than okay," she moans. "Your turn to lay down."

She gets to her knees, and I sit up. She pushes me back on to the bed and turns around so she's facing away. I'm still rock hard, and I push in inch by inch, filling her. She quickly sits and throws her head back.

"Ahhhh! Hold my hands, baby." She reaches back, and I hold them; she's using them as leverage while she rides me backwards. The sensation is like nothing I've ever felt; it's an intense pain and pleasure combined, completely exhilarating, and I feel like I could break in two.

She lets go of my hands and grinds down as hard as she can, rocking back and forth. I grip her hips and surge with frenzy.

"Holy shit. Oh, my...Ahhh!" I can't even see straight, except for little star bursts in my eyelids from squeezing them closed so hard. "Fuuuuuck!"

She moans loudly, and her beautiful voice lets out small whimpers. She's trying to keep it down, but it's not working. She falls back on top of me, and I slowly pull out of her pulsating heat.

"Where did that come from?" She breathes.

I wrap my arms around her chest and caress her breasts slowly. She rolls off and lies on her stomach, her head on the pillow.

"How did you get here?" I manage to ask after my breath finally slows.

"I drove my car." She looks like I've expecting her to run or something to Jeremiah's house.

"Oh. Here I was hoping you crept in all mysteriously."

"Well, kind of. I parked down the road, and they're so drunk out there they didn't even see me sneak by them."

I laugh and kiss her cheek. "I love it."

"But I have to go."

"What? No!"

"Umm, yes! Go to sleep." She sits up and searches for her clothing, quickly dressing.

I pout and run my hand on my chest, down to my still somewhat hardness, gripping my girth. "I can't sleep now."

"Blaine!" she whispers, giggling. "You are insatiable." And with that, she turns on her heel and leaves, closing the door behind her.

"That girl..." I smile and sigh.

CHAPTER TWENTY

My ranch looks like something out of a country fairy tale. Pale pink and white fabric hangs from posts on either side of the seating area, draping across the aisle that I'm about to walk down. Mason jars with small light bulbs in them are hanging with twine from the corners, and big white paper flowers in delicate bunches look like clouds in the evening sky. Each wooden chair has sheer linen wrapped around the back, tied with twine and the same pale pink tulips woven into the twine.

Maria and Kelsey are magic; I'll admit it. You have to spend time on every little detail, or you might miss something. At the end of the aisle an arbour stands, made out of my old fence posts. I wondered where Jeremiah had taken them. It's amazing and rustic, a large spray of pink and white tulips on the top. A whimsical *B + A* is engraved into one of the posts surrounded by a heart, just like the ones people carve into trunks of trees. *See, details.*

In the reception tent, people are everywhere, finishing last minute things, making it perfect for us. Three long rows of tables flow down the space of the tent. The giant beams holding up the peaks are wrapped with the same pink and white fabric, and tiny white lights are underneath the sheets, giving off a pretty glow.

For the centerpieces, bunches and bunches of tulips are set into jars full of water and sliced lemons. Candles float in tiny Mason jars, each with a label and a name on it, placing a guest at a certain seat.

At the head table, a large wooden banner, just like the one at the entrance to the ranch, is hung from the corners of the tent with *B + A* painted onto the wood.

"Well? What do you think?" Maria surprises me, and I turn to hug her.

"This is just beautiful, Maria. I can't thank you enough."

"You better thank your wife; she was the one with all the ideas and spent most of the night and morning out here. I don't even think she's slept!"

I'm sure our rendezvous last night recharged her battery, and I chuckle to myself, thinking of her sneaking into my bed last night.

By four twenty-two, I'm standing in wait. I'm nervous; my palms are sweaty, and I keep fidgeting with the buttons on the cuffs of my shirt, my belt buckle, anything I can get my hands. Jeremiah helped me pick out my clothes—not a first for us, since he got me clothes last year when I was in the hospital. I'm wearing my jeans, boots and a white button-up shirt, and I bought a white Resistol hat just for today.

Jeremiah, Alex and my brothers match me but wear no hats. Also, instead of white shirts, Maria got them all the pale pink like the rest of the fabric and tulips.

"Real men can wear pink," she said when she pulled the shirts out of the bag, and all of them turned up their lips or noses. She won that one.

Riley, Zoe, Leah and Camille are all in matching cotton dresses, pale pink, just as you'd expect. The dresses are knee length, and they're all wearing cowboy boots. Perfectly beautiful.

Each of them begin walking down the aisle in turn, slowly to the soft guitar gently playing behind us. Riley is wearing a white ribbon around her waist, tied in a bow above her belly like a present. She's glowing, and I look at Alex. He smiles at her, and I'm sure he looks like he could cry.

The moment I turn my head back to look down the aisle, I see her. I drop my jaw and instantly cover my mouth with my hands. Like a child coming down the stairs at Christmas and seeing piles of presents, I'm awestruck.

Her father has his arm looped through hers, and he walks her down to me. She's wearing the most beautiful dress I've ever seen, a strapless top that clings to her chest and stomach, flowing down and widening into small tiers of fabric, hanging just above her knees. She's got on matching boots with her bridesmaids. Her long red hair spills over her shoulders in perfect curled tendrils, her bangs swept to the side and pinned by a small silver clip. I can feel the tingle in my eyes when I see that she's wearing my Mom's pearls, and I can see my Dad notices, too, because he almost gasps in his seat when she walks by him.

"Who gives this woman to this man?" the preacher asks.

"Her mother and I." Richard wipes a tear from his eye with a white handkerchief and kisses his daughter on her cheek, then turns to sit down beside his sobbing wife.

"Hi," Addison says, smiling sweetly up at me.

"You are so beautiful." I choke the words out, still in complete shock at what's standing next to me.

"Not too bad yourself," she whispers and squeezes my hand.

The preacher gives his speech about marriage and love, and he reads some beautiful verses from the Bible. The three simplest words he speaks are from 1st Corinthians: *Love never fails.*

"I do believe you two have your own vows?" he asks.

We both nod.

"Addison, if you will." He holds out his hand, and she swallows and inhales deeply.

"Blaine." She looks at me, and I'm locked in her big blues. "Today and every day to come I will love you with everything I am. You are my best friend, the answer to all of my prayers. I promise to cherish you always, encourage and support you, and share in your joys and sorrows. Because of you I laugh, and I smile, I even giggle. You are the reason my heart beats every day. God gave me you. Take this ring as a symbol of my eternal love for you." She takes my hand and slides the titanium band on my finger.

"Blaine..." The preacher motions for me to begin, and I quickly snap out of my trance and clear my throat.

Here goes...

"Addy, I sat down and tried to write on paper how much I love you. No words can describe just how much, and how deeply, I'm devoted to you. No embrace will ever be tight enough, no kiss will ever be passionate enough. Your smile is the first thing I wake up to and the last thing I see at night, and with those things I am complete. I promise to always hold you up and support you, to laugh and cry with you, and share myself wholeheartedly. The Lord gave me you, my sweetheart, my angel, my red rose. To the world this band may just be one small thing, but to me, this one small thing is the world. Please wear it as a symbol of my love for you."

She holds out her trembling hand and tears pour from her eyes. I slide the platinum band on her finger and squeeze her hand tightly in my mine.

"Addison, do you take Blaine to be your husband in love and life for this day and each day to come as long as you shall live?"

"I do." She smiles and wipes her tears.

"Blaine, do you take Addison to be your wife in love and life for this day and each day to come as long as you shall live?"

"I do." I wipe my own tears.

"Family and friends, it's my pleasure to introduce to you Mr. and Mrs. Blackstock! You may kiss your bride!"

Everyone stands to cheer and clap, and I pull her into me as close as I can, kissing her perfect lips and holding her hands in mine. My wife, my beautiful wife.

Weeks ago we poured over music and finally chose the perfect song; it might as well have been written just for us. We decided on Blake Shelton's *"God Gave Me You"*, which is exactly what He did; He gave me to her and her to me. We danced to our song, and all of our loved ones stood in a circle around us. A big dinner, some wine and even line dancing later, we were partying the night away.

We're sent off by everyone late in the night for our two AM flight to Florida, which will connect us to the British Virgin Islands.

I still haven't told her where we're going. She knows about Florida, but that's about as much as I've given. We sit in first class; once the seat belt sign clears, I pull her legs over my lap, and she leans into me.

"How are you, Mrs. Blackstock?"

"Mmm." She smiles and kisses my shoulder. "Cloud nine, my love."

Ditto, I think to myself and lean back in my seat.

We are on layover in Florida for two hours, and it feels like the flight to the BVI takes hardly any time at all. Tortola is breathtakingly beautiful, and I momentarily think of listing my ranch and moving here.

"Look at how blue the water is!" Addison gazes out her window and beams at the view.

"This is where my Mom and Dad went on their honeymoon." I picture my mother here, and it warms my heart.

"Awe, really?" She smiles. "Thank you for choosing this place for us, too."

We check in and enjoy breakfast on our terrace, which is literally feet from the ocean. I've been married for just over twelve hours, and I haven't made love to my new wife yet. Looking over at her, I feel myself start to harden beneath the glass tabletop. "Hey, you."

"Hey, you." She smiles, peeling her eyes for just a second to look at me, then right back to the landscape.

"I want to make love to my wife."

"Oh! Do you?" She laughs and picks up a strawberry. I know exactly what she's going to do with that berry, and she surprises me when she just winks and pops the whole thing in her mouth, biting down and chewing it.

"Okay, well. If my wife would rather do something else..."

"Actually," she says as she sits up in her chair, "let's go out!"

What's that famous saying? *Happy wife, happy life?* Yeah, that's the one.

MEADOWLARKS

I agree, and we go out. Martina gave me a bunch of brochures when I booked our honeymoon.

We swim with dolphins, and it's amazing. It costs a small fortune for something that only lasts about twenty minutes, but it's worth it. Later we tour a replica pirate ship, and I get to set off a cannon, which delights the kid in me.

We decide on dinner at a restaurant instead of eating in, and we choose a bustling place with a wide open patio and wine bottles lining the shelves on the walls. A tasty combination of Caribbean spices and sauces made our meals outstanding; we order steak and fish to share plates, even though we want to order everything on the menu. I try a local beer, which is better than I expect, so I order and drink four more. Champagne is served when nine o'clock hits, and everyone in the bar toasts and drinks. I sure could get used to this place.

"Are you ready to have your wife now?" She leans in and whispers in my ear.

I put my beer down, and raise my hand to ask for our bill.

"I guess that's a yes." She laughs and takes my hand.

When we walk in the suite, the smell of the sea fills the room, and the cool breeze feels so good on my heated skin. I lift her hand and kiss her ring finger, her wedding set glistening in the light of the room.

"Come outside." I take her hand, and we walk out onto our terrace; to the right is a wading pool. The water is filled right to the edges, so it almost looks like it's got a glass lid on it. I undress her slowly; her shorts fall to the ground, and I kiss her shoulder and cheek. Off goes the shirt and, making my way down, I unclasp her bra, and it falls with the rest of the clothes. Lower and lower, I reach her hips and kiss across the small of her back. We opted not to do the garter thing at our reception, so I'm taking the opportunity now to pull down her panties with my teeth. I kiss all the way back up her body, tiny sparks on my lips from her skin with each alluring touch.

She walks down and steps into the pool, the moonlight showering her beautiful body as she slips beneath the water. I take off my khaki shorts and my t-shirt, kick off my shoes and slowly submerge into our own private haven.

"Your vows were the most beautiful words I've ever heard. I had the biggest lump in my throat while you were saying them to me." She sits in my lap, her legs wrapped around my waist and her arms resting on my shoulders.

"I prayed I didn't forget any of them; I practised for days."

"It was perfect. All of it." She touches her nose to mine. "I love you."

I kiss her; just like my vows, it isn't passionate enough, but it never will be with her. Each moment is a big deal, so the next has to be doubled just to outdo the first. My mouth sucks her neck and throat; I bite her shoulders gently and take each breast into my mouth.

She grips my hair and pushes my head harder into her body, making me breathlessly gorge myself on her sweet flesh.

"I want this inside of me, baby." Her hand travels down my body and slips under the water, grips around my raging thickness and rubs it against her delicate skin.

"How badly do you want it?" I breathe and suck her earlobe.

"Make love to me, Blaine. Please."

I lift her with my hands, and she directs me into her, I slowly lower her down, stretching her body so she possesses my own with hers. The water laps over the edge of the pool as she rises and falls rhythmically. The splashing quickens, and I pull her hips down to grind me harder as I enter her deeper.

"Ahhh!" she cries out and throws her head back. When she looks back at me, her eyes are blazing from the hunger and from the moonlight. Her skin, tanned already from just one day in the sun, has been made white by the night sky.

"You feel so good, baby," I hiss, and moan as the intensity builds in my body, spilling out of my pores and filling the pool. She leans back and is almost floating. The angle of her body bends me in a way that makes my eyes roll back in my head; I catch my breath and push my hips up and slam against her. My hand runs down her stomach, and I rub her tenderness with my thumb.

"Ah! Oh, baby!" She reaches for me and holds my thighs as she reaches ecstasy. An orgasm ripples through her, igniting my own climax, and I rumble loudly as I thrust the last of my length as deep as I can go.

I finally made love to my wife. It's probably cliché to say that it feels different now that we're married, but it really does. For me, anyway. I feel closer to her than ever before, and I don't want this instant to end.

I make love to her again in the bed in our villa, just like our last night as an unwed couple at Jeremiah's house. This time I have a headboard to hang on to, and we can both cry out as loudly as we want. I couldn't care less about strangers hearing me please my wife.

The Tortola honeymoon goes by too quickly, and we're both disappointed that we have to return to the real world. On the flight home Addison flicks through the photos we took.

"Look at your face!" She giggles and points to the screen. I'm puckering while sucking a lemon wedge at the wet bar after throwing back tequila shots.

"That one's not going on the wall." I smirk and shudder, remembering the awful bitterness.

She falls asleep on the flight home from Florida's airport. A lock of hair falls on her face, and I lean over to brush it off, tucking it behind her ear. I sit back in my leather seat and watch her sleep peacefully, a tiny smile on her lips as she must be dreaming of something.

A pretty blonde flight attendant walks out of the cabin. "Can I get you anything, sir?"

"I've got everything I need right here." I smile. "Thank you."

"No problem. We'll be descending within the hour." She whispers once she sees that Addison is sleeping and smiles, moving on to the man on the other side of the plane in a business suit.

***

"Home sweet home!" She bounces in her seat when we drive under the banner across the driveway.

"Yep. That also means back to work." We both frown, and she laughs at my exaggerated bottom lip. One last day before she goes back to work; I knew the fairy tale had to end sometime, shaking us back to the real world.

A relaxing night in with pizza and a movie is disturbed when Addison's phone rings, and Riley is on the other end, wanting to know about the honeymoon. She smiles at me, and mouths, "*Sorry!*" before getting up off the couch and going into the kitchen. She leaves me to watch the movie alone—which I do, right to the end where Bruce Willis gets the bad guy. As usual.

In the kitchen I find her sitting on a stool, still on her phone. When I open the fridge to get a beer, she turns and smiles, doing the talking motion with her hand letting me know Riley's chatting her ear off. I'm pouting; I'll admit it. I want my wife all to myself, and learning to share is not something I've really ever had to do.

"Awe, he did? What a sweetie. I know, he's really excited. My parents can't believe the change." She must be talking about Alex.

I point up the staircase. "I'm going to bed."

She frowns and holds up a finger, letting me know she'll be a minute. I know she means a girl-minute, which calculates into a man's hour and then some. I could tease her and take my shirt off, or make some other suggestive motion, but she is too wrapped up with Riley, so I just go upstairs. Slowly moping and pouting like a big baby, I undress and fall under the sheets, letting them drift down on me, and I'm out.

"Blaine!" Her scream pulls me out of bed and in seconds, I'm stumbling down the stairs, my eyes trying to adjust to all the light in the kitchen.

"Blaine, hurry!" She's frantically standing at the bottom clutching hands together under her chin. The dogs are going crazy at the door. "There's someone out there!"

"What? Someone outside?" I run over and whip open the door. Rex and Luca rush out barking like crazy.

"I saw something in the window! Please be careful!" she calls from behind me, and I quickly run back inside and grab a flashlight from the top of the fridge.

The dogs stop barking but sniff all around the house, the hair on their backs standing on end. The hair on my neck is, too. Who would be outside of our house in the middle of the night?

"Who's out there?" I shout into the darkness. Like whoever it is will show themselves; I highly doubt it. It could have been just an animal. *I hope it was just an animal.*

"Well?" She's standing in the doorway, expectantly and still clutching her hands.

"There's nothing out there, baby. I think you're just tired, and when you panicked, the dogs did too." I call them back in the house, closing the door behind them. I lock it, and they follow us back upstairs to our bedroom.

When they sleep at the foot of the bed again, I think of Reid and the night that Addison came home after he attacked her. Officer Herring or someone would have notified us if he was out, wouldn't they? There's got to be some sort of victim's service that would tell her if he was released on bail.

Once she's calmed down and tangled tightly in my arms, she falls asleep, but I don't. The dogs and I are on alert. As soon as the morning comes, I decide I'm calling the police station. At six AM, the alarm rings, and she wakes up for work.

"How did you sleep?"

She stretches and smiles, momentarily forgetting about last night. "Good." Then she looks around the room like she's expecting to see something frightening.

"You're okay, Addy. We were here all night protecting you." I smile and whistle for the dogs who jump up from the floor and stand at the edge of the bed.

"My brave boys." She pets them, and they start panting.
I can relate.

Breakfast is quick and rushed, like usual on mornings that she's running late. The toaster pops, and she's out the door. I stand and wait for her to come back in.

"Oops!" She kisses me and laughs. "I think I'm going to take the Mustang today; I miss driving it."

"Okay, my love. Have a good day." I wave and she's gone. The Mustang rumbles from inside the garage; the beast has awoken, and it emerges, silver glistening in the morning sun. She leaves one hell of a dust trail today.

Once she's out of sight, I check all the windows and doors. Nothing looks out of place, no tamper marks or anything unusual. Still, I call Jeremiah and tell him I might be out when they come for work today. I'm going to talk to Officer Herring and find out anything he can tell me about Reid.

***

"Are you kidding me?" I can feel my face flush.

"I'm sorry, Mr. Blackstock. We tried calling."

"We were out of the country! On our honeymoon. Why didn't the hospital call and tell her then?"

He shakes his head in frustration and apology. "I'm very sorry. He somehow got bail; but he's supposed to be staying with a surety."

Addison is going to flip when she finds out.

"Officer Herring, she thought she saw something outside the window last night. Even the dogs were going crazy."

He narrows his eyes. "Did she see anything specific?"

"No, but she freaked out, and I checked outside. Didn't find anything, but it still gave me the creeps."

"Well, I'll check in with his surety this morning. Make sure everything is on the up and up. I'll give you a call when I get word."

"Thank you, sir." I shake his hand. When I get into my truck, I just sit and let it idle. If I turn left, I go home and start work; if I turn right, I head toward the hospital and tell Addison that the douchebag got released. I decide to turn right. If she finds out from someone else that I knew but didn't tell her, she'll be upset.
Hey, gorgeous. I'm coming by to see you.

Really?! OK, babe. Text me when you're here.

Seven minutes later...
I'm outside. Can you come out? Should I come in?

I'll come out.
"Well, isn't this a nice surprise. My husband visiting me at work." She kisses me. "All the girls swooned when I told them you were coming."
I frown and shift in my seat to face her. "Reid's out."
Her smile fades into an expressionless face. "When?"
"Yesterday morning."
"I told you, Blaine." She holds her finger up in the air. "I just know he was out there."
"Addy, I don't think he was. Why would he be? If he was smart, he wouldn't come near you again." We both know he's far from intelligent, but I try and sound reassuring anyway.
"Why didn't someone tell me?"
"I talked to Office Herring this morning; he said he tried calling."
She takes a big breath and slowly lets it go. "Okay. It'll be okay." And I'm not sure if she's trying to convince me or herself.
"You'll be okay, baby. I promise. If you want to take some time and come home, you can."
"No, I'm needed here."
I take her hand and kiss it softly just as my phone rings.
"Hello?"
"Mr. Blackstock? It's Herring. I've contacted the surety. They tell me he was in the home all night."

"Oh, really." I'm almost hesitant to feel relieved just yet.

"I've also called a neighbor I know personally, and they told me they didn't see his SUV leave at all through the night."

"Well, thank you. That will put us at ease."

Addison motions for me to hand her the phone.

"Addison would like to talk to you." I hand her the phone.

"Officer Herring? Yes, well I was so sure...I know, thank you very much...It was lovely, thank you..." She pulls on the fabric of her scrubs nervously. "Okay. Yes, we will...Have a good day. Bye."

She hands me back the phone. "He said he's sure Reid didn't go anywhere last night. And that he'll look into having surveillance put on him."

"Want to take the rest of the day off?"

She looks like she's almost about to say yes. "I can't. I wish I could, but we're short staffed today."

"Okay, call me if you need anything. Promise?"

"I promise, my darling husband."

"I love you, Mrs. Blackstock. So very much."

CHAPTER TWENTY-ONE

It's nearly midnight on May 29th, and the sound of the phone ringing startles us both. Addison scrambles to reach it on the nightstand.

"Hello?" She sits up quickly, and my eyes take a minute to adjust. "Okay! I'm getting dressed now!" She leaps off the bed and almost slips on the floor before she reaches the closet.

"Addy?"

"Riley's going into labour! I gotta get over there."

My eyes are still trying to focus by the time we pull into Jeremiah's driveway. I get out of the passenger seat and hold the door open for Riley to get in. The three of them were already waiting outside for us.

"Drive safe, and keep me posted." Jer looks nervously into the car at Addison and Alex. "Good luck, Riley!"

"Thank you, Jer." She breathes, holding her large belly in her small hands. "Thank you for staying with Isaac."

Alex and I get into the back, and the tires kick up stones when she throws the car into reverse.

"Whoa!" Riley grips the door.

"Sorry."

"I don't want to have this baby in a car, Cole!"

They both laugh, and Riley quickly softens her voice, breathing slowly. She must be having a contraction; I don't know much, but I've seen enough TV to know that.

"How far apart are you?"

"She was four minutes about half an hour ago." Alex leans up and sticks his head between the front seats. "Babe, you okay?"

She breathes, and I think we all exhale with her.

"I'm okay." She smiles back at him, and he reaches his hand through the center and holds hers.

Addison looks in the rear view, and I can see in her eyes that she's smiling.

Riley and Alex calmly walk up and down the white hallway of the maternity ward, back and forth, stopping every few minutes for a contraction and then starting again.

"She's doing so well." Addison smiles at them as they walk away from the row of chairs we're sitting in.

"Alex looks like he's ready to pass out." I chuckle, and she elbows me.

"Hey, that'll be you someday, too."

"Can't wait." I smirk, and she rolls her eyes. "Practise makes perfect."

She gapes and shakes her head at me.

When I come back from the bathroom, only Addison is left in the hallway. She's standing in front of a door, looking through the window.

"Where'd they go?" I stand behind her and peek in over her shoulder. Alex is standing beside Riley, who's now lying in a bed on her side. I'm not sure if I'm ready to see anything else, so I go and sit back down on the uncomfortable chairs across the hall.

Minutes turn into hours, and after the hundredth time I nod off, Addy wakes me up and tells me we should get something to eat.

"What time is it?"

"It's noon."

Riley's been in labour for twelve hours, and there's still no baby.

"Nothing's happened yet?"

"Not yet, but everything is going smoothly otherwise though. Alex is sleeping in a chair beside her bed. It's so sweet." She smiles, and I take her hand, walking down the hall and into an elevator to eat questionable cafeteria food.

I eat my roast beef sandwich alone, in my orange plastic chair. I stare at the soda machine, wishing I hadn't bought this awful sludge they advertised as coffee and instead got a can of pop. Addison sees some co-workers and stands by the window talking to them. Every so often, she looks over and smiles. I just sit and eat and smile back with a cheek full of sandwich.

At dinner time, I'm exhausted. I'm trying my best to stay enthused about it all, but I really just want to go home. Addison looks tired, too, and when Alex comes out, he frowns. He tells us the doctor thinks it'll be a couple more hours.

"They'll do a c-section if it doesn't improve." He runs his hands through his hair in frustration.

"As long as she's okay, and the baby's okay. That's all that matters, Alex." Addison hugs him and he rests his head on her shoulder, closing his eyes for a moment of peace.

"Listen, you guys should go home." He read my mind. "I'll call you if something changes."

"Okay. Love you."

He smiles and hugs her again. "Love you, too, Addy."

Home sweet home; oh, the glory of those three words. My bed almost envelopes around me, and I cocoon into the blankets, feeling comfort at last. Normally I would associate this bed with sex, and having her beside me would make me want to touch her in any way. But right now, all I want to do is sleep. I think I can hear her saying something to me as I drift away, but I'm too far to make out the words.

Baby Cole is finally brought into the world. Alex called at six AM to tell Addison that Riley had started to push around 4:00. An hour and a half later, he became a father.

She's crying while she's on the phone with him, smiling and wiping her tears with the corner of the blanket. "Oh, Alex I'm so happy! I just love her name." She turns to me. "Scarlett Cordelia Cole."

I smile, happy that the baby is here and everyone is well. They've chosen a beautiful name for her.

By 8:00, we're on the way to the hospital to see our new niece. As expected, she's a beautiful baby. She has a head full of jet black hair just like Riley's, but she's got big blue eyes like Alex. He's sitting in a gliding chair, slowly rocking tiny Scarlett in his arms. I try and tune out the gory details of her birth, and wince when I hear words like tear and blood and stitches.

"Sorry, Blaine." Riley smiles up at me, still beautiful even after everything she's been through in the last thirty-plus hours.

"Mommy!" Isaac peeks through the door, and his eyes brighten when he sees his mother. Jeremiah is behind him, unsure if he should come in the room.

"Baby! Oh, I missed you so much!" Riley hugs him, carefully lifting the hand with the IV in it out of the way of her son. She sees Jer over his shoulder and waves him to come in. "Get in here, Jeremiah!"

He comes in without a sound and whispers hello to everyone, seemingly afraid that if he raises his voice, he'll somehow break the fragile newborn.

Alex laughs. "Jer, you don't have to whisper. She'll have to get used to noise in this family."

Riley sneers at him but then smiles. "He's right."

Addison gets to hold the baby, her small hand around an even tinier head. "Hello, little darling." She smiles down at her and traces her finger along her little ear. "She's perfect. Just perfect."

Riley and Scarlett are able to go home to Jeremiah's house the next day. Alex fumbles around, trying to get her tiny little body buckled into her car seat, careful where the straps went. Once he made sure she was snug, he stood back and admired his work.

Addison had lent her brother her Taurus to drive his new family from the hospital, and she's going to surprise him by selling her Mustang and buying them a new car to have as their own.

"That's what my Dad would want. Alex has proved he's responsible. I don't need two cars." She smiles while she rubs her hand on the trunk of the old Ford. "Wanna go for one last boot?"

I grin and hop in the passenger side; she turns on the ignition and throws the car into reverse. The dust cloud trailing behind us down Porter Road is enormous. The engine roars as we take a corner and spray stones all over the side of the road.

"Whoaaaaa!" I grip the door and hang on for dear life. "If nursing doesn't work out, you might have a shot at NASCAR!"

She laughs and floors it, pulling us back into our seat on the last straight stretch of the road. A few seconds later, the fun ends, and we're on asphalt.

The rush is exhilarating, and we drive around with no destination, down other roads and streets. We are fully enjoying the last time we'll be in this car together. At the lights by the railroad tracks, Addison slows down, and we cruise along with the windows down, the warm June air flowing over our hands and through our hair.

A pause at the streetlights causes a change in the fun.

"Babe?" She narrows her eyes and looks in the rear view. "What kind of car is that behind us?"

I turn in my seat and look. "Ugh…a Lexus?"

"Thought so." As soon as the light turns green, she quickly looks both ways and slams her foot right down on the gas, jolting us forward. "Babe, I think it's Reid."

"What!" I shoot around in my seat again, almost frantic to try and see if it's him. The windows in the SUV are too dark, and I can't tell.

We come to another light, having to stop again, but this time the Lexus pulls up beside us. The dark windows give us no chance to see who is behind the wheel. I can feel my heart start to race; I reach over and hold my door handle like I'm ready to jump out and fling open the door of the Lexus. With my luck, it would be a soccer mom I'd be yanking out and not the piece of shit Reid.

"It's okay, baby," I tell her. "Just breathe." And she does, slowly, through a small opening in her lips. She doesn't look over at the Lexus while it's beside us. As soon as the light turns green, she accelerates, and when I look in the mirror on my door, I feel relief.

"It turned, baby. I don't think it was him. You're okay, my love." I stroke her thigh with my hand, trying to ease her anxiety, hoping I'm successful.

She exhales loudly. "I panicked."

"You were just fine. Ready to go home?"

She nods and smiles; I turn up the radio, and we drive home. When the pavement turns back into dirt, Porter Road is turned into a dust cloud again. One last hurrah.

Jeremiah comes over for dinner, giving Alex and Riley some alone time with their new bundle. Over dessert, which is ice cream, he's convinced me to start practising team roping for a rodeo this summer. Truthfully, he doesn't have to say much to convince me; it's a great idea. He's just as good as me, and we could make more money, too.

The sun hasn't quite set yet, and we clear the table. Addison sits, still eating ice cream and talking on the phone to Riley.

"You know, what you're doing for them is pretty good, bud," I say to him.

He chuckles and opens the dishwasher, tossing the silverware in the plastic basket. "Well, sometimes people need a little help. And I like having them around." He grins. "Maybe she'll convince one of the other Maine girls to move out here too!"

"Cheers to Maine girls."

We laugh.

"Indeed."

After her call and once she's finished her ice cream, Addison joins us in the kitchen.

"Wow, look at this!" She gazes around the kitchen at the empty sink and counter tops. She seems astonished that we figured out between the two of us how to load and start a cycle in the dishwasher.

"We just stopped pushing buttons when we heard water start spraying around in there." Jer laughs and shrugs his shoulder. I laugh, too, because I know he's being completely honest.

"Thanks for dinner. It was good, like always." He pats his stomach. "I should get going, though. I need to get to Lander's before it closes."

We walk out on to the porch and watch him leave.

"See ya tomorrow, buddy," I call to him.

"Ah, shit." He walks back around the front of his truck. "I got a flat tire."

"Well, at least it's only flat on one side," I joke, looking at the tire when I get over to the truck.

He elbows me. "Ass. I got a spare..." He looks at his watch.

"Well, we could change it now; it'll only take a few minutes," I say.

"If you need to go now, you can take my car, Jeremiah." Addison smiles.

He looks hesitant, but after a few seconds, he agrees. "You sure? I can bring it right back."

"No, it's okay. You can bring it back tomorrow. I'm sure it'll be easier to change the tire in the daylight, anyway."

"Thanks, Addison." He catches the keys to the Mustang in the air when she tosses them and grins as he climbs into the driver's seat.

"Careful! It's got a sticky gas pedal!" I laugh, and he pulls out of the driveway, careful not to speed while in view. But a few minutes later, when she's gone back in the house, I hear the roar of the engine and exhaust, and I smile.

***

Her fingernails gently scrape the skin on my back and push down into me while she massages me underneath the spray of the shower head. I lean into the wall, standing under the cascading water, and let it coat my body. I can feel her mouth on my back, my shoulder, and she kisses me on the back of my neck. Her hands are now around my chest, and she leans in, pushing her body right against mine.

I stand straight up and turn my head to kiss her. She is still behind me, rubbing down my abdomen and over my hip bones. When she finds what she's looking for, she slowly strokes and grips me, pulling and caressing my hardening length.

When she's got me completely vertical, which doesn't take much with her touch, I turn around and face her. Her long hair is a tangled wet mess, and I take it all in my hands and pull it over her shoulders and behind her back. I twist it around my hands and wrist so she's nose up, and I kiss and suck her throat and neck anxiously.

"You taste so good," I breathe, in between sucks and licks, and I turn her around. "Lift your leg, baby." I pull her thigh up so she's standing on one foot and press into her body with mine.

I suck and bite her shoulder, tasting her succulent skin.

"Ahh," she moans. "Mmm..."

"I want to tease you." I want her to beg for me to make love to her, to drive her crazy and make those beautiful blue eyes roll back into her head. "Ready?"

She breathes deeply. "Yes, baby."

The tip of my erection trails down her stomach, through the top of her thighs and rubs gently against her delicate flesh. Provoking with each rub, it sends little sparks through me, wanting so badly to just move an inch or two and thrust myself deep inside. But I don't. I persevere and keep on with the beautiful torture.

Her body ripples, and she almost falls when a shock of pleasure progresses through her as my hard tip rubs against her tender skin over and over. While she's crying out and still cresting, I let her thigh back down so she's on two feet, and I move enough to push up and right in to her.

"Blaine! Fuck." She screams for me, her beautiful mouth can even make that word sound delicious. I've caught her off guard, and her warmth is still convulsing on the inside, gripping me as I pull out and thrust in slowly but powerfully.

I bite her neck again. She moans loudly, and I whisper in her ear, telling her how much I love her and how amazing her body feels. My hands squeeze and rub her breasts, hold her stomach and hips, touching anywhere they want to. One hand slides down her body, and I slowly rub against her soft skin again, quickly sending her into a frenzy once more.

This time the pull of her muscles holds me so tightly I have no choice but to let go. I push and push and push until I can't go any deeper. The sensation is so strong, I could burst through the glass walls just from my hands pushing against it. I'm trying to keep myself from losing balance and falling to the tile floor.

The heat from the water and the fog from the orgasm has clouded my head, and I'm almost faint. We stand there for a few moments, my arms wrapped around her body, just breathing and feeling our bodies gently float back down to earth.

Later, Rex and Luca start barking, and I sit up in bed to hear someone pounding on the front door. When I stagger down the stairs, I flip on the kitchen light and see through the door that it's Officer Herring.

"Blaine," he says as soon as I open the door. "Is Addison home?"

"Yeah, she's upstairs sleeping. What's up, Officer?"

He motions his hand in the door. "May I?"

I step aside, letting him in, and I close the door behind him.

"There's been an accident, Blaine. A car registered in her name."

I shake my head, unsure if I just heard him right. "Her car is here." I look outside, and then it hits me. Jeremiah's Dodge. "Jer! What happened?"

"Blaine." He puts his hand on my shoulder; I see it, but I don't feel it. "You need to sit down."

"What happened to Jeremiah?" I'm frantic, keeping my feet planted on the floor.

My commotion alerts Addison, and she comes downstairs, squinting in the light of the kitchen. "Babe? Officer Herring! What's going on?"

I look at Officer Herring, begging him to tell me what happened to my best friend.

"Addison, your car was involved in an accident. I'm so sorry..."

Her hands fly to her mouth and cover it as she gasps.

"Mr. Sanford has been taken to the hospital."

With his words, I rush by him and grab my keys off the island. I'm out the door before either of them can say a word.

"Blaine! Wait!" She calls from the porch, but I get in the truck and breathe insanely, trying to get this damn key in the damn ignition.

"Damn it!" I fumble the keys, and they fall on the floor by my feet.

The passenger door opens and she gets in. "I'm going to come with you"

"Blaine, please, if you're going to go, drive carefully." Herring is standing in the way of the open door, a look of sadness on his face. "Addison..." He looks at her, and she nods, agreeing to something. I have no clue what.

I'm silent the entire way to the hospital. I feel her look over at me a few times, but I can't take my eyes off the road for a second. I need to get to him. I'm still trying to figure out how he was in an accident; I guess I should have let the cop explain what happened.

In the emergency department, I rush to the desk. "Jeremiah Sanford. Where is he?"

"I'm sorry, sir. Are you his family?"

"Yes! I'm his brother," I lie, and the woman behind the desk looks at Addison. She obviously her and smiles kindly.

"Okay, I'll get someone to speak to you." She gets up and walks in the emergency room, behind a frosted glass wall and disappears around the corner.

"Blaine, my love." Addison runs her hands on my forearm, setting her chin on my shoulder. "You have to sit down for a minute, please." She pulls me toward the empty seating area.

"Addy, I just need to see him. See that he's okay. I don't even know what the hell happened."

"I do, and this is all my fault." She starts to cry and puts her face in her hands.

I look at her with wide eyes. "What are you talking about?"

"Officer Herring said he was run down in the parking lot of Lander's." Her eyes pour tears, and she looks away from me. "By...by...Reid."

"What!?" I can't breathe. "What the fuck, Addison? What are you saying?" Just as I stand to my feet, a man comes out the door and walks toward us.

"Mr. Sanford?"

"Where's Jeremiah?" I am desperate.

"Your brother has been in an accident, and he has slipped into a coma." He holds his hands together in front of him and looks at me sympathetically.

"I want to see him."

"Of course. I'll take you in. Are you going to be okay?"

I look at him, wanting to ask him why he would ask such a stupid fucking question. Of course I'm not going to be okay.

Jer is lying in a darkened room. I see more wires and tubes than skin. His head is wrapped in a large bandage, and small sutures hold together a gash on his face. I feel limp, so I sit down on a stool beside his bed, holding his hand in mine.

"Jer? I'm so sorry, buddy. I'm so, so sorry."

He doesn't move. Only his chest rises and falls with the help of a breathing tube. I watch him for at least an hour, or so it seems, anyway. A nurse comes in twice to check him, but I don't acknowledge her presence. I'm a broken mess, just the shell of a man on a stool.

Addison comes in the room and stands on the other side of his bed. I look up at her and quickly put my head down, my forehead resting on his cool hand.

"This is my fault. I should have changed that fucking tire." I inhale deeply and look back up at her. "He wouldn't have been in that car."

"Baby, he wasn't in the car when he was hit."

"What?" I tilt my head to the side. "What do you mean?"

"Officer Herring said that a witness saw Reid idling in the parking lot. When Jeremiah walked out to the car, he..." She starts to cry and wipes her eyes. "He drove right into him."

I let go of his hand and touch his leg under the blue hospital blanket. Hard and cold.

"The doctor said his legs were crushed, and his head must have whipped back and hit the roof of the Mustang."

"Oh my God, Addy!" I can't believe what I'm hearing. "Where is that piece of shit now?" My jaw is clenched, and my heart is hammering rage through my body.

"He was still sitting in his car, Blaine, when the police got there." She shakes her head and looks over at Jeremiah. "They think he was in some sort of shock. Just kept muttering that it wasn't supposed to be *him*."

I just don't get it; why would he do this to Jeremiah? How would he even know who he was? Then it clicks on like a light bulb. "Addy, he thought Jer was *me*."

She looks at me, and her eyes widen. She knows I'm right. It was dark; he saw her car and a man walking out to it. Who else would it be other than her or me driving it?

The doctor comes in the room, followed by Officer Herring and another cop. The doctor half-smiles kindly and checks the screen of Jeremiah's life support, pushing a few buttons and then flashes a small light in his motionless eyes.

I have to look away. The last time I saw those, eyes they were lit up like fireworks, eager to have a rip in the old Ford. Now they're empty, and I can't bear to see him like this. I hold his hand again. Now it's my turn to be at his bedside with worry and desperation.

"Blaine, can I have a word?" Officer Herring nods toward the doorway, and I leave the room with him. "Mr. Surrey—I mean, Reid—has given a full statement of the incident. He told me that he thought Mr. Sanford was you."

"I knew it." I look at the cold floor. "I can't believe this happened."

"He's admitted to everything and has been formally charged with attempted murder."

It doesn't bring me any comfort, but I force a smile anyway. "Thanks. So, what now?"

"Well, he'll be in court on Monday."

"I'll be there." I look into the window at Jeremiah and dig my nails into my palms as hard as I can.

CHAPTER TWENTY-TWO

The next three days are exactly the same as the first day when I found out. There's no change in Jeremiah, and I don't leave the hospital. Alex and Riley visit and cry while sitting beside his bed. Addison goes to work and goes home to get me clothes, then stays at the hospital with me while I stand at his bedside.

"I can't leave him, Addy. He's laying where I should be." I feel the tears coming. When they start rolling down my cheeks, I angrily wipe them and lean back in the chair. "Ugh! I just don't know what to do."

"Blaine, you need to sleep. I will stay with Jeremiah."

"I can't. I just can't. I'm sorry."

On Sunday night, I'm alone in the room with him when the machines he's hooked up to start beeping. A nurse quickly comes in the room.

"What's going on?" I stand and look at her expectantly.

She checks the machine, and then she runs out of the door. In seconds, she is back with the doctor. I stand back and give them room. Like a movie scene, the doctor and nurse are joined by three others, and they all try furiously to bring Jeremiah back.

"Blood pressure is falling to fifty over 33!" one of them shouts. A deafening blur fills the room, and just as fast as the beeping started, it stops. One long, hair-raising tone echoes around the room. As if the hands on the clock above the doorway stop moving, time slows to a standstill. I watch them, hovered over Jeremiah's body; the expressions on their faces are of worry and sadness. I'm expecting at any moment to snap out of it, and a calm to come; they'll tell me he's okay. But it doesn't happen, and the moment slowly starts up again.

"Well? What's going on?" I ask quickly.

They look at me, and the doctor puts his hands on his hips. "I'm very sorry, Blaine. He's gone."

"What? No, he's not." I rush over to his bed, wanting to shake him awake. "Jer! Jer? Please, Jeremiah. Wake up."

"Blaine..." The doctor starts to speak but doesn't finish.

"He was breathing a second ago. Try something else!" I am frenzied with disbelief.

"His heart couldn't hold on anymore, Blaine."

I fall to the ground and put my hands over my face. "No. Jer, no!"

The best man I've ever known, my friend and brother, just died in front of me. Died in the bed that I should have been in, and I'm on the floor where he would have been if things had gone like they were supposed to.

I feel sick, and I reach for a garbage can in the corner of the room, throwing up my grief and whatever little vending machine food I had forced into me.

Addison is on overnights, and someone must have called her down to the ICU.

"Babe!" She rushes to my side and kneels on the floor, holding my head in her arms. "Baby, I'm so sorry!"

She rocks me, and I cry, completely and utterly fatigued, full of sorrow and anger—no, rage. I feel like a little child, limp, and I need help to stand.

His hand is still warm when I touch it again, but this time, there's no other movement. No rising and falling of his chest—nothing. I can't bear to see him, and I need to get out of this fucking room.

Addison drives me home, and when we pass Jer's house, I yell at her to pull over so I can throw up again. She doesn't say much the rest of the way home, just holds my hand. When she parks beside his truck, I almost lose it again. His tire is still flat, and I just want to scream up into the sky. I will never forgive myself, for so many things I could have done differently.

"Blaine, come inside. Please." She stands in front of me and hugs me tightly. Her arms and warmth soothe me, and I hold her.

"I'm sorry," I mumble.

"Don't be sorry. You're supposed to be sad, baby." She tries to comfort me. "I'm going to stay home with you, okay?"

"Someone needs to tell Alex." I clear my throat, swallowing down grief and bile.

"I'll go over. Will you be okay if I leave?"

I nod and let her go. When she leaves, I go into the garage and get my tools to change the tire on his truck. Through glazed eyes and constant sniffling, I finally gather enough strength to push it down. I scream as loud as I can when I pick up the flat tire and heave it across the driveway before I fall to my knees.

"Jeremiah!"

***

His funeral is on a Thursday. Four days after he died and three days after I sat in the court room, listening to a prosecutor give a judge detailed notes about what happened to him. I watch Reid as he sits and listens to his charge escalate from attempted murder to first-degree murder. The only thing he's ever done right was admit his guilt. Another date is set for a few months from now, and when I watch him leave the room, I can finally breathe again. Though he didn't once look at anyone but the judge, it took every part of me not to jump over the rows of benches and choke the life out of him.

The church is packed with all the people Jer loved and all the people that loved him. Martina, his aunt, sits beside me; she's the only blood relative he had left after his parents died. Even Gwen shows up.

I manage to give a eulogy, telling everyone what they already knew. I talk about how great of a man he was, how much fun life was growing up with him, and how very much I was going to miss him with each and every day to come.

"I wish each person could be as lucky as I am to have a best friend like him. Twenty-five years wasn't enough, but I'm thankful for every second I got to spend with him. I love you, Jer."

He's buried in the cemetery, next to his parents. Addison and I chose his headstone and the inscription we thought suited him perfectly.

The first thing I'm going to do
Is spread my wings and fly.
Jeremiah Paul Sanford
November 30, 1981 – June 9, 2012

Three meadowlarks are carved into the dark granite, just like the ones Addison had made on my belt buckle. They are Wyoming's birds, flying fast and free, just like him, a Wyoming boy.

Days turn into weeks, and weeks quickly become the month of August. It's the time of year when Jer and I would usually be well into the rodeo circuit, working hard and hardly working all at the same time. After he died, a lawyer contacted me to tell me that he left everything he owned to me. His house, his farm, truck, everything. I manage to give his truck to Alex. As painful as it was seeing it leave my driveway and not watching Jeremiah drive away, I knew he would want it this way.

I remember the conversation I had with him months ago about Alex asking to move Riley into the house. "It needs life it in again," he'd said, and he was right. Alex, Riley and their little family grow in Jeremiah's house now. They bring it back to life, and the two times I've gone there since, I feel him in the home. He's at the fire pit, on the porch, in each room, and even in those shadowboxes on the bathroom wall with the dried flowers that his mother made.

Reid is found guilty and is sentenced to sixty-seven years in prison with no chance of parole. Coincidentally, the car he crushed Jeremiah against was also a sixty-seven, and it only brings a tiny amount of peace knowing that he'll be confined until he's either too old to function or dead. I'd prefer the latter.

***

On November thirtieth, I crack open a beer and toast the sky, I tip the bottle to the heavens and to Jer on what would be his 31st birthday.

"Miss you, buddy. Happy birthday."

"Hey, handsome." Addison stands behind me and pulls me into a hug. "How are you?"

"I'm good, my love. How was work?"

"Oh, same old." She shrugs and smiles. "Jeremiah's birthday?"

"Yep." I sip the beer and smile.

She puts her bag on the picnic table and roots through it, pulling out a white stick.

"Well, there's an old saying—with death, comes life." And holds up the stick. It has a small pink plus sign on it, and my eyes fly to hers.

"Are you? We are!" My heart is thumping from my chest, and I grab the stick, examining it closer.

"We are, my love."

She smiles, and I pull her into me, kissing and hugging her intensely.

"I love you so much. Thank you."

***

On July 17th, 2013, my son is born. He comes a few days early, surprising everyone. I hold Addison's hand when she pushes and breathes through his delivery, watching his tiny head and body come into the world. He cries, and we sob. The first time I hold him, I just dissolve away, like the first time I saw his mommy. My heart seems to stop, and I'm breathless.

"He's perfect, Addy. I love you so very much."

She smiles, her eyes tired but happy. Once we're alone in her room, she falls asleep, and I rock our son in the chair, studying every inch of his beautiful face. Touching his tiny fingers with my big rough ones, I gently kiss his head of golden hair.

"Hi, my little man." I smell his brand new scent. "You see that beautiful lady over there? That's your mommy. Aren't we so lucky to have her?" He sleeps in my arms for hours. I whisper to him and tell him over and over how much I already love him.

Alex, Riley, and the kids come to see him. Scarlett is walking now, and she teeters up to me, curious about the little blue bundle in my arms.

"Scarlett, that's your little cousin, Seth!" Riley bends to hold her daughter up to see the baby.

Seth Jeremiah Blackstock is seven pounds and 14 ounces of pure wonder. When he opens his eyes to look at me, I feel like I can see the entire world in those baby blues. How can my heart take anymore? My love for him is earth-shattering.

My brothers, their wives and my Dad all visit us in the hospital, too. When Dad holds his grandson, he looks at Addison and gets choked up.

"He looks just like you did, Blaine. I can't get over it."

I picture him thirty-one years ago, in a room just like this, holding me. But when he looks at the bed, it's empty. There's no one to share his joy, just two other boys without their mother. The thought sends a dark feeling through me, and I sit beside Addison on the bed, grabbing her hand to make sure she's actually still there.

The next morning I take my wife and our son home. The dogs bounce anxiously to see exactly what it is I'm carrying in the seat. Addison pets them, letting each of them smell her hands.

Each and every day with Seth is a gift, and watching him grow and make milestones is truly remarkable. Addison was showering when he crawled for the first time. I jumped off of the floor and shouted for her.

"Baby, he's crawling!"

Seth giggles and takes a few more brave movements toward me. His chubby fingers spread on the wooden floor, he reaches for me when I sit down in front of him and extend my hands.

"C'mon, my boy." I smile and wiggle my fingers.

"What was all that about?" Addison says melodically when she gets to the bottom of the stairs, wrapped in a towel. Then she sees him. "Seth! My little man; what a good boy!"

She kneels beside me and clasps his hands together under her chin, as excited as I am. When he reaches my hands, I pull him up and right into my arms. I breathe in his scent and close my eyes; his little warm body feels so small in my arms.

"Good boy."

He giggles again, and I lift him up in the air above my head like an air plane. His eyes widen, and a long string of drool flows from his mouth and lands on my lap.

"Oh, thank you!" I chuckle.

"I can't believe our little boy is crawling." Addison beams and takes him from me. She cradles him, stroking her fingers in his hair lovingly. When she sits on the couch to nurse him, I head upstairs to change.

Today we are going on a date, our first in months. Riley kindly offered to babysit Seth at their house, and as much as I wanted to decline because I'll miss him, I know he'll be fine. We need to get out, even if it's just an hour or two.

Date day consists of going for a ride. She trots beside me on Jax, who has grown into a huge mass, strong and rigid, a real sight to see. Mischief is just a shadow compared to his stature, but we keep up, even when she takes off cantering ahead of us.

When the sun starts to set, we head back home and brush the horses quickly before letting them go back into the pasture. I put away my saddle and our bridles and close the barn door behind me.

Addison is sitting on the picnic table, watching the horses roll in the field, smiling when they stand and shake off the dirt.

"I miss him already."

"I do, too."

"I called. Riley said he's sleeping sweet and sound."

I smirk and lean down to kiss her shoulder. "Well, that gives me more time, doesn't it?"

"And just how are we going to spend that time, Mr. Blackstock?" She grins and bites her lip.

I narrow my eyes and scoop her up in my arms. "Very, *very* wisely."

Addison Cole: From the Pine Tree to the Cowboy State

I scan the auditorium looking for any familiar faces. Finally, I see Mom and Dad, both sitting and smiling while staring back at me. Alex is sitting beside Mom, looking bored as usual. He was pretty much forced to be in attendance today.

Where is Jacob?

Maybe he couldn't find a seat near my parents; I hope he's not running late.

I have the biggest butterflies in my stomach. I hate big events, hate being the center of attention even more so.

Just call my name already, so I can get this over with.

Thankfully I'm a C initial, so it doesn't take long to get to me. Once I hear my name, I'm up and across the stage.

"Congratulations, Ms. Cole!"

"Thank you!"

Mrs. Lydell, my favourite professor throughout the long and gruelling but so-very-worth-it nursing program, hands me my diploma. A quick handshake followed by a few more, and I'm down the steps, free and ready to start my new life.

Addison Cole, RN. Wow. It feels so good that I've finally finished. Now the hard part begins, actually finding a good hospital to hire me.

"My baby girl!" Mom hugs me, crying of course, and Dad wraps his arms around the both of us. Alex stands a few feet away, thumbing the screen of his phone and occasionally eyeing some girls nearby.

"Have you seen Jacob?" I ask.

Mom looks around the auditorium and frowns. "No. We thought he was going to sit with us. Has he called?"

I open my small purse and pull out my phone. No texts or missed calls from him so I send a quick **where are you?** text message to him. My parents look at each other, probably both wanting to tell me he's an asshole and I should just ditch him, but they don't say anything.

A congratulatory dinner is planned, and I quickly drive home to change out of this ridiculous outfit. I'm surprised when I see Jacob's car sitting in the driveway. I park the Mustang next to his Rover.

"Hey there, handsome!" I open the screen door of the small porch and see Luca sitting at the front door. "What are you doing out here?"

The door is locked, and it takes me a minute to find my keys. Once inside, I toss my purse on the small table by the door, kick off my heels and lightly tip-toe upstairs. I bet he's still sleeping, and I'm not going to let this one go easy. I can't believe he missed my graduation.

The millisecond my foot hits the top step, I hear it. My heart starts thumping in my chest so hard and loud it's almost deafening. I'm no idiot; I've seen enough movies to know what is making the sound on the other side of my bedroom door. It's just like in the movies; the woman is always brave, either kicking the door open or bursting in some other way, telling the bitch on her man to get off, grabbing her by the hair.

I breathe slowly, still listening to the heartbreaking whimpers and sighs coming from my bedroom. I shake my hands at my sides, trying to loosen myself a little, letting all the ache fall out of my body.

The old brass knob is cold in my hand. It turns slowly and clicks when it releases the mechanism on the inside.

Here goes, Cole. I breathe.

"Becca?" I can't believe my eyes.

"Oh, my God! Jake!" She screams and flies off the bed, grabbing all the sheets with her, leaving him completely naked.

"Addison, what the fuck are you doing here?" Jacob hisses and doesn't even bother to cover himself.

I'm breathless, standing in the doorway of my own bedroom, having just witnessed one of my best friends sleeping with my boyfriend.

"I...I..." I stammer, my cheeks hot with anger. "My grad; you didn't come." It really isn't answering his question, but it's all I can manage to say.

He gets out of bed, furiously rips a sheet from her hand, and wraps it around his waist. "Get out of here, Bec."

She scampers across the room, grabbing something; I have no idea what since I'm awestruck, looking at him. The person I live with, thought I knew—thought I loved and loved me back; is now unrecognizable.

She doesn't say anything to me when she rushes past, and as much as I would have loved to grab her head and slam it off the door frame, I don't. I don't move at all.

"I asked you a question." He narrows his eyes, and slowly walks toward me, menacingly.

"Are you kidding me!?" My chest heaves from exasperation.

He chuckles. "You think *you're* enough for *me?* Please." He reaches out his hand and strokes my heated cheek with his cold fingers. I wince at the contact, and his eyes flare.

"Such beauty..." He trails his fingers on my skin. "And that body..."

The first hit takes me by surprise, and the second takes my breath away. I curl on the floor and hold my face in my hands as I try to stand back up, crying for him to stop.

He doesn't.

The last blow sends me right out of the bedroom. By some miracle I stop before falling down the wooden staircase.

***

"Mom, I need this." I look at her with puppy eyes, and she melts, just like she always did when I was a little girl and wanted something.

"I know, baby. I know." She strokes a long piece of my hair and twirls it in her fingers. "I'm going to miss you so much!"

I hug her and tell her how much I will miss her too, how much I'll miss the smell of the air from the ocean and everything else about Maine. *Almost* everything anyway.

Alex already has his bags loaded in the trunk of the Mustang. I don't think it's ever had so much stuff crammed into it before.

Dad's in the driveway talking to him, probably giving him a lecture about behaving himself and that he should listen to his big sister and be respectful. It's the same talk he always got, never listened to, and then got all over again before heading out on his next venture.

"Please call if you need anything along the way." Dad smiles and hugs me tightly.

"Well, call regardless!" Mom gushes and starts to cry, kissing Alex's cheek and then rubbing her lipstick mark from his skin. "Be a good boy, Alex."

He'll always be their baby, no matter what he does and how bad he screws up.

I have no idea where we're going, and to be honest, it feels amazing. Just being behind the wheel, no time frame, just the open road with Luca—and Alex.

New York, then Illinois. States fly by, and we try to enjoy each and every one of them. At a small and absolutely adorable diner in Missouri, I call Mom quickly to tell her where we are and let her know we're just fine. Alex walks Luca across the road to an open field and lets him run around.

On the wall is a big map of the United States, the edges brown and torn from all the people passing through, I'm sure.

"Alex, you pick this time," I say once he returns. I smile and point to the map.

"California! California!" He closes his eyes and laughs. His long finger slowly traces the old paper and at one point ends up in the Atlantic.

"Too far." I snort. And he tries again.

"Wyoming. Shit." He frowns when he opens his eyes and sees where his finger ended up.

I found a cute little condo to rent month-by-month; it doesn't take long to realize once we got here that this place is just perfect. It's exactly where I've needed to escape to, to find myself again—to smile again.

It takes a few weeks to somewhat settle in, unpack my clothing and put pictures on the walls. Alex is living out of his bags, which I don't mind, as long as they're not sprawled around the house.

Wyoming is beautiful, and this morning I feel invigorated. I shower and stand in front of the tiny closet, trying to decide what to wear. My hair drips cool water down my back, and I rub the towel through my head, drying it a little.

I thumb through the hangers and finally choose a simple blue cotton dress. It's got a little bit of a low neckline, but I'm feeling good lately, so why not?

I absentmindedly trace my fingers along the little eyelet patterns all along the bottom. It's one of my favourites. When I slide the closet door shut, the mirror on the front is right there, and I'm forced to look at myself.

I stare at the girl in the glass, taking in her features and leaning in close to eye every detail. When I stand back I lift my right arm and look at my ribcage. No more bruises, no more marks anywhere. I remember the pain. I remember every second, and I'm so thankful I don't have anything permanent to remind me daily of the worst day of my life.

"Alex, let's go shopping."

Words every guy loves to hear, right? He snorts but gets up off the couch anyway. What else does he have to do today?

We stroll down the sidewalk, looking at all the stores, and I stop a few times to window shop. Alex is annoyed, but I don't care. After lunch at yet another cute diner, we continue walking and turn the corner on Oakburn Street. There's a feed store beside the grocery store. I elbow Alex and point.

"Let's check that out. Maybe get Luca something."

The little door dings, and I smile to myself. Small towns; they're adorable.

A big counter to my left has a display of plastic cubes with all kinds of bones and biscuits in them. Some are made with beef, some pork, chicken and lamb.

"The chicken ones look good."

I look up and see a handsome man with short dark hair and bold brown eyes standing by the end of the counter. He's smiling and very obviously blushing. I smile and thank him for the suggestion, and I choose three chicken treats for Luca.

The guy behind the counter isn't as cute, but he's smiling and kindly tells me how much I owe him. When I hand him the money, his fingers rub mine, almost as if on purpose, and it creeps me out a little. Alex is completely oblivious to everything, still texting who knows who. He's never without that phone.

"Let's go, Addy." He taps me, annoyed and eager to leave.

I slide my sunglasses on when we get outside. The sun is even brighter than it was five minutes ago. The warmth feels amazing on my skin, and for the first time since we got here, I feel it was meant to be.

"Hey, look!" Alex taps me again and points to a bake sale over at the grocery store. "Buy your little bro some treats now?" He grins and almost skips over to the stand.

It only takes a minute to buy butter tarts and chocolate chip cookies, but getting Alex away from these raging cougars is quite another. He loudly refers to me as his sister a few times, giving them the clear message that he's very available, and I roll my eyes behind my dark glasses.

Alex starts chatting with some woman in too-skinny skinny jeans and a blouse that doesn't leave anything to the imagination. I turn my back to them and lift my head up to the sky, letting the sun soak me and heat my soul.

The small ding of the feed store door catches my attention, and I see the one guy from the counter walking out carrying a bunch of buckets. He puts them in the back of an old truck, and walks back up the steps to hold the door open.

I have to lift my glasses when I see what walks out next. A man with unruly dirty blonde hair, carrying a big bag of food over his shoulder steps through the doorway and down to the truck. His t-shirt is so tight around his arms that I almost feel a quiver in my knees. The messy hair, the jeans, the boots—he's picturesque. I'm breathless.

Where was he when I was in the store? Then again, I probably wouldn't have been able to stand let alone speak if he had suggested what to get Luca instead of the other guy.

As I'm watching him, I'm quickly pulled out of my little bubble when Alex takes the paper bag of goodies out of my hand and pulls out a cookie.

"I'll see ya around, Chelsea." He takes a bite and winks at the panting cougar.

I drop my shades back down on my nose and smirk at the woman. I watch the beautiful man climb in his way too big but way too perfect Ford and drive away.

Afterward, I make a nice spaghetti dinner, which Alex gorges himself on. Then, he leaves the table to get ready for his "date" with Cougar Mom. I clean the table off and start the dishes.

"How's this look?" He stands by the sofa and pops the collar of his shirt.

"Oh, very dapper." I smirk and roll my eyes. "I'm sure it won't take much primping for this one, Alex."

He snorts and slaps his hands together quickly. "Nah. You're probably right. She's hot and ready."

"Eww. Really?" Like this is something I want to hear anything about.

I'm up almost every hour with anxiety, and so far, Alex hasn't come home. I know I'm not his mother, but I wish he would at least check in with me and let me know he's okay.

We're so far from Maine, and he doesn't know anyone around. I pray he stays out of trouble. When I finally do fall asleep, it's again short-lived. But this time when I awake, I'm panting, absolutely ravaged from a delicious dream about the stranger in the Ford.

Those arms, and that body...I flutter my lashes, and my eyes fall back in my head. My body sinks back onto my bed. My blood is thumping, and I can't help but smile when I think of him holding me in my dream, gazing at me and touching me in any way.

***

Alex's whirlwind romance with Cougar Mom lasts only a few days. He comes home, and out comes the phone again.

"Who are you texting all the time?"

"Why do you care? Are you the texting police?" he hisses.

"Pardon me? Don't be an ass; I was just asking." I hiss back. What a little shit! He acts like the world owes him something.

He doesn't say anything back, just kicks his shoes off and puts his dirty-socked feet on the coffee table.

"I'm taking Luca out. See you later."

Luca needs updated shots for Wyoming's dog laws. Thankfully, a vet just around the corner had a spot open for this morning, and I'm able to get him right in. I walk him down the street and smile at the people we pass. Everyone is so friendly; it's almost unreal. I doubt they even lock their doors.

Dr. Jenkins D.V.M. is displayed on the large sign above the building in big blue letters. As we walk through the small parking lot, I see a big black truck, and it looks oddly familiar. When I get closer, I realize where I've seen it before, and my heart starts racing again in my ears and throat.

Calm down, girl. I almost fan myself with my hand, trying not to gawk around for the mesmerizing creature of a man that I saw get in that truck a few days ago. Shakily, I grab the long door handle and inhale as I open it. Luca and I walk in, and I exhale slowly.

Oh, my...

***

ACKNOWLEDGMENTS

There are no words to express the amount of gratitude I have for the following people:

Ross: Your constant support and never-ending encouragement is something I will always cherish. You make me smile...I love you.

Clarissa: I couldn't imagine a life without you in it, you are an amazing friend. Your honesty, support and love for romance fueled my heart and made me want to keep writing.

Elena: You read the bare bones of Meadowlarks (and combed it to make it pretty), and you reported back with honesty and amazing words of reassurance. I've been blessed to have you in my life for all these years.

Alex: My second brother. You're wonderful. Don't change a thing. We need a martini night soon.

Mom: I hope you enjoyed reading your second book ever. I'm glad it was mine.

Ryan: My little brother...You're just awesome. No one can make me laugh the way you do.

My Girls: Mommy loves you. Pure and simple.

To the rest of my supporters, family and friends: You're all amazing. I love you, and I'll always be thankful for you.

Want more? **Breathless: Book Two** of the *Meadowlarks series* is in the works!
Follow Ashley on Twitter @AshCwrites

CPSIA information can be obtained at www.ICGtesting.com
Printed in the USA
LVOW100402250613

340014LV00007B/37/P

9 781626 464186